Arthur Britannicus (Fo

Book 1,

Paul Bannister

Table of Contents

Lord of the Narrow Sea

Prelude: Flight of an Eagle

An occasional scrape of hoof or jingle of harness was the only noise made by the pack mules as they plodded through the night, but the sentry was alert and called a challenge when they were still a hundred paces distant. The swift response came from a bulky figure that walked at the front of the mule train. As the shape moved into the light of the charcoal brazier by the toll bar, the sentry started. A lion's head was advancing on him.

Gaius Misenus Flavialis wore an African lion's mane and pelt over his helmet and shoulders, part of his uniform as proud Eagle bearer of the Ninth Legion, but this night in foggy, damp Britain, he was anything but prideful. His legion had been badly mauled by British rebels led by their queen Boadicea. Four of every five of those Pannonians who fought under the Eagle of the Ninth Spanish legion were dead, or captive and destined for the slave pens. Misenus and a detachment ordered to protect the standard that had once been carried before the great Julius Caesar's army had hacked their way clear of the slaughter and struggled to the rear of the battle. There, the impedimenta guards had already loaded a dozen mules with the military pay chests. Swift action, fog and night helped the Romans to escape with the bullion and their sacred Eagle, and they had headed north into the limestone country of middle Britain. Their intent was to skirt the rebels who blocked the way and deliver the Eagle and silver to the colonial headquarters at Eboracum, on the great road to the north.

Misenus had sent his two pony soldiers ahead for help, and this sentry was the first sign of aid as the group trudged into the mining hamlet of Lutudarense. "How many of you?" Misenus demanded. "Just a dozen, sir," said the sentry. "We'll give you a guide to the fort at Navio. It's another three hours away."

"Get on with it," said the officer wearily, and waved his small command forward. The group stepped through the night with cautious speed, ears and eyes straining for sign of the insurgents they knew were loose in the countryside, so their nerves jangled when, still several miles short of the garrison, two armed figures emerged from the darkness.

The soldiers were fellow legionaries, and their brief report was bad news. A strong enemy force was moving down from the northeast and would probably arrive at Navio within a half day. The garrison, established to protect the valuable silver and lead mines, was sorely depleted and the commander could not hope to hold out. Sensibly, he had sent a warning to divert the pack train and hide the bullion until it could be recovered later. His note suggested concealing it two miles from the fort in a disused fluorite mine. "We know the place, but it will be hard for just anyone to find it, and our miners have been warned not to lead the rebels to it," one of the legionaries assured the aquilifer, who nodded. "One of you, go back to Lutudarense and bring the rest of the detachment, we'll likely need them."

By midday Misenus was standing in the fluorite cavern, which was the dry watercourse of an ancient stream. The gilded silver Eagle, with its proud wings and laurel crown, was taken from its long staff and wrapped reverently in the aquilifer's scarlet wool officer's cloak. Then it was hidden with the chests of coin in the cave floor. Blocks of tumbled limestone buried it all. The mules were led away, the entrance was disguised under another collapse of rubble and the detachment of weary soldiers marched to the garrison. Misenus took a scrap of flattened lead used to record company accounts and pulled out his knife. Best be safe, he thought, as he scratched a crude map of the cavern's location.

The Britons came that evening, and before the sun set, every Roman had been butchered, and the insurgents were looting their bodies. The lion pelt of Misenus was torn and bloodied from the fight put up by the aquilifer, but it still attracted the scavengers. They took it as well as his mail armour, his weapons and his waist purse. A Briton with a blond moustache was still puzzled over an exchange that a wounded legionary had called out before he was finished off. "Treasure! I can show you. It's on the officer's map. Don't kill me!" The plea went unheeded, and a blue-tattooed spearman had cut off the man's words with a thrust through his throat. The warrior with the moustache had hacked down the standard bearer, and it was he who claimed his weapons and goods including the waist pouch, which he shook out on the trampled grass. It contained a few coins, a rough-hewn walrus ivory figurine of the god Mithras and a small sheet of lead marked with odd scratches. A day or two later, the Briton took the sad little pile and his other loot back to his village on the windswept coast of the German Sea. There, he told the story of the battle, and showed the lead sheet with its hurriedly-scratched map. "This must show where a Roman treasure is hidden," he declared to his family, but nobody could decipher the clues. The lead sheet lost its interest for them, and for two long centuries, the Eagle waited under the rock fall, in its cavern beneath the earth.

I. Brigantia

The boy Carausius was sleeping safe in his parents' home when, silent as clouds, the ships of the raiders came through the pre-dawn wolf light. Two vessels pushed through the fog that was settled on the oil-smooth sea and rolled to the rhythmic heave of the oarsmen. Beaded droplets glinted on rigging, cloaks and men's beards; moisture muffled the creak of timbers and the slap of sails. The fog also hid the motion of the oars, which rose and fell like wings easing the raiders towards the looming land, and only the herring gulls that hung mewing above the two carvel-planked longships witnessed the arrival of Hibernian invaders at the seaboard of Britain.

The birds' sea cliff home was the raiders' landfall, a vast chalk promontory that spearheaded itself into the gently heaving waters of the German Sea. South of the headland's prow, the curtain of fog was opening to reveal a village nestled in a wooded fold between two small white cliffs? "That," said the war band's chief, gesturing where a blue smudge of smoke proclaimed the settlement, "will be ours today. Steersman, you head for the ravine."

The red-gold of Sol was warming and brightening the land as the keels of both ships ground up on the white chalk and shingle that shelved below the village. In moments, men were scrambling over the sides to heave their vessels above the wavelets' reach, or were passing shields and weapons to shipmates who waded the last few yards to the beach.

They were Scoti, marauders from the western island of misty Hibernia. Seagoing adventurers experienced in the treacherous tides, storms, and rocks of the isles between their homeland and Britain, they could navigate through fog with the crystal stones that could find the shrouded sun. They knew the songs and chants that listed headlands, bays and other aids to navigation, and they could sail anywhere. They came to this coast because they had heard tales of a god whose followers had gathered wealth but had failed to make themselves safe in the eastern lands of Britain. The marauders had listened, planned, and gone in search of these new sources of plunder. This war band had brought their oak-ribbed ships Fleetwing and Wavehorse around the northernmost tip of the land of the Picts, a place where the green, racing waters of the Atlantic surged into the dark German Sea.

They had battled through that clashing millrace, passing safely by the island's sea-wracked coast with its headlands of spiked sandstone towers. The bards said the place was home to fearsome half-humans who ate the hapless victims of shipwrecks, and the marauders scanned the land carefully as they rowed past. They had turned their broad-beamed vessels south, gliding in summer calm past the loom of the mountains of Alba and by the unseen imperial walls of Antoninus and Hadrian, and they had stayed well offshore, out of sight of Roman signal stations, until their leader felt they were beyond the reach of the frontier garrisons.

Filwen the Bastard, the Scoti warlord, made an imposing figure. His short ponytail of silver hair barely reached the humps of shoulder muscle that bulged beneath his wolf fur cloak, and his arms, sleeved in blue tattoos and clinking with warrior rings made from the weapons of his slaughtered enemies, rippled with power.

He urged his men on, telling them that Britain was rich in coin hoarded by priests faithful to a prophet dead for two centuries or more. The Christus followers had slid from sight, condemned by Rome because they refused to acknowledge the Augustus Caesar as a god, but their treasure was still somewhere, he told them. It would be easy pickings. The Romans, he knew, were hardly able to defend their northernmost province because they'd stripped it almost bare of soldiers, sending them to contain the threats to their empire posed by the hordes from beyond the rivers Rhine and Danube.

Nor were the cowed natives a viable opposition since the punishments that followed the Boadicean revolt. His half-hundred armed men, surprise and a few diversionary firebrands tossed into the thatch would soon overwhelm any settlement's resistance. "We'll have women and slaves tonight," Filwen muttered. He removed the dagger he kept fastened inside his cloak, slipped it into his belt and threw the heavy fur to his servant. "And we'll learn where the temples are, with the silver," he added.

As the ships' sturdy keels ground across the first shingle banks just off the beach, the warlord tugged on his leather helmet with its stitched ridge and green-dyed horsehair plume, pulled his iron breastplate straight and, for luck, tapped the oblong flat of his sword where it hung from a brass chain at his left side. The servant brought the warrior his full length shield of willow faced with waxed leather, but he gestured it away, and took only the ash pole with its spearhead that was half the length of a man's arm. "No shield wall here," he grunted, "just a few fishers, seal hunters and farmers. Now, let's get busy."

The ships were grounded, the raiders were readying, pulling on boiled leather breastplates over their wool tunics. Some carried heavy javelins, most had iron swords, a few possessed a prized, steel Roman gladius, the feared stabbing sword of the legions that had slaughtered Rome's enemies from Aegyptus to Germania. "Leave the shields," Filwen ordered, "and bring fire."

The hamlet in the ravine above the hissing shingle looked Pictish, with reed-thatched round huts of stone, wattle and wood, and several byres for pigs and cattle. Its homely dung heaps steamed gently in the summer morning's cool. Above the settlement, a fold held a dozen or so undersized grey-black sheep and a loom stood outside one hut, alongside a drying frame that held great hanks of dark wool. On the slope in the lee of the northern headland were strips of cultivated farmland where barley and rye glinted gold in the rays of the rising sun. Those same rays flashed off the accoutrements of the raiders as they hurried up the ravine's hard-beaten path, and that caught the eye of a yawning man who'd stepped out of his hut to relieve himself. He gaped at the hurrying invaders as they rounded a slimy retting pond, then his sleep-fuddled brain understood what he was seeing. "Danger! Feraz! Danger!" he yelled, his voice breaking. "There are attackers coming, get out!"

The villager scrambled back into his hut, sliding on the dew-wet turf, but his shouts had alerted others and a boy began running from hut to hut, banging on the rough doors and shouting shrilly. In one of the huts, the child Carausius raised his head from his pillow. His father was scrambling off his sleeping cot and his older brothers' feet thudded on the packed dirt floor. Outside, Filwen was emerging from the ravine, cursing because the surprise had gone. He gestured impatiently at the four who were carrying firebrands to scatter through the settlement. The other raiders, yelling to induce panic, thumped towards the huts where men were emerging, tugging on trews and tunics even as they hefted staves and axes. Carausius' father Aulus, a black-bearded man in knee length breeches, stepped out of the settlement's largest stone building. Over his head, the two faces of Janus Twin stood above the door, protector of both the interior and the exterior.

In one hand Aulus carried his wool cloak, in the other he grasped a horn-handled knife with a long blade shaped like a slender leaf. "Halt!" he bellowed at the onrushing raiders. "Cease this, at once!" Several of the invaders, struck by the obvious authority of the man, slowed and stopped short. Filwen, cursing quietly, stepped forward.

"Who are you?" he demanded of the bearded man. "I am Aulus and this land is Brigantia. That headland is Oceli Promontorium. It is my land," said the chieftain. "Who in the name of hell are you?"

"I am your new master," said Filwen, stepping forward and levelling his spear at Aulus' naked, tattooed chest.

"Not you!" rasped the Briton. He stepped back, circling his arm to bind his cloak around it as an impromptu shield even as he extended his dagger straight out, at arm's length. Behind him, two teenage boys pushed out of the hut's door.

"Kill him, father!" urged one. Filwen stared, laughed, then spat at Aulus' bare feet. "You and your whelps are mine," he declared, twitching the point of his heavy spear. "Put down that dagger, you're slaves now."

Aulus looked across the trodden dirt of the settlement and saw that in amazingly quick time, the raiders had taken control. Several thatched roofs were already flickering flame and would soon be belching smoke into the sky; two raiders were hacking at a villager curled in fetal position on the ground. His axe was lying useless next to his blood-drenched body. Bilic, an unusually tall villager noted for his ability as a seal hunter, was slumped against the side of his hut, impaled through the chest with a javelin delivered so hard, a hands span of the blade protruded from his back. His wife was kneeling next to him, alternately wailing and sobbing deep, wracking gulps.

A clutch of hooting marauders were shooing six or seven women in their night shifts into the foul retting pond below the hamlet, where flax rotted. Other raiders had gathered half-awake men at sword point and were lashing their hands and necks together as they lay on the ground, some pinned under the nailed boot soles of the Scoti. "Put down the dagger, slave," Filwen snarled at Aulus.

The big man nodded, sighed and drooped his head. Then, fast as a striking adder, he stepped inside the raider's spear point and seized the ash shaft, dragging Filwen towards him. He swept his dagger across the Scoti's eyes. The raider, however, was just as fast. Untouched, he half-fell backwards, pulling Aulus off balance. The big man stumbled to his knees and Filwen kicked his wrist, numbing it but failing to make him drop the dagger. Behind their father, the two boys hesitated, then began to move forward, but they were unarmed and three of the raiders were at them, fast. One boy was quicker. He stepped swiftly back inside the hut and slammed shut the door; the other was seized by his long hair and forced to the ground.

Inside the hut, the youth who'd escaped faced his mother. "We're dead," he said simply. The woman looked at him, turned away and said calmly to the ten year old who was watching wide-eyed: 'Caros, my son, you have to run away. Go quickly." She grasped her small son under the arms. "Off you go, my love, through there." She lifted Carausius up to the smoke-blackened rafters and pointed at the vent hole in the thatched roof. "Through there, carefully and run to the smith at the forge. Tell him everything. Go, my darling, go quickly."

A thought struck her, and Clinia looked at her older son, paused, then fumbled in the dirt floor at the base of a support pole. Acting quickly, she scraped free a wool-wrapped scrap of lead, a small sheet of metal with something scratched into it. She whispered urgently: "Hide this, it's important. Your father inherited it. His father told him it shows where a treasure is hidden, but we don't know where to look."

She put the thin lead sheet with its inscrutable markings into the older boy's hand, then turned in alarm. A raider outside had thrown himself against the door, making the whole frame shudder. Dust and soot drifted down from the thatch. Carausius, frozen on the rafter, reacted to the noise and scuttled for the vent hole. As he popped his head into the outside air, he saw his father in front of the hut, moving forward in a crouch, his dagger extended at Filwen. All eyes were on the fighters, nobody saw the boy squirm through the vent, slide onto the mossy reeds and squelch down onto the dung heap alongside the hut.

A sea raider spotted Carausius as he scooted across the settlement but the man turned away. There was loot to be had, women and slaves to be taken. He wanted his share and legging it after a skinny boy across country while the others got the pick of things wasn't for him. The boy could be caught later. He turned, grinning, to watch the fight between Filwen and the Briton, knowing his warlord's skills with sword or spear. "He'll hurt that peasant. They don't call him the Bastard for nothing," he muttered. His eyes flickered sideways, his attention caught by the seal hunter's sobbing wife. Long, chestnut hair, slender shoulders. He licked his lips. He could take her into that hut, he thought. That would be better than chasing some boy. Let Filwen gut the peasant, he had other things in mind. He'd comfort the new widow, act of kindness, he grinned to himself.

The feeling was coming back into Aulus' right hand and the bulge of the dagger's handle again felt solid in his palm, but the chieftain knew his weapon was badly outmatched. He shifted the cloak more firmly around his left forearm, noting that the garment's fastener, a heavy silver and amber brooch that was the symbol of his rank was on the outside, forming a miniature shield. He had no more time for reflection as Filwen thrust hard at him with the long spear point. Aulus was barely able to hurl himself aside as it scraped his bare upper arm. "Close with him," the thought blazed through his mind. "Dust in his eyes. Dust." Aulus dodged another thrust, stumbling sideways. His fingers scrabbled at the ground. The spear thudded into the earth right by his hand, hurled at the instant he began to fall. The Briton's fingers grasped gravel and dirt, he began to straighten to throw his blinding handful and his world went dark.

Filwen had launched the big ash and iron spear with his right hand and in a motion made skilful by long hours of training, had continued his arm's swing to grab the haft of his sword. He instantly drew it across his body, snatching the sword free of its hanger chains. The Scoti whipped his sword backhanded, scything the blade across Aulus' face. The tip took out the Briton's right eye in a gout of blood, smashed through the bridge of his nose and jellied his left eyeball so cleanly, its fluid ran unbloodied down his cheek like the albumen of an egg. The shock of the impact drove the Briton to his knees, stunned, blinded and helpless. Filwen glanced at the watching teenage boy held by his hair, throat tilted to the serving man's blade, then crashed the pommel of his sword onto Aulus' undefended head.

The down thrust shattered the skull, releasing a glob of pulped brain to glisten against the chieftain's dark hair. Aulus slumped face forward into the dirt, twitching in his death spasms. He never felt the jarring impact of the raider's blade as it hacked into the nape of his neck. His killer reached down to free the silver brooch and its bodkin from the cloak wrapped around the dead man's arm, and jabbed it into the wolf fur his servant offered at his gesture. "A memento, a pleasing memento," he said, eyeing the lump of amber set in a triple spiral of heavy silver that was, though he did not know it, symbol of a high chieftain. "Now, let's find where these Druids are with their coin."

II. Peak

Carausius had never been so terrified in all his ten years of life. He heard the roaring cheer from the raiders as his father was slaughtered, and knew what it meant. He felt he'd been seen as he ran for the copse of trees above the village and it lent speed to his flying feet. His chest hurt from his rasping breath, his throat felt raw, his bare legs were scratched from the brambles. His toes were bruised and cut where he'd stubbed them against stones, but he knew he could not stop. He still had several thousand more paces to run until he reached the forge. There, he'd find his friend, the young smith Gimflod and he would know what to do.

The boy ran on, throat burning, chest heaving. A white rat scampered across the forest path in front of him and he started. White? He'd never seen such a thing in his life. He ran on, arms thrashing at the air, lungs on fire, legs knotting painfully with the effort. Finally, the hovel came in sight, tucked under an outcrop of ironstone that provided the smith with his raw material. A heap of turf-covered charcoal smouldered nearby, and Gimflod was patching a leak that was venting smoke through the patchwork of sod.

"Hello, Caros, don't want any air in there," he said cheerily as the boy panted up. Then he looked again, realizing Carausius' distress. In a spate of babbled words, the boy told what he had seen. "My father is dead," he sobbed. The smith closed his eyes as he thought. A man unwilling to make swift decisions, he took time to pace into the forge, thoughtfully pumping the leather bellows. He was reheating the blade of a wheeled ploughshare he was repairing for a wealthy barley farmer and he took comfort in the familiar action as he tried to think. "They're raiders," he said, closing his eyes again. "Let me consider. They will be going inland. They will likely come this way, so we are not safe here. We must go."

At the hamlet, Filwen grunted satisfaction as he surveyed the woman Clinia, whom his men had dragged from Aulus' hut. She was a handsome, full-breasted wench, he thought, and he'd enjoy teaching her new duties, but the real prize was her two sons. "By Mithras, they're twins," he'd muttered when he first saw them together. "They're exactly alike.They'll fetch a fine price on the slave block."

Domnal and Mael stared back at him, sullenly. Their teenage world had been brutally upended. In minutes they'd gone from being the privileged sons of a chieftain to captives at spear point. Their father was lying dead in his blood and their mother had been dragged away to join a coffle of slaves. Now they faced the same fate. Domnal, the older by 20 minutes, stared meaningfully at his brother, then glanced down at his right hand. The older twin was wearing what seemed to be an ugly grey metal ring he'd never seen before. In fact, it was the strip of lead, twisted and hidden in plain sight. Mael raised an eyebrow but said nothing. He knew his twin would explain later, and he understood it had to be important.

Filwen walked around the pair, musing, turned to survey the settlement. "Put the saleable ones over there, the rest are the doomed," he told three of his raiders. "Doomed, lord?" one man asked. "Yes, save the women, younger children and those who can work. Make double sure of those twins. You can kill the old, any strong ones who might make trouble, and any babies," he instructed.

A dozen women were being tied together, ropes looped from neck to neck. Only eight men had survived the invaders' frenzied onslaught, and they were bound at the wrists, seated on the ground under guard. A gaggle of children and infants wailed from one of the huts into which they had been pushed while the raiders hunted from hovel to hovel, digging into floors by the doorposts and hearth stones, the usual places to hide valuables.

Aulus' madder-dyed cloak was spread on the ground and from time to time a raider would drop onto it a cooking pot, household utensil, a mortar and pestle, a few denarii coins or a pathetic piece of jet or silver jewellery. A poor haul. "Get me something to drink," Filwen demanded, and a woman hurried to him with a leather cup of barley beer. He swigged it, then strode through the settlement to stand over the bound menfolk. 'Where is your temple? Where are your priests and their silver?" he demanded. Nobody responded. The Bastard felt his quick rage rise. "You," he stabbed his sword at one of the bound villagers. "Where's your temple? Where is the silver?" The terrified man shook his head, mute and uncomprehending. There was no temple. Filwen

He chopped once, twice, at the man's neck, stepping back as a wash of bright arterial blood sluiced across the dirt. He turned away, his rage vanished as quickly as it had come. "Take them to the Wavehorse, fasten them properly, keep them alive. Leave six guards, and stay alert," he instructed. "We'll try inland for a few days, then we'll be back. If anything happens, send a messenger to find us, we'll be west of here, but this side of the military road. The rest of you, get your shields, food and weapons and be back here quickly. We'll take a few of those women, too."

An hour later, out on the open wold, Gimflod was watching. Alerted by the sun flashing off the blades of their shouldered spears, he saw the first scouts of the raiding party as they breasted a rise two miles away.

"Now, we'll have to go now," he said urgently. He snatched up a cloak, several pieces of dried mackerel and a half loaf he had planned to eat that night. He caught up his valuable hammer and a small leather purse containing a collection of coins. Some silver pieces showed the head of the old emperor Septimius Severus, who'd ruled not so long ago from the palace at Eboracum, the provincial capital that was a day's march to the west. His head was also stamped on the one precious golden aureus in the purse, but no one could tell whose image adorned the worn-down brass coins that made up the rest of Gimflod's meagre fortune. Nevertheless, all were valuable, as only the military and traders usually got their hands on actual money. Barter was the normal form of exchange for lesser folk.

The smith and the boy slipped away down a fold in the land, remaining unseen by the marauders, and began their trek to seek safety. They kept moving cautiously, scanning often as they slipped surreptitiously across the landscape under the wheeling gulls. That night, wrapped in Gimfold's heavy cloak, they slept in a copse under the wind-shelter of a small headland, and awoke soaked in dew and hidden in a thick morning mist.

After two long, cautious days of skulking travel, the pair arrived footsore and hungry at a coastal camp called Peak, where a Roman army detachment was building a signal station. Gimflod swung his bundled cloak over his shoulder and headed towards the weather-beaten legionaries, who viewed them curiously. Quickly, he explained himself to the hard-eyed centurio in charge, as that veteran of a dozen bloody killing fields looked with unexpected sympathy at the boy. "How many do you think there are of them?" the sergeant queried. "Fifty or sixty? We'll settle them, and soon. We'll have them down faster than a tart's knickers."

He called over two of his soldiers and gave them instructions. Within a half hour the pair were provisioned, armed and striding west on the stony causeway towards the great north-south highway, where they would report to the nearest staging post. "There will be cavalry couriers going to the palace at Eboracum and on to Lindum v by nightfall," the sergeant forecast, adding grimly: "There will be a detachment on the raiders soon enough, and the executioner will be busy with any bastards the slavers don't want. Now, let's get you two fed and watered and bedded down for the night. That boy needs rest."

A week went by without incident except that a messenger from a cavalry detachment rode by to say there had been no sign of the raiders, who had looted and burned a few homesteads inland, but now seemed to have left the area, probably on seeing the military.

The soldiers working on the signal beacon continued their task, and they welcomed the smith's skills. On request, the ironworker set up a small forge to repair a few broken tools and bits of personal equipment. The detachment had almost finished the lumber and stone structure that was temporary by Roman standards, and the centurion shrugged at it. "The engineers will be back in a few months with masons to make a proper building, a stone tower with a heavy timber superstructure for the fire signal," he said, nodding to the great iron basket that would hold the fuel for the warning fire.

"This is just for now, to establish an early alert system for pirates, Gaels, Celts, Picts; any of those thieving bastards. If they come at night, we light the fire, and the detachment at the next place along the coast will see that, and pass on the message. If they come in daylight, we throw wet moss on the flames, to create smoke. You can see it for miles. Our signals can outrun any ship, and we can send the message right around the country in a half day. The army keeps detachments a few miles inland, to use the military road north or south, and they can have cavalry at the coast to greet invaders before they've dried their feet on the beach. It's important stuff, so we'll be moving up the coast to build a few more of these."

Gimflod nodded his understanding. The big smith had had time to think and he announced his decision. "It's time for us to be getting back. There will be things to do at our village, and maybe by now the prisoners will have been released."

As the men spoke, a Gallic trading ship with brown leather sails was tacking into the lee of the headland. With its flat bottom and high prow from which a lookout could spot rocks and shoals, it could approach very close to the shore. In these waters protected by the headland from the blustery north-easterly wind, its progress was smooth and unflurried.

Carausius turned to the smith. "I saw a ship like that once before," he recalled. "A tall man with long dark hair came in it, and he came especially to talk to my father." "Was he a trader?" Gimflod asked idly, not really interested. "No, my mother said I was to be very polite, he was a powerful lord of magic." The big smith's interest was captured.

"Magic?"

"Mother said he'd come from the western islands to talk to my father. He seemed to know me, but I'm sure I never met him before."

"Lucky he didn't turn you into a toad," grunted the smith. "What was his name, this sorcerer?" The boy scowled as he tried to remember more.

"It was Myr …… Myrddin," he said, triumphantly. "He made prophecies. He could see the future, my father said, and he walked with kings in high places." The smith shrugged, only half-convinced.

"I suppose he visited your family because your father was an earl. Sorcerers don't visit blacksmiths."

He turned away, interest fading as he watched the trading ship inch closer. Now the water was barely three feet deep and the crew could jump over the side to haul their vessel to the beach. One waited to carry the bearded negotiator, as the Romans called a trader, to do his buying and selling with dry feet and trews. "Talk to him," said the centurion. "He's going south and he can take you back to your settlement for a coin or two."

Gimflod nodded. A tiring trudge back to the site of the tragedy would be hard on the tired boy whose white face reflected his recent nightmare-torn nights. Sailing would be better. The smith had money, so the next morning, with an offshore breeze, they were aboard the trader and headed home, if there was a home left standing.

III. Belgica

As the salt-stained vessel cleared the wind shelter of the great headland, the German Sea and the squally weather began to assert their power, and the negotiator was obliged to tell his steersman to head more easterly. "We can't sail due south in this wind," he explained to his two passengers. "We'll have to head out to sea, then turn back south and west."

The trader was faced with the main drawback of his stout ship. It had no oars and relied only on its bellying mainsail for propulsion. Although the stitched leather sheet was strong enough, tethered as it was to the deck on either side of the mast by halyards, it made the vessel clumsy. The negotiator could not easily sail his desired course when the wind was foul, and as night fell over the heaving sea, Gimflod and Carausius found themselves being carried ever further east and south.

When dawn broke on the second morning of their voyage, revealing a line of threatening squalls, the Gaul's vessel was far from Britain and its steersman was anxious. By noon, however, he was shouting in relief. He spotted a dark line on the horizon. "Land, master," he called to the negotiator, pointing. "Probably Belgica."

He was right. As they neared the land, the steersman let out a whoop of joy. "There's the pharos, the light tower to bring us home. See the colour of the water? That's silt from the outfall of the Rhine. We're close to Forum Hadriani!"

The trader sighed with relief. Every sea voyage was a risk, and coming home was always cause for a gift of thanks to the gods, a vow he privately made to himself. "It's a busy place, Hadrian's Market, a town of a thousand people or more," the negotiator explained to wide-eyed Carausius. "You'll like it, and we'll soon be able to get you a ship back to Britain from here." He could not have been more wrong.

For weeks, everything seemed to conspire to keep the two Britons from going home. Carausius fell sick with a fever almost at the hour he set foot in the bustling settlement, and Gimflod the smith ran through most of his scant supply of coin to pay for room at a tavern and to employ a

Greek physician to care for the boy. By the time Carausius was well enough to travel, they couldn't afford to pay for the voyage.

The smith, however, felt a lessening desire to go back. Hadrian's Market was a vital naval centre, a place between the great rivers Rhine and Meuse, which were linked here by a shortcut canal that was an important waterway in Rome's most northerly city on the continent. The town had become a staging post for the thousands of troops who had made the long voyage from around the great inland body of water the Romans called Mare Nostrum, Our Sea. In the Forum's sheltered green waters were anchored several great warships, a pair of three-decked triremes and a vast five-decked quinqereme, although the work on the mighty rivers was done by troops in smaller, more nimble vessels.

The town was a thriving place, and the smith soon found employment at a shipyard, hammering out the short iron rivets used in clinker-built oar boats or making great round-headed bolts that were used to hold together the foot-thick oaken ribs of the Gallic coasting vessels. These stout ships, smooth-sided and caulked with cattle hair or hemp and sealed with pine tar, were so much stronger than the flexible, clinkered Roman ships that patrolled the coast.

"The Romans aren't sailors," Gimflod explained to Carausius as the pair ate a supper of barley gruel with pork and a loaf of coarse bread. He flinched as he bit down on a scrap of rock from the millstone that had ground the flour. He considered his words: "They're soldiers, and they know about land warfare, but as for sailing… They have to use Greeks or Syrians or Egyptians to do the sailing, because they're the people who know how to do it best.

"They put a few Romans on board their ships as officers, but that's about it. If it's going to be a sea action, they put land soldiers on board the galleys and fight that way. The rowers on those big warships are free men, and well paid and serve a fixed term. Lately, though, with all this crisis, they've been using pressed men from the colonies and conquered lands, but even they get their diploma of freedom after fifteen years or so."

The crisis to which the big smith alluded was serious. The imperial fleets, weakened by centuries of peace in their landlocked home sea had atrophied. Rome's admirals had not developed their fleets' technology or training, and now found themselves unable to handle the sea-wise marauders who were assaulting the empire. Picts from the north and Gaels from Hibernia in the west were raiding Britain. War Danes and Saxons from upper Germania had forced the Romans out of the chain of coastal islands north of the Rhine, while Goths and other tribesmen from the eastern forests and mountains were raiding across the Black Sea, capturing Roman ships and sailing as far as the Greek Sea to plunder Athens, Sparta and even Byzantium, the very gateway to the East.

The insurgents and pirates were winning, and nowhere was worse than the Britannic Sea north of Gaul. Around the narrows of the 21-mile strait between Britain and Gaul, even under the nose of the Roman fleet's headquarters at Bononia, traders were highly likely to find themselves boarded from rowboats that would put out from the land to loot their victims, then scuttle back to safety before they could be intercepted.

Gimflod closed his eyes in thought as he worked the bellows of the shipyard forge. He had heard nothing in half a year, although he had paid a merchant to try to bring back information about the plundered village. He couldn't afford to buy passage on a trading ship back to Britain, and anyway, the boy was sickly, and might not survive a harsh journey. If they attempted the cheaper, shorter crossing from Gaul in a fishing boat, the chances were high that they'd be caught and sold as slaves.

"I might have well as been enslaved by the Gaels," he thought. "I'm not even sure there is anything to go back for, anyway." He resolved to stay put for another year, or at least until the boy's health improved. There were too many unknowns. Unsuspected by the smith and Carausius, they could have strolled across the marketplace to the slave auction block and found answers to many of their questions, for the man who'd brought about their troubles had arrived in the town.

After the raid on Carausius' home village, Filwen put guards to watch his beached ships and the captives, then he and his raiders had marched west into Britain in search of plunder. They'd followed the track across the high wold, taking care to spit and make the sign against evil as they passed a monolith left by the ancient gods, They had sacked and burned several small settlements with profitable results in terms of goods and women. Mostly, they'd killed the men and the babies, but fair-skinned women and children, they knew, brought good prices from the slave traders of northern Africa who journeyed to visit the northern markets. It was worth the trouble of feeding such captives and keeping them alive for the few weeks it would take to get them to market.

Captured soldiers were a different matter. They were usually strong and difficult to control once taken. Worse, they were liable to kill themselves, which took away all the profit, so the raiders preferred to just slaughter them on the spot if they were far from a dealer or a market. Babies were killed as a practical matter. Few would survive a march, and often a nursing mother would be weakened by her infant and a valuable prize would be lost if she died, too.

Fortunately, wholesale slavers usually showed up if they knew of a skirmish, or else they would arrange to meet the Gael to take captives off his hands, and they were used to handling even reluctant slaves. This raid had been good, with plenty of females and older children and those twins, too, so Filwen was pleased. He sent back to his ships a coffle of weeping women, tied together at the neck, and planned to continue west to intercept the great north-south Roman road that linked Londinium to the garrisons at Lincoln and Eboracum and continued north to the Wall of Hadrian.

When his scouts warned him that Roman infantry had been sighted, Filwen promptly doubled back to his ships, knowing his war band could not face organized troops. Before the legionaries reached the great white headland, the raider's sails were to the south, vanishing in the haze.

Over the next few days, auxiliary troops who had been called in by the signal station crew fruitlessly scoured the hinterland while the raiders sailed south to the great river Humber, turning into it around the narrow sand spit that curved like a bird's bill.

They gazed curiously at the abandoned jetties on the Ouse once occupied by Roman navy detachments, and three times a raiding party went ashore to pillage, plundering several villages and two fine villas. At the last, in the hamlet of Selletun, a house slave named Mullinus revealed the hiding place of his master's hoard of silver rather than have his backside roasted on the glowing charcoal of the kitchen brazier. Filwen would have roasted the man anyway, but Mullinus claimed to be able to read and write. Filwen, unlettered, could not test the slave's claim, but reasoned that if the man told the truth he could bring a price at auction.

The Selletun mansion was the last place to burn, as the raider, conscious that the settlement was within a half day's fast march of the provincial capital Eboracum, opted to retreat down river before troops came to investigate the smoke plumes. The two Gallic ships went out on that afternoon's ebb tide, the Humber's silty current rushing them past marshy shores and into the German Sea. Then the steersmen headed the heavily-loaded vessels east and south and so, in two more days, they fetched up across the sea, at the pharos whose light guided the way into Forum Hadriani, its slave market and shipyards.

IV. Hadriani

Filwen the Bastard liked the slave corrals. He liked to see the hatred, fear or despair with which once-proud freemen faced their futures, standing naked on the block as they were sold under the crown, the mocking wreath symbol of their status that showed they were for sale. In more impromptu markets, the official supervising the sale would set a spear in the ground, to signify that slaves were being sold under public authority.

Because the sale was in a province, not in Italy itself, there was no need to whiten the slaves' with chalk as a sign they had come across the sea and were liable to import taxes, but all wore a tablet around their neck describing their age, character and any defects or tendencies, such as theft, or readiness to run away. It also listed skills like carpentry or brick making, that the slave possessed, detailed his native country and name, and offered a six-month guarantee he was free of disease.

Any slave without such a warranty was made to wear a cap for the auction. Filwen noted two captives marked with the shameful pierced ears of the Eastern slave, a sign that they humbly listened to their master. His slaves, he felt, compared well to the other humans on offer. The most prized, after beautiful females or handsome young males, were slaves who could act as jesters, jugglers or other entertainers, with dwarfs and hunchbacks having value as freaks for the amusement of a household.

The Bastard sized up the offerings, watching amused as Clinia, the buxom wife of the dead chieftain Aulus, was stripped of the few scraps of clothing she'd retained before she was pulled out of the cage and onto the auction block. He chuckled at the raucous comments of the men gathered to buy the captives but grunted at the small price brought by his onetime bed mate. He ungraciously took the money the buyer, a shipwright, offered. "You got a bargain there," he said. The man grinned at him. "She'll keep my cabin clean and my bunk warm. I'm off to the northlands in a week or so and a well-padded woman will be useful."

Filwen grunted again. He didn't see the anguished look Clinia cast backwards towards the corrals, searching for her sons, as she was led away by the shipwright's bodyguard. He was looking at his other women captives, wondering if perhaps there were too many slaves on offer at one time, as the market seemed not as profitable as before.

He sent Mullinus and a couple of other prime captives back to the ships without even showing them to the small crowd of buyers. "I'll get more for them another time," he thought. He surveyed the chatting crowd, spotted a couple of affluent-looking prospects, and on a whim, opted to put the twins up. At his nod, Domnal and Mael were pushed forward. "Might as well test the upscale market," the raider thought, whispering to the auctioneer that he had a high reserve price on these two. The man nodded, and appraised the youths. Carausius' 16 years old brothers were identical twins, dark haired and handsome. Both boys were tall and promised to become prime specimens, but their real attraction for the buyers was their similarity, a novelty and a valuable asset for wealthy men who'd enjoy having matching bodyguards or personal slaves.

The Bastard knew that a rich man with scores of slaves flaunted his wealth by having them perform useless or highly-personal tasks like taking care of the master's sandals while he ate, or wiping him clean when he rose from the toilet. One slave might walk ahead on the street to point out obstacles, another's sole task was to prompt his owner with the names of those greeting him. Matched slaves were especially valued, so the competition for these handsome twin slaves was gratifyingly intense and Filwen soon nodded his approval to the auctioneer at the price.

The winning bidder was a swarthy local who did lucrative trade in Baltic amber. To the Gael's satisfaction, the Belg paid with five golden Roman aureii, a gleaming pile of coins that he spilled from the large purse he wore alongside the knife in his belt. "Good currency, that, and not debased," thought Filwen, "and those boys got about five times what a typical male slave fetches. It was a good day when we saw that village."

The twins hardly looked at each other as they were led away by their new master, although Mael could not resist glancing down at Domnal's left sandal, where the scrap of lead given to him by their mother was sewn into the sole. They had puzzled over the marks and letters on the metal, but neither could read Latin and the scratched map meant nothing to them. One day it might, but first they had to keep it safe. All they knew was what their mother had whispered quickly before she was taken in the slave coffle with the other women. "Guard the map," she'd said. "It tells where someone buried gold." One day, the twins promised themselves, they'd find the treasure and buy all their freedoms.

By the time the Gael left the slave market, the rain had begun and it was full dark. All trading was done and Filwen's leather purse was heavy. Time for wine, food and a girl. He glanced at the rain swept square, flinched as a rat scuttled across his path and pulled a little tighter his wolf fur cloak, which was fastened at the shoulder with the heavy amber and silver brooch he'd taken from the dead Aulus.

He glanced to make sure the two crewmen he'd brought as bodyguards stayed close. He saw they walked with their hands on their daggers. The thought made him reach inside his cloak, where he'd had a piece of horn sewn in, to attach his knife and purse. His fingers fumbled around. The scabbard was empty, his dirk was missing. "Where's my short dagger?" he asked his servants. They fumbled at their own tunics. "I don't have it, master," said one. "Not me, master," chimed the other. "Damn," said the raider. "I must have dropped it somewhere."

He turned abruptly from the darkened square where two flickering rush lights advertised the wine shop, to go back into the auction hall, bumping against one of his bodyguards. The sailor murmured: 'No, you don't," and brushed aside Filwen's thick cloak, opening it to the wool tunic underneath.

The old raider knew at once what was happening, and reached again for his missing dagger. His fingers brushed on the empty scabbard just as the punch into his abdomen took the air from his lungs. The blow created a sharp, searing explosion that tore inside him. It hurt deeply as the sailor drove his long knife up and under the Gael's ribcage, tearing through the fat and abdominal muscle, ripping past the lungs and stabbing cleanly into his heart.

The force of the killer's powerful arm lifted the raider to his toes and rocked him backwards. Filwen felt his short ponytail grasped from behind and his head was pulled painfully back. He tried to shove the second sailor aside but his arm was inexplicably weak and as his mind puzzled at the phenomenon, a rasping, sawing sensation stung his upturned throat. The Bastard sucked for air, and heard an odd whistling gurgle from his own slashed windpipe. The world was going dim. There was a gurgling noise like water draining, and a gout of warm blood splashed over the attackers, soaking them from wrist to elbow, spattering the first sailor's face, but Filwen never knew it, nor would he ever know that the heavy purse of gold, the wolf fur and the big amber and silver brooch all had new owners now.

Back at the jetty where Wavehorse and Fleetwing were tied, the two murderers scooped up a leather bucket of seawater to sluice away the blood from their hands and weapons, then went aboard to collect their possessions. No point staying with the ships, in case some officious busybody came asking questions, and although it was a pity to give up their share of the spoils from selling the few remaining captives, the gold they'd taken from the Bastard was plenty.

"We should release these slaves", said the first sailor, "It will give us time. People will think we're hunting them." The other agreed, and paced quietly up the deck to the high prow where the Britons were fastened. Mullinus, the house slave who could read and write, looked up questioningly as his hemp bonds were unfastened. "Go, get off the ship," ordered his liberator.

Mullinus began to move towards the gangplank and the sailor turned away. "I'll take that wolf fur," he told his accomplice. "Curse you, it's mine," was the snarled response. In seconds, the argument escalated and the sound of the scuffle drew a watchman from the dock. He ran up, his heavy stave raised, to stop the fight. Mullinus crouched in the shadows under the gunwale.

The assassins were already in combat, slashing at each other with their knives. The discarded cloak lay a few feet from the slave, who cautiously dragged it to cover himself. The watchman, shouting for support, laid into both men with his stout stave. He knocked one unconscious and found himself in a desperate struggle with the enraged other. Mullinus saw his chance. Wrapped in the heavy, dark cloak, he fled down the gangplank and into the night. Only when he'd run a distance from the riverside jetty did he stop, gasping, to take stock.

The weight that had banged against his shoulder as he ran was a large amber and spiralled-silver brooch pinned to the fur, and the weight inside the cloak that was fastened to a bit of sewn-on horn and had thumped against his thigh was a soft leather purse full of gold aureii. He was free, he was far from his former master, and he was rich.

V. Cenhud

Carausius was 14 now. In the years he'd been away from his native island, he'd turned from stocky boy to burly young man, made strong by the unremitting exercise of working on a transport scow on the Rhine and Meuse rivers, and nourished with good food by his master's wife, who treated the young Briton as the son she'd never had. Cait of Rodda was soft-spoken and as soft-hearted as her husband Cenhud, shipmaster and river pilot, was tough and wary. They had no children, so when Cenhud had been approached by Gimflod the smith about finding better care for the ten years old Carausius, the sailor had seen an opportunity to please his wife. She'd agreed to take on the boy, and had brought him back to health in short order.

Next, she took pride, as a gentle-born woman with some education, in tutoring him in the Frankish and Belgic tongues, and especially in the Latin he'd need as a trader and navigator. Cait called on a friend, a young Celtic matron teasingly known as Celea Altissima because as a child she'd declared she would grow to be very tall, to help her tutor the boy.

Celea worked with Carausius to teach him the principles of geometry laid down by the Greeks. This was a new discipline of earth measurements invaluable to any skilled sailor. Carausius soaked it up like a Kalymnos sponge, just as he did when she taught him his letters. "Lege feliciter," she'd smile at him, 'Read happily." But, for all his new life and activities, he never forgot his homeland and his heritage as the son of a British chieftain, and promised the god Mithras that he'd return and that one day he would avenge his father's death and the disaster that had befallen his family. Yet, even as the boy mourned for his lost parents and his twin brothers, he took on his shipboard duties with the relish and energy of a bright youth enjoying the physical life, clean salt air and stimulation of the Roman port.

And the port was busier than ever before. That year, a dozen years after Rome had celebrated its millennium, Germanic tribes in the forests across the Rhine were contesting for land and the emperors needed to send ever more legions, even while unrest was surging in other provinces. The shifting power brought a spate of new rulers, frontier generals who had the legions to support their imperial ambitions. Senators from patrician clans contemptuously called them 'barracks emperors' for their lack of distinguished family history, but were powerless against them.

Some of the barracks emperors had learned the lessons of Gaius Julius Caesar, from the old days of the Republic. Caesar had paid his legions out of his own fortune, and kept his men loyal. The ones who took note amassed plunder to boost the public funds with which they rewarded the spears that sustained them. Fifteen times in 43 years, usurpers had donned the imperial purple robes, but none had enjoyed lasting success, and all but one had been killed. The sole exception had committed suicide after ruling for a single month, in a year when six different emperors held the throne.

And, the turmoil went on. Only last year the latest candidate, Postumus had seized power over Britain, Gaul and Germany to create his own Gallic Empire based on Cologne and create more headaches for Rome. Adding to all this instability was a mass bloodlust to persecute the treasonous followers of the Jesus god. Their refusal to acknowledge the deity of the Augustus Caesar, a shocking denial they made worse by saying the Jesus was the only god, had kept the empire's executioners busy for a decade, lining the roads with the crucified and creating in the arenas the great spectacles of blood and death that delighted the mob.

"Christians? Don't even think about joining those god-botherers," Cenhud growled at Carausius one day as they tacked their small ship up the wide Scheldt River, against the tidal flow. The scow was carrying home a cargo of amphorae of good Rhenish wine, the tall terracotta jars packed upright in sand to stabilize and protect them. Cenhud warmed to his discourse. "A woodworker, as your only god?" he sneered. "Makes no sense. There are plenty of fine gods, not just one, and every one of them has his own purpose."

'My favourite is Mithras," said the youth. "I've seen his temple. In Eboracum, there was a shrine of polished stone to him on the great road."

"He's a soldier's god," agreed Cenhud, "a good god, and he has high moral standards that even some merchants like, so he has plenty of shrines here, too, built by those who can afford them."

He could see why soldiers wanted the gods to keep them safe, but why, asked Carausius, did the merchants spend so much on gifting the deities? "Simple, it's for profit," grunted the shipmaster, neatly dodging a naval galley winging along under its blue canvas sails. The warship's beaked ram threw up a plume of spray as it travelled fast upstream under sail, oars and the push of the incoming tide. The sound of the coxswain's hammer taps came clearly across the water as he kept the 30 rowers in unison, the oars rising and falling like white wings. "Bloody knee-deep sailors, they're as useless as a bread breastplate," Cenhud grumbled. "Anyway, why sacrifice? Well, those who give to the gods want their favour, just as they want more money. Give the god some honour, he'll favour your venture. You just have to know which god to ask for what.

"If you want your crops fruitful, sacrifice to Ceres, goddess of grain. You want your ship kept safe at sea? Call on Neptune. For myself, I give the nod to Manannan mac Lir. He's the Celts' god of the oceans, and we Celts have sailed further than anyone," he said proudly. "We tell people we were pilots before Pontius. We even established settlements in Hibernia, west of Britain." The seaman stopped abruptly, remembering that his young listener had effectively been orphaned by raiders from that green isle, but Carausius was following his own thoughts as he watched a group of young women washing at the river's bank.

"Some people ask the gods for other things," said Cenhud, quickly changing the subject. "They ask for people to be cursed." Carausius looked around, interested. "They write requests on bits of metal, little scrolls of lead or pewter, asking for revenge on someone. Say you go to the baths and leave your sandals and tunic outside. You come out and the bathhouse slave has nodded off in the steam, and your best leather sandals are missing. Now, it could be the slave sold them to someone, or it could be he's been sleeping, and they got nicked. Getting him a beating won't bring back your sandals, but asking the gods to help certainly can."

The victim, explained Cenhud, could ask a god's help to get the sandals back, by threatening doom on the thief. To improve the chances of the god taking an interest, the victim would transfer ownership of the missing goods to the god. "If you're a thief and you read on a lead scroll nailed up in the baths that the god Mercury, whom the victim chose because he had golden winged sandals, will destroy you within nine days unless you return his footwear, what would you do?" the shipmaster asked.

"You'd not risk his wrath. You'd take the damn things back." "But the sandals wouldn't be yours anymore," protested Carausius. "You've dedicated them to the god." "Ah, that's the best bit," said Cenhud, grinning. "You can borrow them until you meet him in person."

VI. Rat

The news spread like wildfire after the Sarmatians arrived. A squadron of troopships docked at Hadrian's Market and offloaded hundreds of the auxiliaries who had been conscripted for service in the Rhine garrisons, and within minutes of the first stepping ashore, the news they brought set the town buzzing. Major revolts had broken out in Gaul and in Spain, the troops at the Danube were hard-pressed, legions were marching throughout the empire and levies were being raised wherever the tribunes could find men.

A recruiting sergeant called Publio stopped Carausius as he walked across the city square. "You're a fine fellow," he said, "why aren't you enjoying the life of a soldier?" The centurion outlined the benefits: at 17, Carausius was old enough to enlist. He did not need to be a Roman citizen to become a legionary. If he enlisted for the usual 20-year term, he'd not only get regular pay, food and clothing, but his old age would be provided for.

Many old soldiers, the sergeant said truthfully, were given large land grants to farm. He didn't say that they were usually along the frontiers of the empire, where the settler-soldiers were a useful resource and could be called back to the eagles in time of civil disturbance. The sergeant eyed Carausius' physique and mentally matched it to the muster officer's written specifications: a lithe youth with quick eye, broad chest, erect neck, muscular arms and shoulders, hardened feet and strong legs. Height wasn't too important, but bravery was.

"You'd be a proper Roman soldier, not a mere auxiliary in some funny local costume," the centurion flattered Carausius. "One day, you might be a centurion commanding 80 men. You'd draw twice the pay of an ordinary soldier. And, you'd share booty like the money from the sale of captives. You'd be a fine soldier, and think of the women who find the uniform irresistible!" The boy blushed, eager to be convinced.

As he trotted home, a white rat scampered out of a drain and ran across the paving stones in front of him. The youth frowned. He'd seen such a thing before, but where? He shrugged and turned for his house. For no reason he could understand, an image flashed across his mind, of a tall man with long, dark hair, who'd arrived by sea to visit his parents at their home in Britain. The man was called Myrddin, he remembered, a sorcerer who 'walked with kings in high places.' The phrase struck him, his mother had used it when she spoke of the wizard, and the boy gulped in sudden misery at his loss.

One day, he promised himself, he would go back to Britain, one day he would try to put right the things that had been done to his village, his family and even, he mused, his country. He felt the tug of his homeland, and was angry at the murder of his father and the injustice that had dragged him and his family away from their land. It would be a fine thing if he could somehow correct at least some of that wrong, and he made a mental vow that one day.....

That evening, the memory of the rat sighting was obscurely nagging at him and he mentioned it to Cait. "That's good fortune," she said. "The Romans regard a white rat as a bringer of good luck, so it's auspicious to see one. Good fortune comes with such a sighting." Carausius nodded. He was superstitious, and an augury was a message directly from the gods. He would not ignore it, in fact, he was cheered that the gods had even noticed him. Maybe they smiled on his vague plan to return to Britain. Maybe, he let the half-formed thought surface, maybe one day he could avenge his father. A fierce heat ran through his body, surprising him and somehow sealing the impulsive pact he was creating. The sorcerer Myrddin would be part of his life's work, he knew with a certainty he could not explain, and some of that work would be about the return of his homeland to its rightful gods. Carausius shook his head to clear his thoughts. First things first, he thought. He'd join the army.

Persuading Cait to let him enter the military was his next task, and it was a difficult one, but she saw that the teen had a sense of purpose, and gave reluctant blessing. Cenhud was sorry to see his fine steersman go, but recognized that with the turbulence in the empire it was only a question of time before Carausius was press-ganged into service anyway. Better go as a volunteer, he reasoned.

So, a few weeks later, and after some basic training, the young Briton and several dozen other recruits recited the Sacramentum, that powerful oath of allegiance that changed a soldier's life entirely. Once taken, the oath meant the legionary was the absolute subject of his general's will and authority. On pain of death, he must obey in all things. However, he no longer had responsibility for any action he was ordered to do, be it muster, march or murder.

The army had some iron rules. A soldier would not desert and would not steal from the camp. He must take any plunder to the tribunes and would only leave the ranks to fight the enemy or to save a Roman citizen. One rule overrode all others: the safety of the emperor always came first, and the soldier would love nothing or no one, including himself or his children, more than he loved the emperor. One recruit stepped forward and recited the whole oath, then one by one, the others stepped forward and swore they would do it as the first man had said. Carausius uttered the 'me, too' words: "Idem in me," and bound himself irretrievably to the Roman military.

Life as a legionary was tolerable. There was a lot to absorb, and the drill sergeants were harsh, but Carausius was a quick learner. All recruits had to take a Roman name on enlistment, but Carausius already bore one, a small mark in his favour. Years later, he'd add several more names, to honour his mentors and superiors, as it was more usual to have three names: your given (or personal name), the name of your clan and the cognomen which identified your family within the clan. After that, far in the future, all his names would be famous to some, infamous to others...

Meanwhile, the youth had a lot to learn. In the barracks, he surveyed the pile of equipment and weapons for which he was now responsible, beginning with cleaning them. Happily, he didn't have to cope with the heavy, intricate armour worn by officers, but he did have a full torso chain mail shirt to clean and polish. This was worn over a heavy wool tunic that stretched to the knees.

At the neck, he wore a scarf to protect his throat from chafing against the mail, and clasped at his right shoulder for better freedom of movement was his dull red cloak, the sagum. 'Putting on the military sagum' meant readying for war, as the hooded, oiled-wool cloak was the soldier's most important clothing. It served as coat, blanket, groundsheet, impromptu sail or even, wrapped around the forearm, as a makeshift shield. Its frequent, final use was as a burial shroud, but the centurion, a chipper Sabine who oversaw 80 soldiers, didn't mention that to the recruits.

"The best wool goods come from Britain," he told them, "and you're lucky because you have that stuff straight from the emperor's own weaving sheds in Britannia. "It's where they make the scarlet cloaks that are only worn by officers, so smarten up when you see one. The Brits have great respect for our Ruperts. They call them Red Dragons," he said proudly, "and well they might. We're the best troops in the world."

Carausius' military kit had more elements. He had knee breeches, toeless socks and underpants all made of wool, and a pair of ankle-high leather marching boots, closed all around, unlike the classic open-toed caligae, that had given the mad emperor 'Little Boots' Caligula his name when, as a child, he'd been fitted with his own miniature footwear.

The new boots, much prized by the troops, had soles that were nailed in D-shaped patterns that cunningly distributed the force of the footfall from the heel diagonally to the toe, making marching much less tiring. "These," said the sergeant proudly, "are your own LPC's." He paused for the expected question, which duly arrived. "Why?" said the old soldier innocently.

"Leather personnel carriers."

Next came a metal helmet with a horsehair crest, and a heavy metal-reinforced, curved elm wood shield with outer layers of leather and linen and a great bronze boss in its centre. "On the march, you can use this for shelter against the rain, but first you put this leather cover over your shield to keep the wet off it," instructed the sergeant. "If you don't, it will become too heavy to be useful and you'll be fucked. Also, when we march, we count the cadence. Every thousand paces is a mile, and we need to know where we are. By counting, we have a good idea of how far we've travelled at all times, and the officers keep itineraries that tell us how far it is from one place to the next. Exempli gratia, it's 227,000 paces from Londinium to Eboracum, where the mighty Sixth Legion is encamped, bothering the local whores. So, brush up your numbers, and you'll never get lost!

"Now, take a look at the sharp bits." The centurion indicated an array of weapons laid out in a display. "This," he said, hefting a 10lb javelin, "is your pilum. It's called 'Rome's Secret Weapon.' Four feet of wood, plus two feet of nasty pointed iron, and you'll throw it about 20 yards.

This behind the head is a lead weight to give it extra impetus, and the blade's soft, so it bends on impact and is useless if they want to chuck it back at you. It'll either go right through the infantryman's protections, or at least it will stick in, and not easily be yanked loose. You have two of them, and two volleys of these are usually enough to decide any skirmish. It's a proper wog-stopper, but this," he said as he picked up a longer thrusting spear, "is much more use at close range."

The centurion put the spear aside, turned and picked up a short broadsword and its belted scabbard. "If you lose everything else, keep this because ..." he eyed the recruits, "it's what you're all about. This is your gladius, your very own steel sword. It has a point, see?" and he stabbed it at the nearest youth, who jumped back, "and two nasty sharp edges." He swatted the sword, whirring it through the air. "But you usually stab with it because a stab is much more deadly. Cutting at someone, however hard you do it, doesn't often kill because bones and armour cover the vitals. Striking also exposes your arm and side. Thrusting, on the other hand, covers the body and the adversary often gets the point stuck in him before he even sees the sword. Remember: the point always beats the edge. You thrust, you don't cut. Now, pay attention."

The old soldier looped the belt with its scabbard over his head. With a casual, practised move, he slotted the gladius in, over his right shoulder so the sword handle protruded clear, for an easy grab. "It's here, it's handy, and it's out of the way when you're holding your shield on your left. In a scrap, you throw your pilum when I tell you, and you either level your spear or you whip out your sword. Got it?"

Around the barrack room, the youths nodded, fascinated. One day they'd hurl the heavy javelins at barbarians. The ones the spears didn't impale would be impeded by the heavy weapons sticking out of their shields, and then they'd..... a ripple of guilty starts ran around the room as the daydreamers saw the centurion glaring at them. "Pay close attention," he warned. Next, the sergeant picked up a lead-weighted throwing dart. "Six of these. Clip them to the back of your shield. At my word, you hurl them at the hairies. They carry a hell of a lot further than a javelin. On your belt, you'll wear this – and don't stab yourself with it." He lifted a foot-long knife with a crescent-shaped pommel. "This is your pugio, your punching knife, and more politicians have been assassinated with them than anything else, so don't forget to wear it when you're all senators."

Carausius tried to take everything in. There was a military pack which the soldiers hefted on a short carrying pole, plus a water skin, cooking kit, cloak bag, entrenching tools and even a six-foot heavy stake that would form part of the rampart in a marching camp. In full parade gear the Mules of Marius, as the soldiers ironically called themselves after the emperor who'd reformed the army, hefted about 80lbs of equipment. Each man carried about two weeks' worth of basic food supplies, including precious salt and an anchovy-and-fish sauce to flavour his food. Last, in his personal purse, usually worn in front at the waist, he kept his coins and personal small treasures. "That purse," grinned the centurion, "is called a scrotum and the scabbard for your sword is a vagina, and don't let them get together or you'll get no rest!"

In the barracks, talking to the other young recruits in his eight-man section, Carausius learned more about his new life. Legionaries were not just soldiers, it seemed. They were manufacturers, labourers and builders of roads, bridges and forts. To the local populace, they acted as customs officers, tax collectors, administrators, and police officers. Recently, they'd been permitted to marry, so the row of small wooden houses in Forum Hadriani where they'd kept their concubines, were being rebuilt in stone with a pleasant bath house attached.

One high-class concubine, Lautissima Laurea, 'Most Magnificent Lauren,' as the troops called her, had prevailed on several senior officers susceptible to her charms to build her a special love nest. Envious mere footsloggers were not allowed to sample Laurea's tempting goods, though they had glimpsed her gilded nipples under her filmy kirtle, but they avidly discussed the rumours. The best were that she had a 'love swing' above her silk-cushioned couch, enough scented oils and love potions to float a trireme and, since two soldiers had spotted a plump tribune thrillingly dressed and painted like a Frankish whore, they believed she had a whole wardrobe of role-playing costumes. What they didn't know was that the concubine made a nice side income selling a peep show to a few of the locals, who took turns watching the officers' antics through a hidden spyhole.

Those peeping civilians were playing with fire, for they would have been severely punished if their secret had reached military ears. The army had not gone soft. There were formidable disciplinary actions for wayward soldiers, and civilians were far less well regarded and faced even worse punishments. Carausius and his fellow recruits learned some harsh facts. Desertion, the crime most feared by the officers, called for the offender to be clubbed to death by his fellow legionaries, on the premise that the coward's action had put them all at risk. Mutiny, too, called for the worst punishment, and a general could order the decimation of a rebellious legion, when every tenth man selected by an officer walking down the ranks would be cudgelled to death by the previous nine of his comrades. It was a terrible vengeance designed to keep the rest of the troops obedient.

Lesser crimes drew fines, extra duties, demotion or mere reduced rations. The punishment for some minor crimes was to order the soldier to sleep outside the protected environs of the camp, when the dangers of a slit throat from a cutpurse not only gave most offenders a sleepless night but improved the watchfulness of the sentries.

Flogging was called for if a soldier was accused of 'unmanly acts,' and outraged senior officers would order the brutal flagellum, the 'short whip' normally used only on slaves, to be employed on discovered homosexuals. It was a whip that would lay bare the spine itself in a few cuts, and a flogging with the metal-tipped flagellum usually ended in death. Treason, too, was fatal. A captured traitor would be tied inside a sack of snakes and thrown into a river, while cowardice called for execution by crucifixion or beheading.

"It seems harsh," Carausius told a fellow recruit named Aemilius who questioned the brutality, "but I suppose if you do what you're told, you'll be all right. We're just ground pounders, that's all we need to know." Privately, he thought some of the junior officers were sadists, but his intimidating size, energy and intelligence kept him safe from their attentions and as he was scrupulous in following orders, the young soldier found his life not too burdensome. He marched and drilled obediently, he and his comrades built city walls, bridges and roads under the supervision of engineer officers and he learned more and more about the disciplined army that ruled the world. Forum Hadriani was a hot spot in that world, a staging post for legions that were trying to hold back the Germanic tribes from beyond the Rhine. By now, of the empire's 29 legions of 5,000 or more men, eight were massed on the banks of that mighty river, and Carausius' training battalion was readying to join them.

"We've already seen divisions of our legions sent in to reinforce what we have there," said Crassus, the First Spear centurion of the first cohort as he addressed the assembled legionaries. "They've come from everywhere, even....." his glance fell on Carausius, whose impressive stature and front-rank position made him stand out, "... even from Britain. The Second, Sixth and 20th Legions all helped build Hadrian's Wall to keep out people, especially the ones like young Caros here who looks like a bloody great bear - " he paused to allow the ripple of laughter to die down. ""Now, they're in Germania, driving back the spear stoppers who threaten the Roman Peace. And that's where your duties will be taking you, so kiss your boyfriends in the town goodbye, wash your feet and get ready for some marching."

VII. Beobwill

Just a few weeks later, to the bray of military brass, and burdened under their heavy packs, the legionaries lived up to their nickname of Walk-a-Lots, and marched south. They were trailed by the impedimenta of carts and mules carrying food and gear, all accompanied by a crowd of hangers-on, whores, traders, quack doctors and scam artists, and they were headed down the Rhine river to its confluence with the River Main at the great imperial fort of Mainz, long time headquarters of the XXII Primigenia legion, those Goth-killers whose commander had assumed the purple of Gallic emperor.

The familiar march routine was quickly established and, day after day, they rose at first light to the sound of brass trumpets, ate a breakfast of olives, fruit and porridge prepared by the camp cooks, and were lined up with their loaded pack train by full sunrise. The daily six or seven hours' march covered about 20 miles, before the legion halted to make camp and eat a dinner that usually included smoked fish or salted bacon and hard-baked bread, all dishes that would stay preserved on the journey, plus local cheese, vegetables and beer. In winter's rain, the soldiers walked tortoise-style, holding their leather-sheathed, oblong shields above their heads for shelter, their packs swaying easily on the forked carrying sticks they balanced over their left shoulders. The emperor Marius had reformed the army and implemented his idea to speed the march by putting the load on the soldiers, not on the creakingly slow ox-drawn carts. The legionaries, the Mules of Marius, never forgot him. Most never forgave him, either.

At the end of the day's trek, the routine was also always the same. Surveyors, who had gone ahead literally to stake out a place, had invariably chosen higher ground with water and wood nearby. The arriving legionaries would dig a ditch about ten feet deep, throwing up the spoil to form a wall above it. This rampart, wide enough for sentries to walk through, was topped with the sharpened wooden stakes that each man carried, singly or as a pair.

Always, the encampment was plotted in exact fashion, with gates centred on each of the four walls. One faced the line of advance to the enemy; the gates at right angles to it were linked by the main street. An open space of 60 paces was left between the inside of the ramparts and the lines of tents, leather for the officers, canvas for the soldiers, which were laid out in the same pattern, camp after camp. On arrival at the night's camp, every man knew from experience where his quarters, the cookhouse, the latrines or the horse lines would be and could go unerringly to the same marked spaces to erect his tent just as he had hundreds of times before. Equally, he and his officers knew exactly what their duties were each day, at every overnight halt, whether the legion stopped for one night or a whole winter.

For the next 30 months, Carausius moved in a blur of working, fighting and marching to the familiar, raucous, sometimes sentimental soldiers' songs as the swaying columns tramped on, sometimes 40 or 50 miles in a single day. He and his comrades dug ditches and defensive dykes, cleared trees, repaired roads and built bridges, all while the legions pushed through the dripping forests and across the rugged, snowy Jura mountains to the furthest frontier of the Danube river, to hunt the elusive enemy. The Briton and his comrades were in constant danger as Alemanni arrows flickered from ambush in the dank and gloomy forests, but from time to time the legionaries trapped their enemies and brought them to punishing, bloody conflict. Then, they'd face howling barbarians, crazed to fighting pitch on mead or forest mushrooms, confident that if they died, they'd reincarnate to fight another day. Those days, the Romans ruthlessly butchered the Alemanni, taking some captive for cruel and vengeful deaths as they remembered the comrades they had lost to the arrows and spears that had come without warning from the trees.

The young soldier became familiar with the throat-tightening knocking sounds of shield edges banging together as the shield wall was formed, he knew too well the smells of fighting: smoke, crushed grass, ripped guts, excrement and above all the iron-tasting stench of pooled blood. All were frequent, fear-heightened and vivid experiences, and all were stamped deep into Carausius' memory.

By this time, the Briton was no longer the sickly child who had landed at Forum Hadriani. He was a 20 year old hardened soldier, a big man, bearded and brutal, who had won promotion to centurion through his wits and his scarred fists, which were testament to the opponents he had battered into submission. He rejoiced in his ability to perform strenuous physical tasks, could cover 40 or more miles a day on a forced march under full pack, and still be ready to fight at the end of it. Confident but not a blusterer, Carausius had long since seen the close friendships of his old eight-man section erode as he earned promotions, but he had earned grudging admiration from the 80 men of his century for his savage energy and drive and for his willingness to take on any task. Behind his back, they called him 'Car the Bear,' a not-unaffectionate nickname based on his size, usual amiability and quick wrath when wronged. He expected strict discipline, and commanded unquestioning loyalty from his legionaries, from whom he demanded only a few simple obediences. He laid out his rules clearly. "You don't get drunk unless I say you can, you don't steal from each other and you fight hard when I tell you," he told them. "That's it; three rules. Remember them, follow them, and we'll all be better for it." He did not spell out the alternatives, but after a few dissenters had been clubbed into submission by the centurion, the others learned not to question him, for in combat or a brawl he was a fearsome opponent.

The roots of his fighting skills ran deep. During his early days in the army, Carausius had served in the 15th Legion, dedicated to Apollo, at their garrison on the Danube at Carnuntum. This was a vital military and trade outpost on the Amber Road, and was a key link between Rome's Asian frontiers and its central and northern European territories.

Carnuntum was known as the place where the legions had acclaimed Septimius Severus emperor, but the settlement was most famed for its gladiator training school, a complex that was a mixture of barracks and high-security jail. There, convicts, prisoners and slaves, kept in cells barely big enough to turn around in, were brutally trained to fight in the arena. Carausius' commander was a tribune with novel ideas of military instruction, and had sent his soldiers to be tutored by the gladiator trainers, who had taught the legionaries hand to hand tactics not found in the military manuals.

Carausius thrived on the task. He enjoyed the physical challenges, coped well with the discipline, worked hard at the skills, and learned street fighting techniques that would serve him well. "The average gladiator dies after six bouts, but some survive hundreds of times in the arena", the instructors told the soldiers. "If you know their techniques, you can be a killing machine who will one day retire from the army alive, with a nice nut of booty and a piece of land. You will be confident of winning in a hand-to-hand combat, and that will help you to stay calm in a crisis. When you're fighting some Norseman berserker who is crazed on mushrooms or mead before he goes into battle, you'll move better and be more deadly. The best gladiators use these techniques literally for a living. If they don't learn, or do it wrong, they're dragged off by the heels to meet Charon and cross the Styx."

Carausius listened. He liked the idea of surviving when others did not, and he chose to work hard to improve his fighting skills. He practised with extra-heavy weaponry, toughening his considerable muscles even more, so that when he came to fight with swords or spears of regular weight, he fought faster and easier. He learned quickly, associating with both the instructors and the gladiators, learning a few words of each of their native tongues; German, Spanish, Illyrian and a half dozen others. He took care to remember the instructors' individual fighting styles and tricks. Every man, he found had signature moves, every man fought to one of a score or so of patterns. Recognizing that pattern early in a bout gave him an advantage, and he took it.

Carausius was still stationed at Carnutum when he was first noted for his barracks brawling, and it was only a matter of months before his reputation was widely known, and very few would take on the crushing power of the massive fists or the devastating, unexpected blows from a knee, elbow or head butt that could finish the match.

As his legion campaigned, he used his gladiator's techniques in hand to hand combat with Frankish and OstroGoth warriors who fought with a berserk fury that was often fuelled, as his instructors had said, with hallucinogens culled from woodland mushrooms. Then, Carausius was a cool-headed and expert killer, using his own hot hatred of the enemy as motivation, but fighting with a cold, focused intensity. Time and again, the big, bearded centurion was seen where he liked to be, in the front rank, battering his way through the enemy shield wall so his hacking, stabbing comrades could follow to butcher the shattered line of barbarians. Once, in an ambush sprung by a large war band of Saxons, he had not only rallied his men under a slashing hail of arrows, but coolly bought time for them to regroup by challenging one of the ambushers' chieftains to single combat.

That day, the Romans' overconfident tribune had made a bad error, and had brought his men through a defile where the soldiers could not deploy properly if attacked. It had to happen, it tempted the Fates, and the bored, malicious goddesses saw to their own entertainment. The Saxons were concealed and waiting, the Romans were stalled at a blockage of felled trees; there were too few scouts out ahead and none on the flanks, because the defile was too narrow. There was no warning. Saxon arrows and javelins flickered out of the forest and struck with deadly force along almost the whole length of the stalled column, and howling barbarians came in behind them to swamp the standing file. In seconds, the unprepared legionaries were faced with a chaotic hand-to-hand struggle in which the soldiers could not deploy into their battle formation, and the Saxons' superior numbers meant it was inevitable that they would splinter, isolate and butcher the legion. Carausius acted fast under the hail of missiles. He mustered his century to form an armoured tortoise of covering shields and was working to drag the wounded and dying into shelter when he spotted in the Saxon ranks a big man who seemed to be a commander.

"That's the noisy bastard I want," he muttered to his marching companion Juventus, who was struggling to refasten a broken strap on his armour. "I can distract them, take him and put the fear of the gods into his hairy-arsed mates, too." Carausius grinned. "He's like you, that Saxon; big, soft, and full of his own piss and wind. He'll do nicely." Juventus paused as he struggled with a recalcitrant buckle.

"He's a big bastard, and he'll have you for a snack, you ponce," he goaded. "I suppose I'll have to step in and drop him when he puts you on the ground." Carausius spat on the turf.

"If he puts me on the ground, yes, stick a couple of arrows into him. I don't want any of your Roman etiquette-conscious polite ways putting me at risk."

The Briton turned towards the German line, stepped clear and pointed his javelin at the big Saxon. "You are a coward who needs to eat fungus to give you the courage to fight. You are a woman who fights from behind trees," he bellowed in his oddly-accented version of the Germanic tongue. "Come and see what a real man will do to you. Spread your legs for me, you whore, you know you want it." The grammar wasn't right, but the message was clear. And, in an obscene gesture the Germans themselves often used, Carausius extended his middle finger at the big Saxon. The man's cheeks flushed at the insults and he stepped out into the small clearing where the legionaries were frantically trying to pull the wounded inside the shield wall they had formed around the standard bearers.

"I am called Beobwill," the big blond warrior boomed proudly. "We'll see who is the bitch here." He gestured to his war band to stop the javelins and arrows, and strode arrogantly forward. Along the line, the hail of missiles slowed, then ceased. The ambushers leaned forward on their weapons, panting and grateful for the interruption, to watch the sport.

Beobwill, whose plaited blond moustaches hung below his chin, was impressively large and fearsome. He wore bronze and gold bands on his massive, tattooed arms and a shaggy, sleeveless bear's pelt jerkin over his leather breastplate. He wore calf-length trews and supple leather mid-boots laced tightly. His long fair hair under a plundered Roman helmet with its armoured cheek pieces was tied back with a leather lace, and in his broad belt he had a knife of Roman make whose handle was wrapped in kidskin held under gold wire. A war axe with runic inscriptions on its yard-long handle dangled casually from his fist.

Carausius, too, was a big man, and was professionally equipped for war. He had long since discarded the heavy mail coat favoured by most legionaries in favour of the expensive lobster-segmented armour that was much lighter. Internal leather straps held hoops of iron that overlapped horizontally around his torso, front and rear hoops laced together. His shoulders were protected by hinged iron plates and under the protective metal he wore a padded leather jerkin to absorb some of the shock of a sword blow or spear thrust. The leather was liberally smeared with lanolin taken from new fleeces, to allow the armour to move freely over it, and, where it was more exposed, was smeared with beeswax to waterproof it from the constant north European rain.

Like Beobwill, Carausius wore a Roman helmet, but his was an indulgence; a cavalryman's parade piece, with a silver gilt Eagle standing before the polished crest. Over his shoulder, ready for a right-handed draw, was his gladius stabbing sword, of the shorter Mainz armoury variety. A bone-handled dagger with a long, slender, ribbed blade hung at his left side. He had, as was his custom, rubbed sticky pine sap on the handle to improve the grip, a trick he'd learned from the instructors at the gladiator school in Carnuntum. Carausius nodded almost amiably at Beobwill and dropped his great shield to the ground, but retained the heavy javelin with its shaft of squared ash and long bodkin head of needle-sharp iron. His teeth glinted through his dense curly beard as he laughed at his opponent. "Nancy boy, eh? You'd like a man up your arse again, eh, you mincing bum boy?"

The Briton was watching the Saxon carefully and saw the man's eyes narrow and face redden deeply at the insult. 'He can be goaded', Carausius thought calmly. 'I can incite this one to fury'. He turned to Juventus and the line of legionaries and put a hand on his hip. "I think thith one'th a Greek", he lisped, "a proper bum chum." He kept his voice loud enough for both Beobwill and the nearer barbarians to hear. A growl from the mob of tribesmen, whose rough tongue sounded to civilized ears as if they were saying 'ba-ba-ba,' hence the 'bar-barian' tag, told him they may not have understood his words, but they'd certainly picked up on the gesture. The shot had gone home; the disrespect for their champion was assailing their pride. As a few of the legionaries laughed, and the Saxons muttered to each other, the growl spread. Carausius watched carefully as his opponent moved across the trampled, soggy leaves and mud of the clearing. The big barbarian seemed to step very deliberately.

The Briton noted salt stains on the inside of Beobwill's brown wool trews and what looked like a string of dried spit on the outside of one massive calf. "Trews?" he thought. Then the realization hit him. The man was an equestrian. The stains were from his horse. His fighting was not usually done on foot. Carausius' appraising eye took in the man's tight-laced boots with their smooth soles, and he turned quickly away, dropping his javelin, kneeling and pretending to fumble with the weapon. Surreptitiously, he slid out his punching knife and slashed the laces of his marching boots. As he stood, snatching up and brandishing his javelin high to attract Beobwill's furious gaze, he kicked off the footwear. He'd fight barefooted for surer grip in the slippery clearing.

The Saxon saw Carausius' bootless feet as he stepped forward, and recognized that the tactic would give the Briton an advantage in the uncertain footing, but it was too late and he was too proud and suspicious of a trick to stop and unlace his own boots. Instead, without hesitation he roared and rushed forward, scything the big-bladed axe horizontally, and aiming to chop Carausius in half at the waist. The Briton stepped lithely sideways to parry the blow with his javelin, angling the shaft and deflecting the huge force harmlessly upwards, though it shaved a thick, foot-long splinter from the ash. Beobwill staggered slightly as the heavy weapon tugged him off balance and Carausius circled the sweep of his javelin's long blade to slice a cut below the Saxon's elbow. "You're too slow, bitch," he goaded, stepping back.

Beobwill snarled and swung again, less wildly. Carausius took the blow on the iron blade of the javelin and felt the weakened shaft tremble. His eye was diverted for an instant as he glanced at the fresh gouge to assess the damage and Beobwill, shortening his grip on the long axe handle, surged in unexpectedly, chopping and thrusting two-handed. The rush forced the Briton back, his heel hit a fist-sized stone half buried in the loam, and he was unbalanced. Beobwill was fast. His next blow slid off Carausius' helmet, sliced into his unguarded cheek and delivered a numbing blow to his left shoulder, but the armour held. The Briton stumbled backwards, fountaining blood. He was dazed but from long training circled the point of his javelin at the big Saxon, who was snarling and roaring as he came at him again. Beobwill swatted the Briton's javelin aside, smashed the butt of the axe into Carausius' cheekbone and chopped down with the blade.

The blow was a killing one, and only blind instinct saved the Briton as, head ringing with pain, he threw himself backwards. The axe blade scored down his breastplate and thudded through his left foot, severing the two smallest toes before it buried itself in the dirt. Beobwill bellowed in triumph, and the massed Saxons roared in response, rattling their swords and spears against their shields. The Roman ranks, now formed into three battle lines, stood almost mute, sucking in their breath as they watched their bloodied champion stagger towards defeat. Juventus swore softly, and reached down for his short Sarmatian bow. If it came to it, he'd stick the Saxon through the throat, he vowed.

The pain from his mutilated foot had not yet fully reached Carausius' consciousness. His left arm was almost useless, his neck was slick with blood from his flapping cheek where the teeth showed though, and his face was numb where his cheekbone was crushed. He shook his head, spraying blood droplets, and blinked hard, trying to focus his mind as Beobwill wrenched his axe free of the ground. The Saxon moved in again, slower this time, readying for the kill. He shortened his two-handed grip on the axe, whirred it again at his crippled opponent and growled in pleasure as the big blade hacked clean through the ash shaft, causing the long iron spearhead to fly uselessly sideways.

Carausius swayed, head drooping, Beobwill pulled back to swing again and the Briton took his chance. In the blink of an eye, snarling like a hound, he kicked out his right foot, heel hitting the ground first, and booted hard off his left, feeling the toes dig into the soft ground. His trailing leg straightened, and he pushed his hips forward at the same instant that his right foot flattened against the ground. The strike was as fast as an adder's and he extended it by leaning towards the big Saxon, adding to his reach as he aimed inside the Saxon's guard. The lunge, with Carausius' arm extended in the classic posture of the swordsman, thrust the javelin's jagged, broken handle into the Saxon's open mouth. The big man's head snapped backward and a spray of spittle, blood and broken incisors spattered outwards. The Briton continued his forward lunge, releasing the broken shaft and hurling himself onward. He grasped the stinking bear fur with both hands and head-butted Beobwill square on the bridge of his nose. The ornamental silver gilt eagle on Carausius' helmet crushed the Saxon's eyebrow, the shuddering, heavy impact of the blow dropped him stunned to his knees.

In the blood-pumping rush of combat, Carausius felt again the sense of being immortal that he knew in combat. For him, time was oozing by only imperceptibly and the dim light of the ravine seemed bright and clear. He did not feel his wounds, and he felt detached, almost an observer of the events around him. He did not hear his own animal snarls, he felt he had all the time he needed while his opponent appeared to be moving so slowly he could have danced around him. The Briton gave himself a mental nod of approval. The gladiators' street fighting lessons had served him again. Better move on, he told himself semi-scoldingly, although an observer would have considered no time at all had elapsed. Carausius took a half pace sideways, reached back with his right hand and flashed out his gladius from its shouldered sheath. It was so easy and natural, it was as if every pace, every movement were choreographed. Without even the hesitation of a single heartbeat, he thrust the heavy blade through the kneeling Saxon's neck, in the traditional killing stroke for a defeated gladiator.

The steel went in with a sucking sound and a spurt of bright oxygen-rich arterial blood spouted upwards. Carausius twisted the sword and wrenched hard to free it of the clinging muscle, then stepped back. Beobwill's last sound was the harsh rattle of his lungs emptying for their final time. He was dead before he slumped sideways onto the leaf mould.

Carausius touched the lacerated flap of flesh at his cheek, and grimaced. The light seemed to dim, his adrenaline-heightened consciousness seemed to ebb away. He felt crushing pain, here in his face, there in his foot. He stumbled on his maimed, blood-squelching toes but stood upright to face the Saxon ambushers. "Who else wants a piece?" he shouted in his grating, accented German. Around the edges of the throng men began to turn away and slip quietly into the dripping forest. A knocking clatter of metal sounded behind the centurion as his infantrymen touched shield edges and stepped forward a pace. The menacing promise of the oncoming storm of violence broke the spell and a bold ranker shouted to his fellow legionaries: "Let's do them for the Bear!"

The Saxons turned and began to move slowly, then more quickly through the trees, but there were too many and the retreat became a panic. They blocked each other as they tried to edge away from the ravine's track and into the safety of the forest. A tribune shouted to the archers: "Aim for their balls!" before a hissing volley of feathered death thumped into the Saxon ranks. At the officer's next order, a storm of heavy, lead-weighted javelins from the closing Romans thudded into the Saxons' unguarded backs as they flinched away. From the right, two squadrons of Roman cavalry cantered down the column into position, and at a brazen blown command, the horsemen rode their leather-armoured mounts into the flanks of the shuffling barbarians, spitting them on the long lances, chopping and hacking with their heavy cavalry swords, mercilessly doing the butcher's business of slaughter. In minutes, the Germans' forest was their death field, an abattoir where men were slashed into bloody meat and where those Saxons who surrendered soon found themselves chained, enslaved and trudging into a lifetime of misery.

His wounds had bled freely, and once Carausius had been carried by Juventus and two other companions back to the field aid station behind the legion's standards, the lacerations were further cleansed with vinegar before being sewn shut. The days of the journey from the mountains of the Jura back to Mainz were a faint opium-deadened memory, a time of jolting horse-drawn carriages, flaring oil lamps at night, and the voices of the medical attendants as they told over and again of the heroic contest and of the slaughter of the Saxons.

Then, Carausius was in the base hospital at Mainz, a place sunlit in the summer mornings, cool in the day's heat, in a room that smelled pleasantly of the lemons used to repel moths; a haven soothed by the murmuring of bees in the herb garden outside. He spent his days asleep or drowsing, healing gangrene-free, passing the time in a drifting half-world of hurt and recovery. Several weeks went by. He'd made a few tries to walk the quadrangle but putting weight on the mutilated foot was still painful and he'd always have a limp, he supposed, but he was healing.

One person was largely responsible for the soldier's recovery. Campana, a female pharmacist who was a Briton like himself, took a special interest in the big man and used her considerable skills to help him through the process of healing. She gave him henbane and poppy seed to ease his wounds, cleaned them daily with sour wine, hyssop and comfrey and re-bandaged them with fresh Spanish linen. She eased with infusions of Illyrican iris the terrible headaches that beset him and made concoctions of herbs for other specifics. She employed sage to reduce his fevers, created a broth of ginger to ease inflammation, gave him wild cucumber to control pain and a broth of thyme for nausea. She used plenty of fennel, that herb favoured by gladiators, which they believed gave them courage and stamina, as a general tonic, and she flavoured his food with expensive pepper brought far overland from the Indies to Baghdad and onwards to the northern Italian trading centre of Ticinum. Satisfied with her efforts, she watched with proprietary pride as the soldier's condition improved, week by week.

Carausius also took daily hot baths in salt water, to ease his many aches and pains. The medical care, the rest and the excellent barracks food, which included ham, venison, cheese, and plentiful vegetables all combined to help the injured man recover his strength and speed his recovery. Campana supplemented the barracks diet with soup made with barley and beef marrow, and sometimes with expensive but tasty chicken broth, which his nurse insisted had healing qualities. She also gave him a good supply of figs, olives and fermented fish sauce imported from Italy, delicacies she successfully employed to tempt his appetite. The pharmacist had been to Italy and in one of their many conversations - in which they enjoyed speaking in their native British - spoke with awe of a feast she'd attended at the villa of a wealthy prefect. Swans, geese and duck were cooked and served whole, she reported, with boiled parsnips, all of it served on vast platters and in great style. One note jarred her, though. The Romans ate it with their hands, she told him, with a small moue of distaste.

But the feast! She recalled it in loving detail. It had included a whole roasted wild boar, juniper sausage, cakes stuffed with live figpeckers, peas stewed in honey, and edible dormice covered in poppy seeds and honey. Her favourite dish had been a fruit sauce of damsons, prunes and dates from Jericho, she said. Carausius, now rested and relatively free of pain, was relaxed and mellow. He teased his nurse with his own tales of feasting. Once, he told her a story of ordering a lobster and being served with a crustacean possessed of only one claw. "I asked the slave; 'why does this creature only have one claw?' and he told me it had been in a fight and lost the other," he said.

"What did you say?" Campana obligingly asked.

Solemnly, Carausius said, "I told him to bring me the winner."

He spoke, too, of the old Roman Marcus Gavius Apicius, a fabulously wealthy man with a big kitchen staff and an adventurous palate. "Seneca himself wrote of the appetites of Apicius," Carausius told her. "He ate omelettes made with jellyfish; he consumed minced dolphin, boiled parrot and herb-stuffed mouse. He considered brine-pickled sows' wombs a delicacy and he invented the world's most expensive dish: a pie made with larks' tongues."

Campana gasped, Carausius grinned. "It ended badly. Apicius used up his entire fortune of 100 million sestersi – it simply vanished down his gullet. When his secretary told him that he was down to his last ten million or so, Apicius realized that his epicurean days were ending, so he went out like a true Roman: he had one last banquet and then poisoned himself."

The days slid by, sunlit and carefree, marked chiefly by the unexpected news that Carausius had been promoted to tribune, one of the legion's six senior officers, effectively making him second in command. Although he was eager to take up his new duties, it was also good to be away from campaigning, to idle away the time, although the soldier still had a deeply-felt urge to return to Britain that had been renewed by his conversations with his countrywoman. He was both restive for action and employment and at the same time was almost content not to have responsibilities.

Finally, a summons came and his indecision was ended. The Greek physician brought the news, hurrying into Carausius' room off the central courtyard. "A courier, a courier from Rome, for you," he gasped excitedly. The man, whose dusty face was streaked with sweat runnels, was also striped with his mount's dried spume and stank of leather and horse urine. The small red leather cylinder he handed to the Briton was tied and wax-sealed. Carausius had heard in the barracks of such missives in such containers. It was a message from the emperor himself. He unfastened the binding, extracted the single sheet inside and read it quickly. It contained a single, terse command. Carausius was ordered to Rome. The new soldier-emperor Carus Persicus wanted him there, no reason given.

VIII. Rome

Carausius knew of Marcus Aurelius Carus Augustus, called Persicus. He was no hanger and flogger, just a pig-headed boar of a man who didn't put up with Rome's nancified politicians and their ways. The troops liked the no-nonsense soldier and forgave him his violent temper, and in return, he paid attention to the footsloggers and their pay and conditions. They remembered how he'd drowned a military cook in a cauldron of his own foul stew after he found that the man had been selling fresh supplies and instead was serving condemned meat to the troops. The soldiers also spoke admiringly of Carus' personal courage and immense strength. One much-told tale recounted how, enraged during a wrestling match when his opponent squeezed his nut sack, he'd knocked out the man's teeth and beaten his face to pulp before kicking him unconscious. You knew where you stood with a man like that, the soldiers agreed.

Rome hailed him, too, because he had brilliantly defeated a huge Persian army in an action that pushed them back across the Tigris for generations. Carus had destroyed the entire Persian cavalry and brought thousands of them to Rome as slaves, earning himself his 'Persicus' title. Now, the emperor had taken notice of a lowly tribune and summoned him to court.

The injured Briton did what he'd sworn on his army Sacramentum; he obeyed his emperor, and he went to Rome.

The city, with its 2,000 private homes and 46,000 tenement buildings packed like rookeries that overflowed its centre, was jaw-droppingly magnificent. Carausius remembered his boyhood visits to Eboracum in faraway Britannia and how he'd marvelled at the governor's palace and the treasurer's house there, but compared to these mighty temples, public buildings and homes, they were puny, provincial cottages. Every citizen's home, it seemed, was a palace, and the palaces themselves were beyond belief.

With a day to wait before his audience, Carausius seized his chance to view Rome. Slaves were summoned to carry the wounded Briton in a litter, and he toured the city, awestruck and gaping at the magnificence. Every street was paved, every public building was faced with polished limestone or marble and glinting in gold leaf. Drinking fountains stood on the street corners, statues of the great and good adorned the plazas where conjurers and acrobats, each with a small placard announcing the name of the sponsor who'd paid for his efforts - and Carausius knew enough to recognize some of the names as those of politicians eager for votes - entertained the passing throngs of busy citizens.

Nearby, on a smooth clay court, a group of men were playing a spirited game of bowls, throwing stone spheres at a small target ball, while their idling slaves sat in the shade, gossiping and watching the passing scene. A water deliveryman rumbled by with his cart full of dripping amphorae, a drover herded several pigs to market; a stone mason, dusty and muscled, strode by with his apprentice at his heels while a scribe hunched over his little table to write a passionate love letter on behalf of his client, an unlettered farmer who had a cage of songbirds at his feet, ready for sale. A baker hawked his bread, shouting that it had the best bran content in Rome and that he also had a fresh batch especially baked to be eaten with oysters. Then he called his new boast: his just-baked batch infused with fennel would give a customer the courage of a gladiator. It was a claim ignored by a poulterer who was struggling with a handcart on which he'd piled perilously high several crates of squawking chickens.

In this plaza, a fishmonger newly arrived from the great aquaria on the fifth floor of Trajan's Market had brought live carp in a bucket to the caretaker whose sole task was to guard a sculpture of the emperor Julius. If the statue could talk, Carausius mused to himself, it would have been appalled at the noise. The great Caesar himself had had once proposed banning chariots from the city centre because of the racket made by their iron-rimmed wheels, and though the narrow, smelly streets were well-padded thanks to the muffling qualities of horse dung, the clatter was still considerable.

In the open plaza, shaded by Julius' statue, and across from a goldsmith's storefront where two muscular slaves stood guard and warily watched passers-by, a barber was shaving a client. He was stroking his blade with care, and the client's cheek bulged where the barber had put a small apple into the man's cheek to stretch the skin smooth. Carausius had heard that the last client of the day got to eat the apple, too, but he wasn't sure about the truth of that, or even if anybody would want to. More palatable were the offerings of a score of food vendors who hawked cooked chicken and sausages, olives, cheeses and fruit to the parade of pedestrians thronging by, and the soldier sniffed appreciatively at the tempting odours of the foodstuffs.

The throngs themselves were nothing to sniff at, thought Carausius, mentally telling himself not to gape as he eyed the spectrum of humanity. In this city of a million people, capital of the world, were to be found members of every known race. Glossy black Nubians and olive-skinned Assyrians jostled pale-haired Scandinavian mariners; narrow-eyed Huns from the Great Plains beyond Germania strode by ringletted Egyptian astrologers with their elaborately-bound beards, a bearded Syrian played his odd, transverse-stringed harp; sleek Persian traders in bright silks muttered secretively to each other. A knot of elegant, fashionable matrons with elaborately-piled hair, dyed red with beechwood ashes or gold with saffron, all of it modestly draped under the hood of a palla, chatted animatedly through rouged lips while attentive slaves held parasols to screen their mistresses' lily complexions.

Rome's politicians paraded themselves in togas dazzlingly whitened with chalk to stand out from the crowd's dingier garments and here and there, slaves pushed wheeled cages as they delivered exotic animals recently arrived from Africa and India. Most, like the two Caledonian bears Carausius spotted, were destined for the bloodied sand of the arena, a few would become household adornments of the ultra-wealthy.

As usual, the street was crowded and noisome, stinking from the sewage in the drains and cacophonous with the shouts of vendors and pedestrians, the clatter of hooves and the rumble of the iron-clad chariot wheels.

Many in the crowds were purposeful scholars who hurried heedless past the glowing charcoal braziers of the food vendors. They ignored, too, the poultry and game hawkers and the tavern where men lolled over watered wine and a graffiti artist was defacing a wall with libels about his former lover. The academics were on their way to the great library, which was open from the first hour until the sixth. Carausius watched and marvelled. His eyes lit on the less purposeful in the throng, the matrons and their slaves. Those colourful, attractive Roman ladies wandered leisurely through the rows of awning-protected shops that were a part of the vast bath complex built by the tyrant Caracalla, the emperor they called the Enemy of Mankind, although people seemed to enjoy the facility he'd built.

It was a place to linger, a natatorium where as many as 1,600 bathers could enjoy the temperature-controlled pools at one time, and emerge refreshed and cleansed to browse an array of displays of all the goods of the empire. The tribune's eyes were everywhere, taking it in. The place was a wonder, and he'd heard that some nobleman called Maximian planned an even greater and more sumptuous water palace. The man must have some fabulous wealth to go with an ego to match, he thought.

Carausius absently brushed away a swarm of the flies that plagued the city. His attention was on a Bactrian camel being led through the street until he spotted a woman walking unshaded by her attendant slaves and looked twice. Blonde, she wore a blue linen shift, and a fine wool cloak thrown back from the amber and silver brooch that clasped it at her shoulder. An alert sounded in his head and the Briton did a double-take. The brooch was similar to the one his father Aulus had worn nearly two decades before, the symbol of his nobleman's status. Carausius' breath caught and he urged his slaves after her.

Sucia Silvestria was a Romano-British trader's young widow who had maintained her late husband's lucrative links with Rome and this day was enjoying the results of her efforts. She was shopping. Carausius had spotted her on her way to visit an Arab trader who had travelled the western half of the Silk Routes to bring exotic satins, silks, musk and spices to the marketplace of the rulers of the world. The tribune's hurrying litter bearers caught sight of her as she turned onto the smooth flagstoned plaza that fronted the huge complex of the baths. Carausius urged the bearers on as they pushed through the crowds, and at last he came alongside Sucia.

On impulse, he addressed her in British, not Latin. "Wait, please, my lady," he said. Sucia turned, startled to hear her native tongue after so many weeks. She had recently made the long journey from Britain, braving the pirates of the Narrow Sea, descending the Loire and the Rhone rivers to the southern port of Massalia then shipping by galley to Ostia, sea gate to Rome. In all that time she had heard Latin, Greek and

Gaulish, but only her personal slaves could converse in the language with which she was most comfortable. "You are British?" she asked the thick-necked, bearded military man with the bandaged cheek, who was so incongruously sitting in a litter. "Lady," Carausius said, struggling to stand and bow, "I am so born, but it is a long time since I was there, and my command of my own language may be clumsy."

The pair waved their slaves aside and sat on a marble bench, out of the flow of foot traffic, content to talk comfortably. Carausius diffidently indicated the amber and silver brooch at her shoulder. "My father had such a badge," he said quietly. Sucia heard the longing in the burly man's voice. She nodded and, encouraged, Carausius' sudden loneliness and sense of loss of his homeland caused him to indulge in an unusual opening of his heart. "I miss Britain," he said simply. "I remember it only from the days when I was a boy, but it seems every day was summer, every place was green and fresh, with fields of honey-scented clover and trees burdened with apples that were warm from the sun. It seems like a faraway dream, when I had my brothers and my mother there and I was not concerned with war and hurt and killing."

Sucia was touched, and she wove magic for the big soldier, spinning her words into a blanket of comfort and nostalgia as she spoke of their homeland, and how it was not just a faraway island in the northern mists, but was indeed a green and pleasant place. She told her own story, of losing her husband but keeping his trading business, she detailed how she had brought four couples of prized British hunting dogs to Rome, as well as a consignment of fine wool garments, Baltic amber and a quantity of jet mined from the north eastern coastal cliffs near Carausius' old home. She did not mention the high-value goods she kept safely hidden: the blue crystal mined in the limestone peak country of central Britain, or the precious, prized sun stones that seemed to split the light and show sailors the way in sea fogs. These, she traded from Icelanders, just as she acquired mussel pearls from blue-tattooed natives of Britain's lake land. The lake stones were exactly like those in the pearl-studded breast plate which Julius Caesar had brought back to votive at the temple of Venus.

Responding to Sucia's interested questions, Carausius outlined his military career, his wounds and now, his summons to the imperial court. "I have no real idea what the emperor wants with me, but as he's just back from campaigning in the same part of the world as me, I expect it's military matters," he confided. Unseen by either of them, a white rat crouched in a shady corner, quietly watching, its glittering eyes fixed on Carausius. It was a portent he would have been comforted to know about the next day, when he limped hesitantly into the imperial palace.

The Emperor Marcus Aurelius Carus Augustus, called Persicus, was a career cavalryman and former commander of the Praetorian Guard who couldn't stand bullshit. When Carausius, patched and battered, hobbled painfully into his vast reception hall, the emperor roared at his praetorians to get the man a stool at once; couldn't they see he was a fucking hero and had half his foot missing? "I'm a donkey walloper myself, don't care for that marching stuff, but that doesn't mean I haven't been in more tight places than a shepherd's arm", he bellowed at the new tribune cheerfully. He stepped off the dais where an artist had been painting his portrait. He took off the cap that covered his bald head, wiped his greasy hands carelessly on his fine tunic, ridding himself of the remains of the roast chicken and truffles he'd been eating, and came halfway down the room to sit next to the wounded Briton.

"They tell me you're called The Bear," he said. "To you, I'm Persicus, so we are just soldiers together. Now, relax and be welcome. That fellow's painting my grave portrait," he said cheerfully. "I'm going with the new fashion, and getting buried, not climbing onto a pyre like the old Romans. My tomb will be right outside the gates where everyone will remember me. They won't let even the emperor be buried inside the city walls, you know. Anyway, when I'm dead and in my very handsome stone coffin, they'll put this picture over my face so everyone in future will know what I looked like.

"My wife's had about five marble wigs made so they can keep her statue looking fashionable. At least, portraits are easier, though I've had four made already, didn't like any of them, or the damn artists. These two-beer queers know nothing, I don't know why I don't pack them all off to the Danube to be useful for once. I should put them with the army and let them learn a thing or two. Now, tell me about those Saxons and what's happening in your sector of the frontier."

Over the next hour, as Carausius told of his legion's daily trials and routines, Carus pumped the tribune for details about the troops' morale, equipment and supplies. The Briton, who always made his soldiers' welfare a priority, complained about the quality of the food he'd been obliged to give to his men. "Sir, I wouldn't give some of it to a hungry dog. I'm speaking of filthy green pork and rancid cooking oil that would poison you." Carus frowned. "We had problems with some of these provender merchants and their nasty little practices of providing stuff that should have been condemned," he growled, "but after I had a crooked quartermaster or two and a few bent suppliers crucified, the quality suddenly improved. I'll get a tribune onto that matter today and there will be a few more executions if what you report is still going on. Have you had any problems with supplies from the north?"

Next, the emperor turned to the action that had brought the Briton his wounds and gave him news of the commander who had led his legion into ambush. "I've had Gaius Utrius busted, and he's lucky to have kept his head", he said bluntly. "The useless bastard made a right shit dinner out of the situation. He should never have been made tribune in the first place. If he'd paid any attention at all, instead of strutting about smelling his own musk, he'd have seen he was doing exactly what Varus did at the Teutoburger forest. He's just lucky it didn't turn out the same way."

The old cavalryman was speaking of an ambush engineered by a Germanic chieftain who'd lured three legions into a trap. Almost all, including women and children who'd been allowed to accompany the troops, had been slaughtered in the forest or taken for horrific sacrifice to the Teutons' gods. Rome never forgot, but Carausius' commander did. He simply had not learned the lesson, and only the Briton's diversion and delay of the enemy by challenging one of their chieftains to personal combat had bought time and turned a near-certain massacre into a victory. An aide appeared at the emperor's elbow and whispered in his ear. Carus nodded. "Yes, right now. This fellow Carausius will appreciate seeing a real man getting his reward. He's like me; he has a deep affection for his troops."

The courtier returned in moments with a nervous-looking individual with a broken nose, cauliflower ears and battered, scarred cheekbones. He walked with a slight limp, his eyes casting around warily. On balance, he looked like a well-used and inexpert prize-fighter. "This, lord," the aide bowed to the emperor, "is Timminus Radclifori, a gladiator of the Penninus stable who was also trained here in Rome at the Ludus Magnus." "Ah, yes, and is it thirty or is it six?" Carus asked, beaming amiably at the old gladiator. Carausius raised an eyebrow, but the emperor anticipated the question and turned to him. "Gladiators who survive for six years or thirty bouts are freed," he explained. "I retire them myself, and award them a rudis as token of their honourable service." Leaning towards Carausius so the creased, weathered old fighter would not hear, the emperor said out of the side of his mouth, "Few survive more than six bouts, so this is a lucky one."

He turned back to Timminus, who was nodding his head and smiling vacantly, eyes shifting from side to side. "I see," said the emperor, handing over a wooden sword as symbol that from now on, the man's arena days were ended. He patted the fellow on the shoulder. "Enjoy your peaceful years. Go and grow vegetables on your farm and sire a score of children on a fat wife." The gladiator nodded wordlessly, the aide tugged at the man's sleeve and the pair backed away, bowing. "Poor bastard," said the emperor. "We usually keep them on as instructors, but too often they're like him and are brain damaged."

Carus switched his attention to Carausius. "Now, for you my ursine friend, it's the day the Eagle shits, and I have a reward for you. Kneel down there." The emperor motioned for an aide, who brought a cushion holding a small gold crown. "This is the corona aurea," Carus said as he ceremoniously placed the crown on Carausius' head. "We give it to iron-balled bastards like you for victory in single combat, but only if you hold the ground until the fighting's done. You did more than that, and there's a lot of Saxons gone toes-up to prove it. This crown is to show that Rome thanks you, as would the legionaries whose lives you preserved.

"Now, I have a reward of my own for you. I want you in northern Gaul, and you'll command a couple of legions there. I want those fucking pirates, rebels and brigands cleaned out, and I think you're the fellow to do it." The emperor waved a hand and another aide brought him a fustis, the legate's baton of office, resting on a folded white robe with purple stripes. "Here's the whole kit," Carus grinned at the astonished Briton. "You might not be one of those patrician bastards who think they're the only ones fit to command, but you've earned the broad stripes and I can notify the senate that you are noble born." He paused, then added: "In Britannia, anyway. I suppose that will do, and as I'm the emperor now, it fucking well will have to."

IX. Claria

For Carausius, the next month in Rome went by in a blur of preparations as he readied to take up his new command. He called for several trusted officers from his old legion to be transferred to his new headquarters, or 'hindquarters,' as he privately called it, in the northern Gaul port of Bononia. He met Sucia again, pleased at the opportunity to speak in British, and she presented him with a gift. "Caros, my dear, I saw how you admired my brooch," she told him, "and it means much to me, as it is a symbol of my father's family, as was yours. I went to the silversmiths, took some Baltic amber and had this made for you." It was a surprisingly-close replica of his father's badge of office, and Carausius realized he must have spoken of it in such detail that the astute businesswoman had accurately pictured it. It warmed the new legate so much that he embraced and kissed the young widow. She returned his affection with a warmth that surprised them both. In a swamping rush of physical desire, and before either could consider what was happening, he was slipping her robe from her shoulders to cup her breasts and was lifting her kirtle; she was tugging at the belt of his tunic, and their garments were sliding to the floor. Sucia knelt before the big soldier. "I have another gift for you," she smiled up, before she bowed her head and took him into her mouth. The hours passed in passion and two independent souls sealed a friendship that would last for a lifetime.

"I don't have room now for a woman in my life," Carausius told her cautiously but firmly the next morning. "I would want it to be a woman just like you if I had the means and time, but right now, I want all my energy and attention to go to my soldiering. " She raised an eyebrow, meaningfully. Carausius felt a blush rising. "I can get by with visits to the camp concubines," he muttered.

Sucia was not offended. "I hope you find me better than that," she teased him.

"You are wonderfully better, and you are my friend", the young officer said solemnly. "I will kill anyone who offends you, and I will be there whenever and wherever you need me. That is my oath."

The widow smiled. She liked the man's earnest honesty, and although she was not deeply attracted to him, she was flattered by his attention and decided that a close friendship would be acceptable. She had other thoughts about physical relationships, and they involved soft, perfumed female flesh and gentle, caressing hands and lips.

As they spoke of Britain and the brooch, Sucia remembered a chance meeting. "I was at my friend Cassandra's house a few days ago and I met two very pleasing British men. They were slaves, but such slaves! They were handsome, identical twins in their mid-twenties, and they had been taken from their home on the German Sea by Gael raiders. It was horrible. They told me of being sold at auction, and how they've spent more than a decade in service to their masters, when they used to be nobles themselves."

Carausius went as pale as his weather-beaten face allowed. "Did you hear their names?" he asked. "Whose slaves are they?" Sucia flinched as the powerful soldier grasped her wrist, and she understood this was important, urgent to him.

"One was Dominus or some such," she struggled to recall the name. "The other was, err, Baal?"

"Domtal and Mael, by Mithras!" Carausius was on his feet, pacing. "Are you sure? They're my good brothers, and they're here?" Within the hour, Carausius had chivvied a reluctant Sucia across the Palatine Hill to Cassandra's house.

"It's late, we should leave this until morning. The streets are dangerous," she protested.

"I have a sword," said Carausius grimly, moving fast despite his limp, his hurts forgotten. But the quest was fruitless.

Cassandra's guest, the twins' wealthy master, was already at sea with his entourage, on his way back to Belgica and the Rhine estuary. "He would have sailed from Ostia the day before yesterday," Cassandra, obviously intimidated by the big man's urgent questions, told him. All the soldier could do was to get the trader's name and hope to send a messenger and enough gold to buy his brothers' release. "The general Maximian is a soldier I've met. He has connections in Forum Hadriani, that's up there," Cassandra offered. "Perhaps he could help." The next noon, Carausius went to meet the wealthy noble who one day would be emperor, and whose fate was tied to his own, though neither yet knew it.

Marcus Aurelius Valerius Maximianus, or simply Maximian, was younger by a few years than Carausius, but was a big man, too, and they stood eye to eye. They regarded each other warily, assessing their similarities. Both soldiers came from non-patrician backgrounds, one a minor noble's son from provincial Britain, the other the offspring of Illyrian storekeepers. Both were energetic and aggressive but Maximian was utterly, selfishly ruthless.

He had risen to his high rank of praefectus through connections and menace. He was a coarse bully who used his huge hands and massive strength to stamp his will on anyone, man or beast. Once, when his horse kicked him, he broke the animal's teeth with a single blow of his fist. Another time he choked to death an old, arthritic dog that snarled at him when he booted it aside. He was notorious for his very strong sexuality, sampling both women and men, sometimes incurring accusations of rape. His rank and influence ensured that none of them caused him real trouble. One scandal from which he'd incredibly emerged unscathed involved the forcible deflowering of an elderly Vestal, who had afterwards taken poison before she could undergo the statutory punishment for her sect, of being buried alive outside Rome's Collina Gate.

Maximian, also facing the possibility of death for his profane actions, simply used his connections and bullied his way out of trouble. The Vestal, everyone timidly agreed, must have been smitten by the gods and imagined it all. The fact that the body of the general's accuser was found garrotted with his own tunic cord and left on the steps of the Temple of Mithras had no bearing on the case, all agreed, glancing nervously around.

In military matters, Maximian had a notable understanding of tactics, although he was mule-headed about accepting the opinions of others, and was stubbornly unwilling to spend what he called 'book time' studying the scrolls of previous campaigns and victories. He'd work it out for himself, he declared. His soldiers gave him grudging respect, though they muttered that he'd torch his own grandmother to keep warm.

In some ways, Maximian was like Carausius, a pagan and a military man, but the Briton had what Maximian did not: an innate sense of destiny and purpose. The Roman simply wanted to be a soldier and climb the military ladder to power, at any cost. Carausius, on the other hand, was beginning to feel he could do more than just that. He wanted to restore his downtrodden Britain, where his murdered father had been a nobleman and where the people now were being milked by rapacious landowners far away in Rome. Maximian merely lusted after power and had no tiresome philosophical baggage about justice, freedom or betterment of the human condition.

In the event, after a brief meeting, Maximian agreed to have one of his scribes send messages to Belgica to see what could be done about Carausius' twin brothers. It was the best he could do and the favour might be useful to him if he needed the Briton in the future. In a gesture that was hugely cordial for the brutish Maximian, but which also served the purpose of impressing his colonial visitor, the general invited his guest to view the work he was having done to his villa.

The pair strolled through the peaceful atrium, with its fountain and foliage where a slave sat discreetly to provide lulling music from a lyre, and crossed into a large, airy chamber. Nine small boys were working at long, low tables under the imperious supervision of a striking blonde woman. "This," said Maximian with unusual deference, "is the most talented mosaic artist in the whole of the empire. I was only able to induce her to work on my home through the personal intervention of the emperor's wife herself. Carausius, please meet Claria Primanata Scalae of Claros, home of the great Apollo."

The woman stood, brushing grout from her fine linen robe, and said offhandedly: "He's quite wrong, as always. Claros is famous for the temple and oracle of Apollo. It is not the home of Apollo at all." Carausius was taken aback. Everyone he had seen so far deferred to the coarse, brute power of Maximian and this young Ionian was treating him like a servant. He glanced at the hulking soldier and was stunned to see he was almost simpering at being noticed.

To ease the moment and cover his thoughts, Carausius asked Claria, "What exactly are these children doing?" She looked at him coolly. "We're making a mosaic. It takes little boys' fingers to accurately place small, sharp mosaic tesserae. Sidonia," she addressed a young, dark-haired girl who was overseeing the small boys. "This is my handmaid Sidonia Strada, and she keeps my small elves at their work." Claria smiled at the slave. "Pass me a few tesserae, girl," she said. She turned to Carausius. "See for yourself."

She handed him a squared block of marble half the size of his little fingernail. "As you see, we first assemble the designs in panels on these tables, and grout them before we put them in place on the floor. For the mosaic pieces, we use marble, glass, stone, even precious gems where the householder has far too much money and too little taste." She glanced meaningfully at Maximian, who lowered his head. Carausius looked at the half-finished design, a stunning representation of a naked man, perhaps a wounded gladiator, half reclining on the ground, wrist supported on his upraised knee. "It's very beautiful," he said admiringly. Claria looked at him properly for the first time, taking in the battered, scarred face, and flashed a dazzling, sympathetic smile. "It's a change from what people usually want; the picture of a snarling hound at the entrance, with 'Beware of the Dog' written under it."

At that moment, a balding, dark-haired man in an unfashionable, very short tunic entered the room and bowed to the woman. She gestured to him and spoke to Carausius. "This man's from your country, he's a slave but it's only because he doesn't know how to gamble with dice. He had to sell himself to me to pay his debts." The man bowed to the new legate. "Lord," he said. The woman continued: "He's a maker of images, and if he ever gets his lazy British self-working, we'll have a fine mural on that wall."

"I'll see that he works, leave it to me." growled Maximian. Claria brushed him off. "This is my domain. You go and polish your helmet or something." Maximian glared at the muralist, who retreated nervously, and a moment or two later the mosaic artist declared she had to attend to the drying grout work, indicating that the audience was over.

Carausius bowed as Claria swept out, leaving a waft of lavender on the air, and he murmured a comment to Maximian that she was as beautiful as her art. The Roman bridled in an instant. "Keep your dirty mouth shut," he snarled. The Briton, startled, looked directly at the other man and saw hatred blazing from his eyes. It was as if a storm had blown up from nowhere, an instant tempest of aggression out of a clear blue sky. Without rational thought, reacting purely on the instincts that had always served him well, Carausius knew a deep hatred of the brutish Maximian, felt it welling up inside him. They would be, he knew, lifelong enemies and he should be cautious at this moment. Instead he allowed a hot rage to sweep over him. "Have you reason to be possessive of her?" he challenged. Maximian glared like a bull faced with a hostile rival. "Just get out. Get your crippled self out of here." Carausius nodded. "One day, Maximianus, you will feel my wrath, but it will not be because of a woman. I already have my own reasons." The Illyrian stared back at him. "One day, I will strangle you with my bare hands," he retorted. He turned and stamped out of the room, backhanding across the face a slave who stood mutely by the door. Carausius shook his head. He knew he had made a lifelong enemy, and a powerful one at that, although he wasn't sure why. And deep inside his soul, he knew it was foreordained.

X. Tigris

It was a few months since the new emperor Carus and his legions had crossed the River Tigris and Persia, for so long the traditional enemy of Rome, had lain at their feet, ripe for the taking. Carus was still savouring his role. Not so long ago, he had been the prefect of the now-dead emperor Probus' Praetorian Guard. Then, like a miracle from the gods, he had been elected to the purple. It came about when his troops, who were alarmed that the emperor Probus, far away in Rome, was planning to disband their legion and much of the army, acclaimed Carus as the new imperator. Carus wasn't inclined to resist, so assumed the purple.

Probus promptly declared him a rebel and went with a force to Sirmium to capture and execute him. He made a fatal mistake. After he'd arrived at Sirmium, the unpopular Caesar found a need to keep his troops busy, and ordered them to work, draining some foul swampland 'to establish my authority.' His officers protested, but he overruled them. As the officers stood haplessly by, much of Probus' force simply walked away from the stinking mud lands and defected to Carus. The remaining troops judged that now they were inferior in strength to Carus' legions and were vulnerable, so promptly assassinated Probus to establish where their loyalties lay. The popular new emperor was now in full control. Heady with a sense of destiny and with military might in his hands, Carus shrugged aside any need to consult the Senate, and sent an icy letter to Rome announcing that from now on, he was the new ruler of the empire. Then he turned to his soldier's business of extending it into Persia.

Carus secured his back by appointing his sons Carinus and Numerian as junior emperors. "Carinus," he told the young prince, "I'm giving you considerable power as Caesar. Keep your throne in Rome, take no nonsense from the Senate. You're better off at the centre of things than up in Milan where you can't keep a close eye on the politicos. You have the army at your back, so you are in control. Just oversee the western empire and get those damned Gauls subdued. I'm going to seize the east, because there's a great opportunity. The Persians are concerned with trouble on their Indian border, and they've got most of their forces in the wrong place, for them, anyway. The rest are in such disarray with their internal bickering I can settle them piecemeal. Within a couple of years, we should have both the east and the west under control, and we'll act jointly as Augusti over the greatest-ever expansion of the empire."

Carus had cowed the Senate, made new appointments, including that of Carausius, and set about his plans. Within months, the general took his younger son Numerian and the legions east. He crushed the Sarmatians and their fellow Carpiani in a series of conflicts that ended with 20,000 of them in chains and 16,000 more dead on the battlefield, but Carus didn't stop there. He ignored the usual rules of campaigning, pushed his victorious troops through winter conditions across Thrace and Asia Minor, plundered Mesopotamia and took the meek surrender of the wealthy cities of Ctesiphon and Seleucia without drawing his sword, all while the Persians shivered in winter quarters and watched in dismay.

Before long, the Great King of Persia sent five of his ministers as ambassadors to treat for peace. The bejewelled dignitaries entered the Roman camp and demanded to be taken to the conquering emperor. What they found astounded them; a travel-stained soldier was sitting on a horse blanket eating a meal of bacon and hard peas. The only clue to Carus' status was the purple colour of his woollen robe. Unceremoniously and with open indifference, the still-seated Carus continued to chew his leathery bacon as he listened to the ambassadors' flowery greetings and protestations of their desire for peace. Then he stood up, and pulled off his cap. Underneath it, his head was almost totally bald. "Unless your king Varanes pays proper tribute," he told them bluntly, "I'll leave Persia as denuded of trees as this head is of hair. Just tell him that. Now get out of my sight." The ministers backed away, bowing. Persia, they knew, was about to be as humbled as they had been.

Three days later, the threat was ended. Carus lay sick, pallid and sweating on his camp cot. At his side was his son, Numerian and his guard captain Diocletian, a hardened soldier who had shared Carus' service on the Danube and who had a close bond with the emperor. "I'm dying, Diocles," said Carus, using the soldier's family name. "Take care of my sons."

"Yes, lord," said Diocletian. "Trust me, I shall." Outside the pavilion tent, a violent rainstorm was thrashing the canvas and the rumble of heavy thunder reverberated from time to time. "Going out with a bang, eh?" Carus grimaced weakly as he gripped his old comrade's hand. It was his last jest.

The tent walls flickered in the lightning flashes and the guttering oil lamps were frequently extinguished by blasts of cold air that shook the pavilion. As a slave re-lit several of the lights, Diocletian saw his emperor had slipped away into his long sleep. "Be at peace, my friend," he muttered, releasing his hand from the dead man's and pushing the eyelids closed. Numerian, less accustomed to death, looked on in dismay at his father's body. He backed away, stumbled on a rug and blundered into the slave who was re-lighting the lamps, knocking one to the floor. The oil pooled on the carpet, the flames caught, licked the fringe of a silken hanging and in seconds the pavilion was afire. The emperor's body was rescued, but the accident sparked more than a blaze. It ignited a disaster.

Despite the best efforts of Numerian, who assumed his father's crown, rumours ran rife that Carus had been struck by lightning. The superstitious soldiery believed this was a bolt from gods angered by Carus' campaign and they boiled into a state of near-mutiny. A delegation led by the legion's First Spear met the new emperor to tell him they all were in danger. The Tigris should never have been crossed, the gods would smite them all if they continued. "This, Caesar, is the final limit of Rome's boundaries," they told Numerian, who was suddenly uncertain about his hold on power. Under pressure, the young man nervously capitulated to the legions' demands. To the astonishment of the Persian cavalry scouts who watched, the victorious Roman army turned in retreat, marching away from an empire that was helplessly waiting to be claimed.

The long, slow trudge back to the west took eight months before Numerian and his disheartened troops crossed the Bosphorus into Europe and the young emperor spent most of the march in a closed litter or in the semi-darkness of his tent, as his eyes had been badly burned by sunlight. Diocletian still acted as his guard captain, but Numerian's father-in-law Lucius Flavius Aper had taken over as his prefect and mouthpiece, bringing from the guarded, off-limits tent the edicts he claimed came from the young emperor. Diocletian viewed him with suspicion, especially when the prefect unexpectedly declared that the emperor was ailing and must not be disturbed by anybody.

Matters came to a head soon after the army reached the European continent. Diocletian turned to his centurion friend Galba. "The Boar," he said, referring to Aper by his nickname, "is hiding something. I'm going into that tent to see just how sick the emperor really is." With a file of legionaries behind him, the guard captain pushed aside the sentry and entered the pavilion. Numerian lay on his cot, dead. Diocletian thought fast. The emperor may have died of natural causes, but he seemed to have been dead for hours. Aper must be bidding for the throne. "Follow me," he ordered his soldiers. "You two stay here. Let nobody in." The file of soldiers jogged through the way camp and found Aper near the horse lines. "Seize him," Diocletian ordered. "Take him and chain him, keep him away from everybody. Wait for my next orders. Sound assembly."

Within a half hour, the legions were in formation, and Diocletian stepped up onto the parade podium. He upturned his face to the sun and swore an oath in ringing tones that could be heard across the whole parade ground. "In the view of Sol, I swear that I make a true and honest testimony. In no way and at no time have I ever plotted against my emperor, and what I am about to tell you truthfully happened, as Sol is my witness of this. May he blind me if I lie." He looked to his left, and in stern judicial tones, commanded his praetorians: "Bring me that murderer."

They paraded Aper, bewildered and clumsy in his chains. "This man," Diocletian declared loudly, "murdered our beloved emperor Numerian and tried to conceal his crime while he plotted to steal the grass crown. He must die." A whisper ran through the rear ranks as his message was conveyed, then a hush fell. Not one person in the watching thousands moved or made noise. Before Aper could speak any word of defence or explanation, Diocletian unsheathed his stabbing sword and in a single, swift motion thrust it up under the condemned man's ribcage. The chained prisoner dropped to his knees, and looked in wide-eyed surprise at his stooping killer, who had not released his sword and whose face was brought close as a lover's to his.

Diocletian pushed Aper sideways, still not releasing the sword's hilt, and the dying man's eyes closed as if in tired resignation. He vomited a gush of oxygen-bright blood and fell away from his murderer, who lowered the man, still impaled. Aper died in moments. Diocletian straddled the body, put a foot onto the bloodied tunic and jerked his gladius free.

The assembly maintained its utter stillness as the self-appointed judge and executioner wiped his blade on the dead man's shoulder. He turned to the assembly, opened his arms wide, then turned to point as he shouted: "Numerian is dead in that tent, at this man's hand, but I have now avenged him. I have killed the boar!" He was punning on 'aper' which means 'boar,' and on Aper's nickname, but was also dramatizing a well-known prophecy made years before, that he would kill a boar and become emperor.

A centurion standing at the side of his cohort did as he'd been prompted earlier, and bellowed: "Diocletian for emperor!" The chant rumbled through the ranks, rising louder. Diocletian let the shouting continue for more than a minute, then raised his hand for silence. "If it is the will of the gods and of you, my comrades, I will accept," he said. He looked up again at the sun. "It seems we have the blessing of Sol. The gods are with us. I shall lead you to more glory." As swiftly and easily as that, a new emperor was created.

XI. Massalia

By imperial order, the legate Carausius was to leave Rome, and make his way to Gaul and his new command, but the gods had more in store for him before he exited the city. He had considered going by road; it could be a swifter journey. Hadn't the emperor Titus once covered an astonishing 500 miles in 24 hours to get to the bedside of his dying brother? That wasn't likely for Carausius; it would be a sore trial for his battered body, as even the best raeda carriages, with their three horses and padded leather interiors, provided at best a jolting, jarring experience even on the paved military roads. A sea voyage would be longer, somewhat more dangerous, but easier. He was mulling the decision as he limped along the Via Nova to meet an administrator who had been recommended to him as a good choice for intelligence gathering and internal security.

He'd just decided to take the sea voyage option and had turned his mind to what he'd need when a cry from the pedestrian behind caused him to turn. The man jumped sideways. Carausius began to do the same, not knowing what to expect, but his injured foot made him clumsy. With a rumble and roar, the tenement building alongside him collapsed. A cascade of falling brick blasted a dust cloud but tumbled away from him, although a few timbers fell in the Briton's direction. One, turning end over end, struck him on the hip and flattened him, pinning him against the limestone pavement. Rats scuttled for safety, and even dazed as he was, Carausius registered the movement, spotting the flash of one white rodent among the dark ones in the billowing dust.

The big soldier lay trapped by the heavy baulk of timber, although most of its weight was fortunately propped on brick rubble. He dazedly realized he'd have to wait for help. Then the screaming started. Oil lamps inside the building had ignited a blaze and the pinned Briton was hidden in choking smoke. He began to bellow for help before the flames could reach him or the building fell in.

Out of the smoke appeared an incongruously-cheerful face. The man was not tall, but was heavily muscled. He was carrying a hook and an axe, equipment that signified he was one of the vigiles who patrolled Rome looking for business. Fire fighting crews managed by the immensely-rich Marcus Licinus Crassus, the vigiles turned up to fires and haggled with the building's owner until a deal was struck, or they watched the building burn.

"This your house?" the apparition asked Carausius.

"No, it damned well isn't," the soldier said, gritting his teeth. "Get me out from under here."

"Not sure about that, lord," grinned the vigilis, "I'm Stevig, by the way. My mates call me Stupid. I love the smell of the smoke. Got any coin?"

Carausius nodded. "I have gold," he said shortly. "Right, let's get you out of there, it's dangerous," said Stevig chidingly.

"I didn't bloody choose to be under here," said the legate.

"Right," said Stevig, levering up the bulk of timber so the soldier could inch clear. "One gold aureus, please." Carausius shook his head, but paid up just as a second vigilis arrived, a tall, dark-haired man with an accent from the south. "My mate, Murrus Antipodes," Stevig said cheerily. "He was thrown out of eunuch school because he still has a giant hairy nut sack. He claimed it was an apparition, but his master's wife admitted it wasn't." Carausius nodded, swore at the pain in his hip and damaged foot and began to limp away. Antipodes called after him: "I would have helped in the rescue. A tip would be nice."

A week later, scudding across Our Sea in a blue-sailed naval galley headed for southern Gaul, Carausius grinned at the memory. He ached a bit, but it could have been worse, and alongside him, smiling as the wind blew her hair across her eyes, was Sucia. "Being a legate has unexpected privileges," he grinned at her. "No pirate will come near this warship, all we need watch for is the weather, and we'll be in Gaul faster than any trading vessel. Now, tell me about the merchants' road from Cathay."

So Sucia talked of the Silk Routes, a network of rough tracks that linked remote oases across the east, and how caravans of traders moved between them. Few, she told him, covered the entire distance, because it was too long. Instead, most traders repeatedly travelled the same parts of the routes, making arduous journeys over deserts and mountains. "My trader travels between Samarkand and Damascus," she told him, "and he brings me some of the world's most precious fabrics. I send back amber from the Baltic, sun stones from Iceland that show sailors the way, even in fog; the finest wool garments from Britain, and precious black jet from the coast near Eboracum, not far from your birthplace."

What, Carausius wanted to know, was the mysterious dark blue crystal she had showed him, from her workings in Britain's limestone peaks? "It is just the one cavern, formed by an underground river and discovered by the ancients. It contains a band of rare crystal called Blue John that is found nowhere else in the whole world. I have sent beautiful bowls made from it as far as Pompeii and Herculaneum, gifts of imperial purple fit for the emperor. But I will have a gift for you that is just as precious, when we reach Britain. I will give you one the world's most prized hunting dogs." Carausius grinned again. Since he was a boy, he'd loved dogs. As an apprentice to the river pilot Cenhud and as a foot soldier of the legion, he had not been able to have a dog. Now, a legate of Rome, a man who commanded thousands of troops, he could do anything he wanted. And he wanted a big war dog. One day soon, he thought.

As Carausius and Sucia were passing Corsica on their way to the great Gallic port of Massalia, the twins Mael and Domnal were already there, employed in carrying their master's baggage down the gangplank onto the stone quay built by the Greeks and up into the sun washed town of handsome houses with their red terracotta roofs. Southern Gaul, where the high limestone ramparts of the mountains behind the port gleamed in the bright sunlight, was a wonderful place, a world away from the gloomy fogs and rain of their master's Belgic home in the north. "I don't want to go back," Mael whispered to his brother. "We could lose ourselves in a place this big if we could just slip away." Domnal nodded. He didn't care for their master Gracilis, because although the man treated them reasonably well, he was a perverted pederast and sometimes forced the handsome slaves to participate in his performances with catamites. His demands had lessened as they got older because Gracilis' tastes ran to quite young children and the twins were rarely participants these days, but they still wanted their freedom.

"If we're caught, we're dead," Mael told his brother. Domnal nodded. A runaway slave faced crippling punishments, or death, but after more than a decade as Gracilis' body slaves, they were treated with considerable liberty, and escaping shouldn't be difficult. The hard part would be to stay away, and they could do that easier in the Mediterranean seaport than in Belgica. Their chance came that same evening. The amber trader wanted to sample a Gallic whorehouse that a friend had excitedly told him about, and he left the twins under a solitary guard in the tavern where the travellers were staying.

The duo acted decisively. While their guard sat in the public room below, sipping wine and flirting with a whore whom he had no intention of paying, they uncovered Gracilis' strongbox under the floorboards, prized off the hinge with a knife and took the linen-wrapped roll of coin they knew was inside. They had no difficulty in slipping unseen out of an upstairs window, over the red-tiled roofs of the tavern and the next building and dropping into a stable yard where a carpet of horse dung muffled their footsteps.

"Get rid of our slave clothes, be less conspicuous, then we'll pay our way out of here," Domnal said, gesturing at the drab tunics that marked them as belonging to the lowest class of society. "We'll have to steal some. We can't buy clothes dressed like this, people will question how slaves got money. Then we'll find another town and we'll be free. Maybe we can even get back to Britain." The pair made their way out of the harbour area and headed for the upper reaches of the old town, intending to find a bath house. "Romans bathe nudus," Domnal explained to his twin, "so they leave their tunics, togas and sandals with a bath slave. We should have no trouble sneaking through the steam and lifting some new kit."

At first, the gods favoured them. They quickly found a bath house on the Via Lacydon and slipped inside, past a drowsing attendant. The other guardian of the door was inside, doing his rounds and shouting out the time. The changing room was empty, and a dozen or more of the cubicles held vestments of various kinds. Mael scooped up a fine linen tunic, grinning as he whispered to his brother, "Very intelligent: one size fits all, no tailoring needed!" Domnal didn't answer; he'd stripped off his tunic and was reaching for a bather's discarded clothes when a footfall sounded.

Two burly mariners walked into the steamy room, followed by the sleepy slave, who was carrying linens for them. "They're stealing clothes!" the attendant squeaked as he took in the scene. Mael stood paralyzed, and one sailor grabbed his arm. Domnal ran naked, forcing past the attendant and fleeing into the street. His escape ended as quickly as it began. Two watchmen on fire patrol blocked his way. A naked man running from a bath house slave didn't look innocent. Domnal was seized and bound. By morning the twins were standing before a furious Gracilis.

"You ungrateful bastards ran, and you took my gold. I will have one of you flogged to death while the other watches, then I'll sell the survivor to the Moors for their galleys. You," he pointed at Mael, "are to die." Domnal went to his knees to plead for his brother's life, but Gracilis was obdurate. Then Domnal had inspiration. "We have a treasure," he told the trader. "That is, we know of something hidden by the Romans in Britain. It's an old treasure, and we can lead you to it." He was lying, he didn't know what the ancient map told, but it was their best chance to buy time, and perhaps to escape again.

Gracilis took the little metal map and pored over it. He questioned Domnal again and again, but the slave was adamant. He'd lead his master to the loot, but he wouldn't tell where it was, except that it was in Britain. Gracilis shrugged. The slave could die once the treasure was in his hands. Let him do the leading, give him time to reflect. When he got them back to Hadriani, he'd keep them under close guard until he took them to Britain. Two days later, the chained twins, in riveted metal collars that read: 'I have escaped. Send me back to my master Gracilis Turpilanus for a reward,' were escorted onto the Rhone river barge that would take them halfway across Gaul on their way back to Forum Hadriani. Gracilis, with the little lead map firmly in his possession, thought he would plan a trip to Britain in the near future. He had more pressing matters for now, and he also needed to consult someone he could trust about the map, and go through the business of deciphering the clues.

XII. Bononia

The years had been kind to the escaped slave Mullinus. He had used the heavy purse of gold he found in a murdered man's cloak and had prospered. Able to read and to write clumsily but effectively, he had a business as an accounts keeper and administrator. His clients were the wealthy traders who were based in the Belgic crossroads town of Hadrian's Market, where the mighty Rhine and Meuse rivers served as highways for troops and commerce, faster routes even than the great Roman roads that crossed the continent. With the unrest beyond the Rhine, the constant flow of troops through the market town to the frontier made for good business.

Mullinus was prominent in the town, especially in the taverns, where his trademark heavy amber and silver-spiral brooch that pinned his cloak back from his tunic often attracted jocular remarks about 'lord' or 'baron.' People trusted the fellow because of his good nature and open, almost simple looks, and he took full advantage in his dealings. In a decade or so, he'd come to own several taverns that sold watered wine and filched army provisions at great profit. He also ran a discreet whorehouse that serviced only officers and the wealthier merchants, and he did a brisk trade fencing pirated goods brought to him by the corsairs who infested the seas from the Gallic Narrows out to the great Atlanticus. He was a success, he'd worked diligently and now, suddenly, the hard-nosed trader was unable to concentrate on his business. He was smitten by a woman.

Mullinus had spent years indulging his appetites on slave girls or on some of the professional whores who worked to keep his income rolling in, but had never formed an emotional attachment of any depth. This woman was different. He'd noticed her as she shopped the market food stalls for her mistress, a handsome, auburn-haired slave of full figure and flashing smile. "Good teeth and tits," he professionally appraised her. Attracted, he edged closer as she dropped several loaves of bread into her basket. "Is that fresh?" he murmured, pretending interest. The woman looked up and Mullinus melted. "Still warm, lord," she said.

He loved the timbre of her voice, and his ear caught the unexpected accent. Eagerly, he said in British: 'Are you from Britannia?" She stayed mute, staring at his cloak brooch. The colour ebbed from her face but she had enough self-control to murmur a polite response. Mullinus had just met the widow of the true owner of the brooch. Two thunderbolts from the gods had struck at one time. One hit Clinia as she saw her dead husband's unmistakable badge of office, the other skewered Mullinus as he fell in love.

The next stage, buying Clinia from her shipwright master was not easy, as he knew the slave's value from sampling her charms, and he also recognized how much her fellow Briton wanted her, but Mullinus was a skilled negotiator and owned a long purse. The matter took two weeks before the trader took Clinia to his villa and showed her the room that would be hers. "You will not be a slave, but my mistress," he informed her.

Clinia gasped as she entered her new quarters. Mullinus' servants had laid out fresh clothes and sandals for her. A young slave girl stood waiting by the dressing table, where perfumes, an ivory comb and some scented oil were arrayed next to a bowl of fresh flowers and a glass jug of Rhenish wine. "This is not Massalia, where women are forbidden to drink wine," Mullinus smiled. "This is your home. Please me, and you will be its mistress. Abigail here will bathe you and arrange your hair, then she will bring you to me." The woman who had once been chatelaine with good lands on the coast of Britain felt tears well in her eyes as she was again treated with respect. She said humbly, "You will be my lord, and I shall come willingly to your bed."

It was the beginning of a period of great happiness for them both, but it was still several long weeks before Clinia finally could ask her lover where he had obtained the great brooch that had once been symbol of her husband's power. As he told the tale of fleeing from a ship brawl with the enveloping cloak hiding him, Clinia realized that the raider Filwen must be dead. How else would the wolf fur cloak she bitterly remembered, and her husband's badge of office, have come into the hands of two common sailors? But still she did not know the fates of her twin sons, or of Carausius, her little boy. She had spent the past years as a slave to a shipwright as he carried on his trade in the northern islands of Frisia. The twins and her young son could be anywhere. She was not to know that the twins were under close guard in the very town where she now lived, or that her son Caros was an important soldier in Gaul. "Do you know, lord, how I can find my children?" she asked humbly. "I shall find them," Mullinus said grandly. "I have experience of investigating facts."

A few hundred miles to the west, Carausius was on investigations of his own, as he inspected his new command. The recently-appointed legate of two near-complete legions was touring his headquarters fortress of Bononia, on the Gallic coast. He'd come there a few months before, after missing Gracilis and the twins at Massalia. A ship's pilot in the harbour there had reported seeing identical twin slaves going aboard a Rhone barge just days before the legate showed up at the dockside, and Carausius knew he'd lost that chance to reunite with his brothers. In time, he thought, Mithras will bring me to them. First, he had pressing military matters to attend, and right now, he had a parade to inspect.

The big, bearded man with the scarred, broken face and distinct limp wore his white and purple-striped robes well and the troops lined for inspection regarded him with a mix of fear and admiration. Already, in the first few months of possessing his cudgel of office, he'd comprehensively crushed two uprisings of the rebellious Gauls, keeping busy his executioner, a lean, blue-eyed man with a leathery face and southern drawl who would never say where he was born except vaguely that it was 'down in the south a good bit.'

Davius Perseqius Ansonii saw his duty as carnifex was to keep the Roman Peace by making an example of those who broke it, and crucifixion was a fine way to command people's attention. He carried out other forms of execution, too, because the magistrates said crucifixion was too harsh for Roman citizens, though Davius had topped a few that way. Strangulation or being bled out through a slit throat was the privileged mode of exit for citizens, and the nobles had it even easier, merely getting their heads lopped off, he mused. In the early days, though, the mad and bad were simply launched off the Tarpeian Rock, an 80 foot cliff on Rome's Palatine Hill. It was a second-rate spectacle, too brief in Davius' view. Hanging a felon out on a cross for a day or two really pushed the point home better, he thought. You had to let the punters tremble to see what was in store if they got out of line: hours and hours of agony, not a few seconds' flight and a messy landing. His job took skill, it wasn't literally a pushover. He smiled at his own wit.

Davius had dodged his new legate's parade, and was sitting in a harbour front wine shop, talking about his profession with several off-duty sailors of the Classis Britannica, Rome's British Fleet. "We're getting soft," he said. "In the old days, it wasn't just murderers and traitors who got the push, anyone who was badly deformed or mad was regarded as having been cursed by the gods, and he went off the rock, too. Now, I just top rebels, criminal slaves and the occasional poor bastard who knifed someone when he was drunk."

He took a pull at the watered wine and considered his first meeting with the new legate. He'd been called into the great man's presence and found Carausius studying the returns that detailed the numbers of executions. "There are a lot of these," the big, bear-like admiral said mildly.

"I hope there were none of my soldiers among them. Are you a man who likes his work too much?" Davius stiffened.

"All were ordered, lord," he said.

"So many?" persisted Carausius.

"They're Bagaudae, lord, just scum," said Davius. "They'll never like us, but they can fear and respect us. You need to keep a boot on their necks or they'll take advantage." The carnifex was not to know it, but his few words influenced the legate considerably.

Carausius had considered his options. Popularity was not one of his priorities. He knew his soldiers admired and even liked him, and he had an affection for them, having lived life as a walkalot when he was younger. He had no fears of losing the loyalty of his men, but he was unsure about handling civilians. Better, he felt, to be feared than to lose his grip now he was here in his new command. He would follow the crucifixioner's principle and scourge the bandits. Law-abiding citizens need fear nothing from him, but he resolved to go on to make a terrible example of lawbreakers.

In the tavern where he was dodging the column, unaware of how his offhand remarks had affected his commander, Davius faced the mariners' questions about what it was like to be crucified. "Well, it's probably better than being hung upside down and sawn in half. That hurts a lot, because the brain gets enough blood to keep you alive until the saw finally gets well into your chest," he declared. "It's a lot slower than being burned to death, but that hurts quite a bit, too. If you keep the fire down around the perp's legs and feet, it can take a good while before the flames get to the head. You'd be surprised how much blood comes out, it hisses in the flames. A good carnifex can keep them alive a long time. You make the fire take the perp's calves, thighs and hands first, then the torso and finally the face goes up before they die of shock or blood loss. You don't want the fire to be too high too soon or they just suffocate. Do it right and being burned at the stake can take a couple of hours."

The old executioners, he said, put a flammable tunic on the condemned, and lit it. The good emperor Hadrian had ordered a rabbi who defied his edicts to be burned with a pad of wet wool on his chest, to prolong his punishment. "Some old Greek had a brass bull made so he could put the perp inside it, on the fire," the executioner recalled. "It was fitted out so the screams came through the bull's mouth and sounded like the beast was roaring. The fellow who made it asked the tyrant for his pay, and got more than he wanted. He became the bull's first occupant."

But crucifixion, that's what you do, isn't it? asked the sailors, refilling Davius' wooden wine cup. "Now, that's an art," he said. "It's really all about humiliation. You want to shame them. Even old Cicero called it the most cruel and disgusting death, and it's really for slaves, rebels, people like that, enemies of the state. You flog them first, to get the blood flowing. I use a scourge that has bits of metal in the thongs, to strip off the flesh. It weakens them. Then you fasten them to the crosspiece and make them carry it to where they're going to hang around. We have some permanent uprights here, down by the docks, and in Rome they have quite a few outside the Esquiline Gate, near Nero's house. Old Nero, he liked to have the Jesus followers crucified, did for thousands of them and at night he had their bodies set on fire to provide illumination."

"Anyway," Davius continued, "You fasten them to the crosspiece, nailing is better than tying, though nails cost money. Then you march them to the uprights and hoist the crosspiece into place. The executioner paused. "Remember, keep the nails straight so you can use them again later. If you're not tying the perp's arms to the crosspiece, but want to nail him up, you get long spikes, about seven inches, and angle each in through the crease under the fat part of the thumb and up through the wrist where there's a little tunnel. Then you haul the crosspiece up the vertical and fix it. You can also nail the perps through the forearms; that works, too. As for fastening the feet, mostly, I nail their heels to the sides of the post. Don't forget first to run the nail through a little piece of wood before you knock it through the heel, so they can't tear the foot free."

"I sometimes put a little shelf as a footrest on the upright, to take the weight and keep them alive longer, but some people prefer a small seat about halfway. If you do that, you can put a spike on it; it sticks up their rectum or vagina and adds to their fun. As a kindness, I sometimes make women condemned face the upright so they get full pleasure from that spike. After all, it's their last screw." He paused again for a swig of his drink, then resumed, enjoying the familiar, horrified attention.

Crucifixes, he explained, came in various styles, the most commonly used being the Tau, which was shaped like a capital T and had no vertical above the crosspiece, as the so-called Latin crucifix did. There were X and Y shaped crucifixes, or sometimes the executioner's team would simply use a tree. The upright of the Tau had a squared end that slotted into a matching hole on the underside of the crosspiece, and after the condemned had been fastened to it, it was a simple matter to hoist man and crosspiece up as a unit onto the stake.

"It just makes sense, it's efficient. Fastening a perp to the complete crucifix and then having to haul the whole thing upright and drop it into a post hole with him nailed in place is heavy work," said the executioner, musing "I've never favoured those Latin crosses." He paused again, eyeing his rapt audience who, open-mouthed, were soaking in the gory details.

The most efficient way to carry out a swift execution, Davius said, was to fasten the perp's arms above his head, then nail down the feet so he couldn't raise himself up to breathe. Fastened in that way, the condemned usually died within an hour or so, suffocated. It was not, he said, a technique he used often because the whole point was to inflict suffering and shame, and an hour's worth was not much punishment, eh?

One of the sailors got up and left the table, looking pale. Davius, unconcerned, took another draft of wine. "You strip them naked, of course, because they lose their bowels on that spike and that brings insects to add to their enjoyment. How long do they last? I've had them die in a few hours, or take as long as three days. It all depends on how strong they are, how much the flogging took out of them, blood loss, all that. If the relatives see you right, and you know what effect a piece of gold can have on your attitude, you can speed things up by breaking their legs.

"I use an iron club. With no way to take weight on their heels, the hangers get it all on their arms. It compresses the lungs and they suffocate. But you know, don't rush things. You want people to see them suffering, because that makes the punters think twice about staying on the right side of the law. I see this stuff all the time, and I tell you, I pay my taxes and I follow what the boss tells me to do. I've no intention of being fastened up there myself."

The executioner took a last pull at his wine, wiped his mouth on the back of his hand and mused: "Funny thing, really. We're the civilizing influence, but barbarians like the Picts treat their perps kinder. They toss convicted felons into deep water, hands and feet tied. Simple, no blood, and food for the fish, eh? What's wrong with that is that with their way nobody gets a stern lesson, so I suppose they get more criminals than we do."

He laughed and eased himself up from the table. "I've got to see a smith about making some more nails since we did all these rebels. People buy the spikes as amulets, after they've been used on the condemned. They say they bring good health to the wearer." He wiped his mouth with the back of his hand, and laughed. "They don't bring the perps much luck, do they? Well, it's a nice little earner for me, but it does deplete the ironmongery stocks."

XIII. Margus

Word came to the emperor Carinus of his brother's death and of the upstart general who had assumed the imperial purple. Diocletian, he raged, must die. He'd probably poisoned Numerian himself to steal the throne. The courtiers shrank away from their tyrant lord; a cruel, arrogant spendthrift who courted the mob with bread and circuses. Games, theatre, chariot races, naval battles in the Colosseum, parades, free bread and wine were extravagantly put before the common people. The nobles were treated to sumptuous feasts and debauches but few attended willingly, as Carinus was a vicious sadist who delighted in forcing himself on other men's wives and young sons. His palaces were crowded with dyed-blonde prostitutes and actors, pimps and singers; the vast public spaces were bedecked with Milanese roses and violets from Parma, and the rooms were filled with gilded columns and pornographic frescoes. He maintained a warm water swimming pool in which he liked to swim naked among floating flowers, melons and apples while flutists and lyre players serenaded him. Rumour said he enjoyed an incestuous relationship with his sister, although he had one long-serving wife, as well as having had eight others whom he'd murdered or divorced when they became pregnant. The boldest courtiers whispered to each other about his heir, wondering and snickering if he came from Carinus' wife or his sister Paulina.

Vain and arrogant, Carinus wore jewels on every part of his person. A great ruby clasped his cloak, emeralds adorned his shoes, and pearls, sapphires and other gems studded his belt. He painted his face, gilded his fingernails with gold leaf and was everywhere trailed by an entourage of masseuses, hairdressers and wardrobe mistresses. His first delight was to force married noblewomen into humiliating sex with him, his second was to host sumptuous banquets when the wine flowed from fountains and a squadron of slaves stood by to dilute it to taste with spices or honey.

At one legendary feast, Carinus' cooks served more than a thousand pounds of meats that ranged from giraffe to ibex, plus a hundred pounds each of fish and birds as varied as peacock and lark. To demonstrate his power, the tyrant had his former schoolfellows tortured and executed for remembered or imagined insults. He had wealthy men imprisoned for their riches and ordered the murders of men whose wives he coveted. "He was a good soldier once, on the Rhine, but he's become a monster since he returned to Rome," was the consensus spoken only in private and after a careful check for eavesdroppers.

The time came when Carinus needed his military skills, and urgently. Soon after news came of Diocletian's revolt, word arrived from Venezia, where the governor had also risen against the tyrant's rule. Carinus moved fast, and marched north with his legions. At Verona, he swiftly defeated and executed the rebel governor. Then he moved on again to face Diocletian, who had ended his long march back from Persia and was on the frontier, at the River Danube.

The rival generals met on the plains of Margus, near the great river, and matters did not go well at first for the usurper. Diocletian's troops were reduced in numbers from their months of travel and were in generally poor health after an outbreak of dysentery. Carinus threw his fresh troops at them with conviction and broke the ranks of Diocletian's legions. The slaughter was about to begin, and victory seemed assured for the Roman tyrant, but the Fates stepped in and snipped the threads of his life.

Carinus' own officers, led by a tribune whose wife Carinus had raped, turned on him right there on the battlefield. The tribune and a few accomplices hacked down the despised tyrant, the other officers called off their men and both armies halted, the fighting put aside. In the matter of an hour Diocletian went from facing defeat and execution to being acclaimed emperor by both armies. His parade into Rome was a triumph. He'd left the Eternal City as the son of a senator's household slaves. Then his tide of fortune flowed full. He became military governor of Moesia, took the curule chair of a consul, and next became commander of the palace guard. An oracle had forecast great fame for him, "after he killed the boar." With the murder of Aper the Boar, his men knew he was in the protecting hands of the gods. They bowed to the heavens, and acclaimed him. Now he was returning with his legion, clad in imperial purple and bringing an impedimenta train groaning with loot and slaves. Life, he reflected, had been good to him.

Some of it he had earned, for Diocletian was a highly competent soldier and not just a reckless warrior. Instead, he was a manipulator and an artful politician whose skill at misleading opponents about his true motives carried him a long way. After seeing victory snatched away from Carinus when he was assassinated by his own officers, Diocletian had absorbed the lesson. Popularity mattered. Because he'd evaded a civil war, he was shrewd enough to keep many of his predecessor's civil servants in their old offices and transited them into his own administration. He knew how easily a barracks emperor could seize power, and was uncomfortably aware, too, of the number of short-lived emperors who had lived and died by sword or dagger thrust from a onetime friend. He needed, he knew, a wider base of power.

Diocletian saw clearly how this could be attained. For a century, the legions had made and unmade the emperors, electing or selling the imperial crown to any general they favoured. About 40 such 'barracks emperors' had taken the purple, some lasting only months before being deposed in a pool of their own lifeblood. Diocletian's plan was to recruit several co-emperors, to parcel out the empire between them and to rule jointly, each emperor having his own autonomy and army. The checks and balances of such a system would rein in the legions' power and control their insubordination and would remove the monopoly of influence from Rome's corrupt administrators, all to the benefit of the empire as a whole. And, it would keep this barracks emperor in office for much, much longer.

Diocletian had to deal with the pressing business of holding the eastern frontier and he needed to reduce the terrible drain of maintaining it under arms. His first steps were to draw back some troops from the Rhine and Danube to act as a rapid deployment force. Instead of massing troops along the entire frontier, he'd keep them behind the frontiers, use outlying garrisons to warn him of invaders and respond to their attacks by moving troops to meet them.

The need to revamp the military structure made him look for a suitable deputy to be the first of his co-emperors. His fellow countryman, the brutish soldier Maximian, caught his eye. Diocletian knew Maximian would remain loyal because he could not survive without the support of the senior emperor's political skills. "You will be my fellow Augustus,"

Diocletian told him, after greeting him in the old way, each man grasping the other's right wrist. "Your military brawn and your legions will complement my political power. We will rule the empire together. Do your work in Germania and Gaul, then come to Rome to be formally appointed."

His mutual assistance pact sealed, Diocletian returned to his palace in Nicomedia, near the Bosphorus, where he lived and ruled in Oriental splendour as a god, demanding that those admitted to his glorious presence kneel and kiss the hem of his robe and not look at his face, on pain of death. Maximian, the junior emperor in waiting, obediently marched his troops to Milan and turned his eyes to the Rhine. There were battles to be fought, an empire to keep subjugated and barbarians to kill. He had Spain, Africa, Italy and Gaul to rule. He would be busy.

XIV. Seine

Carausius was pondering over his maps of Gaul. He'd been stamping out the fires of revolution for several years now, but matters kept getting worse. Greedy absentee landowners, clerics and lawmakers in distant Rome had sorely gouged the colonials, and the tenants were passing matters on to the peasants. The legate considered the problem: punishing taxation meant that crops and livestock were forfeited when the taxes were unpaid. It had ruined many smallholders, and they had been driven from their homes to become wandering bandits desperate merely to survive. You couldn't blame them for rebelling, he thought, but he wasn't in a position to sympathise. His job was to bring the rebels to heel.

The Bagaudae, a Gallic term for 'aggressors' who already infested the remoter areas of the empire, were runaway slaves, military deserters, highwaymen and brigands, and they had been joined by dispossessed peasants to form sizeable bands who preyed upon travellers, peasants who were still working the land, and even small settlements where there was insufficient force to drive them away. In several cases the bandits had overwhelmed the military forces sent to suppress them, and had sacked un-walled towns. What had started in Brittany had spread down the coast of the Atlanticus, across the wine country of the Loire and almost to the great southern city of Narbonne. Now came news that faraway Spain was in flames, too. It was a major headache for Rome, and for the legate to whom the problem had been handed, but it was only one of several pressing issues that faced Carausius.

While he was tasked with restoring the Roman Peace, he had to consider not just the brigandage on the land, but also the piracy on the seas off northern Gaul. Saxons from Denmark and Germania ruled the sea from the Baltic to the Gallic Strait. Picts and Hibernians from the western islands were raiding Britain, as Carausius knew from bitter personal experience, and Frankish pirates infested the waters all around the Gallic coast. Almost daily, cargoes were being taken, ships' crews and passengers captured and sold into slavery and the trading fleet itself was being hijacked and turned into yet more pirate ships.

"We have to build and man a fleet, we have to increase the size of our legions and we have to find the money to do it," Carausius told his aide, Lycaon. "Then we can clean up the pirates, and send an expedition across Gaul and into Hispania, crucify a few and get some forts built and garrisoned so we can keep these bastards in line. But we need money to do it."

He was still fretting over funding as he watched the Minerva, one of the fleet's few triremes, negotiate the narrow entrance into the harbour, and wondered sourly if theirs had been yet another fruitless patrol. It had not, and he brightened at the sight of several strange vessels that were trailing in, following the trireme, obvious captives. The Minerva's young captain was soon standing before his commander, glowing with pride. This, he thought, would please old Car the Bear. "We took five pirate vessels, sir," he reported, "and we have 38 captives; we had to kill a few, but the good news is what we took from them." The officer fished under his blue naval cloak for his purse and pulled out five gold coins. "Aureii," he said proudly. "We have a whole chest of coin and silver bullion under guard on Minerva."

The tale came out quickly. After two routine stop-and-searches that had yielded some profit, the trireme had trapped three pirate vessels in a bay where they could not out sail the Romans' oared galleys. After a brief fight with each, the warship had hooked on and boarded the corsairs. "They'd been raiding and had looted several coastal settlements. We just liberated the loot and the captives for ourselves. We burned two of their ships, which were holed and sinking anyway."

The idea hit Carausius with almost perceptible force. Instead of chasing away the pirates, he could simply become a pirate himself. He would discover their home bases and intercept the corsairs as they returned, loaded with loot. He'd relieve them of most of it and release them. That way, he could pay his troops, put down the worst of the piracy, continue to increase his treasury and stamp out the land-based rebellions. "Get that money to the treasurer, Allectus," he said thoughtfully. "You've done very well. Now, send just a few of the pirate crews but not the captains or their chosen men to the slave pens. You can discreetly let the pirate captains choose who we should take for the slave pens. That way, we'll keep the pirates active and improve the quality of their crews. But," he warned, "don't enslave the brigands' captives. They're not rebels, they're victims. We need the general goodwill if we're to get information. Give the victims passage to their places, drop them along the coast, they can make their own way home from there. That's enough, go. I have some business to get started."

Carausius wanted to use the captured bullion, and for that he needed to melt it down and issue it as coin. He needed to build a mint as well as a navy and an army, but he was light-hearted at the once-daunting prospects. He had gold. "Lycaon," he called to his adjutant, "get a few amphorae of good wine to the Minerva crew who just came in, announce a weekend's leave for them. Give them a good donative, and let the whorehouses enjoy some extra business. The mariners deserve my thanks. And, by the way, get a couple of flagons of that wine for us. We can drink to the future with better prospects now!"

Carausius sent for his old shipmaster, and Cenhud came gladly from Forum Hadriani to the stone fortress of Bononia. He brought with him the several men Carausius had asked for, Belgic shipbuilders, expert on the rivers of the Rhine and Meuse. Cenhud greeted him warmly. "Caros, my son," he said, "I am so proud of what you are and who you have become." "Old friend, I want someone I can trust to run this operation," the legate explained. "First, I want to build a fleet of warships that can transport my troops along the great rivers. You know how the army uses them in Germania? Even the smallest vessels can move about 40 men, and can cover 60 or more miles a day on the water. When we have that under way, I'll subdue these bastards on the land, then next, you can build me a sea-going fleet, too, and we'll knock out the pirates on the ocean itself."

His land-based plan was simple. Carausius would move military forces swiftly and almost without warning across Gaul and Spain by river, outflanking the rebel hordes and pinning them against impassable water obstacles so his troops could trap and slaughter them. At sea, he'd supplement his big warships with shallow-draught oared vessels that could intercept pirates close to the coast, so he could relieve them of their booty as they came home from their expeditions. His soldiers would have to learn some of the skills of sailors, but as they used the great rivers, they would be the fastest-moving troops the world had seen.

Running ahead of any warnings, they would strike deep and hard into the heart of rebel territories, and be virtually immune to ambush along the way.

The plan was a triumph and cemented the reputation the general had with his troops. They'd always had a grudging admiration for him, and he for them. They regarded him as hard but fair. Now, with a series of stunning victories, Carausius had brought them pride, and they loved him for it. The general himself led the first expedition, down the great Seine in its springtime floods, to the important stronghold at Lyon. He explained his intent to his commander Lycaon. "We'll sail south and meet the scouts who went out a week ago, and we'll leave one force north of where they find the brigands. Then we sail past the Bagaudae in the night, hopefully undetected because they won't be expecting us, and disembark the rest of our force. With the river on our east, the disembarked troops north and us south, we'll almost have them trapped. We'll send cavalry out to the west to spook them, and drive them north or south, where we'll be waiting. And if they don't move, we just advance up the river bank and trap them that way."

The operation went as if its script had been chiselled into marble. The scouts questioned travellers, drovers and shepherds and found that about 1,200 brigands had sacked and burned several small towns west of the Seine and were camped about a half mile from the river. Lycaon took command of the northern force, landing troops and cavalry three miles short of the rebels, while Carausius waited until dusk and, led by several smaller craft with shielded lanterns to guide them, set off under sail and oars to glide past the unsuspecting horde under cover of dark. Landing the horses and the artillery was the most difficult part of the exercise, but it was done before dawn and the cavalry set out north and west to close the circle on the sleeping insurgents. The scouts and the two bodies of legionaries kept in contact with fire and signal flags to synchronize their attack, and the cavalry pushed the rebels eastwards like beaters driving game. Both forces moved forward in double ranks, finding their line of advance impeded only twice by small copses of trees. The westernmost troops curved inwards as they advanced, better to trap the enemy, who were milling in confusion at the sight of the pincering phalanxes of metal coming at them.

Some army deserters with the rebels tried to organize a defensive line, but they were too few and the undisciplined peasants and brigands were more concerned with gathering their loot and their slaves and fleeing, unaware that they were in a noose of steel. Carausius ordered the catapults and ballistae forward, to add to the rebels' panic. The catapults fired huge darts into the massed horde; the ballistae also hurled pots of blazing pitch into the mob. Then the brass trumpets sounded and the legions marched forward.

At 20 paces, they let their heavy javelins fly in first one, then a second volley that destroyed any cohesion the rebels might have had. The infantry followed that deadly hail of missiles with two more, short-range barrages of heavy darts, then, in wedge formation, levelled their spears over the tops of their shields and tramped in a saw tooth array straight into the mob. The legionaries used the heavy bronze bosses of their shields to pound the rebels backwards and their stabbing lances and swords battered and killed the Gauls as they scrambled over each other to escape.

Most of the brigands knelt in surrender. Those who fled found themselves caught between the river and the lances and slashing swords of the cavalry. After several hundred had been hacked down, the rest knelt to beg mercy. Soon, Davius the executioner and his crew were occupied in their grisly work with the ringleaders of the rebellion, but the armourers were even busier, chaining the captives for the slave coffles and their long march to the auction block.

Carausius had created a successful strategy, and over the next several years he sailed the coasts and quartered Gaul on its great rivers, patrolling the Loire, Seine and Rhone to trap bandits, repeat the butchery, liberate the rebels' loot and fatten his coffers. Always, he took along his executioners, whose crosses appeared outside town after town. The rotting corpses nailed up high reminded rebels of the long, cruel arm of Roman retribution. "They can respect us or they can fear us, or both, but they'll not defy us," said the general, reinforcing his own belief that the cruelties were justified because making examples of the lawless saved many other lives.

After an expedition along the Garonne that mopped up much of the brigandage in the southwest, Carausius' ship-borne troops edged along the coastal waters of Our Sea, outflanking the snowy, steep passes of the

Pyrenees. The flotilla emerged without warning at the Ebro River. There, the legionaries surprised and slaughtered the Iberian insurgents who had looted great swathes of countryside right to the gates of Gerona, and marched onwards to capture the gold mines at Leon. The rewards came every month, when ships and a heavily-guarded mule train took back bullion to the riverfront mint at Rouen. There, Allectus was busy producing the best coinage anyone had seen in 200 years. His moneyers were skilled at taking silver or gold and blending them with brass and bronze into an alloy that looked like pure gold. This they would beat into the proper thickness before cutting them into small square blanks. These were slightly larger than the circular dies a moneyer used. He'd place the blank onto the die, then strike it with a mallet to impress one side of the coin. Next, he would put another die on the remaining blank side and hammer down on it to make the second imprint. When the edges were trimmed, the result was one new coin.

"Our money's been taken right down since Septimius Severus," Carausius grumbled to Cenhud as the pair shared a jug of wine and looked over plans for a new warship. "It's been debased so far that it's a joke. Rome's latest double denarius, for example, is just bronze washed over with silver. Nobody wants money like that but it was all we had to give the troops, so why would they fight for us? Now, with decent money, they have every incentive. Remember, Gaius Julius paid his troops with his own money when Rome wouldn't send him their pay, and the boys remembered that, and stayed loyal when he needed them. It was fair, and it made him emperor. Anyway," he grinned, "I make a far more handsome head on a dupondius than old Julius ever did. I'm surprised anyone would want to part with me just for food or wine."

In the next months, Carausius shuttled back and forth between the green-topped, white cliffs of Bononia and Dover, overseeing legions in Britain and Gaul, and driving his sailors to harry the pirates of the narrows. He drove his men hard, he fed them well, he paid them well and they would have eaten out of his hand because he gave them fair rules administered fairly. Shrewdly, the Briton did not hesitate to let his troops know who was responsible for the good money they were getting. He had his own bearded image stamped on the coinage with the legend: 'The new Golden Age is here.' In another minting, aimed at the British jarls who ached for independence from Rome, he called himself 'The Long-

Awaited One,' 'Spirit of Britain,' and 'The Restorer of Britain.' Not only did the coinage propaganda seem to validate Carausius' right to lead, but as he cheerfully explained, "It pays to remind the footsloggers that Rome wasn't always in the disarray it's in these days, and if they want to think the gods sent me to bring back the good old days, so much the better."

The troops loved it, as they were better paid than ever. Payday, known in the barracks as, 'The day the Eagle shits,' was gratifyingly regular and their money was worth something at last. Plus, this general cut them in on the loot from time to time, and he made sure they had good equipment and good food. Being a legionary wasn't half bad, and you could look forward to a guaranteed retirement pension and land, too. Car the Bear was all right, the troops agreed.

Provisioning the troops was uppermost in Carausius' mind as he sat at his writing table in his office above the harbour at Bononia, and he called for Suetonius, a quartermaster recently returned from an expedition to punish rebels near Spain's River Tagus. The officer stood to attention until the legate motioned him to a stool, and they began discussing the problems of getting enough grain for the legions since the crop had been so poor that summer. "How did you enjoy Spain, by the way/" Carausius asked.

"It was boring, all olive groves, a hot and dry place, no women, no loot, a miserable, uninteresting place, all in all," was the quartermaster's view, although, he recalled, they had made one unusual find that still puzzled him. "We came across a whole batch of scrolls, the gods only know where they came from, and I found a curious thing. I saw my own name, Suetonius, written in one. They were all in the Spanish tongue so I had the thing translated. As far as I can tell it was dictated by some old veteran who got a land grant in Spain at retirement," he told his general.

"Turned out the Suetonius in it was Gaius Suetonius Paulinus, the governor of Britain who had to put down a huge revolt in the colony. It was back in Nero's day and it was kept very quiet, they didn't want the public alarmed. Anyway, the story it told was that the rebels were led by a woman, and they destroyed the capital at Colchester, including the temple of Claudius, and slaughtered tens of thousands of people. The Ninth Spain legion, who weren't too shabby - they'd earned their title for fine service in Iberia, went to save the place and were given a thorough kicking by the rebels. It was such a slaughter, almost nobody came back.

"Even the standard bearer and his unit had to flee with the Eagle. Well, the rebels caught him somewhere short of Eboracum, the legion's HQ, where he was headed for safety. What was most interesting was the scroll claimed it's almost certain the rebels never did get the Eagle, or the legion's pay chests, which the aquilifer had hidden. The story I got was written for an old soldier who claimed to have escorted the Eagle bearer for a while. The soldier dictated a testimony, saying he had an idea where the standard might have been concealed by the aquilifer, but he himself didn't witness it, he wasn't there, which was as well because he learned later the Eagle party had been butchered to a man. It could be interesting information, but who knows?"

At mention of Eboracum, the provincial capital of Britain, and a place he'd visited as a child, Carausius got very interested. "Fetch me the scroll," he demanded, "and keep your damn mouth shut about this."

Left alone, he pressed his fingers to his temples. There was a memory.... there was something he felt he had to recall. A drift of smoke floated in through the window, and his memory flashed bright. The wood smoke, scent of his father's house in faraway, long-ago Britain. He was a young boy, sitting beside his father, whose arm was around his thin shoulders. He could feel again the smooth wool of his father's tunic against his cheek. He heard his father's voice, felt the rumble vibrate as his head rested against the man's chest. His father was showing him a scrap of lead, a thin sheet with marks scratched on it. As clearly as if it were happening in the commander's stone chamber of the Bononia fort, Carausius could again visualize the map and its scratching's, and hear in memory his father's voice.

"This is a map, Caros, a treasure map. We have yet to understand what it shows. It is the secret to a very important Roman treasure and brave men died to keep that secret. One day, I shall find it." The boy looked hard at the little sheet of metal, burning its pattern of lines and letters into his sharp young mind. His father hugged his shoulders, approving as he saw the boy's effort. The child glanced up, and snuggled against his father. It was reassuring, comforting to have his father's affection, although the idea of great treasure was a little bewildering. It didn't matter. His father was there, and that was all that really mattered. Carausius the soldier felt his body surge with the memory, and heaved a gusting sigh. The map was as clear to his inner eyes as if it were on the desk in front of him. He knew the gods were putting before him a thing of importance. He would have to think long, and think hard how to proceed. In a straw-lined nest in a nearby wharf side warehouse, a white rat stirred, then slept again.

Far to the east, and a few hours later, the trader Gracilis walked across the atrium of his house in Forum Hadriani to stand under an oil lamp. He took out the scrap of lead he'd taken from his twin slaves in Massilia and studied it yet again. What he saw had been scratched out at knifepoint two centuries before by a desperate man shortly before he was killed. The metal bore a crude sketch of several lines that intersected. At the top of a vertical line was the part-word 'Ebor.' Running diagonally to it, from the southwest, for the metal scroll was a rough map, a second line had an 'N' and an 'AA' inscribed on its length. The third line ran from the 'AA' north and west to another part-word, 'Manc.' Finally, at the bottom of the metal scrap the word 'plumbum' had been scribed, then scratched through and the word 'bluion' was written. None of it meant anything to Gracilis, but it might mean something to the clever administrator, Mullinus, whose lamp in the house across the street was burning, which indicated that he was still awake...

Mullinus looked at the map with a sense of shock. Ebor? Eboracum? A map of the area where he'd been a slave? Was this some sort of trap related to his runaway past? He concealed his feelings from the slave master. "It seems to be a map, where did you get it?" he asked smoothly.

Gracilis was evasive. "Just something I picked up in Gaul from my slaves, it seemed amusing."

"Well," said Mullinus, "leave it with me and I'll do some studying."

"Oh, no call for that, it's just a curio," said Gracilis, hastily pocketing the thing. Then he added, "Do you have any idea at all what it means?" Mullinus, accepting that there was no danger to him, saw no harm in answering, and his vanity pushed him to demonstrate his world knowledge.

"Well, it seems to be a map of part of Britain. I'd say that 'Ebor' is short for Eboracum, and that 'Manc' for Mancunium. They're significant towns there. I've been to Eboracum, you know. Oh, and this word 'plumbum' is Latin for 'lead,' of course. I have no idea what a bluion is." It was about all he could tell Gracilis until he could find a great library with the tax gatherer's scrolls or maps that might give him clues to what the other letters signified. The next time he was in Rome or Milan, he thought. Gracilis left, also thoughtful, and wondering if perhaps he should consider a trading trip to Britain. If there really was a great Roman treasure, and this was the key to finding it...

Mullinus pulled at his chin; he'd have to think about this. Those twin slaves were somehow involved. They were British. Maybe they knew more, even where the treasure was. Clinia was concentrating on her embroidery when the Briton came into her room. "I just had an odd conversation with that fellow Gracilis," he began. "There's something going on, he seemed very agitated when I looked at some old bit of metal, a sort of map, that he showed me." As he detailed the business to her, Clinia thought she'd faint. "Was it scratched on lead, this map? Was it about this size?" she asked quietly, holding up forefinger and thumb. It was Mullinus' turn to be surprised. "How on earth did you know that?" he demanded. "Were you spying at the door?" Clinia took a deep, deep breath to calm herself. "This is the second time the Fates have caused something wonderful to cross our path. You may have found my sons," she said. "Let me tell you about it...."

XV. Aquila

In his headquarters, Carausius was readying for an expedition by sea, but the matter of the Eagle, the sacred aquila, lost by the Ninth Spanish legion had sparked in him a new train of thought. "That is my father's map," he told himself. "The gods must want me to bring about change in Britain, to restore my homeland to its past glories. If they want it, I must fulfil it. This lost Eagle is a symbol, the key to carrying out their wishes, and with their help. I can rule Britain and bring about that restoration!" He felt a growing excitement as he considered the opportunity. If the timing was right, it could work. He'd already started the propaganda war, issuing coinage announcing him as the Long-Awaited One, and he'd had some very positive responses to the idea he'd cautiously floated among his senior officers about restoring the Golden Age of Rome.

The legate's reasoning was simple. Britain was being plundered by the empire, and the natives wanted their pride and independence restored. They were unhappy at being second-rate non-citizens, tired of being bled for tribute. All he needed was the military force, the will and the symbols to inspire men. For a legion to lose its Eagle was a shameful thing, as it represented the pride and power of Rome. If he could find the long-lost icon and parade it at the head of his legions, he'd be restoring some of that pride, and they'd think him a miracle worker. It could be the exact rallying point he'd need to endorse his authority and his claim to be king, an even more potent symbol than reclaiming his British chieftain's status, if he could ever find his father's brooch of rank.

The old scroll was a good starting point. Its story was that the veteran was dying, and wanted his legion's Eagle recovered. The fellow claimed he had been stationed at a place called Lutudarense during the Boadicean revolt and had witnessed the aquilifer and his detachment head out from there 'back to the garrison,' without saying where that base was. The veteran told the scribe he'd heard that the aquilifer had been ordered to hide the sacred Eagle in some old mine near the fort, but the soldiers who presumably hid it had been killed by the rebels.

Even the group at Lutudarense had been overrun and forced to flee. The survivors had been scattered in the turmoil of the uprising, and Carausius shrewdly guessed that the veteran had probably decided to keep quiet about it all so he could find the coin for himself, but his chance never came and he'd been posted back to Spain. There couldn't be too many forts near Lutudarense, wherever that was, Carausius thought. It must be possible to find one with a mine nearby, and the reward would be tremendous if he could find the Eagle. He sketched again, as he had so many times, the simple features of the little map that lived so brightly in his mind. This, he was certain, showed the location of the lost Eagle, and likely of the missing pay chests that had tempted the old veteran to keep his knowledge to himself. He needed to consult his lieutenant.

Allectus, Carausius' chief advisor and treasurer, was in the fortress' airy office above the harbour, where he had brought requisitions and other scrolls. A slave served the two men watered wine, then moved outside at Carausius' gesture. The man halted in the vestibule, seeming to busy himself with a tray of inks and writing implements. The guards posted across the room at the outer door saw nothing amiss, but the slave was listening hard. With a mixture of threats and promised rewards, he had been recruited as one of Maximian's spies and he was gathering what information he could. That day, gold coins could have showered from the sky and it would not have excited him more. Carausius was outlining the story of the lost Eagle to Allectus and the slave was listening to information that could bring his freedom.

"If Maximian hears this, the best thing that will happen to us is that we'll both go off the Tarpeian Rock," Carausius warned his treasurer, "but there's an imperial crown if we're decisive. We need to usurp the fleet for ourselves and set up a new empire, in Britain and northern Gaul, and that Eagle could be the way to do it."

"It would work, lord," Allectus agreed. "The Britons are restive because Rome ignores them. They've never even had anyone in the Senate, although the Gauls had representatives there almost from the minute they were elected to be a province. As for the locals here in Gaul, they're already administered by us and as long as we keep the Bagudae down and the region safe, they won't care who collects their taxes."

Carausius nodded. "The Britons want to be more independent, and to stop being plundered for the emperor's benefit. The populace would be right behind us, and the Eagle could be a great rallying point for the troops. We don't need to answer to those extortionists in Rome, if we have control of our floating wooden walls.

"We could simply take the fleet for ourselves. The men wouldn't know or even care very much, so long as they have their pay days. It could take months before they realize that Rome isn't issuing their orders, especially if we base the whole flotilla outside Gaul.

"When we have the Narrow Sea to shelter behind, there would be no way for Maximian to reach us. He can't face our naval forces right now, and even if he builds an armada it will be another year or more before the crews are trained well enough to have a chance against us. Anyway, the emperor has enough on his hands with those troublemakers on the Danube; he'll not want to start another campaign."

The two men looked at each other. They were committed now, co-conspirators whose lives would be brutally forfeit if their plans were revealed. Carausius stretched out his right hand, and grasped the wrist of Allectus, who returned the old Roman handshake. They could only go forward now. The agreement was sealed. They'd not just steal the fleet; they would find the Eagle and use it to steal an empire.

As they turned back to the tablum to study lists of supplies and troop dispositions, the wide-eyed slave by the door was moving away across the anteroom, mentally revising what he had overheard. Maximian's agent would pay handsomely, he knew. He just had to be cautious that he wasn't betrayed in turn.

Carausius carried the thoughts of creating an empire with him on a brisk, bright morning as he led a squadron of his new fleet out into the strait. He sniffed appreciatively at the clean salt air as he ran through a mental checklist. Finding the Eagle was only a part of it; he needed to mop up these pirates, make a reconnaissance around Britain, recruit some allies, finish off the rebels in Gaul and Spain, and move some troops into Britain to replace the legions Rome had pulled out for service beyond the Rhine. He'd need to reinforce Bononia, too. There was a lot to do, and he'd earn his salt, but first, he had to sort out these pirates and boost the coffers. "There will be plenty of expenses, and Rome certainly won't be paying for what I want to do. I'll be needing the coin," he thought grimly.

In Forum Hadriani, the trader Gracilis was cold to the scribe Mullinus and his offers. "I bought those twins legally and with proper money. They are mine and they are definitely not for sale," he declared. "I don't care who their mother is, where they came from or what they are. I intend to punish them for stealing my money and running away, but I have a use for them first and they will stay confined until I decide otherwise." Clinia, he said, could not visit them; the security risk was too great. He privately thought that they'd blurt the secret of the map to her and he may be forced to turn it over. Anyway, he told Mullinus, there was no time. He planned to leave Belgica on a trading mission very soon. No, he would not say where he was going, it was a commercial secret and he was a very busy man, so good day to you, magister.

Mullinus left, thoughtfully fingering the big amber and silver brooch at his shoulder. Clinia had sketched what she remembered of the leaden map that her husband had guarded so carefully and that Mullinus had viewed for Gracilis. The 'Ebor' and 'Manc' clues were solid enough. Perhaps, mused Mullinus, he, too, should plan a trade mission to Britannia. It was probably safe enough to go back to Eboracum after all these years. Who would remember a house slave taken in a raid decades ago? There could be a Roman treasure to be found. The risk was worth it.

XVI. Portland Bill

The vessels on the port flank of the Channel Fleet emerged from a small bank of sea fog to surprise the raiders, and the admiral's plan to intercept the Franks had succeeded. The Roman flotilla, patrolling to catch pirates, had been carefully positioned near a great curving beach that jutted from the British shore like the bill of an ibis. Four Frankish corsairs with their high prows, wide beams and shallow draughts were returning under full leather sails from a series of successful raids on the coast. When they saw Carausius' nine new warships, easily identified by their uniform blue canvas, they turned as one, sharply away. The Romans held their line astride the pirates' escape south to Gaul and contained the raiders like beaters driving partridge. A brisk south-westerly closed the seaway to the open ocean, and the loom of the land was hard under their larboard side. They could only sail forward and east. They did not know that the Roman fleet had them trapped like fish in a net.

A navigator wise in these waters had told the legate of the deadly three-mile bank of shingle that extended a murderous wall into the sea, and had brought the fleet to that killing station. "It has the name Portland Bill, lord," he explained, "and it's a ship wrecker. As the tide comes in or out, the swirls on both sides of the Bill crash straight into the flood going east to the German Sea, or the ebb going west into the Atlanticus," the old sailor said. "It squeezes the tide, makes vast whirlpools, and it creates a sea-torrent as fast as a cantering horse. It's all great waves and sea spouts where the currents clash. Ships can't live in that. Worse for them, this wind has the pirates caught between the land and the race. They can't go west against the blast, they can't go east or north because of the Bill and the shore, and we're here in the south. When we close on them and the land, we just have to use our oars to drive them where their sails can't help them. "

Carausius readied his fleet for the capture. He ordered the decks soused with water, and sand to be scattered over them, for better grip in the upcoming battle. He called for the long-poled, bladed hooks that could slash the enemy's rigging to be broken loose, and oars to be shipped above the leather sheets that kept the waves from entering by the holes. The rowers were to rest as the galleys moved forward under sail only. "We have time. Feed the men. Get the cooks to bring bacon and beans," he directed. "I want none of that admiral's ham." The aide grinned. Admiral's ham was what sailors called fish, which few of them liked, even though there was usually a supply of cod drying on the bows of the ships as they sailed.

The ballistae and catapults were uncovered, rope-slung grappling hooks readied and the collapsible fighting towers quickly erected at bow and stern. "Bring up more javelins, and get three sheaves of arrows for each archer," the legate commanded. "Pass that on down the fleet, and tell them: we want these ships captured, not sunk." The orders went out through signallers using red flags and cloaks, or, if the vessels were close enough, were shouted through brass megaphones. Carausius wanted captives and loot, as well as the vessels themselves. He reasoned that if he faced them with shipwreck and drowning, he might force the pirates' surrender, so could take ships, slaves and cargo and increase both his war chest and the size of his fleet.

One of the corsairs broke from the others and in a desperate bid to escape, headed directly for the centre of the Roman line, the green sea foaming white under her bows. The others sailed closer to the coast and dropped their sails. Under bare poles, they watched to see what their opponents would do. Carausius' captain used a speaking trumpet to relay the legate's orders to the squadron. The three central galleys were to surround and take the fleeing pirate; the others were to maintain station.

The red tunics of the soldiers on the centre galleys, which had the names Concordia, Salamina and Minerva lettered across on their sterns, stood out from the blue-green dress of the sailors and an observer could discern the beehive of activity by following the swarm of colours. The infantrymen readied themselves, taking up throwing javelins, checking that their swords moved freely in their scabbards and looking to the fastenings of their armour. The sailors moving between them quickly erected the fighting towers, and wore their ships around to intercept the oncoming pirate. On the trireme Minerva, a blue-clad swarm lowered the boarding bridge at the prow, where the collapsible fighting tower had been left unassembled.

Carausius' captain Cassius Sextus was a grizzled centurion with a transverse crest on his leather helmet and salt-stained segmented armour like his legate's. He was squinting at the trireme where the great boarding bridge jutted forward. "I wouldn't want one of those old ramps on my ship, lord," he said. "They make the ship handle badly, and can sink you in rough seas. I thought they'd all been pensioned off, because they must have been around since Romulus." Carausius nodded. He recalled that the Greek mathematician Archimedes had devised something similar during the defence of Syracuse, centuries before. His war engines had been used to grapple and sink the consul Marcellus' warships. He'd also used great mirrors as burning glasses to focus the sun and set fire to the invaders' ships. Not much opportunity for that in these gloomy northern climates, he thought.

Carausius looked closer at the boarding ramp, which was hinged to the foot of the mast and was being lowered on pulleys to project over the Minerva's prow. A long fang-like spike designed to snag the enemy deck projected from the underside at the front of the gangplank. "I suppose a heavier ship wouldn't be too affected," the legate mused. "Still, I wouldn't want the great clumsy thing, lord," said Cassius.

"Those," he said, pointing where the other vessels had assembled their fighting towers at prow and stern and archers were already swarming, "are much more efficient. I say fire into the enemy, then go alongside. We shoot a few grappling hooks into them and haul them to us, and then we board, all along the side, all at once, and overwhelm them." Cassius rapped his cudgel of office on the gunwale to attract the steersman's attention. "Steer small," he ordered, "and hold our station."

The lighter biremes Concordia and Salamina were almost at the pirate ship, approaching from both sides. Minerva, heavier and less agile, had eased to go head-on at the corsair. The first flight of stones from the warships' ballistae thumped into the pirate's deck-less vessel, taking down several sailors, then a shower of heavy darts from the catapults thudded in. The throwing crews abandoned their machines as the distance shortened, and the archers in the fighting towers began pouring their long, broadhead-tipped arrows into the mass of pirates cowering unprotected. At the same time, at twenty paces' range, the soldiers at the gunwales hurled their weighted, iron-bladed javelins.

Moments later, the rowers on all three decks of the big trireme clattered their oars inboard. The four ships came grinding together. On the corsair, men were screaming, pierced and pinned by the missiles, but a few were running to the ship's sides to fight off the boarders. It was a swift and bloody action. The first infantrymen were already over the ships' sides and stabbing from behind their shields, and the pirate vessel shook under the impact of Minerva's boarding bridge.

A score of nimble marines in leather helmets ran across the ramp shield less, with stabbing sword in one hand and leaf-shaped long knife in the other. The pirates were being assailed from three sides and couldn't surrender fast enough, but the armoured soldiers at their flanks had their bloodlust roused. They battered their heavy knobbed shields forward, knocking aside the raiders' swords, and thrust their stabbing gladii in, under rib cages and chins. They stamped their nailed boots down on fallen, wounded men as they moved forward across the narrow deck, literally crushing the resistance.

Carausius grinned as he watched from his flagship trireme, Isis. "Amazing how soft the human head is, eh?" he asked his centurion. "There's a fellow there just put his sword through from the jaw to the top of that bastard's skull. The point stuck right out. All right, sound the horn and call the dogs off. We can make some money from pirates as slaves, but not from them as dead men."

To the north, the three other Frankish ships had re-hoisted their patched leather sails and were tacking in a desperate bid to gain sea room. The legate waved for his beaters' line to close in. "If we get close, use the sharp hooks to grab the halyards," he instructed his centurion, "then row like Pluto away." The plan was simple. The Romans would slash the ropes that supported the yards and the raiders' sails would fall, crippling the oar less ships. The ploy wasn't needed. The hapless pirates saw their doom approaching, and turned for the shore. Two ran their ships up onto the limestone shingle and the raiders leaped overboard and stumbled ashore, to try an escape.

The third ship was handled badly. She turned broadside in the surf, rolled on her beam ends and foundered in the shallows. Her crew scrambled ashore and ran.   Carausius ordered two warships in close and set about releasing the 40 or so captives the pirates had taken.   All had come from southern Britain, all opted to stay ashore and make their way home. The marines relieved the swamped ship of what cargo they could salvage, then stove in her planking to cripple her. The other three ships were loaded with captives, and manned with prize crews. The legate ordered them to stand offshore until the wind eased, then to make their way back to Bononia, giving the deadly Bill plenty of sea room. Satisfied, Carausius reformed his flotilla and set course for Gaul, to hunt down more raiders.

XVII. Colosseum

In Rome, the general Maximian was administering a savage beating to a house slave who'd spilled his cup of spiced wine. He battered the man with his big fists, knocking him to the ground, then ordered him to stand, before pounding him again, bloodying the man's face as the slave cowered, mute and terrified. "You clumsy ninny, I'll flog you and send you to the Colosseum for the bears," he roared. Maximian's wife Eutropia came into the atrium to see what was happening. "Leave him, darling," she pleaded. "Just have him chained up for a day or two without water. The steward will see to it. Let me look at your poor hands." She gestured to a slave to bring water and a towel, gently eased the brutish soldier onto a stool and knelt to wash and salve his bruises. Two male slaves hauled their battered companion out as the steward shooed them from the master's presence.

"He's lucky I'm not Pollio," grumbled her husband. "He throws slaves to his moray eels to be eaten alive. Anyway, you'd be in a bad mood if you hadn't had a bullion train for months. I have no idea what that swine Carausius is doing up there in Gaul, but the emperor's been asking me some awkward questions about him. We haven't been getting any slaves or silver from up north for months. I've sent messages to the bastard but there's been no response. It puts you on edge."

The butler eased his way into the room. "My lord," he said timidly, "there is unfortunate news about the slave who spilled your wine; he is drunk, my lord. It seems he has been stealing from you, helping himself to the wine." Maximian swore furiously, his wife ended her ministrations and silently exited. "Send the thief to the arena," the general said, shortly. "I'll watch the beasts tear him apart."

Two days later Maximian was entering the Colosseum, a place where hundreds of thousands had died for the amusement of the mob. He passed the arcaded fornices where prostitutes both male and female gathered to offer their bodies in the dens they'd made in the arches of the great edifice. It was long past the ninth hour, the official opening time, after which prostitution was legal. He glanced over the chattering crowd of pimped-out boys, dancers and tavern girls in braided wigs made from Celt or German hair. The law said that prostitutes must dye their hair blonde or wear blonde wigs to signify their legal, but disreputable, trade. High-class women in search of sexual thrills were in the habit of stealing out at night in such wigs, he mused, which rather undermined the lawmakers' intent to stigmatize and humiliate the whores. Another failure of the high-minded, he thought.

His eyes rested on a slender Sarmatian whose gilded nipples showed through her filmy tunic. He glanced at the tariff board above her den, and was tempted, but he hurried on, brushing impatiently at the flying insects that sought his sweat, even as he saw his own name painted in red on several walls, official graffiti that advertised his political standing. Soon, he was taking his privileged seat just above the sand of the arena where he caught the familiar stench of dung and blood. The nervousness many people harboured about sitting too near the front wasn't about the smell, he thought. That caution followed the action of the crazed emperor Caligula, who had once ordered his guards to thrust a whole section of the crowd into the arena to be killed by wild beasts, because he was bored and there were insufficient criminal victims to provide a suitably gory spectacle.

Maximian's reserved section occupied the first rows above the sand, a highly prestigious place designed to display the great and good to the public. It was also conveniently close to one of the vomitoria, those cleverly-designed exits that allowed the crowds to leave quickly and easily. An outpouring of people was moving through it at the moment, having just turned their thumbs upwards like a drawn sword, to vote for the death of the losing gladiator. Now they were headed for the latrines and the food vendors.

Maximian approved. Too often, he reflected sourly, the sponsors tucked their thumbs in, symbolically sheathing a sword, to spare the fighters. He preferred to see gladiators fight to the death, but the people who put on the shows didn't want to waste money, and training a fighting man was expensive. Below him, a slave dressed as Charon, boatman of the Underworld, was loading the body of the slaughtered slave onto a small cart as the other gladiator, bloodied and limping, moved out of the arena, which was buzzing with talk and boos.

An overweight senator in a freshly-chalked, gleaming white toga nodded to him from along the row. Maximian returned the greeting, noting with amusement that the man was wearing an obvious, glossy black wig. Probably hair from India, he mused. People did the damnedest things to be fashionable. Old Pliny had once declared that using leeches left to rot in red wine for six weeks or so would make your hair black, and half of Rome had tried it. Probably turn your scalp black, too, thought Maximian. No wonder people wore wigs instead. He became aware that the man in the shiny hairpiece seemed to want to talk. He moved closer. "Did you see that?" the politician asked. "Quite scandalous, I think."

The big soldier shook his head. "I've only just arrived," he said.

"Oh," said the senator. "Well, that prick of a referee effectively killed the winner."

Maximian angled his head questioningly, and raised an eyebrow. The summa rudis refereed gladiatorial bouts, and the rules were many and detailed, making for bouts that were only rarely fights to the death. If the gladiator had put up a good fight, he was even honoured in defeat. It was all in the rules. Only once, at the pleasure of the emperor Titus, had both gladiators been declared victors, after an epic and long drawn-out duel. Otherwise, the rules were strictly obeyed. One of the key conditions allowed a beaten gladiator to submit, and his life would be spared if the munerarius who'd paid for the bout approved it and was popular enough to sway the crowd's verdict.

One common rule allowed a fighter who'd slipped and fallen but had not been floored by his opponent to get up, retrieve his weapons and continue combat. The referee in the arena would wave away the standing gladiator until this happened. He controlled the fight, and this was what had annoyed the senator.

"That fellow Diodorus," he said, gesturing at the corpse now being wheeled out by slaves dressed as Pluto, lord of the dead, and Mercury, escorter of souls to the Underworld, "had won the fight. He'd flattened the Greek Demetrius, knocked away his shield and grabbed his sword. Demetrius was down, lying bleeding on the sand. He managed to raise his forefinger to submit, and Diodorus did the correct thing and stepped back. He was waiting with both their swords in his hands to see if the thumbs went up, telling him to kill his opponent, but the referee must have had a bet on the fight. He made the most amazing ruling, signalled that Demetrius fell accidentally, and ordered Diodorus away. Then he kicked the Greek's sword back to him. Diodorus turned to protest to the referee, and didn't see the Greek advance and cut him down. The referee quickly signalled that the bout was ended and nodded to Demetrius to finish the man off."

The crowd, said the irate senator, booed the decision, but it was too late for the dying gladiator. The referee had handed the palm leaf of victory to the surviving fighter and didn't even wait for the slave dressed as Mercury to test the defeated man's body with a white-hot iron to see that he wasn't faking death. He briskly strode out, off the sand. "Daylight robbery," agreed Maximian to the sputtering senator. "They'll probably put that on his tombstone."

He nodded again to the senator, and turned back to his seat, then glanced up at the glare of the sun. Too hot, too bright, he thought. He spotted a rigging crew working, and motioned for a slave. "Get those people to pull the awning forward, give me more shade," he commanded. The man hurried off to carry out the instruction and Maximian settled in his seat, thinking with satisfaction how he'd enjoy witnessing his thieving slave's painful end, even though it was against the law to send a slave to death in the arena. "If the magistrates find out, they'll not dare to censure me," he thought grimly, "I'd have them on the sand, too."

Over his head, a handful of mariners skilled in handling large sails were working the rigging to move the vast canvas awnings that protected the crowd from the afternoon sun. It was a cushy job to be one of those chosen to come to Rome and serve out your time, the nobleman thought, considering the hardships of life at sea. He watched with interest as the sailors swung around in the rigging and the shade they created moved across him. One of the sailors approached, knuckling his forehead. "Is that sufficient, lord?" he asked, obviously seeking a reward.

"Fine," the general grunted, then a thought struck him. "Where is your accent from?" he demanded.

"I'm British, lord," said the man.

"Were you serving there?"

"No, lord, I was in Gaul. I sailed with the Classis Britannica, under the lord Carausius."

Maximian leaned forward, and caught the man's blue tunic, getting a smear of tallow on his fingers from its waterproofing. "And how," he said dangerously, "has my lord Carausius been keeping?" What the frightened sailor told the menacing big nobleman about the captured raiders and their siphoned-off loot sent Maximian striding out of the arena in a fury. He headed for the Senate house to find the jurist Marcus Vettius. "That bastard legate Carausius has been making himself rich at my expense. He's got his own mint up there in Gaul, melting down the bullion that should be in my damned coffers," he stormed. "Get him brought back here. I'll court martial the swine, then I'll personally strangle him. Car the thieving Bear! I'll put him in the arena with real bloody bears!" He kicked at an ivory-inlaid stool in rage. Robbed, by that insolent Briton! And, he'd missed seeing that clumsy thieving slave torn apart. What a bloody day!

Nine hundred miles to the north, in Forum Hadriani, the twins' master was viewing them with an evil eye. "We're going to Britain, and you had better lead me straight to that treasure. If you're lying, you'll have your backs opened and I'll show the world your spines before I have you crucified. And if you try to run again, I'll have you hanged upside down over a fire before you're flogged and crucified. Am I clear?" The twins looked back at Gracilis and he was shocked to see hate, not fear, blazing in their eyes. Infuriated, he cudgelled Domnal across the side of the head, flooring him. Mael dropped to his brother's side and looked up. "If you want the treasure, you do not hit him again," he said quietly. "I'm telling you this, listen and learn or you will be a poorer man. We'll go to Britain and we won't run, we'll lead you to the treasure and you'll release us. If you don't agree, we'll find a way, despite you, to kill ourselves and you'll be missing two valuable slaves as well as an emperor's bullion."

Gracilis stared into the slave's level, cold eyes, turned abruptly, dropped his cudgel and walked away. Two days later, with the twins collared, chained, and locked in a wooden cage on the deck of Gracilis' trading ship Venta, the merchant ordered his captain to set course for Londinium. He sailed just a day before Mullinus and Clinia arrived at the same dockside in a litter, with a small entourage of slaves. The couple were there to board a Frankish trader's stout vessel, and they were bound for Colchester. In Britannia's civil service headquarters, they knew they'd find a library and archive of tax rolls for British towns.

In the east, Maximian was still simmering. Carausius had ignored Maximian's summons and the general had been forced to bottle his rage at insolently being ignored because he had major concerns of his own. He'd been sent to the Danube to turn back the rising tide of Goths, Vandals, and assorted barbarians who were pushing at the eastern borders of the empire, and it was a close-run thing. His campaign in Moesia had been a success, but he was chronically short of manpower, and he felt he was merely filling holes in an ever-weakening dyke. He had a burning hatred for Carausius by now, as the flow from Britain and north Gaul of trained soldiers as well as of needed currency had totally dried up and his reputation and career were jeopardised. "With those resources, I could put down these insurgents once and for all, secure this border and clean up the bandits in Gaul and Spain, including that poxed whore's son thief Carausius," he told his battle group commander.

"There's something else," he told his subordinate, recalling what his spymaster had told him. "I heard a story from Darius of a treasure and a lost Eagle that is hidden in Britain. Talk to him, get someone with a brain onto it, find out the truth and report back. I have others working on this, but we might need to send a few trusted men to finish off the job. I don't want some superstition being used to rally a rabble, and I certainly don't want that prick Carausius waving an Eagle he's recovered like he's the new Messiah."

The 'new Messiah' admiral by now held a large swathe of northern Gaul and his fleet and war chest had steadily grown as he captured and crucified or sold into slavery the Gaels, Franks and Bagaudae marauders who infested the northern territory and sea coasts. Their freedom to prey on traders or to raid the coast to loot anything they could have been severely curtailed by Carausius' ever-more-efficient naval force. He had been less successful at holding back the German and Danish invaders, and they had seized the Frisian Islands, driving out Rome's soldiers and settlers, but Carausius' primary mission was to keep open the trade routes from Our Sea to northern Gaul and Britain. And, he privately thought, to build up his forces to sustain his political ambitions. Britain, he thought was ripe for a new emperor who would treat them as a nation, not as a milk cow to be drained for rapacious nobles back in Italy or to fund military expeditions on the Rhine. He mused on another idea that had been implanted in his mind by Allectus. "You know, lord," the smooth-tongued treasurer had murmured, "how soldiers take a Latin name when they swear fealty to the emperor? It might be provident to assume a more British name to underscore your ties to the nation." At first, Carausius had dismissed the idea, but on balance, he thought it a sound idea. A week or two after the germ was implanted, he overheard two sentries refer to him as 'The Bear,' a nickname he knew was respectful enough. 'Ursus the bear,' he thought, or 'Arth,' as 'bear' was in the British tongue. "Artorius' was still too Roman, but maybe 'Arthur?' It would fit well enough with his string of names…

The province was growing richer, attracting invaders as well as the greed of Rome. That wealth, Carausius reasoned, would sustain the island once it became independent of the empire. Affluent Britons were tired of being taxed by remote rulers, and they needed protection from barbarians. The role of protector and liberator appealed to the bear-like soldier and the military possibility of keeping Rome at bay with his skilled fleet was obvious to him. He had discussed the idea with Allectus, now it was time to persuade the legions to muster behind him, and he finally had the bullion to do that.

Carausius set out on a series of visits to garrison towns to hand out generous donatives to the troops, coins that carried propaganda slogans announcing the arrival of the new saviour. "Old Julius knew the tactic," he confided to friends. "He paid his troops from his own coffers, and they backed him all the way to the imperial throne." Privately, though, he remembered that the donatives paid by emperors to the urban plebs could be a two-edged sword. When Marcus Aurleius ended a long absence to make his triumphal entrance into Rome 100 years before, the mob had held up eight fingers and chanted 'Eight, eight, eight!' at him, demanding and eventually forcing him to hand over the eight gold coins they had decided would be a suitable gift to each of them to mark his return.

Carausius resolved that he wouldn't be dictated to by the stinking unwashed. He'd enter the city with a show of force at his back. He'd hand out tokens for food, as happened at some of the games, but he was not inclined to empty his treasury to just anyone. The troops had earned his loyalty, the mob had not.

By the time the emperor Diocletian donned the laurel crown and began his long reign, the legate Carausius had sailed all around Britain. He had made alliances and reconnoitred the strategic routes and places for his legions in any future campaign against the Picts who lived beyond the Wall. He had travelled inland several times to meet local chieftains, to give them gifts of silver and to enlist their aid. 'Help me throw off the Roman yoke that is bleeding Britain white, and I will keep the peace in the south, and give you large land grants north of the wall of Antoninus." The chieftains had listened warily, and when they had questioned why they should need him to give them land held by Picts, the big general had allowed his battered face to break into a smile. "This," he said, tapping his sword, "is one reason. And those," gesturing at his warships off the beach, "are another."

On the way along the coast south through the German Sea, the legate ordered his shipmaster to land him and a party of marines at a certain ravine by a great chalk promontory. Carausius was going to see again the place where he had once been the boy affectionately nicknamed Caros. The trireme closed on the land in the lee of the cliff while the other three ships of the squadron stood offshore, and Carausius, armour discarded, splashed ashore through chest-deep water. A slave hurried to the legate, carrying his dry cloak, and he pinned it with the amber and silver replica badge of a British jarl that a woman had given him, to replace his father's lost symbol of office. The legate and his escort walked through the overgrowth and tumbled stones that had once been a settlement and scrambled up the slope to a small headland. Carausius looked north and east, where a smear of smoke showed, and told his aide Quintus: "This is Brigantia. My father was killed here, my mother and brothers were taken captive here. I ran that way as a boy, to save my life. There was a forge over there, and the smith took me to safety, across the German Sea."

"There could be a forge there today, lord," said the aide. "That's smoke all right." The legate nodded. "I could use a stretch of the legs, even with my bad foot," he said. "Let's take a walk." From the shadows under an elderberry bush, a white rat watched, eyes bright, as the big warlord strode by.

Few things surprised the burly commander, but the sight of Gimflod working the bellows in the old forge came as a major shock. "I came back. Couldn't stand the Belgae," the big smith confessed after the initial greetings and assessments were done. "It was a good choice for me, Caros. I have plenty to do, and the garrison at Eboracum is my best client. I make weapons now, beautiful swords, no more boring work churning out ship's nails and bolts."

Carausius picked up a sword the smith had made, tested its balance and admired the swirling feathery patterns in the steel that spread elegantly from the central channel down the blade. "It's a fine weapon," he told the smith.

"It's just five strips of iron, a lot of hammering to fold them all together, over and over, and a lot of reheating," grinned Gimflod. "The strips give it strength," he explained. "The channel reduces weight and makes it stronger, while the hammering produces a friction weld and takes out the impurities. It gives you a sword that's strong, not brittle. It flexes, it holds an edge and it will completely ruin your opponent's day."

On impulse, Carausius demanded: "Make me one. Make me a sword at least two hand spans longer than this," sliding out his regulation gladius from its scabbard to demonstrate, "with just the exact balance you have in that," he pointed to the masterpiece the smith had made. He continued: "Make a ricasso here," pointing to the part of the blade just below the guard which he wanted left unsharpened, "so I can grip it with my other hand, and swing it two-handed. How long will all that take?" Gimflod looked at the pile of cast iron blooms waiting to be worked, and grimaced. "For you, Caros," he said, eyes closed as he thought, "ten weeks."

"Take it to the palace at Eboracum then," said the legate. "I can't wait. I'll see you, and it, there around the Ides of August."

XVIII. Colchester

Back in Colchester, the legate was making his plans. "We've got to subdue those cattle thieving oat-munchers up there, trans vallum," Carausius grumbled to Allectus. "They pushed us back from Antoninus' wall, and they're lapping at the foot of Hadrian's defences. He had 12,000 men to keep the bastards out; he had Dacians, Tungrians, Spaniards and Gauls. He even had hundreds of those excellent Hamian archers. All I have is a handful of auxiliaries only good for exacting customs duties. I get reports all the time of cattle raids, of Roman citizens and locals taken for slaves, settlements burned. If they breach the vallum, we'll have more than our hands full to round up and contain the bastards, they'll spread everywhere. We need to go up there and put about the lash, and for that, we need more troops. Those Picts aren't all rubbish; we'll need a decent force for a foray." He paused, then smiled quietly to himself as he remembered a joke.

"Did I tell you about Hadrian on the day he finished the wall? He was walking along it, proud as could be, when a small Pict came out of the woods and challenged him to fight. Hadrian sent out a guard detail to bring the impertinent fellow back alive for a flogging. They vanished into the woods, there was a horrible clanking and screaming and the little Pict came out dusting his hands. "Send out some good ones this time, Roman!' he shouted." Allectus nodded, intent on the story.

Carausius took a swig of wine and continued: "Hadrian sent out 20, then 50 men, but none came back until finally, one bloodied legionary staggered out of the woods, battered and limping. 'Look out, Hadrian," he shouted. "It's an ambush, there's two of them!' "

Allectus laughed at the tale, as Carausius took another draught of wine and asked: "How's the coinage going?" Allectus nodded. His mint at Lyon was productive, and the two men were in Colchester to establish a second mint there. The treasurer planned a third money-making operation in Londinium to create more of the good coin that attracted and kept recruits. "The metal's the thing," he said. "The head that's stamped on it doesn't matter. If the weight of silver's right, the coin is worth its value and is acceptable. We do have a reasonable supply of bullion, lord," he told Carausius, "but we could always use more."

"We'll have to take more Picts and pirates to market," grunted the legate. "The trouble is, too many captured soldiers kill themselves before they'll go under the crown, and many of the ones that do submit are rebellious." The two men shared the same thought, of the dangers of unrest. Two centuries before, the gladiator Spartacus had led a slave uprising that cost Rome dearly before it was put down. The empire had reacted brutally to deliver a message to would-be insurgents. In one day, the legions hoisted 6,000 rebels on crucifixes that lined 130 long miles of the Appian Way, all the way from Capua to Rome. People said the screams of their ghosts haunted the road for a hundred years.

Carausius knew the story, and changed the subject. "Next week, I'm off north. I want to take a look at the garrison at Eboracum, see what we'll need to improve if we're going across the Wall to stamp the bastards down. But right now," he said, "I'm going to the baths." Which was where, at that exact moment, Fate was taking the trader Mullinus after his long afternoon spent poring over dusty tax records.

The limping, thick-necked soldier with the mutilated face and crushed cheekbone collided with the smooth-shaven, clerkish escaped slave as they rounded a limestone column outside the baths. Mullinus recovered first and apologized, Carausius was waving away the polite words when his eyes locked on Mullinus' brooch. At the same time, the trader saw Carausius' near-replica of the badge. The soldier's hand shot out and grasped Mullinus' cloak. "Where," he said, in a voice that promised murder, "did you find that?"

Mullinus took in the purple-striped robe, the battered face and the inherent menace of the big man. He spoke placatingly. "This came to me, lord, in the land of the Belgae. I am a negotiator there, I trade in fine goods."

"That," said Carausius thickly, stabbing with a blunt forefinger at the brooch, "was taken from my family. It is the mark of my rank, and it was stolen in blood."

Mullinus thought quickly. He wanted no inquest into the history of the brooch or of himself. The soldier was obviously powerful and important, he could be either fatally dangerous, or a fine ally. He spoke smoothly before the other man could call for the vigiles to arrest him as a thief. "If it is yours, lord, it would be right and just, and I should be pleased to reunite you with such a valuable piece of your family history, as my gift," he said slowly, his mind churning.

He was unpinning the brooch when the thought hit Mullinus with almost palpable force. His hand shook as he fumbled with the bodkin pin. "Your mother," he said, a quaver in his voice. "Is her name Clinia?" Somewhere, the Fates who control the threads of men's lives paused in their spinning, glanced at each other and smiled grimly.

Once she could comprehend the lightning strike shock of the situation and had dried her tears, Clinia could not tear her eyes away from her fine son. A legate, commander of a fleet and of legions, the child Caros she had long mourned was not only miraculously back with her, but was taking charge of her quest and had promised to find and free her twins. "Mother, I'll gut this Belgic merchant who holds my brothers slave. I'll strangle him with his own guts if he resists me," Carausius growled. "I've sent plenty to the crucifix, and if he doesn't cooperate, I'll take such action against him that he'll be grateful to be crucified." The big soldier had already dispatched messengers to Eboracum and Londinium to locate the merchant Gracilis and his twin slaves. "We'll have Domnal and Mael safe in this villa before any of us are a month older," he promised.

The quest was more pressing than finding the Eagle, but Carausius didn't ignore that mission. He sent Mullinus and a handful of slaves, with soldiers to watch them, back to the treasurer's house. There, Mullinus had been combing the scrolls for mention of this mysterious Lutudarense, the first clue in the search for the Eagle. "Keep a sharp look out for this fellow Gracilis," he told Mullinus. "He might also come to Colchester to search the tax rolls. He probably knows all that we do about where the Eagle is hidden." To his orderly, he quietly directed, "Watch Mullinus closely. He might be playing his own game here. We don't want him locating the Eagle and slipping away alone to collect it. Any problems, chain him up. I've dealt with his type before."

The search for Lutudarense took two days, and the place name finally turned up in an invoice. The document was for the sale of a 200lbs pig of lead, and it detailed the markings stamped into the ingot. A literate slave found the invoice, and brought it to the magister. "Could this be it, master?" the slave said, showing the papyrus of river-grown reeds that said "TI CL TR IVT BR EX ARG." "I read it as 'Tiberii Claudi Trifernae Britannicum ex Argentaris: 'Product of Tiberius Claudius Triferna, Lutudarensian British lead from the lead-silver works.' "

Lutudarense, it seemed from the buyer's paper trail, was north, a place near the limestone peaks and the spa town of Aquae Arnemetiae in north-central Britain. Carausius weighed matters. The lost Eagle was most important, and it might be several more weeks before the twins were located and recovered. He opted not to wait, but to go north at once. Carausius, his mother Clinia, Mullinus and an entourage of soldiers and slaves readied for travel. At that exact hour, the merchant Gracilis was haunting Roman tax offices in Londinium, seeking to decipher the map, and Maximian's hired killers were on a Colchester quayside, asking questions and seeking Carausius, Mullinus and Clinia to steal it.

Preparations were slowed, but several days later, a spacious four-wheeled raeda, a covered carriage pulled by four horses, was ready to convey Clinia and her body slaves, while the men would ride horseback, and the household slaves, soldiers and baggage mules could trot behind. "We'll go via the military road to the west as far as the Ryknield Way and go north on it," Carausius decreed. "That will bring us close to this lead mine, and we can find more when we are there."

The group was readying for the road when the tramp of nailed military boots sounded outside their compound. The gate guards challenged the newcomers, who responded, and the gate was opened to reveal Mael and Domnal grinning excitedly at the anticipated reunion with their mother. A shackled Gracilis trailed miserably behind them, under the eyes of a file of soldiers. "We have your man, lord," said the centurion who headed the detachment. "Found him in a brothel with a young boy, the dirty pederast." Carausius grunted his approval at the catch and his disgust with the Belgic trader.

"Did you search him?" he demanded. The twins knew what the centurion wanted. "We have it here," said Domnal, producing the scrap of scratched lead. "Give it to me," Carausius ordered.

"Who are you?" said Domnal truculently.

"Ah," said the legate, bulking large over the man. "I am your small brother."

He quickly untangled their stories, and pondered whether to execute Gracilis. "He doesn't deserve to die. He did nothing wrong," Clinia insisted to her sons. "He bought you honestly; he didn't abuse you until you stole from him and tried to run." "We didn't ask to be slaves," said Domnal, angrily. "We were stolen, and he paid off the thieves." At the end of the argument, Carausius ordered his soldiers to free the Belgic trader and take him back to the Colchester docks. "Put him on the first ship to anywhere," he instructed them. "He probably knew they'd been captured. He shouldn't have bought them. If he comes back, he's to be nailed up." Gracilis nodded, white-faced and accepting. He knew how close he'd been to suffering the brutal legate's wrath. He'd make his way back to the Meuse, grateful just to be alive, but he might also have a word with a connected trader he knew. Information could be as valuable as goods, sometimes...

For Clinia and her sons, the journey north went quickly, as the big carriage ate up the miles of metalled road. On the fourth day, 140 miles into their journey, the group rolled up to the great mansio and staging post at the crossroads town of Letocetum, where the military road met the Ryknield Way that ran diagonally across Britain from Gloucester to the moors and wolds of the north east. They spent two nights at the crossroads mansio to rest the soldiers, mules and slaves, change horses and allow Carausius to discuss military matters with the garrison commander. The next stages of the journey were not as swift as the great high road had allowed, because the route crossed hilly ground, but still the road was to exacting Roman standards, as Carausius proudly pointed out to his twin brothers.

"Twelve feet wide, six layers deep, and where we can, we use iron ore. It rusts together to make a metal surface that will last a thousand years. And there's 50,000 miles of these roads in the empire!"

"Just counted the mileposts, did you?" Mael joked. He didn't care where they were going, or how fast. He and Domnal were blissfully happy to be free men again after long years of slavery. All three brothers spat on the ground, shook hands and vowed to make a new future. Reunited, they were going in search of a gilded silver Eagle that could make one of them into an emperor.

XIX. Navio

Vast grain farms that had been worked for the past two centuries to feed Rome's hungry legions lined both sides of the old road and the small caravan passed a dozen teams of plodding oxen pulling high-sided farm wagons, and field after field of stalks that held a golden harvest. From time to time, a farmstead or potter's barn marked the landscape, but the land was generally innocent of habitation. Carausius and the twins rode ahead of the iron-tired raeda, whose leather top Clinia had ordered closed to protect her from the dust kicked up by the horses. Alongside, marching in step, were a dozen sweating legionaries ordered as extra protection by Carausius after an odd incident just before they left Colchester. The slaves followed, leading the pack mules. Mullinus and another file of soldiers brought up the rear.

Carausius puzzled over the Colchester incident. Three nights before, two robbers who seemed to be unusually heavily armed for their task had been surprised by two of the four sentries Carausius had considered enough protection for the party. They were trying to break into the mansio where the legate and his group were staying. Challenged, they'd turned to fight, and the sentries, reinforced by their comrades, ran them both through.

One of the robbers, dying, had coughed out 'Gracilis,' the name of the trader who'd once owned the twins. Carausius presumed the trader had attempted to regain his slaves, but the matter was puzzling. He had enlisted more troops for protection and was still pondering the matter, uneasy that somehow someone knew of the purpose of his expedition, when a local, hired as a guide during their short stay at the waystation, kicked his mule up alongside Carausius' horse.

"This is Ryknield Street, lord," he told the legate. "It is a very ancient way, improved by the Caesars, that would take us almost to Eboracum, but soon we have to turn off to the west. In a half day or so, we will come to the lead mine at Lutudarense." "What's after that?" demanded Carausius.

"Well, lord, further west there's Aquae Arnemetiae, where the springs are sacred to the goddess, or you could go north from the mine to the fort at Navio."

Carausius took in what the guide had said, mentally mapping the geography he'd described, and a synapse fired in the legate's brain with an almost perceptible 'snap.' He sawed at his horse's bridle and shouted for the convoy to halt. The twins rode up alongside him and he pulled out the scrap of lead and leaned on the pommel of his four-horned saddle as he gestured at the little map.

"It's obvious now," he said. "We guessed that this "Ebor' here is Eboracum, in the northeast. This line that runs diagonally from it with the 'N' must be the road to Navio and it goes on southwest to 'AA' – that has to be Aquae Arnemetiae. That 'Manc' up there is obviously Mancunium, and it's probably only included to establish the general area. The thing we're looking for must be near Navio." He turned to the guide. "Ever been to Navio?"

"Yes lord, a few times. There's a fort there that guards the mines where they extract lead and silver."

Carausius considered that for a moment, then slapped his road-dusty trews. "That," he said quietly to the twins, "is why the old ground pounder or whoever made this map wrote 'plumbum' then scratched it out. He was leaving a clue that the Eagle was in a lead mine, then he changed his mind. Well, we know from the Spaniard's scroll that it was going to be hidden in a mine of some sort, so all we have to do is find a place in that area where they dig out something that isn't for making water pipes."

The group's spirits were high as they rode into the small, square fort at Navio, which was sited above a sharp bend in a rippling river. The countryside around was spectacular, with sheep-dotted fields among limestone outcrops, deep valleys, and a dramatic, wind-funnelling gorge that rose sharply to a ridgeline tor whose steep face was constantly loosing trickles of scree. They handed their animals over to the garrison slaves to be stabled and tended, washed off the travel dust and joined the soldiers in the barracks for a surprisingly good meal. Fresh bread, local ham and green beans, cheese, honey cakes and Gallic wine restored them before they rolled themselves in their hooded wool cloaks and settled to sleep in the dormitory.

The next morning, Carausius brought his search for the Eagle into tight focus. His instruction to the bull centurion Pattalus, who commanded the small garrison, was brief. "Make me a list and a map of the mines within a half day's march of here, but only include very old workings. Nothing recent, and nothing that is a lead mine." Pattalus, who was serving out his time in remote, damp Britannia after an unfortunate incident in southern Gaul involving his tribune's wife and a mistake about just when the man would return home, blinked, saluted by punching his fist and forearm across his heart, and stamped out. He returned an hour later with three possible locations gleaned from questioning several of his men who were locals.

One mine was flooded, so Carausius ignored it for the present. The next was the most distant, at four hours' steady marching, so the legate thought it an unlikely choice. The third sounded promising. A fluorospar mine that produced a coloured semi-precious quartz, it was only rarely worked these days. "They don't do much with it," said the centurion. "I think the old Romans did more, a dozen emperors ago. We don't go around there much, the locals are very possessive, they have legends about the gods who guard the area, some old stories of sacred ground that must not be disturbed. We had a few incidents where a patrol was shot at, and we had to flog a few locals to teach them to keep their arrows to themselves. Since then, they've been quiet and we've more or less left them alone."

Carausius nodded. It seemed likely to him that some echo from the past still sounded in men's memories. He'd be cautious about advertising his presence around the mine. It would be wise to dismiss the guides as quickly as possible, and to carry out this first of his explorations secretly, he thought. He gave instructions to his men and to the centurion, and all were ready within the hour, Carausius' file of troops and several slaves equipped with picks and shovels. Mounted scouts were sent out ahead with orders to keep discreet watch against attack.

The centurion called his troop together. "Right, you lot, it's time for bohica, bend over, here it comes again," he told them cheerfully, "a bit of marching, a bit of digging, more pleasure is in your future." The men grumbled good-naturedly as Pattalus led the whole group to the place, just a couple of miles from the fort walls. "They call it the Blue John mine," he remarked casually as they squinted against the sunlight to sight the cavern entrance half-hidden in a fold of land. The legate, thunderbolt-surprised, jolted upright and almost slipped from his mount. Somehow, he suppressed his emotions, and said nothing. Could he be so lucky, to strike the exact place at his first attempt?

When they arrived at the mine, almost unnoticeable in a jumble of tumbled limestone, Carausius made a play of being disappointed. He shrugged his shoulders for effect and murmured non-commitally that it didn't look good. "We'll go through the motions, and just use our slaves," he told the centurion, "Don't waste your time, take your men and we'll see you back at the fort in a few hours." The old soldier, relieved at not having to stay with the officer, nodded his thanks, gave the salute of the fist across the chest and rode away with his patrol.

Mael and Domnal approached. "Why's he going?" Mael asked. "We've found the bloody place," said Carausius. "It's the Blue-Ion mine, just like the 'bluion' on the map. Get those oil lamps, we need to take a look, and get everyone out of sight, as soon as possible." Inside, the cavern was a winding, narrow place, carved by an ancient stream through the limestone. The animals were led in, and sentries under specific orders to stay unseen were posted by the entrance. Only then did the work party set off.

They were able to walk easily down into the old workings, following a time-worn path left by miners who'd extracted a glistening stone used to make crystal bowls and ornaments. A quarter mile in, the path ended, blocked by a rock fall. It had been two centuries since they were made, but the scrape marks of hammers and iron pry bars on the cavern ceiling were still discernible in the lamplight to someone who was looking for them, and the tumbled rock below seemed to confirm the site.

"Remove those rocks, and carefully," the twins instructed the slaves. It took almost an hour until an elm and leather pay chest with bronze bindings showed, then another, and another. All contained gold and silver coin and ingots. Carausius ignored the bullion. What he was seeking was far more valuable. His breath halted as he glimpsed red wool where a slave levered at a chunk of limestone. "Stop that," he commanded, and dropped into the trench where the men were working.

His pounding blood made thunder in his ears and the place seemed suddenly brightly lit. His breath hurt his throat and an exultation he only felt in the joyous, total surrender to the bloodlust of battle washed over him like heavy surf. 'This is the instrument of my emperor's crown. This will make me master of Britain," he thought. He clawed at the rocks where the red fabric showed. Someone a long time before had made a secure stone cradle for the Eagle, and had carefully stacked more rocks above and around to protect it before the ceiling had been collapsed. The gleaming standard was unharmed in its stony nest, wrapped just as the long-ago aquilifer had left it, safe in his own military officer's scarlet cloak.

Carausius reverently lifted out the gilded silver Eagle with its upraised wings and laurel wreath, and dropped to one knee. "Mithras, I shall sacrifice a bull to you, in thanks," he promised, giddy with relief and excitement. The Eagle that could rally the support he needed to become emperor was in his hands.

XX. Danube

Beyond the Danube River, the general Maximian was fighting a desperate rear-guard action. A vast horde of Saxons and Alemanni barbarians had threatened to outflank and surround his battered, half-strength legion, now down to fewer than 3,000 men, and he'd been forced to withdraw from the shallow valley where they had been confronted. Javelins and arrows were beating down like deadly hail on the legionaries, threatening to turn the trampled meadow into a slaughter yard.

Their general ordered the Romans to form the testudo, the tortoise-like protection created when the ranks held their curved, oblong shields above their heads, overlapping them to form an armoured carapace. The divisions quickly established the great metal shells and, protected under them, retreated, edging away slowly to preserve their formation. The outer ranks, however, were being ground away as the plunging horde of the enemy made inroads, slashing and stabbing at their exposed knees and feet, and the occasional unfortunate was dragged into the hostiles' mob when hands grabbed the shaft of his outstretched spear. Some of those so disarmed were not hacked to death at once, but were hustled through the abattoir of the killing fields to the barbarians' rear ranks. They would be kept in cages for agonizing later sacrifice to the forest gods.

The testudos kept inching backwards, legionaries stabbing and thrusting at the pressing warriors. The situation under the lofted shields was a half-light nightmare of clattering, banging noise, triumphant Saxon howls and shouts, and the curses and moans of the Roman wounded. From time to time, a heavy javelin would find a gap, or a soldier would stumble, and an incoming missile would transfix a shoulder, thigh or throat, but the Romans kept dragging the wounded with them, kept closing the ranks, kept steadily moving, even at the cost of trampling a fallen comrade underfoot. They were edging towards the relative safety of the treeline, where they could reform in the sheltering forest and begin firing back with their own spears and arrows. The general Maximian wanted to tear out his own beard. This was not going the way he'd planned. Where the hell was the cavalry he'd called to loop around from the Roman rear? The big soldier swore he'd have that commander's nuts skewered on a spear if the horsemen didn't show soon.

He turned to the tribune Flavius Constantius, his son-in-law since marrying Maximian's daughter Theodora, and waved his sword in the direction he expected to see the mounted troops. "Send someone to tell that bastard mule thrasher Marcus Aemilius to pull his sodding finger out. No, go yourself. Tell him I want the cavalry getting significant, and now, or he'll answer to me!" he ordered. Flavius, blanching at the fury in the big general's voice, saluted and ran for his horse, beckoning two aides to accompany him, but before he could straddle the animal, brass trumpets sounded and the cavalry appeared from the right flank, trotting into place.

"Testudos down, get those javelins working!" Maximian bellowed in his huge parade ground roar. The centurions didn't need to repeat the order, the soldiers heard it themselves. The heavy shields clattered down, and the front ranks accepted the rain of Saxon missiles for a few moments, as they banged shield edges together to form the protective fighting wall. Within seconds, a rattle of lead-weighted, iron-pointed javelins hurled from the second and third ranks began clattering into the barbarian mass. A few of the Germans cowered away from the deadly hail, but most shouted defiance and kept coming. They were still focused on the obstacle of Maximian's steadfast shield wall when the cavalry tore into their left flank. The barbarians fell back from the trampling hooves and thrusting spears, and the movement spread like a wave rippling against a seawall. The flood of attacking tribesmen diverted, ebbed and broke under the cavalry charge and they were rolled up in a scrum of hacking swords, blood and terror.

Some of the Saxons wheeled to face the new threat, and Maximian pushed his way right through the Roman war hedge, to stand alone in front of his troops. All the while, he was bellowing his bull-like roar and waving his sword, to signal the advance. His men heard him, saw the purple-dyed horsehair crest of his helmet and recognized their general. Maximian stepped up alone, close to the front rank of the Saxons and a bearded blond giant dropped his shield and, motioning with his war axe, accepted the wordless challenge. He swung once, the Roman feinted to one side, reversed and hacked up backhanded with his sword under the man's braided beard, noting dispassionately as his blade bit that the Saxon had threaded small beads into the blond hair.

Maximian leaned into the swing and hauled his spatha across the man's Adam's apple, slicing so deeply he felt the blade jar and scrape against the bones of the Saxon's spine. The impact of the heavy cavalry sword opened a gaping red mouth in the man's throat and threw the warrior backwards in a bright spray of arterial blood. He was dying as he hit the ground, his blood releasing with a sound like water going down a drain. His death spasms caused the Saxon's feet to drum hard on the leaf mould for a few seconds, then he shuddered and was still. A growling animal shout welled from the throats of the watching Roman ranks, Maximian, his face spattered red, hauled his wet-bladed sword free of the dead man's neck and brandished it, scattering a swathe of crimson droplets. Another long-haired Saxon came at him, screaming. Maximian brought his shield edge up hard, under the man's jaw, snapping his head back, then swung his sword right to left across the man's face, hurling him backwards and dropping him like a felled tree. The Romans involuntarily stepped forward, quivering like leashed hounds eager for the release.

Javelins and darts were still flying over their heads from the legion's rear ranks and into the wavering Saxons when a communal, primitive blood lust swamped and overwhelmed the troops. The bruised legion acted as if they were possessed by a single will, one urgent, demanding need. They lunged forward in line, lowering their heads and smashing the heavy bronze bosses of their shields into enemy ranks that were still half-turned to the cavalry threat. The legionaries were inflamed and mindless, berserk with fighting madness, angered at being forced into retreat and reckless with the overwhelming desire to chop, thrust and kill to dispel their humiliation. They plunged into the fur-clad mass of the enemy, battering with their shields, stabbing and punching over and around them with their sharp-pointed, two-edged gladii.

Irresistible, the Romans moved into the press of Saxons, knocking them down, stamping their nailed boots hard on bodies and heads as they went underfoot. The barbarians were trampled and kicked to death even as they were coughing up their blood from spear and sword thrusts. In minutes, the battle went from near-triumph to utter disaster for the

Alemanni. The legionaries clubbed and smashed their way into the heart of the horde, hacking and cutting to turn men into bloody meat, while the Roman cavalry's feared heavy horses, biting, rearing and slashing with their wicked hooves, created white-eyed panic on the flank. In moments, the horde of Alemanni wheeled like a flock of starlings, broke and tried to flee. The Roman cavalrymen abandoned their lances in the bodies of the barbarians who had suffered the first impetus and thrust into the mob to swing and scythe like terrifying reapers with their heavy long swords, Panicked, fleeing men were hacked down from behind, their skulls split open, spines broken, great ragged wounds slashed into unprotected backs, necks and shoulders. The horsemen rode the fugitives down, swinging, chopping and clubbing before kicking on to slaughter the next, until the field was choked and heaped with butchered bodies.

A light rain started, but it did nothing to hide the stench of human dung, the iron-taint smell of spilled blood and the scent of trampled, crushed grass that rose over the killing ground. Maximian pulled off his helmet with its confining cheek plates, wiped the sweat and rain from his eyes and forehead and inhaled disgustedly. "The smell of shit," he grunted. "Battlefields always smell of shit."

The thought was with him again months later, as he led his procession into Rome. Battlefields stank, he mused, but this smelled a lot better. It was the month of Aprilis, once called Neroneus after the half-mad emperor. It was the 286th year of Julius Caesar's calendar. Wafts of honeysuckle and yellow jasmine gave the city some pleasing, positively rural scents that almost overpowered the stench of the dung heaps. The emperor Carus was gone, Diocletian was visiting Rome from his domed Oriental palace in Nicomedia and wore the Tyrian purple now, and that was good.

The emperor was Maximian's fellow countryman from Dalmatia and the pair had formed useful alliances in the past. This day would seal their latest union. Diocletian's cunning brain would be allied with the brutish general's military brawn to benefit them both, and now it was time to celebrate. Today's procession lauded Maximian's last-ditch victory over the Saxons on the lower Danube, a crushing triumph which had led to a series of mopping-up engagements as far as the northern stretches of the Rhine as he'd cornered the barbarians and overwhelmed them. The military defeats, the barbarian kings made vassals, the pitiful files of chained slaves and the horrors of the crucifix-lined roads would ensure a long peace in that part of the empire and, for the victorious general, a purple-draped seat at the emperor's right hand.

Things had been better managed, thought Maximian, since he'd punished his cavalry commander for sluggishly carrying out his orders. He'd broken the man to the ranks and set him to cleaning stables when they got back to barracks at Mainz. When the aristocratic officer protested too strongly and had hinted at reprisals later, the big general had called for the legion to parade in full order. Maximian next commanded the unfortunate equestrian to be brought to him on horseback. He had ordered the officer from his mount and removed its bridle. The general casually dropped the leather reins around the man's neck and, as he kicked and fought, lifted him from the ground and strangled him with them.

The legion, stiffly at attention, witnessed the execution stony-faced before they were paraded century by century past the corpse. There could be no misunderstanding their general's message. Maximian's son-in-law Flavius was the new cavalry commander and, thought the emperor-elect grimly, was satisfyingly more attentive to his orders than he used to be.

This bright, balmy April day, Maximian was leading his triumph into Rome, through the arch of Marcus Aurelius, whose names he had taken, with five once-proud barbarian kings shuffling in chains as they trailed behind his chariot on their way to execution. He glanced at the tombs, forbidden inside the city walls that ringed them outside. A cluster of the mausoleums of the dead stood by the great arch, elbowing each other, it seemed, to have their occupants noticed by the traffic into and out of the city. Romans, he mused, were preoccupied with being remembered after death, though he noted wryly that their living descendants did little to keep their memorials clean. The tombs' walls served as billboards, and among the red-painted advertisements for gladiator fights, a whorehouse, a bakery and an assortment of political advertisements, his own new names stood clear and proud, painted hastily a day or two before by a team he had ordered assembled for the task at this and a handful of other gates.

Maximian had underscored his new status by assuming the Valerian family name of the emperor, a bow to the Augustus who claimed to be the reincarnation of Jupiter, and it paid to let the populace know it. So there, painted over the scatological messages and the libellous, boastful statements of who had done what to whom at that place, all left by the great unwashed, was his new name and claimed patrimony, painted prominently large. 'Marcus Aurelius Valerius Maximianus Herculius,' it said. Maximian grunted to himself. "I'm a Valerian now, like Diocletian," he thought with satisfaction. "I'm Hercules to his so-called Jupiter.'

The god-emperor waited to formally greet the general as well as to survey the wagons piled high with loot that preceded the chained columns of captives, all of it good news for the treasury. "Marcus Aurelius Valerius Maximianus Herculius," Diocletian unknowingly repeated the graffiti, kissing him on both cheeks, "it gives me great joy to welcome you to our home city, whose enemies you have so confounded. For the populace of Rome, for its gods and its Senate, I formally appoint you Caesar, and welcome your sword and strong arm to protect and defend the empire." The appointment made Maximian junior emperor to the Augustus but Diocletian had privately assured him that in a decent time he would also be declared Augustus, to oversee half the empire.

Diocletian was shrewd to share power, for he knew he was vulnerable. He had no son, only a daughter who was not eligible by her sex to assume the purple. He had needed to find a co-ruler from outside his family, and he privately admitted that it would be useful to have a general more capable than himself, as the frontiers of the empire were in flames from Syria to the Danube. Diocletian might not be a military genius, but he was a good administrator, and as a matter of practical security, he separated the military and the civil service. He created new administrative centres closer to the frontiers where they would be more effective and standardized the imperial taxes, quietly increasing them as he did so. In time, he planned to divide the empire between four rulers, to insure against any one faction and its legions rising against him. There had been, he thought grimly, too many barracks emperors who had been elected then murdered at the whim of the soldiery. He had no plans to die soon…

Maximian was his Serbian countryman, an unsophisticated brute but a canny military man who did not pose a political threat to the Augustus. He'll be my attack dog, thought Diocletian. For his part, Maximian was uncomfortable around Rome's smooth, epigram-quoting courtiers who, he knew, sneered at his lack of education. He was a fighting man, a good general. He knew it, and his men knew it. He was happiest in the field, not among Rome's patrician officers, poncing office stallions to a man, he thought. He was even less comfortable in the snake pit of the Senate, where the lawmakers carried knives under their togas and would not hesitate to assassinate you either politically or physically.

Only yesterday, there had been an assassination attempt. People were talking of a would-be killer who had been captured when he fainted while trying to escape. In fact, all Rome was now laughing about the Ashen Assassin. The man, Josephus Lindinius, was the younger son of a political family and had made an attempt on the life of a senate rival of his father's. During the blundering, clumsy attack, Josephus had seized his victim's robe with one hand and swung his large dagger with the other. The victim had twisted away unharmed, and had unbalanced his attacker at the exact moment that he struck. The hapless Josephus had hacked off two of his own fingers and a part of his hand that carried a seahawk tattoo.

The severed digits, the tattoo and the blood trail made him easy to identify and follow and two praetorian guards had caught him on the bank of the Tiber, where he'd fainted from blood loss. Today, he and his father were to be thrown off the Tarpeian Rock and the rest of their family would be forced to witness the event. Maximian thought he might go along to watch, partly for the pleasure of watching some unfortunate's death, partly because he despised such ambush tactics. He wore his sword openly, and that was the way he wanted it. Send me back among Marius' Mules, my honest ground pounders, he thought. He automatically touched the iron of his sword hilt for luck. A sword; that was what he understood.

XXI. Eboracum

Carausius also had a sword on his mind, although he had not yet seen it. He'd heard that a wonderful feather-patterned weapon forged for him by the blade-smith Gimflod was ready and he sent a messenger into Eboracum, bidding the smith to bring the blade to him in nearby Selletun. The legate was safely away from Navio, his successful foray to find and recover the Eagle still unheralded. It was a secret still known only to a few. He was well aware of the huge political and emotional significance of possessing the recovered symbol of Roman pride, and planned a dramatic, triumphal entry into the capital of North Britain. He wanted all to witness him returning the lost Eagle of the Ninth to its rightful place as an icon, not just of military pride restored, but also as a sign of better days to come. It would signify a return to honourable, ancient Roman standards and reinforce him as the legitimate claimant to rule Britain. It was time, he thought, to declare himself consul, or better yet, emperor of Britain and northern Gaul.

The Britons were ready for change. They were suffering under the hard rule of collapsing Rome. The landowners were being too heavily taxed, bled white to sustain the opulent lifestyles of far-away nobles and to pay for military activities along borders like the Danube and Rhine. In turn, the landowners were forced to pass on the demands to their tenants. A series of Rome-appointed governors of the province had made matters worse by openly maintaining their own proud lifestyle at the locals' expense, and treating them poorly in return. Carausius had recognized a pattern. It was, he thought, going the way of Gaul, where peasants who had been dispossessed of their land or who'd been subjected to barbarian attacks had begun roaming the country as marauders. The Briton shook his head as he recalled the blood he'd spilled and the drastic, cruel measures he'd been required to take to suppress those bandits. He could see that happening in Britain if matters did not change, because British history was not so different. Centuries before, when the Romans had been unable to subdue the Britons, they had recruited their barons and jarls, giving them princedoms and kingships in return for their aid in keeping their fellow countrymen quiet. Then, when the place was subdued, the subject kings were discreetly disposed of.

It had happened exactly that way to the husband of Britain's queen, Boadicea. An independent king who was the ally of Rome, and who helped persuade his fellow monarchs to accept to the Roman yoke, King Pratsutagas of the Iceni had died mysteriously and conveniently, just when his usefulness to Rome had ended and his rewards were due. It was the Romans' way. They recruited the chieftains and kings, flattered and made them important, and when the region was secure, disposed of them. Most believed Pratsutagas had been poisoned at the orders of the governor Suetonius. The dead monarch's will stipulated that his kingdom was to be left jointly to the emperor and to his own two daughters, who would reign as Rome's ally, as he had. The Romans ignored his wishes, their financiers called in the dead king's loans and his clan was ruined. Irritated by the royal family's protests, the governor ordered a demonstration of Rome's control. Soldiers flogged the widowed queen, publicly raped her daughters and chained up the royal kin as slaves.

After the humiliations and the display of callous, brutal power, Suetonius contemptuously left the smouldering Iceni and went off to campaign in Anglesey, to put down the British Druids who had formed a seat of power there. He misread the tribes' mood, and his error cost the lives of 60,000 Romans and their colonists. While the governor's XIVth legionaries were slaughtering unarmed Druids and burning down the sacred groves of oaks in Wales, Boadicea raised rebellion, burned the administrative capital of Colchester and sacked Verulam. She destroyed Londinium and its piling bridge over the Thames, and her 100,000 warriors and their terrible chariots butchered the Ninth Spanish legion sent from Eboracum to suppress the uprising. A few survivors hid the legion's sacred Eagle, but they in turn were killed, taking the secret of the standard's hiding place with them to the grave. The legionary icon went missing for two centuries until Carausius tracked it down.

Now, the renegade admiral had the silver-gilt Eagle and he planned to use it to rally Britons to him to overthrow their Roman masters. He foresaw few problems with such a rebellion as he had the legions stationed in Britain solidly behind him and his well-filled pay chests. The navy could keep a Roman invasion at bay, he knew. The greater threat to the island's independence, he suspected, would come from the hordes of

Germanic tribes that would be released westwards once the Romans retreated from the Rhine, as they inevitably must. Dark times were coming, and he was readying for them. First, in just a few days, he would parade the iconic, inspirational Eagle into Eboracum, the fortress keystone of the northern frontier defences. He would rally Britain from there, as its new emperor. He would cast his lot as a rogue emperor, and risk his life and fortune for great rewards. It was what soldiers did, he grinned to himself, mentally adding 'And I'm a good soldier. I deserve a great reward.'

The wealthy trader Mullinus had once lived near Eboracum, and knew the district well. He arranged for the legate and his entourage to stay for a few days unnoticed at a secluded villa a short distance downriver, in the hamlet of Selletun while Carausius' agents arranged matters for the triumphal parade and entry. A messenger also met Gimflod as promised at the full moon of August and brought him and the masterpiece sword he had created to the villa. The same envoy had also quietly informed the trader Sucia of the legate's arrival, and she was hurrying to Selletun to meet her friend.

Meanwhile, Carausius sent a courier south to his treasurer Allectus, with special orders for him. He planned to dispatch to the Colchester mint the old Ninth Legion's pay chests and their high-quality bullion once he could detail a proper guard for them. "The quality of this coin is superb," he told his brothers as they fingered the contents of the five ironbound, elm and leather pay chests they'd uncovered in the cavern at Navio, running the heavy coins through their hands. "It's all from long before Septimius Severus started the devaluation we've had to suffer. I'll get Allectus to re-mint some as donatives to keep the army happy, and have him turn the rest into mementoes celebrating the recovery of the Eagle. That will get the message out; we can use a bit of propaganda. I'll tell him to mint them with my new Roman lineage. I'm the Expected One who's to restore the golden age of Britain, just as it was in the good days of the old rule, and I'll have my British name 'Arthur' on there, too, underlining my roots in this island."

The brothers grinned at each other. "He's decided we're descended from the Antonine emperors," said Mael. "That's why he's Marcus Aurelius Carausius Arthur and you're just dumb Domnal." The older brother swiped at his twin. Mael dodged the blow. "No, really," he said.

'All the recent emperors, Diocletian, Probus, Carus, Carinus and Numerian were called Marcus Aurelius. You'd think they could be a bit more original." Carausius, brows knitted as he ran though his mental list, was not distracted. "We need to make some big pay increases, too. There's enough gold in here to make aureii for the legions in Britain. It won't matter that they're forgeries, the country's basically a closed-currency market anyway. We can boost the gold supply when we get the Welsh mine at Dolaucothi working again. Remind me to get a decent garrison set up in the fort there.

"Also, we should establish a garrison again at Cadbury in the old fort. We'll need to establish a supply point for the beacon and stronghold there, it's a major gateway to the west, and I hear that the old place isn't in too bad shape. Then there's the north. We need to get the Picts off our backs, mollify them or make some treaty with them to keep them quiet while we sort out the situation in Gaul. If we can get the port and forts at Bononia and Rouen reinforced and command the hinterland, those bastards in Rome will likely leave us alone for a while; they have enough problems with the eastern front.

"And, remind me about getting that Gallic mint up to speed, we'll need coin if we're to raise more soldiers over there." Another thought struck the legate. "Get me a proper scribe, I'm tired of having to remember everything myself and these bits of metal and pieces of shaved wood are hopeless for keeping track of memoranda. Find me someone who can record and monitor things, and can send out my directives. It wouldn't hurt if he had some languages, and was someone with half a brain. It would be even more useful if you found someone with standing who could be an ambassador to those painted Picts. I want someone with a bit of initiative, who can carry my message and persuade the buggers to take a break from thieving cattle and burning hayricks for a while. Just don't get me another bloody soldier who can only dumbly obey orders. Now, let's take a look at this new sword."

The weapon was a marvel. "Balanced at the guard within the weight of ten grains of sand," Gimflod boasted recklessly. As the legate had demanded, the weapon was longer by far than a standard gladius, the stabbing sword of the legions that had been adopted as the murderous weapon of gladiators. "You asked for at least two hands breadths more, lord," said Gimflod, closing his eyes as he thought, "but I made it almost a hand span longer than that to get it exactly right."

Carausius hefted the sword. It was longer than the standard 24 inch Spanish Sword of the old republic, but had elements of both the shorter, broader Mainz and Pompeii blades which followed it. It had two slightly curved cutting edges and came to a tapered point. An ornate, knobbed hilt was ridged for the fingers and fitted with a small ring to protect a digit wrapped over the guard as the user pulled back after thrusting. The grip itself was perforated leather wrapped tightly and retained at guard and pommel with wire overlaid with ferrules of beaten gold. The polished bronze pommel was more than just for use as a club; it also acted as a counterweight to the length of the blade. It seemed to Carausius that most of the sword's three pounds of weight was in the handle, making the weapon easy to wield.

The blade itself was a masterwork. It carried a contrasting featherlike pattern along its length, from the sword's deadly point through its leaf-shaped blade to the section of unsharpened steel just below the guard that was called a ricasso. This last was created at Carausius' demand, to give him the opportunity to use the long sword two-handed. He admired aloud the pattern of the steel.

"It's from a Damascene blade-smith who showed me his secrets," explained Gimflod. "The sad bastard. If he'd been a better dice player, I would never have known how to do this, but he lost the bet and had to show me." The smith explained that he melted ore to produce a bloom of loosely-bonded iron that was like a sponge, networked with channels filled with the molten glass that resulted from impurities in the iron. The bloom was reheated into malleability, hammered to drive out the glass, then was shaped into rods.

The smith took five of those rods and twisted them into one blade, fusing them together by heating, folding and hammering them flat. The pounding friction of the hammer blows super-heated the metal and made a powerful weld, while the mixed metals and carbon created the blade's swirling patterns. Gimflod next ground a groove down both faces of the blade, which both lightened and strengthened the steel and allowed an easier break of the suction when the sword was thrust into an opponent's clinging flesh.

He stamped Carausius' names into the blade below the hilt, filed the cutting edges to lethal level and reheated the whole thing. The last stages, tempering it to harden the steel and allow it to hold an edge, were to plunge the sword into a bath of boiling salts, then to quench it in oil. This allowed it to cool evenly, so the blade did not warp or fracture. He repeated the process, this time using layered clay to coat the blade, except for the edges, before reheating it. The clay slowed the cooling and made the steel slightly softer, increasing flexibility while the unprotected edge stayed hard. "A good blade bends under pressure. A poor one is brittle, and snaps," the smith explained.

Finally, Gimflod set the guard over the blade's shoulders, snugged it in place with the hilt and locked the whole together with the heavy pommel. A local leather-smith had created an iron-reinforced scabbard that carried a tooled and painted Celtic pattern similar to the swirled silver and amber brooch of British office that the legate wore.

Now, the blade-smith was looking on, beaming, as Carausius whipped his new sword through the air. "I shall call this sword Exalter," he declared. "It will bring me joy and triumph."

"There's one other thing, lord," the smith said. "I haven't been able to get one myself, but I've heard of a new device to keep the blade extra sharp." The legate looked up. He only knew of the strickle, a stick smeared thickly with pig grease and rolled in fine sand that was used to sharpen all kinds of blades. "What's that?" he asked.

"The southern people use a wheel, lord, a cranked wheel of stone. You turn the wheel and apply the blade. The stone moves, the blade stays still. It's faster and makes a better edge."

Carausius nodded. "Make one," he said thoughtfully. "If it works, we'll equip the troops with the things. Now, send in that woman."

The legate had spied the negotiator Sucia, a woman he'd befriended in Rome years before, crossing the wet stones of the courtyard. She ran a lucrative trade in precious things: freshwater pearls, jet and crystal for adornment, sun stone crystals from Iceland that let sailors find the sun to navigate through fog, fine British woollen clothing and something Carausius craved, British hunting dogs. "I remembered your promise," he told her after the greetings were dispensed with.

"I did not forget either, and you have come at a very good time," she smiled. "This week, you will have one of the best dogs I have ever had trained."

"You too, have come at a very good time," grinned Carausius, for once relaxed and mellow. "I have chests of coin, including gold, and you can charge what you damned well like!"

Some of that coin was scattered by the prefects to the roadside crowd as Carausius made his entrance into Eboracum two days later, heralded with the blare of brass and stirring thump of kettledrums. Allectus and the tribunes had done their work well. At their instruction, as the paymasters handed out donatives of gold, the legions had been asked by their officers whether they had any reluctance in acclaiming as their British emperor Carausius Arthur, the restorer of the lost Eagle and source of the stream of loot that had come their way. The alternative, the scarlet-cloaked officers pointed out to the parade, was meekly to accept the arrival of a stranger sent by Diocletian from his faraway Asian palace. That stranger would rule the armies of the west and would bring Britain again under the crushing heel of rapacious Rome.

The legionaries needed no persuasion. Car the Bear was popular anyway. A soldier's soldier, bluff, blunt and brutal when it was needed, he had always been mindful of his troops' welfare, pay and equipment. He had carefully settled retired veterans not only in border territories where they acted as a military reserve in time of need, but had given many of them generous land grants close to military bases. There, they acted as living examples to serving soldiers of the fine retirement that waited at the end of their service. Any footslogger who wondered why he'd taken the oath only had to glance at the prosperous farms and taverns owned by old soldiers to have his question answered. The general would look after him, not just by being successful in battle or in acquiring plunder, but also when the fighting was done and the gladius and helmet were hung over the fireplace.

The stage was set. The soldiers had the message: this was a good leader in war, and in peace too. Just follow his lead, and his orders. So all was readied, with Carausius' usual shrewd management. The capital's colonial amphitheatre was packed with troops, the priests had made the sacrifices and declared themselves content with the auguries, the officers had addressed the men and their new emperor with the recovered Eagle was on his way to a triumphal entrance and popular acclaim.

Carausius was a splendid sight at the head of his marching columns, a lord of war in burnished, segmented armour, mounted high on a heavy-hoofed, black Frisian charger. The golden crown he had won for single combat was wreathed with his imperial laurel leaves. It gleamed above his purple and white cloak, itself pinned with the emblem of a British jarl. Behind him, protected by an elite squad of troopers in burnished bronze and carried by a standard bearer who wore a black-maned lion's pelt over his armour, came the restored Eagle of the Ninth Spanish legion, symbol of recovered pride and Carausius' new power.

Carausius' genius at inspiring his troops was evident in a subtle sign. When he'd uncovered the Eagle in its stony nest, it was wrapped in the red cloak of a long-dead centurion, the iconic garment of a Red Dragon. Carausius had ordered the Eagle to be wrapped again in the fine red wool for its journey to Eboracum. Once there, he had a seamstress cut the cloak into chevron-shaped pieces and sew them onto braided leather cords. Only the handful of guards who had accompanied him on his quest for the Eagle were entitled to wear these distinctions.

Those men, proud elite of the Eagle, were gathered closest around it on its triumphal entry into the city, and every soldier who saw them knew about and envied the badge of honour that hung at the neck of their breastplates. The strutting guard and their accompanying legion processed past the gladiator cemetery and crossed the fine stone bridge over the yew-lined River Ouse. The drizzle of rain had stopped as if in celebration, and the usually-bustling port was at a standstill as masters and slaves stopped their work to watch the parade entering the city. The columns, swaying with the rhythm of the march, their usual obscene marching chants silenced by centurions mindful of the solemnity of the day, swung through the great east gate in Eboracum's white limestone walls between the human walls of a cheering mob. Carausius, prideful and glorious lord of war, was about to lead his troops into the expectant amphitheatre when a hawk flew low in front of him.

In its claws was a struggling white rat. The warlord's eyes followed the sight, and he watched, absorbed, as the bird fought for height then released its writhing prey. The rat fell onto turf alongside the pavement, paused a moment, then ran rapidly and unharmed right across Carausius' path. He did not pause his horse's pacing, but gestured his aide Lycaon alongside. "Did you see that?" he asked.

"I did, lord," said the soldier, shaking his head in wonder. "The gods have properly endorsed you. A white rat across your path is a sign of huge good fortune. The great Pliny himself declared it so. This is a remarkable day!"

Like a breeze, the word went down the columns of the stunning augury. Infantry, cavalry, musicians, all buzzed with the news as they tramped stolidly forward: we have the Eagle back, and the gods have sent a great sign of their favour.

Carausius, despite the pomp and splendour of the occasion, was distracted. The white rat was good fortune? He'd seen white rats before. Once, he suddenly recalled, was when he was running for his life from the raiders who'd killed his father. Another time was when he'd just decided to join the army. Both times were turning points in his life, and his adoptive mother Cait had explained to him that the rat was an augury of good fortune, a sign that pointed the way to his future. Now, at this hinge of his personal history, as he made open claim to be emperor, a white rat had landed at his feet, delivered almost literally from the heavens. Surely that was a sign of the gods' approval?

Another thought struck him, as an image of a tall man with long black hair entered his mind as bright and clear as if the man stood in front of him. "The sorcerer Myrddin, who came to our house when I was a boy," he murmured. "Is he somehow behind this symbolism? What did he want with my father?" By now, the parade was entering the arch of the amphitheatre, and Carausius mentally shook himself back to the present. As he rode through the archway, a roar went up from the crowd inside the stadium, drowning even the blasts of the acclamatory trumpets. The ranks of waiting legionaries clattered spears against their shields and bellowed for their general.

As suddenly as the wall of sound had thundered out, it stopped. In a single heartbeat, all went quiet. The Eagle had entered the arena, and the crowds on the instant hushed.

They gaped in awed, reverent silence at the glinting, golden Eagle carried tall behind Carausius, there at the head of the disciplined, swaying columns of marching troops. The Eagle of the Ninth Spanish, proud standard of a legion once commanded by the great Julius Caesar himself, a sacred emblem lost two centuries ago had finally come home to Eboracum's fortress on the hill.

As if a signal had been given, the crowd raised its voice again, in one gigantic wave of noise, a shouted acclaim that drove grey doves circling from the city's roofs, over the temples, theatres, baths and the palace of the old emperor Septimius Severus, who must surely be smiling down from his seat next to Jupiter. The Eagle was back, unconquered, and the miracle of its recovery was enhanced even more.

The standard was brought by the Expected One, a British jarl who had promised to rebuild the glory of the nation. The gods had given him the standard, so the glorious promised future would be fulfilled. It was an emotional, throat-aching moment that sent tears down the weathered cheeks of the soldiery as they witnessed this public restoration of their pride. Acclaiming Carausius emperor was the work of a few bellowed moments during a tidal wave of emotion. A new era was dawning, the assurance was there from the gods, the rat, and their general, their emperor.

XXII. Guinevia

Sucia had brought not one, but two, a matched couple of hunting dogs for him, littermate males and near-identical big hounds that delighted Carausius. "They are not war dogs, though they are dangerous," she warned the legate. "The Molossian dogs of Epirus were supposed to be the world's best war dogs, but they are just brainless fear-biters. The legions have used them to break enemy lines, but those dogs are only good at being ferocious when they're half-starved and stupid with hunger.

"If it comes to a dogfight between one of them and a British hunting dog like these, it's no contest. These fellows will snap a Molossian's neck. We use them on wild game. Two or three will bring down a great boar. They work together. One will grab an ear, another will take the opposite ear, and as the boar turns, they'll take out his throat or tear into his groin. Even alone, one can run down a deer. They are agile and highly intelligent. As a guardian of your home and hearth, they really are unsurpassed."

Carausius looked at the part-mastiffs lying by his feet. They seemed already to understand he was their new master. Weighing about 100 lbs, the dogs were large, but not ponderously huge. They had jaws big and powerful enough to crush a wolf's skull, long, strong limbs and large paws. They owned glossy grey-blue and black coats spotted like a leopard's, with a white blaze on the broad chest. In unison, the dogs wagged their plumed tails as Carausius clicked his tongue to make a noise at them. Each dog had bright, intelligent brown eyes that gazed fearlessly at him, the soldier noted.

"They are trained to the hunt, and will stay silent on command. They'll alert you to game, and follow hand or arm signals, even from a distance," Sucia said. "Their mouths are soft, so they can retrieve game birds undamaged, and they're very quick. This dog caught a sparrow on the wing a few weeks ago. I opened his jaws and it flew away, unharmed, which is more than I can say for the squirrels he's caught." Carausius nodded his great, scarred head.

"I shall call this one Axis," he declared, "because I am going to make Britain revolve around me, and that is a good name. And I shall call that one Javelin, because that too will be a part of me. I shall be as true as a spear and I shall reach my goal with an unstoppable force."

The dogs looked up as he spoke, seeming to understand his intent. Carausius looked at them and felt his heart swell. He had waited for years until the time was right to have dogs, and these hounds were exactly what he had hoped to have. He could never guess that one day, they would save his life.

The priority of his plan for Britain, Carausius told his lieutenant Allectus, was to deal with the Picts for a while and pacify the northern border, either by treaty or by force. Only then could he dare to move his legions to settle the problems in Gaul, where he expected soon to face the Caesar Maximian. "We must lock that Pictish back door," he told the twins Domnal and Mael, whom he had made his advisors, and who were in the room for the council of war. "To defeat Maximian will take all our strength. If we make even small errors, we'll lose, and we'll be dead on the field or crucified later. I can't tell you strongly enough how dangerous Maximian is to us. We can only stand a chance of beating him if we have all our strength, no distractions, no dilution of our forces. That means we must get the Picts in line first, before we take on Maximian. We simply can't afford to fight on two fronts. Are you understanding me?" Both twins nodded, then glanced at each other.

Domnal looked worried, his brother noted, so Mael plunged in: "Yes, well, Caros," he said, "about the Picts. You wanted us to find you a scribe to get your orders out, be a go-between, to help you deal with them..."

"Yes, yes, get it out, Mael," snapped the legate, impatiently.

"We have a very suitable scribe," said his brother, hurriedly, "who speaks Pictish and Latin, and Belgic."

"Excellent, bring him in", said Carausius, turning away to his littered writing table.

Mael was back moments later, ushering in the scribe. The legate's mouth opened. "This is Guinevia Avenae, brother, an adept of the god Ogmia, lord of letters and law. She is a Druid priestess of Nicevenn, witch goddess of the Wild Hunt. She was born a Pict, not just Trans vallum, but beyond even the wall of Antoninus, at the very limit of Rome's northern advance."

Carausius was about to explode in rage at being brought a female scribe, and a nun at that, but he looked at her again and held his protest. She was attractive, he admitted to himself, slender, fair, with startling blue eyes. She moves, he thought, like a dancer. She had an aura of calm dignity, and met his appraisal with a level gaze, displaying an uncowed self-possession. It was a quality few displayed when they first came into the general's intimidating presence. Carausius continued his assessment, his mind moving fast. He recognized that his brothers were nervous at presenting their candidate and smiled inwardly. He was coarse, powerful and violent, but he was no fool, and his years as a military officer had made him a shrewd judge of people. This woman, he thought, has a core like a steel blade under that pleasing exterior, but did he want a woman to hold such an important post? Forget about her acting as his scribe and aide, no doubt she could do that, but was she also capable of carrying out the role for which he really needed someone, as an emissary to settle those nuisance Picts?

She registered his appraisal and addressed him in near-flawless Latin much better than his own. "You are dismayed, lord, to see a female scribe? Juvenal himself wrote of clerks, secretaries and copyists who were women. Even the Greeks and Egyptians afforded female librariae much prestige. The Egyptians called us 'Mistresses of the House of Books,' and sometimes, 'Ordainers of the Universe.' We were honoured, as keepers of knowledge and warriors against the oblivion of the past should be."

Carausius stayed silent, but nodded his head at the gentle rebuke. His mind moved quickly. He wanted more than a scribe; he wanted to build a bridge to those Pict porridge-eaters. His unspoken plan was to appoint an emissary who could persuade them to leave the borderlands quiet for a while. He'd expected he'd have to do the orthodox thing, and send a military emissary, but this obvious noblewoman who was one of their own might do a better job. What more subtle indication of his confidence and wish for peace could there be than to send a woman, and a noble-born Pict at that? Moreover, she might have connections among the clan chiefs, might even be related to some of them, their gene pool couldn't be that deep.

Best of all, the pagan nun not only spoke the language, she understood the clans' mentality and she might prove a better means to soothe their fears than sending some clanking armour-clad tribune, dripping with swords and symbols of aggression. The savages, he mused, could see it as a veiled hint of his confidence: 'We don't need to send a soldier to deal with you, but think what could happen if we did...' Why not take this unusual course? As for being a secretary and manager of the accounts and rosters, she could only do a better job and be a lot less trouble than those useless, semi-literate bin rats he had on the task right now.

Guinevia again read his thoughts. "I can help you greatly. I command Latin, British, Pictish and some of the Frankish and Belgic tongues. My work for the goddess and with the great seer Myrddin gave me an education, you see."

"You are an adept?" he blurted, surprised and impressed by the reference to the magician Myrddin Emrys, a Druid sorcerer of fearful power and mystery. It was said that he was a cambion, the offspring of an incubus and a king's daughter and had inherited supernatural powers. The man famously prophesied that Britain would soon return to the glory days of the old gods, those long-gone days before the advent of the Romans. The sect in which he held high office was once the potent focus of anti-Roman resistance, and Britain was the wellspring of their religion. When the Roman governor Suetonius had marched to Mona to slaughter the Druids, the Iceni queen Boadicea had put the Romans' settlements to the sword and had come close to recapturing Britain.

Now, the Druids were a shadow of their former selves, but Myrddin still had tremendous power. He was the living incarnation, or by the religion's beliefs, the reincarnation of generations of Celtic power that stretched back millennia across Gaul to Dalmatia and beyond. Some said he had been driven to madness, others said he was the direct voice of Britain's oldest deities, deliberately sired by a demon they had sent to restore their hold on their ancient lands. All feared the sorcerer's power and Carausius marvelled to himself that this small woman had been accepted as an apprentice of the fearful magician.

"You are adept, and a Pict?' he heard himself repeat, interrupting his own musings. She nodded and in her voice he heard the pride of unconquered generations. "I am from Perth, or Bertha as the Latin has it, where we halted the Romans in their northern progress. Our kings are crowned there, at Scone, and my clan is noble. I am a Pict, an acolyte of Myrddin, and I am on my journey of decades to become a full Druid".

The legate shook his head in wonder at himself. He was, he felt, in the presence of a formidable force wrapped in the black gown and wearing the golden necklace of one who was dedicated to the worship of the sun and moon. "Please," he said, drawing startled looks from Allectus and the twins at the unusual diffidence in his voice, "please come and help me make a peace with your people."

Guinevia permitted herself a small smile. "That will be a most useful thing to do," she said gravely. Carausius gusted a sigh. He felt as if he'd just emerged from a wrestling match, and he wasn't too sure who'd been pinned. And, he felt the pricklings of desire. This calm, collected woman had power not unlike his own and he knew he wanted to possess her. She smiled a small smile at him. She knew, and there was promise in that look.

Time passed, and the woman was better than he'd dared to hope. In a matter of weeks, she had established connections with the major Caledonian tribes who lived beyond the great Forth where the abandoned Antonine Wall crumbled its turf walls into the ground. She was about to travel to her home settlement, through the Four Kingdoms that lay between the walls of Hadrian and Antoninus, a Roman-backed buffer state that had held the north British and the Picts at bay. Guinevia was going beyond the Antonine, to her own land on the River Tay. There, her father, a local chieftain, would host a gathering of the Painted Ones to discuss a truce. She had trained a handful of slaves into a staff of sorts to untangle the legion's records and accounts. Their work had brought about discoveries of corruption that caused three dishonest quartermasters to be flogged to death for embezzlement. She'd sent Carausius' directives to troops scattered from Hadrian's Wall to Bononia and even further south in Gaul, and had impressed the treasurer Allectus with her understanding of financial management as well as of the importance of propaganda.

One of her suggestions especially pleased the legate, and now the mint at Colchester was busy producing coin that celebrated 'Carausius and his Brothers.' Allectus explained it to Mael as he showed the twin a sample of the new coinage. "Since we heard that Maximian had been raised to be

Caesar, we expect it's only a question of time before he's made up to full Augustus. Diocletian has split the workload with him, giving him the west while he lives like a sultan in Nicomedia, in the east. He knows he can't keep Maximian as junior emperor for ever, he'll have to give him the full authority as an Augustus, and soon. So, there will be two emperors running the Roman Empire."

"Our idea," he continued, slyly taking some credit for Guinevia's suggestion, "is that we issue coinage that puts Carausius alongside the pair of them. We issue coinage of the three Brother Emperors. It will have your brother's head on there along with Maximian's and Diocletian's. That way, it will make it official that they are all co-emperors, at least in the minds of the troops in Gaul and Britannia, and the soldiers are all that matter. Even if Maximian doesn't become Augustus, it will take so long before anyone who matters knows about it…" he let his voice tail off.

That wasn't the only propaganda stroke. The treasurer and the pagan priestess took the campaign even further, and issued coins with acronyms that to the initiated, or to the soldiery to whom it was explained, represented such slogans as 'Rome Renewed,' or a quote from the poet Virgil that said 'A New Generation Has Arrived From Heaven Above." The slogans, read out to the troops at parades so there could be no misunderstandings, gave Carausius' self-assumed ascension the heft and dignity of a prophecy fulfilled, and linked him to ancient Roman tradition. They were explicit and shrewd claims that influenced the superstitious soldiery to accept him even more enthusiastically. They understood that the gods willed it, so their emperor could not be defeated. The masterstroke though, was the generous donative issued to the legions, of coins struck from Welsh gold. Those coins vaunted Carausius as 'British Emperor of the Restored Eagle.'

"Absolute stunning brilliance," Mael told his twin later as he passed on the news. "The hump-a-lots get a very nice bonus and a huge boost to their pride, and Carausius is confirmed as the god-supported emperor who got the Eagle back after 200 years. The footsloggers get to understand that the gods favour him, one of their own, more than any emperor for two centuries or more, probably all the way back to Claudius. It tells the legions that they simply cannot be defeated. He's the Messiah, the Expected One, and the gods are with him. Soldiers will fight well if they get decent food and regular pay, old Julius knew that and paid them out of his own purse, but they'll be invincible if they know they have the backing of Mars and his friends."

Mael was right. Recruits flocked to garrisons in Britain and Gaul, where Carausius' paymasters were pouring out a torrent of coin minted from pirated bullion and from the surprising output of the opencast that was the Welsh gold mine at Dolaucothi. This supply of precious gold supplemented the silver output from other British workings in Derbyshire, Devon, Somerset and Gloucestershire. The native production was added to by healthy trade balances from across the Narrow Sea, where British exports that included lead vital to the Roman water supply pipes brought back the bullion that was paying the soldiers' wages. "They all want to be on the winning side," Allectus gloated. "That's where the loot, the women and the glory are."

That same message was spread purposefully by Guinevia when she met the Caledonian chieftains. She was already respected and held in awe as an adept of the Druid Myrddin. Now, as effective proconsul of the emperor, she displayed temporal as well as spiritual power. The priestess approached the chieftains gently, but she also flashed the steel of her resolve. She took them gifts of small gold ingots stamped with their emperor's image, and gave the dozen or so senior jarls a fine-tooled sword made by Gimflod and his apprentices. She also made two simple, credible promises to the wary chieftains. The first was: 'Cooperate with Carausius while he settles his other business, and great rewards will come to you when he rules Rome.' The second vow was grimly sombre: 'Break your oath and cause him trouble while his back is turned, and you will rot on crucifixes along the wall of Hadrian.'

The quarrelsome, prideful, tattooed and painted clan chiefs came to heel, took the oaths, kissed the silver pentagram ring of power the priestess wore on her left hand and left their bloody thumbprints on the vellum agreement that she put in front of them. Then the assembly participated in a gore-spattered ceremony that sacrificed , Nicevennand Ogmia, god of dangerous, sacred words. The pact was sealed between man, emperor and the gods.

A travel-stained, exhausted Guinevia brought back the news to Eboracum: the Wall would be inviolate, and Carausius could take his campaign into Gaul, confident of peace at home. What she did not tell him was that before her great council with the chieftains, she'd gone first to a remote western island. She had sailed there at peril in a cockleshell skiff, confident that she would be kept safe by the intercession of the sea god Manannan mac Lir. She had gone to see her mentor, Myrddin Emrys.

The Druid sorcerer had welcomed his initiate, instructed her in some new mysteries of the oak and mistletoe, giving her a silver pentagram ring of power as token of them, and had alerted her to the significance of the familiar; a white rat, that he had conjured to support and enhance her missions. One day, she knew, she would find the new powers extremely useful, and she mentally welcomed the comforting presence of the rat. And, being a woman, she speculated about Carausius. A fine man, she thought, and one who needed affection, but he did not yet know it, she mused. One day, she would help him discover that need.

XXIII. Gaul

Smoke gusted from the pharos that guided the way into Bononia's harbour and the blue-sailed trireme, oars shipped and under a small headsail, slipped past the great mortared stones of the sea wall. The new Emperor Carausius, regal in his Tyrian purple cloak, nodded to the shipmaster his approval for a job well done. The mariner had pushed his crew hard and had succeeded in reaching port at high tide, which was the only time when the entrance to the Gallic harbour was navigable to larger vessels. It had been a busy few weeks, with parades in Eboracum, Aquae Sulis, Londinium and Colchester to display the recovered Eagle, and the emperor was eager to show it to the troops in Gaul.

Now, accompanied by his aide Guinevia, he was in Bononia, the dangerous sea voyage was behind them and there was much to do. The emperor gestured impatiently to a centurion to ready the gangplank. He was in a hurry to be ashore and receive news of Maximian's activities. He'd considered a triumphant entrance with the Eagle mounted on the prow of his ship but opted, considering that the vagaries of wind and sea could upset his timing, to parade it before the troops later in a more formal and predictable land-based operation. No point, he thought, to undermine the magic by going aground on a falling tide. Anyway, right now, he wanted news, not celebrations.

Had the emperor of the west taken action against him yet? He had to know.

He strode past the honour guard lined up on the quay, clapping his arm diagonally across his chest in salute, but hardly sparing time to glance at their gleaming turnout. Inside the square of the keep, Lucius Cornelius, the prefect in charge of the fortress, snapped another honour guard to attention. Carausius paid them as little mind as he had the first squad. "News for me?" His anxiety to know how his enemies were disposed made his demand brusque. "Where's Maximian?"

The prefect saluted his emperor. "Over the Rhine, lord. He's had to destroy a Theban legion for mutiny, and now he's putting out fires in the east again."

"Mithras be blessed for that," said the self-appointed Emperor of Britain and northern Gaul. "I hope the bastard gets his nuts roasted."

"There's a message for you from Rome, lord. We had a courier a day and a half ago," said the prefect. "I didn't send the dispatch on, as we knew you were coming here today. It's waiting in your quarters." His entourage trailed behind as the emperor strode rapidly into the barracks tower, his limp scarcely evident as he hurried up to the commander's chambers.

Guards at the door stiffened and saluted, body slaves sidled back against the walls. Carausius picked up the heavy, sewn-leather package and slashed the stitches and the Senatorial seals apart with his punching knife. The missive from the senatorial jurist Marcus Vettius bluntly 'requested and required' him to return to Rome with all speed, no reason given. "Court martial," the emperor muttered. "The boneheads have finally worked out why they're not getting any income from Britain. Well, their rapacious days are ending."

He crumpled the summons and dropped it on the tiled floor. "The hell with them. I'm not going back to have my shoulders relieved of their weight." He turned to his aide Lycaon. "Get the scribe here, bring Allectus, too. And, I want the quartermaster. Get me a full report on our readiness; garrison strength, equipment, supplies, the condition of the grain crop, the infirmary list and anything the scouts and spies have on the Bagaudae situation between here and the Seine. I want it all in an hour."

The pagan priestess Guinevia Avenae had never been to Gaul, and was unsure if her gods could hear her, away from her own settings, so she quickly made sacrifice to her deities to ask their protection and guidance in this place that was a spiritual stronghold of the Druids. She located an old temple to Minerva and had a slave visit the livestock market. Soon, her preparations were complete. First, she offered a lamb to the witch goddess Nicevenn, leader of the Wild Hunt at Samhain, the night of the dead. Handling the little creature tenderly, and with merciful swiftness, she slashed its throat and raised her bloodied hands to the ruined ceiling. She quietly muttered an incantation as she dedicated the gift to her goddess, then expertly gutted the carcass and burned its entrails, adding incense, inhaling the smoke and closing her eyes in meditation.

Her second sacrifice, to Ogmia, god of dangerous, persuasive words that can enchain, was less gory. She pricked her thumb, wrote in her own blood on a piece of papyrus the acronym that represented the secret vow of her sect, then burned the scrip in a small dish. She pulverized the ashes with her thumb, scattered them on a scrap of linen and examined the patterns. They made the rough outline of a crown, a wonderful augury. All the omens, she felt, were good, and she glanced upwards again to the water-stained plaster ceiling of the old temple, seeing with pleasure that a small vapour cloud had formed. It was the usual sign that her magic was working. Nicevenn and Ogmia had come with her and were satisfied, and she happily carried the thought with her as she stepped lightly back to her quarters.

Carausius was in process of sending military orders across the continent and as his appointed scribe, Guinevia had been busy improving her command of the Gallic and Belgic languages so she could clearly communicate news of the recovered Eagle to potential allies. The emperor came into her scriptorium to collect the latest batch of scrolls and to see a new thing she had created for him, a codex. The creation was a collection of sewn-together pages that were much easier to view than unrolling a long and cumbersome scroll, and Carausius appreciated the convenience of being able to easily view inventories of stores and supplies in the handmade book. He thumbed through it and grunted, then turned his attention to the tools of Guinevia's trade, picking up an ochre-stained mortar that was used to grind natural pigments. Its pestle stood next to a finished cake of colour that was bound together with gum and Carausius prodded it with his finger, testing the texture.

Guinevia smiled at his interest and showed Carausius the stylus and the reed pen she used. "This," she said, displaying the pointed stylus with its opposite, flattened end, "is for writing on wax tablets. That's just for note-taking, really. You can smooth the wax and erase any mistakes with the flattened end. You put the wax tablets into these wooden frames, they're hinged so you can write page after page of notes. A good secretary is careful not to clatter them together while the master is speaking. The reed pen is for writing permanent records. You cut a slit or crush the end of the reed so it takes up moisture easier. You dip it in water, then brush it across the cake of colour, or in this case, black. In this horn, I use ink made from iron gall or charcoal or soot mixed with water and acacia gum."

Some scribes, she said, used wood as a writing material, employing shavings or even a thin tablet, but for the imperial missives, she used papyrus made from river reeds glued together and smoothed. For an important document that would be a permanent record, she used vellum, the scraped skin of sheep, goat or calf. "I prefer papyrus because you can wipe away mistakes with a wet finger. It takes a knife to scrape away a mistake on vellum, plus a bit of smoothing with pumice stone."

Carausius was close enough to catch a scent of the dried lavender Guinevia kept in the chest in which she stored her clothes. He inhaled again to catch more, and detected the dab of crocus oil she had put behind her ears. Her fair hair, he noted, was shining and clean, and the nape of her neck as she bent over the vellum was white and looked invitingly soft. He nodded and cleared his throat, then refocused his thoughts. He handed the priestess a piece of papyrus he had received from a spy in Mainz. There, he knew, on the west bank of the great Rhine river that formed the frontier, the Romans maintained a military base that commanded both the town and a great bridge with a span of 500 paces. This crossing, one of the four bridges along the long length of the river, was a chokepoint in the defence of the empire, and Carausius spent purses of gold to be kept informed of the Romans' activities there.

"This report is barely a week old," he said, passing the document to Guinevia. "The couriers can make good time when they need to. It's Frankish, and I don't know that tongue well. Can you read it?"

"Somewhat, lord," she replied, taking the note and scanning it. "It says essentially that Maximian is much occupied with the Alemanni on the Danube, and is not expected to return for months. The region is quiet."

Carausius grunted. "What I thought." he said. 'You have done well, thank you."

Guinevia bowed her head and dropped a curtsey. "Thank you, great lord," she said playfully. Almost without willing it, Carausius reached out and took her hand to raise her up again. His throat ached. As she rose, he scooped her into his arms and tilted up her chin. Her eyes were calm as they looked up into his, her breath wafted sweet and warm against his face "I think we should use the sleeping chamber," she said quietly, and turned, still holding his hand as she led him across the room.

The sunlight woke Carausius. "Middle of the afternoon, I must be mad," he grumbled. He looked at Guinevia's calm profile as she slept, her shining barley-golden hair gracing the pillow beside him, and felt a surge of unexpected tenderness swamp him. He grunted again, and swung his legs from under the coverlet, flinching as his bare feet hit the frigid stone of the floor, then he was grabbing and dragging on his tunic even as he shouted for his aide Lycaon. "Get the senior officers to me in a half hour. We have some planning to do."

The emperor looked around the attentive faces. "First things first," he said. "Let's deal with the basics: objective, intelligence, personnel, communications, supply and transport," he said, ticking off the items on his fingers. "We're clear on one thing: everyone here knows the objective. We want to force Rome to the negotiating table to give us Britain and Gaul right down to the TransAlpine province. If we turn back Maximian's legions, we'll get the territory because they won't have the reserves to retake it. To them, keeping the barbarians behind the Rhine and Danube is the priority, so they'll negotiate if we can put Maximian's western forces out of the picture. That's the desired result. Next up, it's vital that we know who's where and what they're doing. Intelligence gathering is your job, Allectus. Get your spies and scouts working; you have the gold to do it.

"Personnel and communications are in the aegis of the tribunes Quirinus and Cragus. Divide the duties between you, and put some extra focus on recruitment. We can't have too many legionaries. See if you can get experienced troops. If we pay enough, we might lure some auxiliaries across from Belgica and the Rhine frontier, the way we got those German cavalrymen. Barbarian mercenaries will come for the loot. Plus, Maximian doesn't treat his infantry well, and that could help us to tempt defectors and deserters. It's always good to get soldiers who are already trained.

"Suetonius, you're the quartermaster and you're responsible for supplies. Talk to me later about that, I have some ideas about iron rations and establishing supply dumps in critical places. We don't need to have the men humping a month's worth of rations as well as all their other gear. There's the usual danger that some will eat it too quickly, and others will steal. We need to control the supplies, it's more efficient and will give us a little more mobility.

The emperor looked down at the scribbled list on the tablum before him. "We'll need to get the coopers busy making staves, too, we have a desperate shortage of barrels for things like salted ham, figs, dried fruit, sardines and salted mackerel, plus salt itself. Also, get the potters making amphorae to store the olive oil and wine, and pack the damned things properly, in sand inside the chests; we're losing too much to breakage. See to it, too, that we have ample charcoal, the smiths are complaining. The inventory of grain sacks for hard bread and grain is fine, I'm told. After all that, we have not had any decent garum for the boys for months. They want their fish sauce, it's about the only way to make bland food taste good, it's useful for morale, so whatever it takes, ship some barrels in, even if you have to use negotiators to get it out of Milan or Massilia.

"Talking of morale, I'm hearing complaints about the latrines. Make sure they're properly maintained, get some punishment details working on them. Oh, we'll be needing one vital small thing, that's more sponges for the men's personal latrine use. Hygiene's of the utmost importance so see to it that the water channels by the latrines are kept fresh for washing those sponges, I want no sickness that we can avoid so easily.

"Lastly, we have transport. Papinius Statius, you see to the baggage trains. I'm inclined not to rely too much on oxen because they slow us down too much, but they're a necessary evil for the artillery and heavies. Only use them where you have no other options. Get out into the countryside and commandeer wagons and carts that the mules can pull. Mules are best, but they can't move the heaviest impedimenta and I have a feeling we'll need siege engines as well as bridging equipment. I want as much mobility as we can arrange, so we'll try to move some of that big equipment by water. It might mean building some sheer-legs or cranes to load them, so look into making some demountable ones. We also need someone to oversee our river craft. Cenhud the Belge will act as pilot master, but I'll put a tribune in charge of the infantry on the ships. Scribe, did you get that? Remind me about finding the right tribune for the river craft."

The innovative plan, the emperor explained, was to use the great rivers to move troops quickly, as much as 60 miles a day, as he had in the past, only this time he'd employ a hundred or more rivercraft to move a great mass of men and equipment. He could not hope to slip unnoticed past Maximian's legions, but he could surprise them by swiftly bringing unexpected force and throwing a loop of steel around them before they were properly ready. Marching the troops, even on the great roads that criss-crossed the continent to link Rome to its remotest outposts, limited the legions' movements to about 30 miles a day or less, and wore out the troops in a prolonged campaign. Using the great waterways would keep the troops fresher and would move them further and faster.

Carausius planned to seize several large cities like Narbonne, Nimes and Rouen, where the Romans operated a mint. The seizures would serve both strategic and bargaining purposes, and taxes and tribute from them would boost his coffers. Lastly, he instructed Bononia's garrison commander Lucius Cornelius to supply and reinforce the citadel so it could be held against siege with a minimal number of troops. Done right, the port could still act as a forward headquarters so the fleet could continue to move against the pirates along the coast. Cornelius should, the emperor specified, keep a good portion of the fleet as well as a squadron of Gaulish merchant ships across the narrows in Dover, where all would be safe from any surprise land attack. "Don't forget to guard against a seaborne attack, too," he cautioned. "Maximian's no fool, he might well come that way."

Maximian indeed was not a fool. Away in the eastern mountains and forests, he had out-marched the Alemanni invaders, trapped them as they came through the gap of the River Drava and butchered them without pity. Later generations of mountain people would claim that carrion crows returned to the killing field for a dozen years, long remembering the feast they once had there.

Rome celebrated Maximian's victory at the same time they acclaimed the Augustus, who took pleasure in his fresh status as a god. Diocletian promptly decreed that those lucky enough to be admitted to his presence must kneel to kiss the hem of his robe, and none was to raise their eyes to look into his. He introduced new, elaborate levels of court ceremonial, ordered some imposing new public buildings erected to his glory and generally ensured that his deity was acknowledged and worshipped properly. He had to consider what to do about those Christians, too. They refused to acknowledge the deity of any but their own carpenter-god and it was a poor example for the rest of the empire. He'd have to take steps to bring them to heel, he thought. The newly-minted god-emperor also boosted his own standing somewhat by declaring general Maximian a Hercules to his own Jupiter. That sent a message to the mere mortals of the cowed Senate that Diocletian-Jupiter did the planning, while Maximian-Hercules dutifully carried out the great tasks he was set, and they'd better stay subservient, or things could change, and painfully, for them.

The new Hercules wasted no time in carrying out his tasks. Maximian turned away from the eastern borders of the empire and moved his legions to Gaul and Spain. "A dirty business," he wrote to his Syrian wife Eutropia. "These are rebel citizens of the empire. There is no glory here, and there will be no glory in bringing Carausius to justice. First, I have to put down southern Gaul and Spain, then I'll see to that Briton. It won't take long." The emperor was badly wrong about the timing. Putting down the insurgents took months. There was resistance, disease, and foul weather that bogged the Spanish roads. There were, too, guerrillas who cut his supply lines, so, it was no swift campaign, and throughout it, the grim general left rows of crucified rebels nailed to the poplar trees that lined and shaded the Rome-built roads of Gaul.

He also erected crosses with their sun-scorched, stinking burdens all across the dusty Spanish plain. When that was finally finished, two more years had gone by during which Carausius was untroubled by Maximian's troops, but there was still more work for the emperor. The barbarians had again crossed the Rhine, and in great force. Two vast armies, one of Heruli and Chaibones, the other of Alemanni boosted by some Carpiani, had forded the river and were sacking Roman settlements.

Maximian turned his campaign-hardened legions east one more time. He confronted the Alemanni in the forests of eastern Gaul, and carried out a classic military operation. He battered the enemy with artillery and heavy infantry, then sent his cavalry to outflank and roll up their ranks before they chopped the fleeing rabble into bloody ruin. The second horde of invaders lay to the north, and was trapped between the German Sea and the wide river Rhine, unable to retreat and reluctant to advance against the Romans. Maximian did not hurry to meet them. Instead, he contained the invaders, who quickly denuded the land of its crops and, as the Roman expected, died where they camped, ravaged by starvation and dysentery. Maximian never needed to confront them. His main task was to round up several thousand to send back to Milan as slaves. He contemptuously allowed the ragged, emaciated remainder to straggle back to their native forests.

The emperor marched his weary troops north to Cologne and settled them into winter quarters on the Rhine. "Hang up your breastplates and brain buckets and relax for a few months. It's time to grow your seam squirrels and pants rabbits," he told them cheerfully, referring to the inevitable flea and tick infestations that came to troops in barracks. "Enjoy it while you can."

Next spring he planned to drive deep into Germania with fire and sword, destroy all he found, scorch the earth and batter the barbarians into final, abject submission. After that, he could turn his attention and his veterans to the business of recapturing northern Gaul, and then Britain. The detail he'd sent had not been able to prevent Carausius from finding and parading that damned recovered Eagle in front of his superstitious troops, and they'd paid for that with their lives, but he was still a great general and he'd do what he knew best. He'd crush the usurper under his nailed military boot. He'd left Carausius alone for long enough. Now it was time to put him down, take what he wanted and build his own empire.

XXIV. Fishbourne

Carausius had used the lengthy breathing space to full advantage. He abandoned his plans to occupy Narbonne because of the proximity of Maximian's superior force as it hurried by, moving at double pace from Spain to the Danube, but he marched into Rouen, emptied the mint and spread coin from it lavishly through northern Gaul, buying the loyalty of the legion at Bononia that had once been Maximian's. The usurper emperor considered it politic to validate his claim in the eyes of his troops, so put on a ceremony to declare the founding of a British nation liberated from the emperors in Milan and Nicomedia, and free even from the new Roman centres of administrative power in Mediolanum, Antioch and Trier. It was a careful distinction Carausius made, as it implied that the twin emperors had turned their backs on Rome and its values but he, sent from heaven above, had not.

The soldiers responded well to the implication that they were the last of Rome's loyal legions, and happily took the generous donatives of gold that kept them bound to Carausius' cause. The tribunes of the 30th Ulpia legion paraded their gilded silver Eagle through Bononia alongside the recovered Ninth Spanish's Eagle and the standards of detachments from Carausius' three British legions, the Second Augusta, the Sixth Victrix and the 20th Valerian. The new Empire of Britain covered the island itself and a large part of northern Gaul, and on the battlements of Bononia, a ship's mast proudly displayed the multiple banners of the legions.

With the dice rolled and Carausius committed to his course, he re-crossed the Narrow Sea to make the formal proclamations of empire in Britain and to begin the lengthy business of establishing its administration. Mindful of the reports he had received of the new pomp of Diocletian's court, he ordered his own palace near Chichester to be upgraded into a fitting symbol of his power and influence, then journeyed north to Eboracum to meet the Pictish chieftains who were surprisingly keeping both their word and the peace along the Wall. Further south, as spring arrived, the Emperor Diocletian exchanged the imperial wreath for his military helmet and breastplate and came from the east with an armoured host. He sailed his convoy from Nicomedia and up the familiar Adriatic, where he was building a great new palace near his birthplace at Split, to make the passage through the Alps into Germania. At the same time, his co-emperor Maximian was readying for battle with another invading wave of Alemanni on the upper Danube.

The twin pincers of the Caesars caught the barbarian armies unprepared. They crushed them, soaking the slaughter fields in Saxon blood. After their triumphs, the Romans were merciless. They burned field crops and granaries, razed settlements, took slaves, butchered livestock and crucified any man found with weapons. Tens of thousands of Carpiani were resettled in the north, where territory devastated in earlier campaigns had been depopulated. The campaign to scorch the land subdued the inhabitants, added a huge swathe of new possessions to the empire and allowed the twin emperors to create a military frontier on the further, eastern bank of the Rhine.

This they fortified and supplied from Mainz to Cologne via a great metalled road that allowed swift movement of troops, couriers and supplies. At Diocletian's command, Maximian reduced the number of troops along the border itself, instead holding strike forces back from it a short distance behind the outlying garrisons that would warn of invasion. The response forces would activate when needed and use the new road system for rapid deployments. It meant more troops were needed, but it led to better stability in general and Diocletian's newly-raised tax levels paid for it all.

There was one more thing to do to prevent invasions. Maximian settled a long strip of northern border territory with Frisian and Chamavi tribes who pledged allegiance to Rome and formed a buffer against any wandering barbarian hordes. Now, with the frontier secured, the junior emperor could turn his attention to the upstart who'd stolen Britain. He'd start with those rebel Franks who had allied themselves to the enemy of Rome.

Carausius was enjoying the fruits of his boldness. As well as living luxuriously in the north, in the Eboracum palace built a century or so before by Septimius Severus, he had ordered expensive improvements and additions to his south coast palace at Fishbourne. This, with its 100 rooms, was easily the largest Roman villa north of the Alps, and compared favourably with Nero's fabled Golden House in Rome or the Sicilian villa at Piazza Armerina, where, Carausius heard, residents even enjoyed thermal baths from natural hot springs.

The emperor had ordered a fine bath at his own palace, and he loved the building's design and finish. Each day, he made time to examine the work being done by the builders, from the hypocaust that supplied underfloor heating to the fountains that graced the vast formal garden and courtyard and the atria of the living quarters. The arched and colonnaded dining hall was a beautiful airy space, the public hall and marble-faced reception rooms were opulent and huge, but the breathtaking showpiece was the integral bath house, an enclosure magnificent with pillars of polished Tibur stone decorated with gold leaf that graced the pre-plunge washrooms and the great bath itself, where 100 bathers could simultaneously take the water.

The colonnaded fronts of the four wings that made up the palace - which measured about 150 paces square - had a triumphal entrance and a great assembly hall. With its courtyard garden, luxurious guest houses, fish ponds, granaries, military supply base and accommodations, it was a suitably imposing palace for an emperor, and Carausius revelled in it. For the first time in his life, he had time for relaxation, and one of his favourite pastimes was to take his big dogs Axis and Javelin into the forests to hunt deer, boar, wolf or, rarely, bear. It was when the emperor and his lover Guinevia were on a deer hunt that the dogs' training truly showed itself.

The duo had dallied behind the half-dozen spearmen who had accompanied them when the party set off in high excitement, chasing a magnificent red stag. The pair were embracing, laughingly fumbling at each other's clothes. The sunlit forest clearing was quiet, the lovers were engrossed, and the dogs were lying a few paces away, when Axis let out a low growl and Javelin's head swivelled to stare into the undergrowth. Carausius half-heard his dog's warning, and waved a 'silent!' signal behind Guinevia's bare shoulders, not wanting the distraction. He didn't see the dogs rise to their feet and move almost without motion, their eyes flickering between their master's hand signal and the brush 30 or so paces away, across the clearing.

Carausius didn't see the bulky black shape as it emerged from the bushes, but he looked up as a whiff of musty, rank fur struck his nostrils.

What he saw was a black bear, its rheumy eyes blinking at the sunlight in the clearing, its wet doglike nose lifted to scent the air. In an instant his mind was racing, and he put his fingers over Guinevia's warm lips. The bear, he realized, was upwind and had not yet scented them properly. Its eyes were poor and had not seen the lovers on the turf in front of it, but its hearing, he thought bitterly, would be good enough to catch any noise of movement he made towards his boar spear. He glanced at his dogs, which were crouched low, quivering, teeth bared in silent snarls. He made another hand gesture, a circling motion that told the dogs to move to the side. They flitted across the grass like shadows, and the bear turned its head suspiciously in their direction.

Carausius moved his own head slowly, eyes seeking his heavy spear. Four paces away. He could get it and be in time turn to face the bear before it arrived, but Guinevia? He pressed his mouth to her ear. "Stay still. Keep lying here," he breathed.

Axis was glancing to him. He brought up his hand in the 'Kill' signal and waved the dogs' release. They leaped forward at the bear. It turned to the movement and started to its hind legs. Carausius had the spear haft in hand and was turned towards the wild beast in time to see the racing dogs launch. The bear swatted at Javelin, who flew sideways, rolled and was back on his feet and lunging. The diversion had let Axis in and his great jaws were sunk in the bear's thick fur at the throat. The big dog was tearing at it, the bear was clawing at its tormentor. Javelin hit the beast from the side and all three were entangled and growling ferociously as the man raced up, saw the moment and plunged his heavy boar spear under the bear's ribs. He strained his great strength and lifted the beast, with both dogs still attached, like a harvester throwing hay. The spearhead burst the bear's heart. Axis, bloodied from the beast's claws, was bleeding from his shoulders but had torn an ugly slash across the predator's throat. Javelin had the bear's snout in his jaws and was shaking his head, tearing painfully at the dying beast that was pumping its blood onto the grass.

As fast as that, the attack and kill were ended. Carausius gave the spearhead a final twist, then called his dogs away. He turned to Guinevia, who was white-faced with shock. "The dogs did well, eh?" he said, wiping his hands on the grass to remove some of the gore that had spattered up.

"I've never seen anything like it," she whispered. "So silent, so quick."

"Aye," said the emperor, "and they've ruined his pelt." But he was smiling even as he complained. Sucia had done a fine job training his hounds. He was still to learn just how valuable that training was, and how it would save his life.

Safely back in Fishbourne, where the emperor proudly relayed the story and showed the torn bear skin, prompting a few witticisms about a Bear killing a bear, Carausius was relaxed enough to tolerate the good-natured jibes, for he was enjoying life as never before. Just as he took deep pleasure in the lovemaking he shared with Guinevia, who had bewitched him with her spells and who was increasingly important in the daily running of the new administration, he and she both took a good deal of pleasure in the palace, and they both especially enjoyed wandering into the north wing, to watch the Ionian artist Claria Primanata, who had been brought at considerable expense from her faraway home, to construct a vast floor mosaic of sea creatures, one of a dozen the emperor had commissioned for the palace.

The Greek oversaw a squad of nimble-fingered small boys who placed coloured fragments of pottery to her meticulous designs, which were all in the Italian style. The boys were working at low tables, where they put down the pieces onto a coloured design painted on papyrus, the whole thing contained in a frame. They fixed the mosaic fragments together with grout as they worked on one panel at a time. When it was done, the finished section was lifted out and laid over an older floor which had a black and white pattern but which had the advantage of being a level surface, a constant problem in creating a mosaic floor. Then, the edges between the latest section and the previous one were carefully joined and grouted. Claria's ocean-themed artwork was dominated by the image of a trident-carrying Cupid riding on a dolphin and was intended to remind the viewer of the sea power of the emperor-admiral. On the walls above it, a vast sea-themed mural was also being created.

Claria's slave Celvinius Ionis, a portrait painter who had been forced to sell himself into slavery because of an unfortunate gambling habit, was recording scenes from the emperor's waterborne life. Here was the boy fleeing for his life across the German Sea, here was the river pilot on the great Rhine. Next in the mural came the Lord of the Narrow Sea as an admiral suppressing pirates. Here, he was fearlessly leading his fleet around the stormy northern horn of Pictland, where terrible cannibals waited to murder and eat the victims of shipwreck.

Celvinius had slyly added an image or two of his own. A bear or two were half-hidden in woodland scenes, a figure that looked suspiciously like Guinevia could be seen on close examination to be hovering a few inches off the ground, and there was even a depiction of the mad emperor Caligula's 'conquest of the sea.' The painter had pictured him ordering his soldiers to do battle with the waves and defeat Neptune before setting them to collect seashells, which he had displayed in Rome as evidence of his triumph. Now, the muralist was working on a vast wall-painting to show the fleet in Bononia, but he was handicapped by a lack of knowledge of the city and was waiting for an opportunity to interview Allectus to get a description of it.

The sorceress Guinevia glided in, followed by several inky-fingered slaves, their arms wrapped around bundles of scrolls. "More decrees to sign, lord," she said, gesturing for a slave to hold out the portable writing table he carried. She looked around. "I like the mosaic a great deal." She flashed a motherly smile at the talented young Ionian, who dropped her usual haughtiness to respond with a gracious inclination of the head. "The mural is very effective, too, in its way," Guinevia said thoughtfully. "Although it's not classical art." She fingered the decorative gold pestle shaped like a bull's horns that hung around her neck.

The slave Celvinius tugged at his too-short tunic. "I am attempting to capture the essence, lady," he said, his tone bordering on insolence.

"Wash your mouth out," Guinevia snapped. "Cross me and I could send the witch goddess to turn your sleep into nightmares." Claria looked up at the rebuke of her slave. "Keep your thoughts to yourself, ink drinker," she told him. "You are just a monkey with a colouring reed." Celvinius, whose life had been privileged before his downfall, flushed. He'd remember the rebuke, he promised himself.

The scowl faded from his face as a fellow artist, an Illyrican named Barbanata, came quietly into the room. Her fingers were blackened with charcoal dust, for she had been sketching two of the sculptures on the terraces above the palace's small harbour. "What about these?" she asked him, her smile lighting her face. His mood lifted. The two muralists were planning a mythological theme for one of the great public rooms. It was to be an illusionist, theatrical backdrop of an idyllic landscape that would incorporate griffons, cupids and deities in a view of the real landscape around the palace.

Barbanata showed him her preliminary sketches of the two sculptures and quietly indicated a small figure she had inserted almost invisibly against a backdrop of trees. In a few careful strokes, she had sketched Guinevia casting a spell, as a small cloud of vapour formed above her head. Celvinius laughed out loud. "Perfect," he said, his annoyance forgotten. "That should go right on the wall."

Carausius ignored the laughter and turned away to busy himself with his scrolls and an inventory codex. Increasing activity by sea raiders from Hibernia and Saxonia concerned him, and that, plus the immediate threat from Maximian and the likely invasion of Germanic tribes had him actively fortifying the Saxon Shore. This was the south-east coastline of Britain where Saxon settlers lived, and the closest point to the continental mass of Gaul and the Belgic lands.

The emperor's chief base of the Shore was at Dover, which overlooked the straits of the Narrow Sea. It was situated under white coastal cliffs, the turf-topped chalk battlements of Britain, where the wide river Dour flowed into the tidal race. The Romans had built two 60 feet tall sandstone lighthouses on top of the heights to guide vessels into the tidal river, where quays stretched for a mile inland. A large fort with 80 or so rooms for the garrison, granaries and supplies commanded the river mouth, but it had been there for a century and a half and was showing signs of disrepair that could compromise its military usefulness. Carausius ordered additions and reinforcements to the structure, to be built Roman-style with layered stone, tile and brick and to include substantial round bastions and a deep ditch.

He had also sent builders across the narrows to Bononia to duplicate the Dover lighthouse and fortifications. At night, the signal fires would shine to each other across the sea channel, and patrols of the fleet could move between their two bases with relative surety and safety.

The emperor pored over the coastal charts with his aide Lycaon, as the dogs Axis and Javelin slumbered and twitched, sleeping close together near the glowing brazier. "The raiders are a nuisance, but if we put garrisons at the river mouths and in the most likely landing places, I think we can control them," he muttered. "The real threat is not the raiders, it's that Rome attempts to take this from us, and even if with the help of the gods, we can defeat them, there will still be waves of Germanic tribes flooding this way.

"If we are to hold this country of ours, we need to do more than win a few battles. We have to make the island a fortress so we can live the way we want, not as milk cows for Rome or as slaves of the Teutons, Saxons and the rest who would steal our land. We must reinforce our borders. I'll put strong points all the way to The Wash, up there above Colchester. I'd keep a strong cavalry force there, too, as reserves we can get quickly to meet the bandits at their beach head and hold them until we can get foot soldiers in. There are signal towers along the northern coast; I even saw one being built there, as a boy. It was impressive, a great iron basket full of fuel to signal with fire by night and smoke by day.

"The old Romans knew their job. They built more beacons that went inland to Eboracum and Lincoln so the signal could quickly reach those garrisons, and I've ordered those old towers manned and refurbished. We can shuttle the hump-a-lots from the garrisons up or down the military road north to the border or south to Londinium to meet any invader. It's a good tactic, to have a swift response force behind the frontier, and I'm told that Maximian is using it on the Rhine.

"Here on the Shore, we must cover the rivers, especially the Thames. We'll need to build signal towers along that estuary, so the Londinium garrison gets plenty of warning if Maximian comes that way. Better put in a big log boom, too, so we can close off the river if we need to. I suppose that goes for other ports, too."

He checked off further points along the coast, nine fortresses in all, plus some beacon stations, holding down the curling edge of the chart with an ink horn as he plotted a number of smaller strategic garrisons. One critical spot to reinforce, and soon, was the Great Port that was an outlying part of Winchester's defences. It was a vital defensive link and an important harbour with its mysterious two high tides a day that sailors said were created by the shape of the coastline and the depth of the Atlanticus.

In Gaul, across the Narrow Sea, the emperor wanted reinforcements moved up and strong points improved near the estuaries of the Seine and the Somme, as well as at the mouth of the Belgic river Scheldt. The emperor looked at the army lists and sighed. Not enough troops to reinforce garrisons everywhere, he thought. The dozen or so forts westwards along the coast of northern Gaul would have to take their chances. Vessels from the great fortress and naval base at Bononia could scour that white-cliffed coast for pirates but Carausius didn't want to stretch his land reserves too thin by extending his military coverage any further west.

"The threats will come from Maximian's legions on land, from the east and south, and from a fleet that will come from the east. They'll not sail the long way around, through the Pillars of Hercules and up the coast of Spain. He'll be building his vessels in the east, not in the Inland Sea. The naval attack will certainly come from the Rhine coast. One day soon, we'll need a strong fleet there to take on Maximian," he forecast grimly to Allectus and a group of senior officers. "When that happens, I don't want to be caught with my trews around my ankles. We should keep most of the fleet at Dover, so it can't be attacked by land forces while it's in port in Gaul."

He paused, tapping the scroll as he thought. "I should probably take some coin to the tribes, refresh the alliances, and especially meet that fellow Gennobaudes on the Rhine, to keep him enthusiastic about our treaty. He has some influence with the tribes, you know. Maybe I can persuade them to send some infantry, too." On an impulse, Carausius added. "I might mix in a bit of pleasure, do some hunting in the Ardennes with the locals, establish the contacts and create some more goodwill. I'll take the dogs."

Only a few days later, Carausius sailed across the Narrow Sea, collected an honour guard of two centuries of smartly turned-out legionaries, and with them, his hounds and his twin brothers headed for the Belgic forests, and serious trouble.

A hundred miles east of Carausius' small column, as it made its way the Via Agrippa towards the territory of the Belgae, the Frankish king Gennobaudes was sickly grey with fear. He knew he was lucky his head was still attached to his shoulders. It had all happened so quickly, he thought mournfully. Maximian and his legions had rolled up the tribal forces along the Rhine, and butchered, crucified and enslaved thousands. There had been a few rumours, but the Romans had surrounded and controlled the tribes and before any real warning could reach the Belgic king, Roman cavalry was at his town walls and messengers were delivering him a harsh ultimatum. Unprepared, he had no choice, and had opened the gates....

On the very day that Carausius arrived at the Belgic king Mosae's small citadel, the Caesar Maximian was sitting on a throne just a few days' march to the east. It was the royal seat of Mosae's overlord, Gennobaudes, and the cowed monarch was kneeling humbly before the Roman. The business did not take long. The Frank kissed the tip of Maximian's sword, solemnly promised allegiance to Rome and was installed as tenant king. At least, he thought sourly, he was alive. Maximian suppressed a sneer as he viewed Gennobaudes' vassals lined up along the walls of the receiving room and waiting to re-swear their oaths of allegiance. They knelt one by one, their hair shaped with lime water into towering horsetails that nodded as they kissed their king's feet. It all had all happened as the Caesar and his red-cloaked Dragons had expected. They'd suppressed the restive tribes, taken out the leaders, and appointed a few puppet rulers to do their dirty work. The long lines of crucifixes outside the city walls with their still-moaning victims explained the enthusiasm of the chieftains to surrender.

A tangible result of the Roman success was to be seen in the long wagon train loaded with plunder and guarded by a half-legion of Saxon auxiliaries that went south to Milan, a snake of miserable, chained slaves a full half-mile long dragging behind it. Maximian watched the head of the coffle trudge past, briskly swung himself astride his new Frisian warhorse and nodded for the trumpeter to sound the march. No time to waste; with his great convoy of three legions and their impedimenta, he was impatient to move in another direction, west into Gaul to put the cities of Rouen and Bononia back under his control, and to bring that rebel bastard Carausius to heel. A messenger from king Mosae had been captured by his troops, and he had been carrying notice that Carausius was at his master's citadel and wanted an audience. Just possibly, Maximian thought, he could catch the Briton away from his army. He clenched his fist at the thought. There would be one more crucifix adorning a field somewhere, he promised himself.

The dogs next to him heard or perhaps scented something first. Carausius was standing on the parapet of the town ruled by the minor Belgic king Mosae, looking down at the camp the British troops had established on a meadow outside the protection of the town walls. The light was fading, the air was still and quiet, and he was pondering how he should best contact the high king Gennobaudes who was, he presumed, two or three more days' march to the east. First Axis, then Javelin growled deep in their throats. The emperor looked to see what had disturbed him, but saw nothing. A sentry made alert by the presence of his commander leaned over the parapet, peering into the dusk. "Lord," he said, "I think there's something."

Even before the man spoke, Carausius, instincts honed by years of campaigning, was alerted by a prickle at the nape of his neck. In the dusk-darkened woods, just inside the line of the trees and virtually invisible to searching eyes, squads of archers equipped with bales of odd-looking arrows were standing quietly. Their heavy-headed arrows each carried a thick hank of greasy wool tied below the head, the whole flammable package coated with pitch. A platoon of soldiers carrying shielded containers of smouldering charcoal moved quietly along the groups of archers and blew the charcoal into glowing life. The bowmen touched their arrows to the glow, the lanolin-soaked wool ignited, the pitch contained the fire and the archers aimed the heavy arrows high as they stepped out of the trees and into the open.

Carausius, uneasy, was scanning the dusk purposefully when he caught a glimmer of something. It flared, then another few points of light flickered and bloomed crimson beside it. The first red-glowing point arced upwards and plunged steeply down into the British tent lines. Five, six more fire arrows followed the first, then a whole flight of them looped into the air as the thin, sharp noise of bowstrings twanged and plinked in the dusk. The missiles were dropping into the orderly squares of the camp, catching alight the tightly woven wool that had been waterproofed with lanolin and beeswax. Suddenly, it seemed as if only the few leather-canopied ridge tents of the officers were not yet on fire. Men were scrambling out, snatching up weapons, tripping over guy lines in the dusk, calling out the alarm. Carausius was bellowing for the citadel guard and the sentry beside him was clashing his sword pommel on a signal gong when from the treeline a rank of horsemen burst into the open.

Alongside them as they cantered, Roman infantrymen were clinging to the rear pommels of the saddles, being carried at speed across the open ground. Their feet bounced across the turf in great leaps as they were dragged along. In moments, the horsemen and their foot soldier passengers were at the transit camp's rampart and ditch, forcing down the wooden palings, hacking at the few duty sentries at the gates. Within a minute or so, the cavalry was in among the tent lines, the whole scene lit eerily by the flames of the blazing camp as the horsemen thudded along the open lanes, shouting, slashing and spreading chaos.

Several knots of the emperor's men formed a resistance of sorts, retreating as they faced the horses but the majority of the Briton's escort was being chopped down. Two groups coalesced into one unit and fought grimly as, shield-less, they stepped back and back to the barred citadel gates. The prefect Lycaon was inside the walls to aid their escape. Snarling like a beast, he forced the gate guards at sword point to ignore the local commander's orders and opened a small wicket set into the great gate of the citadel. One by one, the retreating fighters backed through. Defenders began arriving on the walls above the gate, and fired arrows and javelins down at the pressing Romans, but they could not save the last few soldiers, who died outside as the wicket was bolted fast.

XXV. Ardennes

The night had been a busy and difficult one, and it was almost first light, but King Mosae and Carausius had the walls secured. The little citadel was sited on one of the short, steep hills that were plentiful on the Belgic plains and the Briton had a good view when the sun finally came up. With practised efficiency, the Roman invaders had established their camp. A ring of soldiers had the citadel surrounded and they could be seen already erecting a palisade to circle the entire town, keeping the besieged safely trapped and their own rear protected. Maximian had joined forces with his son in law Flavius and they had arrived with almost 9,000 men. The rebel Briton was caught in their noose of steel. "He'll know I'm here," Carausius thought bitterly, "he has certainly questioned his captives. How in great Jove's name did he find me?" Everything was clarified a few hours later, when an emissary from Maximian arrived to parley.

The herald met the citadel commander and two of his officers outside the gates, and he carefully iterated the grim terms Maximian demanded. The town would be spared being put to fire and sword, the herald said, if Carausius and his twin brothers, with King Mosae and all his family were handed over naked, in chains. They were to be told their fate before being handed over, the herald specified. . They would be eaten alive by pigs. "You must tell your king and the rebels that my lord has a small herd of feral hogs and it takes them just eight minutes to eat a man, meat, guts and bones," the herald told the emissaries. "It's very entertaining to watch and it is a most effective way of keeping discipline. Before you bring the captives, you must cut off their hair, and knock out all their teeth. All of them. My lord's pigs don't digest hair and teeth well, and he does not want them upset. He said specifically that he did not want the swine's' digestion fouled by the rebels' rotting teeth. You must bring them ready for the feast.'

The herald eyed the commander and his aides. "Be absolutely sure to inform your king and his guests, the filth who rebelled against my lord, how and why they are to be readied or you too will suffer the same death.

We will question them before they are fed to the animals, so we will know if you properly explained their fate to them."

As far as the rest of the citadel's occupants were concerned, the emperor's envoy declared that the garrison would be decimated for its rebellion, and the treasury, granaries and storehouses filled with the salt, fleeces and leather gathered as taxes were to be emptied and loaded for transport away. Fifty of the citizens, he said, would be sent to the slave pens as token punishment for giving succour to the rebels. The younger townswomen were to be brought to the market place so the victors could make their choices.

King Mosae mumbled terrified defiance when he heard the terms, and although his officers looked warily at each other to see if anyone were bold enough to mutiny at once, none did, so the waiting emissary was sent back and the siege began. With trained efficiency, the besiegers speedily began pulling down buildings for material to continue the construction of their palisade around the town, working behind impromptu walls that covered them from the defending archers. They blocked the new aqueduct which supplied most of the town's water and engineers began constructing platforms for the siege engines that were in Maximian's baggage train. Work parties tramped off to cut timber in the nearby forests, others set about building siege towers, screens and ramps. In short order, the big catapults were readied, and by mid-afternoon were hurling rocks over the walls, destroying buildings and causing chaos from the resulting fires.

The catapults, called 'wild asses' for the terrible kick they made, also threw burning material into the town and Maximian ordered forward a dozen batteries of ballistae to support them. These were crossbow-like weapons that fired rounded river stones or large arrow-headed bolts with great precision. He directed them against the archers on the walls above the huge gate and turned one battery of wild asses to batter at the gate with rocks.

,

The walls themselves were too high for a quick assault, so Maximian ordered miners to begin burrowing under a corner tower. His intent was to dig out a vast cavern under the foundation, support the excavation with timber, then burn through the supports. This would cause the collapse of both the cavern and the fortification which stood above it.

Meanwhile, under the cover of a constant barrage of fire against the men on the parapets, pioneers crouched beneath protective roofs to fill and hard-pack the ditch in front of the wall so they could roll their heavy machinery right up to the stonework.

In the swarming beehive of activity, one man was everywhere; Maximian personally oversaw the digging and dragging, the firing and the construction crews. Untiring, and conspicuous in his crested helmet and purple cloak, the emperor strode about, contemptuous of the defenders' fire, urging on his engineers to complete the siege tower that would allow his own archers to shoot down on the defenders.

"Come on, you donkey-dicked mouse launchers," he shouted, grinning as he addressed a sweating detachment, who were dragging huge catapults into prepared positions. "We'll soon be inside, and then it's women, wine and loot. All we need is a little more effort from you charts and darts fellows to get those walls down." The centurion in charge of a battery of ballistae acknowledged the instruction, fired a bolt and with it tumbled a defender from the wall. "What's your name?" Maximian demanded, nodding in pleasure at the shot.

"I am Maximus Heatonius, lord, marine of the Fifth Pontus."

"What's a sea soldier doing here?" the emperor demanded, half-joking.

"Just lucky, Caesar," the man responded, straight-faced, as his commander laughed and turned away to the next task.

Within the week, the attackers' siege tower was ready to be pushed into place across the in-filled ditch, and the protective, heavy-roofed galleries were being rolled to where they would shield the battering ram crews who would swing their iron-headed beam against the town gates.

Inside the walls, grimy with smoke and sweat, the twins Mael and Domnal were working with hooks and axes, pulling down buildings to make firebreaks. Carausius, streaked with smoke and grime and bloodied from numerous small injuries, stood alongside the Belgic king and looked at the Roman activity that continued even though it was almost nightfall. "We should try a sally against them, destroy some of their equipment, slow them down," the Briton urged.

"I don't have the men for it," said the king.

"We'll have no men at all if we don't do something. We don't have a lot of other possibilities," Carausius retorted. He was mindful that the three scouts he'd sent to bring reinforcements from Bononia had been captured as they tried to slip through the enemy lines.

That unwelcome news arrived when their severed heads had been catapulted over the walls two days before. "We can't hold out until winter, it's too long. We can't break out against such force and we don't really have much hope of relief from either my Bononia troops or your King Gennobaudes, if he's even in the picture any more. I suspect that Maximian's neutralized him somehow. Our best hope might be to poison their drinking water or spread some kind of plague, but the danger there is we might catch it, too."

Mosae looked thoughtful, excused himself and went to speak to a wise woman in the town. He had not told the Briton that his men had reported hearing the sounds of miners undercutting the tower in the west corner. It wasn't wise to share everything. Carausius also looked thoughtful, wondering about his own plans. The town, he knew, could hardly hold out for much longer. He might stand a chance of escape in the chaos of murder and raping when the Romans broke in, but he and his two brothers would be better advised to slip away sooner, if they could, as the twins were too noticeable for a discreet exit when the place was on alert.

The big soldier considered some possibilities, to get over, under or through the walls unnoticed. Through meant using the gates, and they were under constant guard. Going over the wall might be possible, but they were very high. Tunnelling under them might be more profitable. He'd start with the latrines. The Romans had improved the town, and their sanitation systems were first rate. Although the streets were often foul with waste thrown out of windows, the latrines were a stone-built system of trenches sluiced by running water that had, Carausius reasoned, to go somewhere outside the walls. With the dogs Axis and Javelin at his heels as always, he went to investigate, and started for the west tower, where a barracks latrine was sited.

The Briton didn't know it, but the earth under his feet concealed a raging furnace. The Roman miners had carved their cavern under the tower, supported the workings with wooden pit props and drilled small ventilation holes to the surface. They'd dragged bundles of kindling into the cavern to stoke the fire, and just hours before, they had soaked the props in pitch and set them alight. They had, however, miscalculated. The ventilation shafts had created a venturi effect that sucked in air in a blast that superheated the fires, and they were raging, not smouldering. They had created a furnace that was burning far, far faster than they had planned.

Above the hidden inferno, and oblivious to the wisps of smoke that emerged from the cavern's ground-level vents, Carausius looked at the path of the stone-lined trench of the latrine in the crypt of the tower. He deduced it would clear the wall about 20 feet west of where he stood. He moved out of the building and stood under the wall, seeking the trench's exit. There it was, barred with iron, an impassable barrier. He turned to go back into the tower when a flash of white scampered across his path. He frowned. Another white rat? Both dogs had seen the rodent but made no move to chase. Instead, acting as one, the dogs looked up at their master and whined, then cowered against the town wall. Carausius stooped to reassure them, and the action saved his life.

At the very moment he moved, an earth-shaking rumble began as the cavern below him collapsed into itself, knocking the soldier to the ground. The tower shook and swayed, then crumpled inwards. The pit props had burned through as if vaporized, the cavern imploded under the tower's weight and the whole structure turned into rubble. Blocks of stone thundered down within a few feet of the crouching man and his terrified dogs, but not a single piece hit them. Shaken, Carausius stood upright, coughing, and took stock. The tower was no more, it was just a heap of rubble from which choking billows of dust were spewing. The iron bars of the latrine grille lay sideways, and an open exit beckoned.

A hundred paces away, outside the walls, Maximian was cursing, raving and shouting orders. The tower had collapsed far sooner than expected, and his planned coordinated attack was in ruins, too. He raved that he wanted the siege tower in place, he wanted that fucking ram battering the fucking gate down. The rubble didn't give him enough of a ramp into the town, it was too defensible from the walls on either side, those fucking engineers had fucked everything up, get the fucking archers busy and keep those fuckers' heads down on the walls. Splinter that gate, I don't care if it's dark, the fucking goblins won't get you.

Their commander's ravings spurred the Roman camp to swarm like a wasps' nest that had just been kicked over. Carausius looked into the dust-choked exit in front of him and didn't hesitate. "This way, boys," he called to the dogs. He ducked past the latrine gate into the dark, and slipped into the fog of stone dust that was drifting on the night breeze out from the walls.

The fleeing emperor grimaced. He'd only had to kill one person, a legionary he had chanced upon in the miasma of dust and smoke, and his new longsword Exalter had done a splendid job on the fellow's throat. He'd surprised the man with the sword's extra reach and a two-handed, backhand swing. He supposed he should chalk up some credit to Axis and Javelin, as the dogs had alerted him to the sentry's silent presence, stopping, stiffening and giving low growls before Carausius could blunder into the soldier. Instead, the Briton had quietly drawn his sword, edged along the palisade the man was guarding and taken out his voice box before the sentry could get even level his spear. He'd gathered up the man's cloak and helmet, cleared the containing palisade and had travelled fast, ignoring the pain in his foot.

He'd gone across country all night and through the whole of the next day. Now he was into the karst country of the Ardennes, a well-watered place of dense forest, limestone caves and relative safety. With the stolen cloak and helmet, he could claim to be a courier once he reached the Via Agrippa, that great road which he knew ran to Bononia. He had a couple of days of hunger, but twice, the dogs caught rabbits, and the man and beasts shared the raw, warm flesh. Once, he found wild plums, and there was plenty of water. The big soldier was used to hunger, and he made good time. It would not be long before he reached the road, and could find transport.

The battering ram's heavy iron head had finally smashed through the reinforced elm gates of the citadel, splintering them above the great locking beam and allowing axe men to hack at it and the defenders inside the gate. Above the heads of the sweating, panting squad who swung the ram on its chains, the heavy planks of the wheeled gallery that protected them banged and shivered under the impact of rocks and timbers hurled down from the fighting platforms inside the wall, but nothing broke through.

Inside the citadel, the defenders were being thinned by a rain of arrows and iron-headed javelins fired down from the tall wooden siege tower that now overtopped the walls. A few dozen invading infantry led by a red-cloaked officer were scrambling up the scree of the tumbled corner tower, half-hidden in the choking dust that still hung in the air. Maximian felt it, his instincts all told him that in moments he would be through the defences. Then, he promised himself grimly, he'd hunt down the rebel Briton who'd been a thorn in his side for so long. He's drag him back to Rome, shackled like an animal. Forget about the pigs, for now.

The infantry climbing the collapsed tower were at the parapet, almost unnoticed in the dust and chaos. The officer jumped down into the courtyard and led them at the dead run for the inside of the gate. Several went down under defenders' arrows, but the rest were flanking the gate defenders, swinging and stabbing in a bloodlust frenzy. It took only moments for the resistance to melt away. Some defenders ran, a few dropped their weapons and tried to surrender, but were cut down where they cowered. The red-cloaked officer and three of his men heaved at the locking bar, pulling it loose. The wrecked gate was pushed open from outside, and the slaughter, screaming and horror began.

Domnal and Mael had never trained as soldiers although they had lived active, often hard, lives for a long time as slaves. They were strong men, but they were into their years and their foot speed had long passed. They were not fighters, they were not fleet-footed runners, and they were doomed. Squads of Romans systematically scouring the town had trapped them as they tried to cross the east wall, and now they were squatting under guard in the open forum with hundreds more townspeople, waiting dully to see what the conquerors would do.

King Mosae had been recognized when his body slaves put up resistance, and he was taken alive. He had been beaten and raggedly castrated, and was presently manacled naked to the outside wall of the Temple of Mars where passing soldiers jeered and spat at him. Smoke was billowing across the marketplace and a centurion with a file of infantry began pulling men out of the crowd of captives in the forum for a crew to create a firebreak.

"Get over there, you'll be tearing down houses," he ordered them. The twins were selected, the centurion's eyes narrowing as he saw their similarity. The prisoners were marched rapidly through the paved streets and ordered to strip the reed thatch from a row of low houses before sparks could ignite them. Soon, half a hundred men were ripping and tearing at the buildings to make the firebreak. Mael was working alongside his brother and saw a chance. "When I tell you, drop through the roof," he whispered. He watched, could see no soldier observing them and hissed the command.

Domnal vanished, his twin took another swift scan and followed him. In the disorder of the smoke and destruction, it was the work of moments to climb through the window hole at the side of the house, crouch, and slip into the next street unseen. The twins worked their way cautiously west, staying close to the fires and the concealing smoke, until they cleared the wall and ditch. Then it was a matter of walking coolly across open ground, hoping to avoid a challenge.

The Fates' good fortune was with them. The soldiers were too occupied with fighting the fires that threatened their loot, as well as doing some freelance pillaging for themselves. By the minute, more captives were being herded into the forum, and a couple of men walking openly across the deserted siege lines were of no great interest. The twins turned aside before they reached the impedimenta, where they correctly anticipated that a rear-guard would be on the lookout for thieves. By nightfall, they had reached the forests to the west. If they had known it, they were following closely in their brother's limping footsteps.

King Mosae was in torment. He had been stripped, crudely emasculated, flogged brutally, then crucified. The Romans had driven iron nails through his forearms and both heels, and hoisted him on a cross high on the ramparts of his own palace, so he could be seen from a distance. Maximian's tribune Flavius had delayed feeding the king to the pigs, and had ordered the flogging and crucifixion to force from him where Carausius was hidden. Mosae badly wanted to reveal the whereabouts of the fugitive, but he simply did not know, and he'd not been able to convince Flavius of that truth. He'd tried, but the Roman was disbelieving. Now, the king was suffering agonies.

Each time he tried to ease the brutal pain in his feet by letting his arms take the weight, his chest was compressed and he began to suffocate. When he pushed down against the long nails that ran through his heels and into the sides of the upright of the cross, the agony in his feet and legs was like fire. The muscles of his back were torn and weeping blood, the white of his ribs showed through where the metal tips of the flagellum had ripped away the flesh during his whipping. He groaned and moved his head from side to side and the infantryman posted to keep the onlookers from helping him glanced up. "He won't last another half day," the soldier thought. "If the pigs want him alive, we'll have to get him down soon."

Inside the smoke-reeking tower of the keep, which had escaped major damage in the fires that swept the citadel, Flavius was speaking to his father in law and commander. "Mosae really doesn't know, lord," he told Maximian nervously, "and I'm fairly sure Carausius is not in the town." "Did you get his brothers?" the Caesar demanded, knowing the answer. "We're still searching through the captives, lord," Flavius evaded. Maximian turned away in disgust. He'd wasted too much time in this place to capture Carausius, and the bastard wasn't to be found. These muttonheads couldn't even find a pair of twins among the captives. This could seriously damage his chances of being promoted to Augustus, if his senior emperor was displeased with his failure.

"Take a hundred of the strongest-looking captives and decimate them. Make their own comrades kill each tenth man. Then ask them where Carausius is. If they won't tell you, decimate the survivors and ask again. Keep doing it until you find out." "Yes, Caesar," said Flavius, 'but why the strongest?"

"Because, idiot, they're the ones who'll give us the most trouble as slaves."

The butchery continued as the dying king hung above his conquered citadel, and Maximian strolled down to the forum to look over the captive women. He pointed to a white-faced girl of about 14, to a pretty, Jewish seamstress who was twisting her hands and nervously biting her lip, and to an expensively-robed young matron who was holding her child. "Take those three to my quarters, strip and wash them," he ordered an archer. "Get them properly clean. I'll be there when I've had a drink. Kill the brat if that one resists at all." He stepped close to the seamstress, fondled her buttocks and sniffed at her hair as the woman stood silent and trembling. Maximian leaned even closer and murmured into her ear: "Don't worry about what will be going into your mouth. It isn't pork."

The man for whom his former hosts were dying because they did not know where he was, had crossed the River Scheldt hanging onto the tails of his two big dogs, and came out of the forests at the great Roman road to Bononia. He turned north. He knew that every 15 miles or so there would be a way station mansio of four or five rooms with a bath house, a facility built for officials travelling on government business. There, he could hope to bluff or bribe his way onto horseback and move faster and with less pain.

Carausius was in luck. Two miles along the Via Agrippa, he came to a way station. The administrator looked askance at the limping, dirtied soldier with the two panting hounds at his heel until he heard the man's story of being beset by bandits as he came from the siege. The big man's natural authority, gold piece and demand for a remount all worked, and the emperor was on his way, knowing life would be easier at the next mansio when he would have a horse to exchange. In a day or so, with luck, he could be in Bononia, with his legions, his sorceress and his crown.

The twins had much less luck. They were across a clearing in the forest when they were spotted by an outlaw. He'd heard a stag belling his rutting challenge and had been moving with extreme care to find the creature and shoot it, when the twins came into his view. The ruffian saw their dirtied, expensive clothes and smelled money. What went on in the forest was nobody's business, he thought. He quietly stood two arrows upright in the loam at his feet, then notched a third on his bowstring and drew it back to his ear. The twins never had a chance. The poacher's three-bladed iron broad-head sliced through Mael's throat, dropping him to the ground in a choking gush of blood. Domnal, three paces ahead, turned at the smacking wet sound and stepped back to his fallen brother.

He dropped to his knees, disbelieving the sight, and on an instinct, had half-turned towards the bowman, pointing at him, hand outstretched in a silent motion to stop the death he knew was coming, when the second arrow, swiftly reloaded, struck him in the armpit. The impact knocked him sideways but he struggled to his feet. He was facing the archer when the third arrow hammered into the Briton's eye socket, burst through his brain and left a hand's width of arrowhead and shaft protruding from the back of his skull. He was dead even before he slumped to the ground, where his face, part-buried in the leaf mould, seemed to have a puzzled expression.

The outlaw ran to check the two bodies, and empty their purses. He growled irritably when he found they had almost nothing of value but their clothes and swore to himself at the problem he now had, of recovering his arrow from this fellow's skull.

XXVI. Aemelius

Forum Hadriani was bustling with activity. The Belgic town was crowded, but its shipyard was frantic with activity, with all manner of men bustling, fetching and carrying. There were slaves moving timbers, carpenters sawing and shaping ships' spars and ribs, and ropemakers working in their narrow ropewalks to twist hemp into the long lengths needed to run smooth and unspliced through pulleys and blocks. Smoke billowed where half-naked smiths glistened with sweat as they pumped bellows to blow charcoal to glowing heat and forge red-hot iron into blades and armour, barrel hoops, bolts and nails. Sail makers sat cross-legged like tailors to work their awls or stood over vast tables using cutting tools to shape wide spreads of canvas. Elsewhere, sweating riggers hauled upright then stepped ships' masts, anxious sea captains viewed the progress critically, and list-bearing chandlers bustled to bring equipment and the thousand and one tools and fittings needed to create just one seaworthy vessel.

The warship hulls were especially difficult to build, needing oak-built bows reinforced with bands of iron or brass, and double-planked hulls caulked with linen or animal hair before all was sealed with pitch. Then the whole hull had to be enveloped in lead sheeting carefully nailed with small copper fasteners that would not rust away, and everything, hull building, rigging, provisioning and arming, was done at forced, urgent pace.

The emperor wanted an armada to invade Britain and destroy the stolen fleet, and he wanted it before the winter storms came that would pin his squadrons in harbour for months. He needed hundreds of flat-bottomed invasion barges and he needed to man them. Those thousands of men would require feeding and clothing, and specialist clothing at that. They would require supplies of grain to make bread, and cattle, sheep and pigs to provision them now and after the invasion. It would call for salt, wine and beer, olive oil, fish sauce and fresh greens. The quartermasters demanded iron hoops and staves for the barrels to store those supplies, draft animals to move them, warehouses to store them, and men to tally and guard the food, for the preparations had to be plentiful for a campaign that might take months.

Maximian had his own priorities, of timber and pitch for the ships, steel for the weapons, cordage, leather, wool, canvas and iron for the men, their ships and their tents. The demands were endless. There were barracks and store rooms to be built, latrines to be dug and dumps of food and fuel created. Over it all, the officers had to drill and discipline their men, some of them raw recruits freshly marched in from the corners of the empire, an unpromising lot of untutored yokels awed and gaping at the novel sights, sounds and smells.

So the shipwrights worked frantically, recruits were drilled, stores gathered, barracks built and reinforcements brought in by road and river. A procession of ox carts dragged by lowing cattle trundled into the Forum, some loaded high with grain, others bringing reeking piles of leather from the tanneries downstream. Shepherds mustered a bleating flock destined for the slaughterhouse as a half-legion of auxiliaries from faraway Macedonia, dusty and thirsty from the day's march, tramped into town under the arch and square twin towers of the north gate.

They passed two Thracian shipmasters who eyed their old rivals warily but the mercenaries didn't notice. The soldiers' eyes were searching eagerly under the principal street's cloisters for the taverns and whorehouses they'd visit once the centurion fell them out. The concubine Laurea, wrapped in a russet-hued cloak that owed its colour to dye made from ironstone, watched from a window to assess the officers who marched at the head of the column. Black-bearded, olive-skinned Greeks; she'd heard they all liked boys best, but surely there were some among those handsome men who'd pay for her ash blonde assets, and not just for the dominatrix play-acting, either.

She was tiring of the middle-aged, portly Roman officers who were her chief clients. These Greeks had bodies like gods, she thought. Maybe she could pretend to be a boy? Two houses further along the street, the pederast trader Gracilis, who had returned home from Britain gratefully still in possession of his head, was also assessing the incoming troops. They'd want boys, he thought, it was the Greek disease. There would be profit in them, not like the money he'd made off those slave twins, but good profits nonetheless.

The twins were in Maximian's mind, too. The Augustus had ordered him to bring them in with Carausius, and he hated to fail. All three had vanished. The Briton had escaped him, he knew. His spies in Bononia had reported Carausius' safe return there, along with the upstart's actions in ordering most of his fleet to transfer across the strait to Dover, and his further, lavish spending of coin to recruit more mercenaries. Readying for me, the Caesar thought sourly. He'd need plenty of bullion for that. But those twins? There were no reports of them in Bononia, there had been no sightings of them anywhere and they were not among the dead at the sack of King Mosae's citadel. It was irritating, and he'd have to report failure to the Augustus but he had to focus on having this fleet built, and go through the tedious business of manning it with proper sailors, not Roman mariners who had few real sailing skills. He'd have to scour the slave pens for Greeks and Spaniards and Egyptians, he supposed, and he'd send word to the Roman governors in places like North Africa to find mariners for him. He called for Flavius and gave him some new orders.

Carausius, too, had his headaches. News had come from Britain that the Picts had broken their treaty and were rampaging through the border country, burning and looting, and his stretched-thin forces were having a hard time attempting to contain them. It wasn't much better in Gaul. Maximian's troops had re-taken Rouen and its mint. Fortunately, spies had brought warning to Allectus, who'd decamped by the river just hours before the Romans arrived. He'd had time to empty the mint, loading ingots of bullion and a new supply of coins onto several swift cargo vessels and sailing away, but the city was now lost. In the west, Spanish and Frankish bandits were roaming the land, causing more problems. About the only good news on that front was that the British fleet had managed to get the Narrow Sea's piracy problem mostly under control, so at least the emperor could concentrate his naval forces on readying for the threat from the flotilla Maximian was building.

The Briton had tried a couple of sallies at the shipyards, hoping to destroy the Romans' part-built fleet, but had been driven off by the shore batteries that commanded the entrances. He'd probably have to wait until Maximian sailed, and fight his battles at sea. A bustle at the west gate attracted his attention, and he saw that a courier had arrived on horseback. The news he brought required prompt action. Bandits and a strong force of deserters from Maximian's legions were making major trouble along the coastlands of Gaul. He'd have to confront them before his small garrisons were ousted from the ports, which could lead to losing command of the Narrow Sea. Carausius called for his new aide, Aemilius, who'd once been a young recruit with him. His previous captain, Lycaon was either a slave or rotting on a Belgian crucifix, he supposed, taken captive or killed when King Mosae's citadel fell. He wondered again what had happened to the twins. Probably enslaved once more, or maybe they too were crucifix decorations. Certainly, Maximian wouldn't have been merciful. He sighed at having to deliver the news to their mother, then brought himself back to the present. Aemilius was waiting for orders and the emperor mentally shrugged. There was nothing he could do for his brothers right now, he thought, pragmatically.

Scouts reported that a force of Bagudae bandits were camped with their wagons kraaled in a semi-orderly manner on both sides of a broad river and, to judge by the wagon ruts on either bank of it, they were protecting a ford. The spies reported the bandits at around 600 men, a manageable number for Carausius' two centuries of disciplined troops and squadron of equestrians. The scouts also reported that they'd ridden both upstream and down, but had found no traces of another ford for some miles. The emperor nodded. The bandits probably had some locals in their ranks, and knew what they were doing. Camped as they were, they could use the river as protection if attacked from either direction, simply by retreating across the ford, which would be relatively easy to defend.

Carausius elected to camp for the night where he was, to rest his march-weary men and give him time to survey the killing field for himself. "Set up camp on that hill with quadruple sentries and put outposts there and there," pointing, "so we have no surprises. And, I want a strong guard posted outside each gate." In a few hours, while the emperor rode out to view the enemy, the ditch was dug, the rampart built, the palisade and sentry path were in place and most of the tents had been pitched in the usual places inside the temporary fort. Carausius and his entourage arrived at a low hilltop half a mile from the enemy.

The bandits must have some military leadership, he thought as he viewed their position; the camp was well established. They'd dug some defensive ditches and had circled their supply wagons to provide cover from archers. They didn't seem to have any cavalry, though. Carausius had heard from several drovers brought in by his scouts that the brigands were led by a couple of landowners who'd been crushed by taxes and the theft of their lands by predatory lawmakers in Rome. He thought sourly that they should have sided with him against Rome instead of causing him all this trouble, but whatever their cause, he couldn't tolerate them doing the any more damage.

Axis sniffed at the air and growled; Javelin stiffened. Carausius paid attention to his two big dogs, and scanned the bandit camp to see what had caught their attention. There was a wagon set off by itself and a pack of dogs was chained along a picket line from it. "War dogs, lord," said Aemilius quietly. "They could be a problem." The emperor grunted. The bandits were copying the tactics of the Romans. They liked to break the enemy ranks with half-starved, ferocious fighting dogs.

A favourite technique was to strap a container of burning oil to the leather-clad dog's back and send him into the enemy lines, where he'd especially disrupt the cavalry horses. Or, they'd send in whole attack formations of big mastiffs wearing armour that sprouted sharp blades and knife points. Some dogs were even trained to attack the bellies or hamstrings of horses, to bring down the riders.

The troops hated the dogs, the biggest of which, the Molossian, was supposed to have descended from mastiffs which had mated with tigers. These 'Samson Dogs' needed two or three handlers to hold them, and when one launched itself at an infantryman with its great spiked collar and sharp-bladed ankle rings, the soldier was in real danger of being disembowelled. Carausius nodded at his aide's remark, then turned and unexpectedly grinned at him. "Here's something for you," he said, "that shows the power of learning. Guinevia told me she had read of war dogs in ancient Persia, and she told me of a plan to deal with them. This is what you must do…"

The British emperor's troops stayed in camp for two days. The bandits sent spies to survey them, and the British scouts in turn watched their enemies, reporting that some had melted away during the night but there were still about 500 of the raiders, drinking and preparing their weapons. Carausius inspected the camp with his tribunes Quirinus and Cragus Grabelius, pausing to gesture at a grindstone on which the soldiers were sharpening their blades. "A Persian invention," he said. "You make the wheel spin with that crank. It's faster and gives a better edge than the old greased and sanded strickle stick."

Cragus, who came from Lycia, legendary home of the fire breathing female Chimerae, was making a small joke about the sparks that flew from the blade being sharpened when the trio were accosted by the baggage master. "Caesar," he saluted the emperor, "am I to be responsible for all these scratching mongrels that Aemilius keeps bringing in? I don't know how I can transport them."

Carausius shook his head. "They won't be a problem after tomorrow. Just live with it for now, and keep the flea-ridden things away from my tent. Now, gentlemen," he turned to his tribunes, "let's see how the stores situation is being managed."

The wolf light of a dull dawn had broken, Carausius' troops were formed in battle array, the emperor was in full war gear, and he rode his big Frisian horse down the armoured lines. He wore his golden crown of courage around the eagle-crested cavalryman's parade helmet, a crest he'd once used to break a Saxon warrior's nose, stunning him before administering the fatal sword thrust. This day, Carausius had thrown back his imperial purple cloak, fastened with the massive silver and amber badge of a British warlord, and displayed his gleaming hooped armour. He punched the sky with his sword Exalter to emphasize the words he delivered in a parade ground below.

"I want these bastards ground into offal," he said. "I don't want to have the bother of crucifying them. They're not soldiers, and they don't have proper weapons. It will be like fighting nine year old girls, and you will crush them. When you're ordered, and not before, launch the javelins and the darts. At my command, and in an orderly manner, move forward in wedge formation. Use your shield bosses to knock them down when we get close, then finish them off with your sword. Thrust, don't slash. That's the killing stroke, and remember that the point beats the edge. Above all, keep moving forward. If your man isn't dead, stamp on his dirty black head as you go over him. The next rank will kill him. Stick together in formation, and you're unbeatable. One last thing: we don't stop to plunder. Do this as I tell you, and we will have everything."

He sent the cavalry to the British right wing and detailed the harried Aemilius and the 20 or so slaves who were holding a pack of barking, yelping mongrels off to the left to face the war dogs he could see the bandits had assembled. At his trumpeter's signal, the emperor's infantry knocked their shield edges together and began a steady tramp forward, the heavy scuta forming a moving wall of elm, leather and bronze. At 100 paces or so, as he'd anticipated, the enemy made the first move and released their attack dogs.

Aemilius looked to his emperor, Carausius raised his arm, and the Britons' ragged pack of mongrels was set free. Some ran at the oncoming fighting dogs, others simply stood and scratched, but the effect on the bandits' canine corps was electric. In seconds, the war dogs had diverted their rush and were among the mongrels, snarling and snapping at their own pack-mates as they fought to mount the handful of bitches which were in heat. The emperor's ranks tramped forward, past the humping, scrambling dogs, a ripple of laughter moving through the soldiers. They'd heard the story of the pagan priestess and her plan, and one wit shouted: "Tell Car the Bear that I'd sooner fuck than fight, too!"

The ranks roared, and the raiders' horde, many of whom were half-drunk on honey wine or had heads spinning from the forest mushrooms they'd used to dull their fears, looked on in dismay. Their big attacking plan had been effortlessly frustrated. They muttered in anger and rattled their weapons. Then the soldiers were close, the centurions waved for the missiles to be launched, and the screaming started as the first javelins began thumping down on the unprotected bandits.

Most of the Bagudae were opportunist marauders capable only of taking on unarmed villagers. Lacking proper armour, with few shields, no training and little discipline, they could never successfully face professional soldiers. Not even their superior numbers could save them, and the predictable butchery began.

The weighted javelins came battering in, spearing and pinning the bandits, who howled and flinched away. A wave of movement started on their left side as a group of Gauls began to run for the ford, thinking to put the river between themselves and the bloody ruin they saw approaching. The soldiers came closer, and launched another volley of javelins, piling up Frankish wounded and dead and obstructing the struggling mob. As the infantry got closer yet, they began hurling the heavy darts they carried clipped behind their shields. The retreating marauders seemed to swirl in confusion, uncertain where to turn to escape the deadly missiles. The decisive moment was now.

Carausius' cavalry tribune waved his horsemen forward, and they swept in from the right in two waves, crouched over their horses, long lances levelled, boots dangling, swords still scabbarded and banging at the horses' sides. The first surge crashed into the panicked mass of bandits, parting them like a wagon through a wheat field. The second wave, arriving moments later, brought with them infantry who clung to the cavalrymen's pommels as they raced in. The initial impact of the battle-trained fighting stallions with their slashing hooves and snapping teeth allied to their riders' spears and heavy swords shattered the mob. Then the second wave of foot soldiers crashed onto the panicked Franks like an Atlantic roller pounding on a rocky shoreline. The thumping impact of the infantry shook the marauders' flank and the enveloping attackers cut off their retreat towards the ford. In moments, the action turned into a heaving slaughter.

As the bandits reacted to the flank attack, the shield wall of Carausius' first rank arrived on their front in a wedge array that was shaped like the teeth of a handsaw. The piercing formation let the legionaries penetrate and break the ragged Frankish defences, and the bandits were cut down where they stood, backed up against the river. Lashed by the flail of a blizzard of arrows, forced into shrinking clusters of desperate men by the slashing, stabbing thrusts that came from the pressing shield wall, the Franks could hardly even see to fight as they flinched away from the horrors of death-dealing missiles and swords. The river was streaked pink with skeins of blood by the time the survivors began throwing down their weapons and wading in surrender back to the riverbanks. Soon, the armourers were working with chains, and the ravens were gathering to feast on the dead.

XXVII. Dover

Axis the dog, leg cocked, was marking a stack of red clay roof tiles stamped with the 'CLBR" of the Classis Britannica, the quartermaster's mark for all British Fleet possessions, when Carausius came out of the barracks at Dover. "Good thing I'm the emperor, boy," he grumbled. "That's probably dumb insolence." The emperor was in a good mood. Guinevia was well pregnant and had assured him that the child would be a boy. She had cast rune stones and consulted an oracle, and the omens were excellent. "Caros," she had told him, "this child will be an emperor, too. He will make this nation even greater." A man needed to hear that; a son, and one with a destiny. Life was good. The pity was he was so busy he hardly had time to take it all in. Just look at all this muddle. Building materials were everywhere, he thought, great piles of squared stone, heavy timbers, kiln-fired bricks and corrugated roof tiles. Well, he'd ordered huge construction works done all along the coast, and the troops were getting on with it. It wasn't just roads and bridges, either. Carausius had been pondering the problem of supplying the garrisons along northern frontier, or at least creating a secure, speedy pipeline for heavy supplies, and remembered his youthful days on the great rivers of Europe, and how efficient it was to use waterways. The obvious need was for a river that ran north from Londinium to Eboracum, but they all seemed to run east and west. Then, inspiration struck, and he decided to build a canal. The idea was hardly conceived before he acted, and dispatched a full legion plus three times as many slaves to dig a ditch, a 130 mile canal that would run from Cambridge to Eboracum.

The inland waterway, ironically called the Caros Dyke by diggers who knew the emperor's diminutive name, would supply the legions on the northern frontier. It would be used to transport heavy loads of wool for clothing, leather for shoes, shields and tents, lead and iron for the armourers, oil jars, salt, sacks of corn and barrels of salted beef and pork from the rich agricultural lands of the east and south. All of it would move by barge faster and safer than by it could go by road. It would need a handful of garrisons along the length of the canal to protect the precious cargoes from marauders and thieves, so the cargo barges' first task was to carry building materials, and they were another of the emperor's priorities.

The forts of the Saxon Shore were being rebuilt and reinforced, too, because Carausius knew that Maximian, just a score of miles away across the narrows, was progressing with his plans. The junior Caesar's fleet was nearly ready, and spies reported that he had been moving troops to the coast between Ostend and Bononia, readying them for invasion. The British fleet would have to stop them at sea, and Carausius was confident it was up to the task. Years of fighting piracy in the waters around Britain had given him a skilled, toughened navy. He knew that Maximian needed a covering fleet to protect his invasion barges, and he knew too that his old enemy had a weakness. He was blinded by hatred of the Briton and would not wait a moment longer than he must before attacking, even if it was not the cautious option. Maximian would know he could not face the British fleet ship for ship, but he would likely gamble on a swift crossing before the defenders' squadrons could be brought into play. Carausius, however, had spent gold generously to monitor Maximian's movements and was sure that he would have full warning from his spies of the emperor's moves. There would be no surprise.

The British ships, not the chalk ramparts of the southern sea cliffs, were the nation's best defensive walls. So long as they were in place, they would dominate the Narrow Sea. Rome, Carausius knew, could not overcome his wooden walls, but it would not hurt to make a pre-emptive strike before any invader got close to the beaches under the white cliffs. That needed planning. Also to be considered was the matter of the devious Picts, who had treacherously broken their treaties after taking his silver. They'd long since crossed Antoninus' wall, now they were in the buffer state, the land of the Four Kingdoms between the walls and threatened to breach Hadrian's more southerly defences, too. Carausius had ordered troops mustered at Eboracum to prepare for a campaign against the northern raiders and was wondering if he could stretch his naval reserves enough to send an expedition up there to provide seaborne support. He felt he had a breathing space before he needed to face Maximian, as he knew the Roman was not yet ready for him, and he had a plan to set back that individual's invasion timetable even more.

Tomorrow, he'd begin the journey to Eboracum, get the legions organized himself and take them, under the sacred Eagle standards, to bring the Picts to heel. Get boots on the ground, he thought, it was necessary to mount another campaign to secure a kingdom. While he was up there, the tribunes Quirinus and Cragus would lead a surprise strike across the Narrow Sea against Maximian's fleet.

Similar thoughts of aggression were in Maximian's mind. His shipbuilding program was moving along well, and almost too quickly. He had been forced to move a number of finished transports away from the crowded quays at Forum Hadriani because he needed the dock space. He'd started sending the vessels west a short distance to an anchorage in the outfall of the Scheldt river, using only skeleton crews because of his shortage of trained sailors. He mentally cursed Carausius again for stealing the whole damned British fleet and its valuable sailors, it was a setback to be overcome, and even if, during the invasion, he used only a handful of mariners on each loaded troopship to work the vessels across the straits, he still didn't have enough trained sailors.

So, he had to wait a while longer, until troop transporters from Rome could bring him some skilled mariners, Phoenicians and Egyptians, most likely, who should have been recruited in answer to his missives back to Milan.

For now, Maximian's newly-built invasion barges and their skeleton crews were using the summer's fair weather to creep under their short sails down the Belgic coast and into haven in the estuary of the big river Scheldt. A temporary sail makers' loft and makeshift shipyard was operating there, fitting cordage and doing all the dozens of commissioning jobs that a new ship needed.

There were other things, though. With all the distractions of equipping an invasion force, it was understandable that Maximian had overlooked a few details, and the junior officers who'd noticed them were too afraid of his savage temper to bring up the matter. Maybe he'd decided things should be run this way, they told each other, best not to irritate the boss by questioning his actions. They told each other how, only a week ago he'd found that a slave had stolen one of the Caesar's imported Syrian figs. Maximian's response was to spear another fig on the end of his sword, force it between the man's teeth and order him to eat it. As the trembling slave bit down on the fruit, the emperor thrust the blade deep into the back of his throat. The man took ten minutes to die, choking and drowning in his own blood. Maximian ordered the fig to be retrieved and nailed to the wall of his palace kitchen. "Better than a notice to the others," he grunted, handing his sword to a slave to be cleaned.

The message was not lost on the several troopers who saw that the new fleet anchored in the Scheldt was guarded only by soldiers on the river banks and a few watchmen on the vessels themselves. A waterborne attack would leave the land soldiers as mere spectators. Who'd tell the bad-tempered emperor? Not our job to incur the boss' wrath, the legionaries muttered to each other. Let the Ruperts tell him, they get paid for it, it's their responsibility. But the Ruperts didn't notice.

Spies brought the news of the vulnerable fleet to Quirinus when he sailed into Bononia from Dover, and he acted quickly. By morning, he had mustered six of the nimble, 30 ft. sailboats the army used on the bigger rivers, and tied them off, a pair to each trireme, to be towed up the coast. Taking an idea from the great Julius, who'd employed the technique when he sent scout vessels to spy out Britain before his invasion, he ordered the ships, their rigging, masts and sails to be painted sea-green. Even the crews were ordered to wear green clothing and to smear their faces, too, camouflaging themselves as well as their ships. The slopped-on paint was hardly dry before they set sail at dusk, towing the still-tacky fire ships, which had been the last to be painted.

The convoy made good time with the easterly flood of the Atlanticus and, near-invisible and unchallenged, were off the mouth of the Scheldt before the first of the wolf light. Then the sailors began to carry out the careful instructions they had been given, instructions that had been repeated until their officers were convinced they were understood. First, they sluiced inside the fire ships' hulls with a highly-flammable distillation of pitch called Greek Fire. Next, they unwrapped lanolin-soaked wool and bundles of kindling that had been covered to keep them dry, and spread them along the length of the keel. When that was done, they stretched canvas tightly from gunwale to gunwale to cover it everything. Last, they poured oil over the sheets, which they kept furled, as the sailboats were being towed under bare poles.

Quirinus stood the ships in as the gloom lifted. In the minutes while they closed on the new fleet that was anchored and lashed together just off the main channel, he ordered the six river boats' oil-soaked sails hoisted to catch the breeze off the sea. The gleaming new wood of the anchored invasion barges showed clearly through the dawn gloom. Flames flared on the raiders' ships as sailors lashed the steerboards in place, lit the canvas-covered fuel, and scrambled overboard to swim back to the triremes, which stayed cautiously upwind. The fire ship squadron were carried in on the tide, pushed by the breeze, and sailed like ghosts, the flames in their bellies not yet burned through the covering canvas. When it did, the breeze fanned the flames quickly, they licked upwards with hunger, the sails caught, and moments later the fire ships were jostling the anchored fleet where a few drowsy watchmen were stumbling to find bailing pans to splash seawater on the fires.

It was all too little, too late. One fire ship wedged itself between the bows of a tethered pair of transport barges, and the fire spread at the speed of a cantering horse. Other blazing vessels scraped down the clean new wooden sides of the targets, dropping deadly embers and tangling their blazing spars with the anchored barges' rigging. A fire ship was caught in a line of wicker fish traps and stayed fast, a blazing beacon that illuminated the scene.

One enterprising watchman found an axe and used it to chop the anchor ropes free on several tethered ships, but they simply drifted into the same long line of fish traps alongside the blazing fire ship blazed and were engulfed. From the shore, alarmed legionaries shouted and ineffectively fired arrows, until two small rowboats filled with archers pulled out to challenge the raiders. Quirinus ordered his trireme to row straight at them, and crushed one under his vessel's iron-clad forefoot. The other hastily turned back to shore. On the smooth waters that mirrored the blazing destruction, there was no real resistance possible. Within an hour, when the retreating triremes had rounded the low Belgic shoreline, entered the open sea and caught the ebb tide west, most of Rome's newest fleet had burned to the waterline and sunk, or was turned into beached, charred and ruined wrecks.

The raid had its effects. Maximian was incensed and had two prefects executed for failing to protect his lost ships. The Saxons on the Rhine were cheered and began a new series of harassments that diverted the Caesar into retaliatory actions that cost him dearly when half a legion was isolated by the enemy and froze to death in a sudden winter storm. And the garrison in Bononia received an unexpected legation.

The tribune Quirinus was at his writing table when the guard saluted and announced that there were visitors, lord. Probably they were local aldermen, the soldier thought, and they were waiting in the courtyard. The tribune assumed it was a local magistrate and deputation come to complain that the men had stolen chickens again, and impatiently told the man to show them in. Instead, three Gallic chieftains strode into the chamber.

Briefly, they wanted a truce. They had, they indicated when a suitable interpreter could be fetched, been interested to hear that these soldiers of the emperor had destroyed the ships of those soldiers of the other emperor, his brother. One of the splendidly-moustached Gauls produced a coin to support what he said. 'Carausius and his Brothers' was the abbreviated legend over the images of the Briton, Diocletian and Maximian.

"Family squabble," said Quirinus hurriedly. "All is well. In fact," he had an inspiration, 'look at this." He rummaged through his purse to find another of his emperor's recent mintings. "Rome Renewed," said the legend on the coin he handed to the puzzled chieftains. "It's a new age of Saturn," he explained to them. "Says it right here. The bad, old Rome is gone. The brother emperors are all in agreement, and they are changing the ways people have been treated. This will be a time of cooperation, prosperity, that sort of thing."

Quirinus glanced around. The propaganda seemed to have been accepted at face value. He called his servant to bring some of that very good Rhenish wine, several flagons of it, and quickly. The chieftains looked at each other warily. They had received news of the slaughter of the bandits, they acknowledged. It was better for all, they said, if the brigandage was stopped. Now that they could see that Rome was having a change of heart, and the great Carausius was strong enough even to chastise his brother emperors, they would order a halt to the raids that reprehensible elements from Spain and Brittany had been conducting. Gaul would have peace, at least until the spring, if the legate agreed? The four men drank to the new order, and to peace. Quirinus sighed inwardly, relieved. The dispatch to his emperor arrived in Eboracum within five days. Carausius already knew of the damage to Maximian's fleet, now he heard with pleasure and some surprise mixed with scepticism that Gaul would be quiet while he turned his attention north to put down those treacherous Picts.

XXVIII. Stirling

Hadrian's famous Wall was Rome's only stone frontier, and ran 74 miles from sea to sea, but for all of its short-lived useful life it was never intended to keep the Picts out, merely to deter raiders and control and tax travellers. The rampart that formed the spiritual and physical northern boundary of the empire began as a series of 15 forts that were gradually, through the efforts of three legions and part of the British fleet, linked by a high battlement right across the country. It was originally called 'The Aelian Rampart' after the Spaniard Hadrian's family name, for he was properly called Publius Aelius Hadrianus and was heir to a fortune made from the clan's Iberian olive groves. The family was important and influential enough that the emperor Trajan himself had been Hadrian's guardian.

Publius Aelius Hadrianus' Wall stretched from the bridge named for him – Pons Aelius – in the east to Bowness, on the Solway Firth in the west, the latter short stretch made of turf and timber, not stone, but all of it boasted watchtowers every one-third of a mile, with fortified, manned gateways at every mile or so. The rampart itself was 15 Roman feet high, ten feet wide for much of its length and sat behind a wide berm that had forward of it a deep defensive ditch. Where possible, the builders used local landscape features to make it more formidable, building it, for example, along the crest of a ridge. When the legions had finished building the Wall itself, they turned their attention to the land south of it, and dug a parallel, 20 feet wide flat-bottomed ditch with earth ramparts on either side, to protect the rear and create a zone controlled by the military. In its glory, it was a wonder of the world. When Carausius came to inspect it, however, the legendary frontier barrier once simply called The Entrenchment was in a sorry, neglected state.

"We just don't have enough soldiers to man the whole thing properly, lord," a harried cavalry commander told the emperor. "The fact is, the Wall was mostly abandoned after only a handful of years, when Antoninus built another wall of turf and timber about 100 miles further north of here. We did return to this as the frontier after a while, but it's never really been a proper military fortification, more a customs barrier." The emperor, standing in the wooden gateway of a mile-castle, could see for himself the outlines in the ground where a onetime fortification had been dismantled, the stone and timber removed for use elsewhere and the ground sealed with a layer of clean clay and turf, ready for rebuilding. Standard Operating Procedure, he thought. Army orders were that nothing was to be left for the enemy to use. He turned back to the equestrian. "We're going north, beyond the Antonine, so we'll take a look what's there. I don't suppose there's much."

Two weeks later, Carausius found he was right. Antoninus' timber palisade had gone, rotted into the ground in the two centuries since it had been abandoned and the turf walls had crumbled into the ditch. About all that was left were some gently-sloping old excavations with trees growing out of them. A grown man would hardly break stride as he crossed the onetime barrier that marked the high tide line of Roman conquest. Nothing here to use, thought the emperor, tapping his horse's sides to move on, and glancing across to the raeda carriage where his mistress Guinevia and a wet-nurse tended his baby son. Carausius smiled to himself. She was so excited to be travelling back to her homeland, and to be taking their son Milo to meet his grandfather. Not many soldiers made a military expedition a family outing, he chuckled to himself. Well, I'm the emperor, and she's my best advisor. So be it.

The legion continued its march north behind its sacred gilded Eagle, along the old road of Dere Street, which was in fine condition even after a century without maintenance. The troops crossed the Forth River and turned north to the huge dolerite crag that outcropped steeply from the plain at Stirling. The old Romans had built a strongpoint there, on the site of a hill fort so ancient it had probably been built by the gods.

A temple of good, square Roman stone still stood there, the structure intact, roof a little damaged, the floor inches deep in animal droppings where it had been used as a byre. Its inscriptions showed it had been dedicated to Mithras, the legionaries' god who was born from rock, so Guinevia, a pagan sorceress who had daily been growing more animated as they marched deeper into her native land, insisted on making sacrifice in the old place of worship. It was, she explained, a site of ancient magic, a perfect place to consult the auguries for the coming campaign. All she would need was a day or two to purify it first, and as she was in her homeland, the gods would hear her voice. The emperor shrugged. He and most of his legionaries worshipped Mithras. It was appropriate. He ordered detachments down into the plain and woods to forage for fresh beef and venison, and decided to spend a week or two on the natural fortification of the great rock while he sent out scouts in search of enemy war bands.

Inside the temple, shafts of sunlight that fell through broken roof tiles dramatically illuminated the stone altar which Guinevia had readied for the ceremony. She had overseen a work party of legionaries eager to clean up the old temple to their god, and the restoration had gone well. Under the dung that had padded the floor, a wonderful mosaic was revealed, an image of the sacrifice of a bull. In it, as a radiant-haloed Sol looked on, Mithras in his Phrygian cap was pulling back the head of a bull with one hand while thrusting his dagger into its throat with the other. Relatively undamaged, the floor's black and white image glinted in the shafts of Sol-sent light, as did the bronze of an incense burner and a drinking horn on the altar. Beside them, a small silver bowl held sacred mushrooms and a glass flask stoppered with a pine cone contained the wine that would substitute for the blood of a sacrificed bull.

Carausius and a congregation of soldiers listened respectfully while Guinevia called on her witch goddess Nicevenn to witness, and she dedicated the sacrifice to Mithras, asking him to observe that they had re-purified his temple as true believers. From somewhere, a small cloud of vapour had gathered under the arch of the broken roof. Guinevia looked up at it and smiled, and the congregants who noticed shuddered, and made protective signs. The priestess walked to the side wall of the temple, where soldiers had brought in three Picts as possible offerings.

Two of the captives were miserable dark creatures taken as they herded some scrawny brown sheep and she dismissed them as unsuitable. The third, a gross-bellied mule trader called Leoni, a man with an oversized bald head and large teeth, was more acceptable. She gestured at him. The soldiers quickly stripped away his coarse blue striped wool gown, bound his hands before him with a length of leather and pushed him towards the altar. Sixty or more legionaries crowded around in a rough circle.

Guinevia motioned to a bearded centurion who was the pater, or head, of the legion's Mithraic devotees. As a woman, she could not belong to the cult, so would not make the sacrifice, but she could read the auguries, and her role as a priestess fitted her to conduct the ceremony. The centurion stepped forward with a slender-bladed skinning knife half-hidden at his side and looked again at the priestess. She caught his gaze and nodded. The pater moved quietly, almost humbly towards Leoni. The muleteer, dazed and nervous had no warning of what was to come, and the pater looked into the prisoner's eyes. Leoni blinked stupidly in the centurion's almost-hypnotic gaze and never saw the man's movement as he punched the knife forward, then across. The soldier drew the knife steadily, unhurriedly from right to left in a long slash across the muleteer's gross white belly. Leoni's mouth opened in an O of shock and he looked down as a blue-green spill of guts cascaded to his knees. He stooped, clutching the slippery, warm intestines with his bound hands, then whimpered and looked up at the unmoving, impassive centurion almost questioningly.

A little blood flowed over the backs of the fat man's hands. Then the prisoner was on his knees, weakly trying to scoop up his steaming entrails. The soldier looked again at Guinevia. She nodded. As gently as a lover, the big centurion leaned forward and jabbed the knife carefully under the man's jaw, into the left carotid artery. Suddenly, there was blood. Bright, oxygenated arterial blood, it spurted in a thin jet, pulsing with the man's pounding heartbeat, then sheeted over his bare shoulder and chest. The victim somehow staggered to his feet, his bluish guts flopping and trailing, his bound hands clutching at the side of his neck where the blade had entered. He took three paces, weaving like a drunk, stumbled and sank slowly to his knees.

For the first time, he spoke, breaking the silence that had gripped everyone in the old temple since Guinevia uttered her incantations. "I'll tell Mother," he said thickly. It was all anyone said, then, as the sacrificed Leoni died, he mewed like a cat. Several legionaries sniggered, drawing reproving looks from the pater. High above the sorceress' head, unnoticed, the vapour cloud seemed to pulse with a dim light several times, then dissipated.

Guinevia waved the circle of soldiers back and carefully studied the blood trail and spatters across the cleared stone floor. She approached the dead man, who was facedown, and motioned again, still silent, to the centurion. He eased his foot under the bloated body and tipped it onto its back. The corpse gave off a death rattle as trapped air exited the body.

Guinevia leaned in to examine the man's spilled guts, and glanced briefly at the fatted heart and enlarged liver. She looked more closely at the lungs, which were marbled grey and crimson, and surveyed the small bag of the stomach, which was fairly full of what looked like cabbage and greyish meat. The entrails made a repulsive, still-steaming snake that flowed from the corpse. Nobody spoke. Carausius found he was holding his breath. The priestess moved lightly around to the other side of the body, mindless of the puddling blood that wet the hem of her robe, and examined the man's open eyes. She straightened up, looked across the corpse at Carausius, smiled and said: "The auguries, great Caesar, are good. The gods are with you." As the soldiers roared their relief and approval, a white rat moved slowly across the rear of the temple.

A week later, Carausius remembered those auguries and their interpretation sourly. The gods were with him? His situation, it seemed, could not be much worse. He was tied by the wrists to the tail of his own horse, being dragged like a slave. Every so often, the rider above him would turn and spit, or slash him across the face with the willow withy he carried. Around them was a war band of Pictish raiders who were driving along four other prisoners, one of them his aide Aemilius. Four more of their hunting party lay dead and mutilated in the woods a few miles back. The gods, the captive emperor thought, had turned their backs, and it had all happened, as these things do, very quickly.

It was only a couple of hours since Carausius had opted to go and hunt deer or wild boar. His scouts were still out somewhere, the men were enjoying a make-and-mend day, he'd heard a stag belling in the distant wood and thought some fresh venison, or even hare or pork would be welcome. Hunting was a good thing for soldiers, a training session as well as a welcome means of filling the larder. It kept horse and rider in good shape, built camaraderie and trust in the spearman alongside you and taught the party to work together. The group was in high spirits as they rode, although they had not yet sighted any game. Aemilius was riding alongside his emperor as they trotted through a small wooded ravine. He was telling a convoluted story of waking up thick-headed in the bed of the wife of a man who'd come seeking trade with the military when the forest around them exploded into an ambush. The volley of spears and arrows put six of the nine riders on the ground in the first moments, and when the Pict war band emerged howling from the trees, Carausius remembered bitterly, things had gone from bad to worse.

His warhorse Ranter had stepped in a rabbit hole and stumbled, throwing the emperor clumsily into Aemilius, who was right alongside him. Both men had fallen and suddenly only one of their party was in position to put up a defence. He died almost at once, with two short, thick boar spears through his chest. The Picts clubbed Carausius senseless as he scrambled to his feet and tried to fight, and when he came to consciousness he was bound and helpless. The Picts had disarmed and robbed the five survivors, finished off the badly wounded of the hunters and plundered and mutilated their bodies. They gathered up the spoils and the prisoners, then goaded them to their best speed away from the military camp and its likely patrols. The hapless Britons were driven like animals, whipped and threatened if they lagged, forced to a gruelling pace. It was a long day, and dusk was falling when the weary captives sighted the fires by the Roman bridge over the Tay river.

Under guttering rush lights in the timbered hall that was the residence of the chieftain, a Pict named Calderian waited. His thumbprint, Carausius knew, was on the broken treaty the Caledonians had agreed with him. The Pict looked at the emperor with interest. Carausius, his face striped purple from the lashes he'd received, stared back at the traitor and anger overwhelmed him. "You agreed a treaty with me; you are not man enough to keep your word. One day, I shall cut out your tongue."

Calderian shot back: "That was no treaty, there was no agreement!" The big man gestured his bound hands, imposing a moment's silence on his captor. "Listening to you speak, hearing your falsehoods, is like watching a snake eat its own vomit," he rumbled, but the Pict, his pale face flushed, cut him off.

"You are a caged Bear now, and you will dance to my tune. You were foolish to invade my land," he gritted. "For that foolishness, and for your upstart insolence, I shall make an example of you. Beheading is too easy. I shall have you drowned in the cauldron tomorrow as we feast and watch." He turned aside, signalling for the prisoners to be taken away.

The Britons were held, chained and under guard, in a stone and thatch structure oddly similar to that in which the emperor had lived as a boy. He remembered his escape out of that hut from the sea raiders and assessed his chances this time. Not too good, he thought. As he lay down to rest, uncomfortable in his irons, he wondered what had happened to his hounds Axis and Javelin, who that morning had run alongside the hunters' horses. Now it seemed a lifetime ago. He asked Aemilius, who told him he'd seen the dogs slinking behind 'like wolves, lord,' as the captives were dragged towards the Tay. With that news, the emperor settled down to doze. He was bruised, exhausted and hungry but somehow comforted.

Next morning, Guinevia, waking in her father's compound, was the first of Carausius' company to learn what had happened, but it came as no great shock. She had slept fitfully and knew the gods had a message for her, but she was curiously calm. Matters were bad, but they would be remedied, she knew. As the sun took the mist from the fields, a clansman came to her sleeping quarters at to summon her. She took her baby son to the wet nurse and walked calmly across the cobbled yard. The old chieftain, who had heard the news from two clansmen, who had seen the troop of captives pass and had followed their tracks back to the killing ground, was thoughtful when he relayed the news to his daughter.

"You are not just his lover, you managed that treaty," he reminded her. "If the ones who broke it are fearful of your master's vengeance, they might seek to kill you." Guinevia was dismissive of the idea. "I am a Druid, adept of the witch goddess. I was trained by the sorcerer Myrddin," she reminded him. "I have the power of rivers and mountains and I have wielded the iron sickle to cut mistletoe. They will not dare to touch me."

She dispatched two slaves by pony to Stirling, with a missive reporting the emperor's capture, and set out with her guards for Bertha, the onetime Roman camp, now the village where treacherous Calderian ruled. She arrived in time to see the last minutes of Aemilius' lingering death. The Picts had fastened him in a green wicker cage roughly shaped like a man, then hung it on a chain over a fire. The unfortunate Roman roasted to death, moaning, soon after his hair and eyelids had burned away. The dashing young centurion Crassus, who was noted for his luck at both women and dice, died next; his chest crushed under great stones that the painted savages piled onto him.

Guinevia hid her horror and remained impassive and outwardly calm, as she waited for Calderian to emerge from his sleeping quarters. Carausius, she knew, would not be killed until the chieftain was present. It was afternoon before he emerged, pallid and yawning. He registered the sorceress' presence and was alarmed, but walked to her and inclined his head. "It is an honour to have you here for the ceremony, mother," he said.

"Ceremony?" Guinevia snapped. "This to me looks like foul butchery. There is no honour to the gods in this."

Calderian hesitated, reconsidering his defiance, then stiffened his resolve and ordered the emperor brought out. "I shall kill your emperor myself," he said. "We shall see about the gods."

XXIX. Selsey

Search parties had gone out at dusk when the emperor had failed to return from the hunt and the camp was disturbed all night with the comings and goings of horsemen. The tribune Cragus feared the worst, and found it soon after dawn. A patrol was drawn by the circling, cawing ravens to the mutilated bodies of their comrades, but the soldiers realized that the emperor and several others were not among the dead. Cragus deduced that Carausius had been taken prisoner, so ordered a dozen detachments to sweep the countryside. He detailed one squadron to head directly and with all speed to the next major settlement, at Perth. Those horsemen met the mounted slaves hurrying with their dispatch to Stirling. When he heard of their mission, the prefect in charge had the initiative to open the package and read Guinevia's message. He ordered two cavalrymen and one of the slaves to continue to the camp at Stirling with Guinevia's note and scribbled his own report for them to deliver, detailing his plans. He would ride to rescue Carausius, who was likely at the old Roman camp at Bertha. He indicated that he was taking a guide, and sending the other with the note to bring reinforcements to him. With Guinevia's slave showing the way, he pushed his column forward at a steady hand-gallop.

Three burly guards forced Carausius out of the hut at spear-point and pushed him to kneel in front of Calderian. The Pict walked around him and noticed the fine, nailed boots he wore. "Take those from him," he ordered. As the marching boots came off, he saw the Briton's mutilated foot where a Saxon's sword had hacked off two of his toes. He laughed. "We can even that up for you," he sneered, drawing his own blade.

Guinevia stepped forward. "If you harm him, I will call on the witch goddess Nicevenn to curse you," she said calmly. "She will turn your eyes into suppurating pools of pus and your lying, false tongue into corpse marrow. Turning on the guards she continued. "Touch him, and you and your shrivelled souls will be the playthings of Rodak, the hideous boar goblin of the Underworld, and you will spend your agonized eternity howling and crying for mercy as you thrash in molten iron and sulphur."

The guards, turning pale at the threats to their souls, backed away, making the sign against the evil eye but Calderian, though nervous, would not accept such a total loss of face. He half turned away, then suddenly swung his sword, chopping down into Carausius' unguarded ankle. The Briton yelled in agony and rolled sideways. Guinevia grasped at the Pict's sword arm, but he pushed her away and turned to hack again at the prone captive. Before he could strike, two grey-black blurs raced across the packed dirt of the courtyard and flattened themselves growling, fangs bared, in front of the Pict.

Carausius, trying to rise, saw his dogs face Calderian. He did not hesitate. "Axis, Javelin!" he shouted, gesturing a hand to his chin. The dogs saw the familiar silent hunting sign to which they'd been trained, and stayed crouched and quivering for the release. The Pict saw his death in their menace but was frozen motionless. Carausius gestured again, a chopping motion, and the big dogs leaped simultaneously in a deadly choreograph of attack.

Their bodies knocked Calderian backwards, jarring his sword loose. Even before his shoulders hit the ground, two sets of great jaws were tearing into him. One had his windpipe, the other's teeth clashed against the Pict's, tearing his gums as the dog seized his lower jaw. The hounds shook the man like a rat, flopping his head wildly as they savaged him. The teeth of the first closed through Calderian's trachea and larynx, ripping out his whole voice box and pulling it away in a froth of blood and saliva. The other dog, growling as it braced its paws for leverage against the man's chest, tore his jaw half away, leaving the Pict choking in his own lifeblood, helpless and so shocked he was unable even to raise his arms in defence.

Deep-chested rumbling growls came from both dogs as they harried the dying man, and changed the targets of their savage, flesh-ripping attacks. Axis tore into Calderian's groin, Javelin, foaming blood and spume, shook him violently by the nape, breaking his neck. The man had no voice even to whimper as his lifeblood pooled out steaming onto the packed dirt of the compound. Carausius lay nearby, propped on one elbow. He watched impassive, silent as his terrible hounds worried the mutilated Pict for a minute or so longer, then whistled sharply, three piercing notes, and called them off.

The prefect at the head of the column that galloped into the settlement could scarcely take in the sight. His emperor was propped against the wall of a hut, his foot wrapped in a gory cloak. Two blood-splashed, mottled grey dogs crouched protectively by him, snarling ferociously at any movement. Nearby a dead man with only half a face and a torn-apart crotch lay slumped on his side in a puddle of congealing blood, his head at an odd angle. Standing over the corpse and facing a dozen mesmerized, unmoving Pictish brigands, was a woman in an otter fur cloak that trailed blood from its lowest hem.

Over the woman's head at the height of two men was a small vapour cloud that had mysteriously formed in the grey morning. Her arm was outstretched, her forefinger, on which a silver pentagram ring glowed in the poor light, was pointing at each of the transfixed men in turn. She was keening in the Latin and British tongues, invoking the names of the pagan witches and demons from the deps of hell, who would seize them and theirs if they moved even a single step.

She chanted of her witch goddess Nicevenn, leader of the Wild Hunt that roamed the world with its hounds from Hell on Samhain, the night of the dead. She threatened the shaking, terrified Picts, chanting in a hypnotic and remorseless drone how she and her Druid powers would send them to flee in terror alongside Nicevenn's damned down the long, black slopes of eternity. Their bodies would be so foul, she promised, that even Sterculius, Roman god of sewage would turn aside in disgust, and their eyes would liquify into pools of corruption at the very moment they turned to watch his rejection. She used the eloquence of her god Ogmia to shackle with brutal chains of words. She held her shaken listeners attentive and captive and her emperor safe from their swords with the awful power of her threats until the troops arrived. The drone went on as the prefect dismounted to stand by his commander, and the British troops circled around the Picts to herd them at sword-point. Only then did Guinevia fall silent, lower her accusatory outstretched arm and bow her head in relief. And nobody heard as she smiled to herself and murmured, "I don't think the Jesus-botherers can do that."

The wounded Carausius was taken to safety, the legions tramped out into the glens of Caledonia and the tribune Cragus conducted a textbook campaign. He destroyed the Picts' army, their crops, their huts and their morale, all in a matter of months. He cleared the region between the walls of Hadrian and Antoninus with flying columns of cavalry that surprised and defeated the wandering warbands. He encircled the rocky strongpoint of the Votadini that controlled the Forth valley, expecting to conduct a long siege of the steep-sided stronghold, but the resistance melted away after a lucky shot from a ballista toppled the Votadini king, Alpin from a high wall. Cragus took the fortress' surrender, lined the cliff with burdened crucifixes and moved next to crush the Damnoni tribesmen who had gathered to the west. Then he turned north against the greater body of their kin, who were encamped behind the presumed safety of the estuary.

Cragus remembered his history, and how the legions had conquered the wide Thames river at Londinium with a pontoon bridge. Under cover first of darkness and then of the morning's sea fog, he constructed a floating highway from lashed-together fishing vessels to cross the wide waters. The bridge and the fog allowed him to evade the eyes of Damnoni scouts who watched the upstream crossings, and his force arrived unsuspected on the clan's eastern flank. The battle to which he brought them effectively ended after the Picts' initial berserk charge was broken on the curved shields and long spears of the legion's front rank. Their impetus spent, the tribesmen backed away and Cragus waved his veterans to step forward, stamping, chopping and thrusting in mechanical precision as they wreaked bloody ruin on the rabble. Cragus herded hundreds of captives into the slave pens and marched east and north along the line of old Roman forts to roll up the rest of the resistance. He left behind him a wasteland of scorched earth, plundered crops and ruined hamlets and brought back another procession of manacled slaves.

All the while, Carausius was immobilized, recovering from the ankle wound he'd received from the treacherous Calderian. The sword had cut deep, but the tendons seemed to have survived. British military medics had washed the wound carefully in vinegar, sewed it up and splinted and immobilized the joint. The emperor instructed them to do what the pharmacist Campana had done for his facial and foot injuries in the hospital in Mainz. She had applied henbane and poppy seed to the wounds, cleaned them daily with sour wine, hyssop and comfrey and re-bandaged them daily in fresh linen. "I came out of that without infection," he told his medics, rubbing his scarred cheek. "Do the same now, I don't want my flesh to rot, I want to keep my leg." The treatments worked and within a month, although unable to walk without pain, the emperor was in a raeda carriage trundling south, first to Colchester, then on to coastal Fishbourne where he wanted to meet his staff and supervise the reinforcement of the Saxon Shore defences.

Couriers sailed daily across the narrows from Gaul or rode from the corners of Britain to Carausius' palace, bringing intelligence from the mainland and from the line of garrisons that guarded the southern and eastern ramparts of his empire. His well-rewarded spies along the Rhine and Scheldt rivers also told him of the progress Maximian was making, rebuilding his burned fleet, and the Briton knew that another naval crisis and invasion was brewing. But, for all his concerns, he made time to take pleasure in the great palace, where the artisans he had brought to work there were moving ahead.

The mosaic artist Claria had been joined by a dark-haired Carthaginian astrologer, Cinea Carbonia, whose task was to create a detailed star chart that would be set in the tiny tiles to show the heavens just as they were on the night Carausius was born. On the walls above the mosaic, fresh murals displayed scenes from his life and career. Among them were painted images of his golden crown of courage, his recovery of the legion's Eagle and his imperial wreath. The artist was careful too, to leave space for the triumphs still to come, and like a good courtier, diligently mentioned that plan and the plentiful spaces to the emperor.

The forward planning was intelligent. The emperor of Britain was preparing to create new triumphs, and therefore was a frequent presence around the shipyards of Dover and Portus Magnus, where he was overseeing modifications to his refitted fleet. The shipmaster Cenhud had given the emperor some ideas, and he wanted them implemented. "The Romans are largely building ships of the kind they use in the Inland Sea, lord," Cenhud explained. "They are useful in rivers like the Rhine, because they are nimble. They are also much easier to build, but they are not such effective sea-going warships as the Gaulish vessels we use."

The difference, the old shipmaster explained, was in the way the Gauls built their ships. They used oak frames and nailed the planking of the hull to them carvel-style, butting the edges together to make a strong, smooth-sided vessel that was not stiff or brittle but would flex enough to survive in bad seas. The planking finished, they caulked the seams, hammering fibrous material like cattle hair between the heavy timbers. It was a longer process than the lap-straked, or clinker-built vessels the Romans built, where each plank of the hull overlapped the next. That made for an easier build, and the clinkered ships were lighter and more nimble but they were also weaker, and did not do as well in heavy weather, flexing overmuch in heavy seas.

Another vital difference was in the materials. Because of the strength of the Gauls' ribbed ships, the hull planking could be heavy oak that was much stronger than the lighter pine boards used in the clinker-built boats. "Clinkered pine or cedar, Caros, is fine for small boats. Warships need oak, and oak bound in iron at that, better for ramming enemy vessels," the shipmaster concluded. That, thought Carausius grimly, was where the great land general Maximian would learn a hard lesson from the seagoing Britons. He went back to the shipyards, hobbling but mobile, and supervised certain changes to the ships of his fleet.

Maximian did not have the efficient spy network of his rival, so was unaware of Carausius' actions. The Roman had moved forward impatiently with his ship building efforts, and ridden his men hard. Now, he judged he was ready for the invasion and recapture of Britain and ordered his fleet to sail from Gaul.

The Roman had brought his newly-built troop barges down from Forum Hadriani. Eager to start, and champing at the bit after an eleven-day delay caused by foul weather, he had ignored his mariners' advice and seized on a brief window between the storms to launch his invasion. He'd taken on troops along the Belgic coast and intended when he left the staging area off Ostend to sail northwest, weathering northerly around the south eastern tip of the British coast and into the mouth of the Thames river. His swift attack would plunge arrow-straight for the capital. Nothing could go wrong and Maximian gloated at the thought of seeing Carausius' death.

The triremes that headed the Roman's armada made a brave sight as they entered the Gallic Strait and moved northeast against its fast-flowing ebb tide. Triple-banked oars under the blue sails dipped and swayed in rhythm, the tap of the hammer or sound of the horn that kept the rowers synchronized carried through the blustering wind, and the glint of the soldiers' polished armour caught the rays of the watery sun. But all was not going well. The nasty northerly wind and high spring tides combined to wreck Maximian's plan. The near-gale that rose unexpectedly quickly joined with seasonal strong currents to send a great salt river racing westwards. The German Sea poured out like a wall of water from a breached dam. It raced around headlands and churned up vast ridges of white-foamed waves as it forced itself into the narrows of the strait before racing to its spreading release in the wide Atlanticus.

Maximian's bigger ships could cope with crossing such powerful elements, but his more fragile, unhandy and flat-bottomed troop barges should never have put out into that rapid-moving mass of water. They simply could not successfully battle across the wind and tide to the Thames. They were forced west with the flow, but fast as they went with the wind and tide, they could not outrun the warnings of the beacons lighted at sight of them all along the Foreland of Kent. The invaders were swept past. There was no place safely to come ashore on this coast, where the British fleet waited to put out of their strongpoint at Dover. The frustrated Romans could see British cavalry archers trotting along the coastal battlements of chalk cliffs, keeping pace as the enemy army was carried along in their unseaworthy barges, helpless on the rapids of the ebb tide.

Maximian viewed the line of smoking beacons that sent their wind-horizontal signals from headland to headland ahead of him, and cursed. He saw answering smoke signals across the strait to the south, where the fleet's secondary base at Bononia was also alerted. No surprise attack today, he thought bitterly, cursing the incompetence of the Egyptian shipmaster who had overseen the timing of the operation. He'd have him nailed to the prow of his ship for the return journey, he vowed. "We'll have to find somewhere suitable for landing further west, once we get rid of these horsemen," he declared. "We can't have them whistling up troops while we're still wading ashore."

He looked at the straggling sails of his flotilla, and ordered his signal officer to flag them to close up, while telling his own shipmaster to slow and wait for them. In the waist of his ship, soldiers were throwing up, already seasick in the jostling, heaving waves. The invasion fleet swept along, the smaller ships and barges powerless against the thrusting tidal race, and the sails of the British fleet could be seen astern as they clawed out of Dover harbour in pursuit. A lookout in the fighting tower already erected in the prow of Maximian's flagship called out a warning. Sails were putting out from Bononia, too.

With enemies on two sides, Maximian opted to forge ahead. 'Make for Portus Magnus,' he said, naming the great British harbour that sheltered behind an island off the southern coast. He was gambling that Carausius had gathered most of his fleet at Dover to repel an attack at the south eastern tip of Britain. Now that he'd been carried past the Britons there, his way might be clear to steal into their hopefully less-defended port to the west. He looked around. More of his soldiers were vomiting, the seasickness was worsening. Would his men even be ready to fight if they got ashore?

Astern, the British fleet was standing out into the narrows and angling south of him, and the sails from Bononia were also out into open sea, shepherding him away from their coast. Carausius, he thought, is cutting diagonally across my wake. He's not heading to intercept me.

The Roman was correct. The British emperor's plan was to drive the Roman fleet west and north onto the island's rock ledges or into the whirlpools, eddies and pyramid-shaped waves they created. And he knew the exact place to do it. The tide churned, the Romans ran with the millrace of water, butting head-on into green rollers. Explosions of white spume towered over their bows from time to time, and the shallow-keeled barges struggled for a grip on the water so they could claw across the wind. Every seasick soldier hoped for a landfall, their officers looked at the steep chalk cliffs with their footings in narrow strips of shingle and prayed they'd find a beach where they could land troops.

The experienced British sailors herded the invaders like sheepdogs, lying their warships close to the wind, closing in to nip at the heels of the flock, harrying them from east and south until their admiral emperor, who had destroyed many pirates in these very waters, judged the moment right and ordered them to attack. In its first engagement as a national fleet, the British came down like pack wolves on a sheepfold.

Carausius had learned how the Romans fought naval battles, and he knew they were no sailors. Because he had taken the seasoned mariners of their British fleet with him, he guessed that the replacements they'd had to recruit from Greece, Phoenicia and Egypt would likely use the familiar, old tactics which called for them to ram an opponent with the sharp beak at the prow of their warships, to hook onto the enemy and board him or to cripple the opponent by cutting down his sail halyards.

The oak-ribbed hulls and oak planking of the heavier British warships were for all practical purposes impervious to any ramming the Romans' lighter ships could inflict. Additionally, Carausius' ship's chandlers and quartermasters had fitted chains to protect the rigging and keep the crossed spars in place if their ropes should be severed. Against the threat of boarders, or of rigging-cutting blades, they carried long spars to fend off any ship that drew too close. They had also equipped their ships with something else.

Every warship of the British fleet had mounted several great catapults on platforms alongside the collapsible fighting towers that were erected at bow and stern before an engagement. The ballistae were terrible, powerful giant crossbows that could fire either iron bolts or shaped stone balls and were lethal enough to crumble a mortared wall or shatter a ship's hull. Carausius had ordered loopholes cut in the gunwales of his warships and solid breastworks fitted above them so the crews of the highly-accurate ballistae could aim and fire their deadly missiles while protected and unimpeded. In long hours of practice, squads had been drilled to operate speedily the winches that drew back the catapults' animal sinew bowstrings and to reload the heavy iron bolts equally swiftly.

For their part, in the weeks before the engagement, the tribunes had experimented with different warheads to see which would best penetrate a ship's hull, and determined that blunt projectiles best shattered pine boards, while bodkin-tipped arrows were the missiles of choice against mail or leather armour. Supplies of both were piled at intervals near the catapults. Some of the artillerymen had also loaded round stones onto their ships, choosing river stones and some shaped granite as the best projectiles for density and accuracy. Lastly, a detachment of slingshot men who were trained to hurl lead missiles that were the shape and size of eggs were deployed on each ship, to work with the archers as snipers.

The legion's officers had seen to it that every infantryman was equipped with five javelins, heavy, iron-pointed weapons that had a round lead ball attached just below the arm-length spike, to add extra impetus at the strike. The spearhead itself was of softer iron, so it would bend on impact and could not easily be pulled out. This had the benefit of impeding the target if that unfortunate to have survived the strike. Neither could the bent javelin be re-used quickly against the thrower. Some of the newer javelins had a wooden pin securing the blade to the shaft. On impact, the pin broke, making the javelin useless to the enemy. All the British sailors needed was to get close.

As the signals officer waved the red cloak that finally turned the two halves of the British fleet towards the enemy, the Romans were off the indented coast where Carausius' great palace of Fishbourne stood. The signal beacons had flared and smoked their warnings for hours, and the emperor's household steward had assembled the house and farm slaves, armed the retainers and taken them all to the headland to watch for invaders. Guinevia, who had formed a friendship with the mosaic artist Claria, looked west across the water at the island of Hayling. "It reminds me greatly of the northland, beyond the Wall," she said, "I was born there, but I could live in a place like this."

"Stop the dreaming. Right now, we need all your magic," said the Ionian. "The emperor has to stop the Roman fleet or we will all be on the auction block. Can you do anything to help?"

Guinevia nodded. "I can do something," she said simply.

The sorceress looked east to survey the approaching sails, then south, gauging the speed of their approach, the wind and the flow of the speeding tide. Below her feet where she stood at the edge of a bluff, a line of ragged sea foam, swirling currents and clashing waves marked hidden, underwater ledges. They blocked and diverted the great power of the current and created a killing ground for sailors. Long green rollers threw up great pillars of white water as they hit the obstructions, giving more warning that the ledges' wicked stone teeth would tear out the heart and snap the spine of any ship thrown onto them. Those undersea fangs extended out into the strait for two long miles. "It would be best if the Romans did not see that," Gunevia murmured to herself. And she closed her eyes to begin her enchantments.

The Romans were being dogged ever more closely, and Maximian was cursing his inexperienced sailors. The invasion fleet was being forced nearer and nearer to the shore, and was straggling. Along the line to the rear three British ships, spray bursting over their bows, had already closed on a trireme that was attempting to shepherd the struggling troop barges. The British sea wolves tore into the rear quarter of the trireme and a volley of iron bolts slammed low into the vessel's hull. Some hit the oars, throwing the rowers off their benches and causing the ship to slew and roll. An alert artilleryman who had waited his chance, fired his ballista's great rock at the Roman hull just as the ship rolled away from him, revealing itself below the waterline. The smooth round river rock smashed through the planking, the ship rolled back level and suddenly green seawater was gushing into the vessel's waist.

One group of sailors tried to fother the stove-in planking by bandaging the hull with a sail. They draped the canvas over the bow, then dragged both ends along opposite sides of the ship, wrapping it right around the hull. They used the power of the inrushing seawater to push a plug of bundled woollen cloaks into the shattered planking. One brave mariner was hanging upside down over the ship's side adjusting the plug, when an iron bolt fired at 30 yards' range went straight through his body and pinned him to the pine boards. The shipmate holding him by the legs vomited in shock and fell backwards. The plug slipped out, the saltwater gushed in, and the trireme fell away, sluggish as it started to settle, its fate sealed. The British ships turned and, like wolves among sheep, began carving into the smaller, fragile troop carriers.

Aboard his flagship Minerva, Carausius grabbed the arm of the shipmaster and pointed a mile ahead of the struggling Roman squadron. "Where has that come from?" he demanded. A dense sea fog was creeping across the water, promising concealment for the west-fleeing Romans who were still running with the racing tide. "How can that be?" he swore. He'd managed to trap the Romans between his warships, the shore and the teeth of the deadly Bill that lay in their path, and now a fog might let them escape him. "Where in the name of Manannan did that come from?" he asked the sky.

On the shore, Claria knew. She had watched in awe as the black-robed Druid priestess of the witch goddess of the Wild Hunt worked her spells. The slaves were huddled away in fear, the palace steward, pale faced, had waved the retainers back to a safe place but the pagan priestess was oblivious to it all. Almost unseeing, she stooped and took up a handful of sandy soil from the cliff top. She stepped forward towards the edge, and threw it high into the wind, causing a small haziness as it was snatched away. Her eyes were rolled back in her head, perspiration stood out on her forehead, a low ululation came from her mouth and her body shuddered with effort. Finally, eyes closed, she threw both her hands forward, opening her fingers as she released her two-fisted spell. The silver pentagram ring of Myrddin seemed to pulse and glow in the misted light and the slaves later swore to each other that sparks had crackled from her fingertips. Guinevia slumped over, hands on knees, exhausted. She remained still for minutes, eyes closed, breathing hard, before she finally straightened her back. Her eyes were unfocused and it took minutes more before she could view the result, and success, of her enchantments.

The sea fog she had conjured rose out of the depths ruled by Manannan mac Lir. Spreading like thick smoke, it cloaked the ocean around the claw-like promontory whose tailings stretched far into the strait. Inside the cold, near-impenetrable fog, the waters of the strait clashed in a thrashing maelstrom that told of the furious power of the tide. Above the heaving turbulence of the water, the fog by contrast held an eerie stillness, and no current of air seemed to move. Water droplets waited to bead and condense on the rigging and spars of the ships that entered the enveloping gloom, and the churning white and green waves thrashed above rocky underwater teeth that were waiting to snatch the lives of mariners driven by the tide into the confusing, concealing dimness.

Carausius punched his fist into his opposite, open palm. "Got the bastards," he exulted. "That sea fog is exactly what we want. They're caught, they have no local pilots, they don't know and they can't see. They're going onto that promontory blind. It's happened to me like this once before. We trapped pirates on a bill just like this years ago, on this very coast."

He assessed matters. The triremes still outside the fog bank were trying to fight off the British sea wolves while the barges scurried past, but the warships were being frustrated by the skilled British crews. Their vessels were relatively undamaged from the occasional ramming and the crews had successfully fended off all the Romans' boarding attempts with their long poles. The frustrated fighting parties that crowded the invaders' decks were paying a price, They were under bombardment from the Britons' heavy javelins, arrows and egg-sized, leaden slingshot missiles, and the dead, dying and wounded were piling up, clogging the open ships and hampering the crews who worked them. The British orders to kill officers and steersmen with the accurate ballistae was effective too, evidenced by the erratic wakes left by some warships and the bloodied steerboards at their sterns.

As Carausius watched, a prefect in a splendid coat of polished mail took a bodkin bolt square in the chest. The armour wasn't proof against the heavy arrow with its needle point nose. Sparks like those struck in a forge flew from the links of mail, and the man was hurled backwards. The bodkin head and several inches of shaft protruded from the prefect's back, having passed right through his mail and his body. The legate nodded grimly. The ballistae were accurate and immensely powerful. That officer would take no further part in any actions.

A furlong's distance away, two triremes were ablaze from end to end, caught by lobbed buckets of Greek Fire, and worse, terrible damage was being inflicted on the lightly-built troopships, whose sides were splintering under the deadly fire of the catapult projectiles. One large river rock, fired head-on, hit exactly on the bow of a troop-carrying barge. It struck the stem with so much force that the strakes of the whole boat opened like flower petals, the green sea poured in, and the barge went down in a spread of planking.

The fight, Carausius saw, was well on its way to being won, but he'd soon have to call off his sea wolves because the eerie mist that hid the teeth of the bill were getting closer. He hung on to the last, determined to keep the Romans headed where he wanted them to go. Finally, he gave the signal to turn away for the safety of the open strait. Maximian saw the British manoeuvre and sighed with relief. He could vanish into the sea fog and still have enough troops to establish a beachhead or even capture a harbour and await reinforcements. He signalled his flotilla onwards, ordered his rowers to pull harder, and his trireme, boosted by the sea race, charged unknowing into the fog that concealed the ship-killing rocks.

XXX. Constantius

Maximian didn't die, but he lost his newly-built fleet and his hopes of a glorious re-taking of Britain, at least for the time being. Not even half of his warships escaped the deadly teeth of the coastal rocks, and some that did had been so damaged in the sea battle, they worked their seams open in the heavy swells and sank anyway. It was a desperate struggle for the remnant of the fleet to rescue survivors, or to haul as many of the foundering troopships to safety as they could, and when the mysterious sea fog had cleared, screaming hordes of gulls arrived to feast on the awful things that floated in the sea wrack.

The emperor returned to Gaul with blood in his eye and fury in his heart. For a month, his slaves and those around him lived in trembling fear of his rages, but Maximian eventually calmed and began planning his next campaigns. A lull in the Alemanni incursions along the Rhine border meant he was able to pull back six of the 18 legions stationed there. "Put them on bandit duty," he instructed his tribune Crassus. "Clean up the Bagaudae insurgents in eastern Gaul, then quietly move a couple of legions close to Bononia. I want to surprise those bastards who stole our fleet." Maximian knew that northern Gaul would never be subjugated while his enemy could cross at will to reinforce his troops from the sea with all the reserves of the Britons' island. He would put down the bandits in the countryside, seize Carausius' headquarters in Gaul and crush the Gallic rebels. Only then would he ready another invasion fleet for Britain. The Roman began gathering bullion, troops and supplies. He would first destroy the stone warship that was the sea fort of Bononia. Building a second fleet could come later.

In Britain, The Expected One was enjoying his good fortune. Carausius–Arthur wore the circlet of a Roman emperor and the badge of a noble British jarl. The populace was at peace, pride was restored, the golden age his coins promised seemed to have arrived. He had recovered the long-lost Eagle, and brought down the gods' favour and had defended the island from the tyrants who had extorted them so heavily while treating them like third class provincials. For the first time, a British ruler had pacified and unified the country, built trade and demonstrated that the nation could withstand the war eagles of Rome.

Britain's own legions, its navy, the fortifications along the Saxon Shore and the watch beacons up the eastern coast meant that any who came from Germania or Saxony must come as peaceful settlers, not as raiders. Even the Picts were quiet since the tribune Cragus had taken the Eagles beyond the Wall to punish the northern tribes and bring back hundreds of slaves and a score of their chieftains' sons as hostages. The Celts, too, were subdued. A legion sent from Chester had worked with several squadrons of the fleet against Hibernian sea raiders in the northwest. In a shockingly swift campaign, they had trapped, crucified and enslaved enough of the wild men of the western island that they would not soon break the British Peace.

Carausius also ordered improvements to the fabric of his nation, rebuilding ruined roads and bridges, channelling clean water into the towns and restoring long-neglected temples to the old gods. In return, those deities smiled with good harvests, good weather and a lack of plague. The coinage of silver and gold was so fine that merchants from as far as Phoenicia came, confident in the exchanges and eager to trade. Even the emperor Diocletian in distant Nicomedia turned a blind eye to importers doing business with the rebel province because where else could one obtain such fine woollen goods, not to mention the other luxuries from the far north?

Against this golden prospect of British peace and plenty, the junior emperor Maximian brooded in Gaul over his defeat by the usurper, and was putting his plans into action. He gave his best general, his adopted son Constantius Chlorus, some specific orders. First, a force was sent into the delta of the Rhone river, to secure the eastern marches against the Franks on whom Carausius might call for aid. When they were in place, half a Roman legion was sent to move swiftly down the rivers Aisne, Oise and Somme in oared boats, travelling on the spring floods as fast as a cantering horse. Two thousand more men came in sea barges, creeping unheralded down the coast from Ostend to Bononia, and no spies successfully slipped out of the Belgic seaport to carry warnings to Gaul, although a handful tried.

They were crucified to die slowly at the roadsides where they were caught breaking the emperor's embargo, setting a vivid example for others tempted to disobey imperial edicts. South of Ostend, another full legion of Maximian's troops marched up the old emperor Agrippa's fine high road to Bononia, screened by cavalry and confident in their numbers.

The combined strike was lightning fast and came at wolf light. The ship-borne squads of artillerymen and foot soldiers who had arrived several miles along the coast had landed unnoticed after dark and moved quietly into position, secreting themselves and a battery of ballistae in coastal woods a short distance west of Bononia. They emerged when the trotting cavalry arrived at daylight and trapped the British squadron in harbour, just as Maximian had planned.

He had explained matters to Constantius, who was known as Chlorus, 'The Pale,' for his ultra-white skin that never seemed to take a tan. "I've had spies' reports and sketches for weeks, and this is what we'll do," he said, tracing with his forefinger on a sketched map of the citadel of Bononia. "The fortress is on a bluff behind the entrance to the harbour, and it guards the harbour well, but they've missed something. They haven't properly defended the harbour entrance, which is about 100 paces from the quayside. All that's where the ships come into harbour is a small fortification, enough for maybe ten men, and we can seize that easily enough. We also won't have much trouble cutting Bononia off from the hinterland, either. The place relies on being supplied and reinforced from the sea, from Britannia and as long as it is, we probably won't be able to invest it. So we need to command the harbour."

Maximian glanced up at Chlorus, who nodded. "Now, here," the emperor continued, jabbing at the map, "is the sea entrance. It's about 300 paces wide, and ships can only enter and leave at high tide, when even the deepest water is not much, about the height of two men. At low tide, the harbour is virtually dry. I want to stop that entrance, block it with a barrier and stop all traffic through it. If they cannot resupply the citadel from the straits, if we can isolate them, we have them."

Chlorus managed matters well, the attack was swift, and the surprise worked. The Roman artillerymen emerged when the tide was falling, the cavalry protected them from the garrison's foot soldiers and a detachment of chosen men made short work of seizing and manning the small fortification at the harbour entrance. By the time the tide was high enough for the ships in the harbour to sail out, it was too late. The artillery was in place commanding the sea approach from one side of the entrance, the fort on the other was in Roman hands. The British ships were bottled up under the threat of the rock-throwing ballistae. The Bononia commander hesitated to act, thinking this might just be a raid, and the ships were safe enough under the walls of the fortress. Matters changed rapidly.

Within a few more hours, the land around the citadel was swarming with legionaries who had force-marched that day a full 40 miles up the great road. They reinforced the ship-borne troops who had sailed in along the coast and provided security for the hundreds of engineers who drove a double row of pilings across the tidal entrance.

Before the stout fence was even partway complete, thousands of soldiers and slaves laboured to fill the gap between the pilings with rocks and shingle. No ship could cross that mole, and the Romans fortified and garrisoned the ends so that no land attack could take and destroy it. While the sappers were pushing the cork into the bottleneck of the harbour, a corps of engineers was readying the siegeworks. They first dug a canal trench to divert water from the Liane river, and created a moat around the land side of the city. This they reinforced with two more walls, a tower-fortified double rampart and ditch to contain the besieged and another wall behind their own army to protect themselves against any relieving attack from Gallic or British land forces.

This defensive wall was a maze of mantraps and misleading blind alleys backed up with a minefield of the spiked coltrops that crippled horses. Within two weeks, the city and port were solidly isolated, the catapults were established and their missiles were crunching away at the city walls. Approach trenches were snaking forward and ramps and siege towers were well along in construction.

Constantius Chlorus had the garrison trapped, but he knew that many of them could be persuaded to defect to his forces, so he wanted to keep casualties low. The ballistae engineers were busy lobbing firebombs and boulders into the besieged citadel when he called for a parley. Lucius Cornelius, the garrison commander, knew the general of old, and came out himself to talk. The meeting was curiously cordial. "Look, old friend," the wily Constantius said, "I want to save your ground pounders. I need them on the Rhine. Surrender and they can redeem themselves. They'll have to re-take the Sacramentum and swear allegiance again to the Augusti Maximian and Diocletian. We'll let bygones be bygones. I can argue with my boss that Carausius seduced them and all will be well enough for them. It's for the best. Just look where you are. You can't get out, the Gauls won't help you, Carausius can't get enough troops together in time to save you and you can't sail away."

He paused and looked pointedly at the bustling sappers. "You know how it works," he said sympathetically. "We have the ramps almost finished to storm the place, and even if that fails, we'll be through the walls in a week with the artillery. Why sacrifice the foot sloggers?" The general looked candidly at Lucius. "You and your senior officers will likely be busted for a year or two, but at least you'll walk away alive, and you'll save your men. It isn't a bad bargain."

Constantius was persuasive, and the besieged commander could see the truth of what he said. He'd carried out sieges himself and he knew how inevitable was the result of a well-conducted one. Lucius took a short time to think matters through but honestly could see no other viable way without losing a lot of lives that would be useful to Rome. His army career was damaged, but maybe if he proved cooperative.....

He walked back to the big general and clapped his fist across his chest in salute. "You have it, if my men take their weapons with them and they stay in their own units. No crucifixions, no slavery for our troops. You can have the citizens - do what you want with them." The agreement was made and the next morning, brass horns blaring, the garrison marched out to a reshaped future, one in which they would be fighting for another Caesar.

Constantius sighed with relief and gave orders to begin the lengthy business of dismantling the siege works. What he had not told the gullible Lucius was that he was under Maximian's explicit orders to give generous terms to the Bononia garrison to encourage the rebels in Britain to surrender too. "If they see we can be magnanimous to a defeated foe, they'll not fight as desperately as they would if their lives were on the line," he mused. "Ah well, get on with dismantling this stuff, we'll probably need it on the other side of the narrows."

He went back to the garrison mansio where he had a pretty, dark-eyed Gaulish girl waiting for him, as ordered. Spoils of war, he thought happily. He hoped she struggled, a little. It was always more enjoyable when they tried to resist, and they probably secretly enjoyed the split lip and the bruising, anyway. He licked his own lips, remembering. He thought he might take another walk around the slave pens tomorrow, see what other women were in there. The surrender had gone well.

That evening, at high tide, the surge of the sea broke down the mole across the mouth of the harbour. Constantius wasn't surprised. His engineers had been warning him for a week that it could collapse, but he didn't want to be seen reinforcing the barrier in case it gave the besieged some new ideas. If the garrison had waited a single day, they could have escaped or been reinforced from Britain.

The weeping women in the slave pens and the few dozen Gauls who were to be crucified at the dockside for trading with the enemy, looked bitterly at the surging water. If only they'd been allowed to hold out for another day. One of those already hanging from a crucifix was especially bitter. The garrison commander Lucius Cornelius was writhing in agony from the flogging, from the pain of the nails through his wrists and heels and the sheer humiliation of being hung out naked on his own fortress wall. That morning, he'd been more shocked than anyone when a squad of Constantius' legionaries had surrounded him as he marched out of the gates at the head of his men. One or two of his soldiers had growled, but they had fallen quiet as a detachment of Roman archers raised their bows.

The victorious general Constantius stepped onto a wooden chest, the better to be seen. "This man broke the Sacramentum," he bellowed. "He did not do as you did, and follow orders. He turned traitor to his emperor after taking a sacred oath to obey him. He must pay for that. You men, move on. Assemble over there, at the officers' orders". Minutes later, the general was speaking directly to the defeated commander. "We really can't have someone like you walking away, can we?" Constantius used a reasonable tone as he addressed the ashen-faced Lucius. "The footsloggers were just obeying orders, but you and those five," he pointed to five senior officers held at spear point, "Well, you should have known better."

He paused. "Old friend, be damned. You're a cheap little chancing traitor." The general spat on the ground and addressed the rigid centurion on his right. "Give them all a sample of the flagellum then nail them up, Romans or not. They've forfeited all privileges. And, I don't want anybody breaking their legs for a day or two. Keep them alive. They can think about what they've done and take their time regretting it. Anyway, it will be something for their troops to look at."

News of the fall of Bononia came to Carausius just after he'd come out of the baths at Dover, still vaguely irritated because his ruminations had been disturbed by a couple of voluble merchants who seemed to be in love with the sound of their own voices and by the actions of several youths who'd been diving in and splashing rowdily. A slave was tying his sandals for him when a courier arrived, streaked with horse spume, road dust and sweat. The man stamped to attention and handed over a packet stitched into leather and sealed. "Urgent, Caesar," he said. "From Londinium."

The emperor's moodiness vanished like mist in the sun. He read the dispatch's contents twice and chewed his lip in thought. He'd suspected the worst since the lighthouse across the narrows had been extinguished a couple of nights ago, but the wind was foul and the ships he'd sent to investigate had not yet returned. Word had arrived via a trader on the payroll of his spymaster, Allectus. Bononia was gone, and the troops had been pardoned and allowed to march out under full arms, so it was total surrender.

Carausius calculated. He'd lost the 30th Ulpia, he supposed, scratch that legion off the army list. Summer was here, a good time for Maximian to send an invasion force, and he'd be better prepared for the sea crossing this time. He'd likely bring the force he already had in Bononia, 25 short miles away, and he'd quickly bring in more troops from the east, if he had not already started those movements. He'd only have to wait to bring invasion barges down from Ostend or wherever he'd stowed them. Say, three weeks... Best to move a readiness force south right away and make sure the coastal defences were truly prepared. The 2nd Augusta had been in place for a week or more, he could bring into play most of the 20th Valerian, plus what there was of the Ninth Spanish with their iconic Eagle, and hope the Picts up there beyond the Wall kept quiet for a while. The fleet was in reasonable shape, though he'd lost the squadron he'd stationed in Gaul. He commanded a sentry to fetch Allectus. "We'll need more coin, for certain," he thought grimly, tugging his big naval cloak around himself as he stepped into the sea wind.

XXXI. Boadicea

"I want the usual subjects covered, gentlemen," the emperor told the commanders standing around a large table top map of the Narrow Sea and its hinterlands. "That's objective, intelligence, personnel, communications, supply and transport. The objective is simple, and it's as unadorned as nature intended. We must hold what we have and turn back any invader. Intelligence is next, a vital area that Allectus will oversee with his spies. As matters stand, our best course is to be readying for conflict right now. We don't need to wait for more warnings, what's happening is obvious enough and if things change, Allectus' overpaid informants will keep us abreast. It looks like Maximian will be fully ready to move within a matter of weeks, while the weather's good, so we know what we have to do in the meantime.

"Cragus, you will handle personnel and communications. I've ordered the Valerian and the Spanish legions brought down from the north, sort them out, and see to it that the coast beacons are properly manned and on full standby. There's a whole division of Germanic cavalry outside Londinium, so move them up as a swift response group. And, I want log booms chained and ready to be fixed across the Thames to stop any seaborne invasion coming that way." He nodded to the other tribune. "Quirinus, you are in charge of equipment and supplies, and I'll need provisions at once for three legions for a month. Get supply dumps set up in the coastal forts and make sure we have more dumps in the hinterland so we don't have to drag everything with us and can move fast if we have to. Also, liaise with the Kentish ironworks and with the admirals in Dover and Portus Magnus over getting enough chains to them as protection for the ships' cordage. We'll need them made safe against cutting, the Romans have that tactic. I've had complaints from the shipyards over chain shortages, so give the appropriate people a kick up the arse.

"That leaves Papinius to deal with the transport needs, so you work closely with Quirinus over those supplies. You'll need to requisition animals and wagons from the locals, but don't tread on the wrong toes, we want the chieftains' cooperation not their moaning that all their draught animals have gone and they can't get their crops in. Finally, I shall oversee the fleet. If we can send the bastards to the sea bed, we won't need a land campaign".

Carausius did more than just ready the fleet, however. He used Britain's good stone roads to travel rapidly around half of the country to impress the war lords with the urgency and importance of this campaign. Emissaries went ahead of him to arrange the councils and at his overnight stops the emperor met the jarls, bretwaldas, eorldormen, barons and lords of the British.

Using the raised, paved highways, with relays of couriers' horses exchanged at the frequent staging posts and sometimes employing a fast three or four-horse raeta carriage in which he could doze, the emperor moved from Dover to Londinium, to Colchester and Lincoln. He continued north after a council in Lincoln's hilltop fortress to a conclave in the governor's palace in Eboracum attended by the powerful lords of the Picts and Brigantes, Parisi and Coriani. Next, he crossed the high spine of Britain and across its rich north-western farmlands to meet the Welsh captains and kings at the 20th Valerian Legion's red sandstone stronghold on the Dee at Chester.

Those talks were successful, and Carausius was saddle-weary but satisfied as he turned southeast to traverse the limestone peaks of central Britain for a crucial meeting with the Catuvellauni. His message to them delivered and agreed, he next turned south down the arrow-straight Via Fossa that once marked Rome's western frontier in Britannia, and crossed the brown River Severn. His destination was the vast military camp at Caerleon, a stop he hastily added to his journey after receiving a late dispatch from his scribe, the pagan sorceress Guinevia.

The blunt, bluff soldier approached the citadel walls of the Legio II Augusta with some anxiety. His meeting, set up by the Druid's adept, was with her mentor the great sorcerer Myrddin, He had agreed to sail from the sacred Druidic island in northern Wales to meet the emperor because he felt the hand of the gods was on Carausius and the nation would benefit. Guinevia had doubted the wisdom of travelling on the dangerous sea, but the tall Druid had waved aside her objections. "I am protected," he told her loftily. "Anyway, it will be less tiring and much swifter than moving across the mountains. There is no danger to me. The gods will be with me. This soldier is their instrument in uniting Britain and in restoring them."

Certainly, Myrddin's influence with Manannan mac Lir, deity of the waters, was obvious to the awed sailors who conducted the great sorcerer. They swore they had never made such a swift and perfect journey around the usually storm-wracked Welsh headlands, for they sailed on a sea mysteriously calm that took them with perfect winds into the tranquil, dun waters of the Severn Sea. From that wide channel, Myrddin's ship was wafted effortlessly into the sparkling River Usk and smoothly up to the vast Roman castra of Caerleon, the military strongpoint that dominates the western lands.

Carausius was escorted by one of his tribunes to the airy quarters assigned to the great Druid. He was unsurprised to find that Myrddin was exactly as Guinevia had described him, tall, with long dark hair neatly plaited, a hawk's nose and piercing, crystal-blue eyes under shaggy dark brows. He moved quickly and with the grace of an athlete. Involuntarily, the autocratic emperor general deferred to him, so overwhelming was the aura of power that cloaked the wizard. Myrddin gestured aside the politeness's and led Carausius to a tablum on which he had weighted down the corners of a vellum chart. The astonished emperor recognized it as a map of Britain, Hibernia and Gaul, but such a map! Instead of being the usual Roman linear list of way stations, with scale and distance incidental, this was the view that would have been shared by an eagle flying high above the land. Myrddin moved a long forefinger across the chart.

"Bononia," he murmured, tapping the mapped markings of the Gallic coast. His digit moved across the Narrow Sea. "Dover, Winchester, Fishbourne. These places are ancient, and are connected by nature's lines of power. They are not there by accident. Rivers, forests and mountains have powerful spirits, just as high places are sacred. The old gods had their reasons for establishing the places where they were worshipped, they are sites where power can be harnessed and nature can be co-opted. If you act as the gods wish, you will restore Britain. You will be Carausius of Britain." The title resonated with Carausius, who was seeing clearly for the first time the geography he had previously had to imagine, and was studying the great chart, burning it into his memory. The map seemed to swell under his eyes as he heard the echo of the sorcerer's words. 'Carausius of Britain.' "Your battle will come here," Myrddin prophesied, tapping the line of the coast west of Dover. "Be prepared."

Carausius shook his head and prodded at the map. "London. It will be there. Maximian will try for the Thames and the capital," he said shortly. "That is where I have to muster my forces."

The Druid, with secret amusement in his eyes, shook his head. "Manannan mac Lir can be persuaded. The gods want Britain to be saved by the sea and you must crush her enemies in the way they wish. Then you will be a great king. There is more. The gods are with you now, but you will one day not be with them." Carausius shook his head. What was this nonsense? How he could ever turn his back on Mithras and Jupiter, on the spirits of Britain's mountains and rivers and the whole pantheon of gods who protected him? The thoughts were unspoken, but the sorcerer understood them.

"You will be Carausius of Britain; you will bring peace and fortune to your nation. When you are dead you will lie in one of its holiest places under its great mountain and in Britain's true heart, but the price will be to deny your gods. It is an awful toll, and it is not one that will bring you happiness, but you must know it and you must accept it, even if you do not understand. Britain requires it."

A slave entered silently, carrying a flagon of mulled wine and two drinking glasses chased with hunting scenes. Myrddin turned, and in an instant the near-electric atmosphere in the chamber seemed to lift. "Take a glass of wine," the seer said sociably. Carausius, shaken by the prophecies, shook his head to clear it. "Yes, yes," he muttered, accepting the drink and turning to look out of the window. Myrddin, goblet in hand, stepped up beside him. "I have summoned the great chieftains of Gwent and Powys, the blood shield Gaels of Lleyn and, oh, enough warriors to make the difference. And I have spoken with the gods. Your course is to do what soldiers do. Mine is to shape matters to the will of the gods. If it is done properly, this nation can move into sunlit times again. Should you fail, there will indeed be darkness in the hearts of men." The sorcerer put down his glass, turned to a slave who held his cloak and shrugged himself into its folds. He raised his long fingers in ironic blessing. "Do your duty, Arthur of Britain," he said. He turned abruptly and was moving away before Carausius could even respond.

The emperor brooded on the sorcerer's words and tried to escape the feelings of doom that beset him when he analysed them. Finally, he took the pragmatic view. If he performed his military tasks, and Myrddin carried out his occult ones, the gods would support them. His spirits lifted as he continued his journey, stopping a night or two later at Bath to sacrifice at the great temple of Sulis Minerva. Under the symbols of the moon goddess Luna and her healer acolyte, he sacrificed a goat and prayed for his nation and its safety in the upcoming struggle.

From Bath, he took a hard day's ride south, following his soldier's need to inspect the garrison on the commanding limestone hill at Cadbury. "This," he told his guard captain, "could be the keystone that holds our kingdom. From here, we command the west and south, but more importantly, this is a place of the power of the gods. If we fight here, we will win, because Britain's own deities will come to our assistance".

The ancient earthwork defences dug by a people whose bones had long since crumbled into the earth had recently been maintained and improved. The primary defences were four lines of ditch and bank topped at the summit by a tall stone wall 16 feet thick. The big soldier scanned it with a professional eye. It was dotted with fighting platforms, and was further guarded by timber palisades and watchtowers that the emperor had ordered built a few years before. The whole defensive girdle surrounded a vast plateau fully 18 acres broad, where sheep nibbled the turf.

Carausius limped on his bad foot as he made his way up the steep road that pierced the ringed defences, passing through wooden towers with double gates and around turnbacks that would fatally trap an enemy. At last, he found himself on the hilltop, facing a large timber hall and a small palace. Over it all towered a signal station, its iron cage holding the lumber and protected dry kindling that would send a fiery message across the lowlands. That call to arms would start a chain of fires to set men hastening to rally against invaders. "The engineers have done a fine job," he told his tribune.

"The Romans, lord, left us some good stonework," said the man, gesturing at the foot-square, tapered blocks that made such durable walls. "And the ancients made it spacious enough for a thousand fighting men."

Carausius nodded. "Keep this place strong, and well-supplied," he ordered. "It is our bulwark in the west. I'll send you more troops, but in time of emergency, you'll have half the men of the region gathered here. Make sure the granaries are stocked, and get some cattle brought in, too. And get an extra well or two dug," he added. The tribune nodded. Car the Bear knew his business all right, but there would be plenty of work to do. He just hoped they had time enough before the trouble started.

For several more days, the emperor conferred with the region's chieftains, impressing on them his needs and hopes for Britain, then took his leave on a foggy day to finish his journey. At long last, exhausted but satisfied his plans had been accepted, he finished his circuit of the island at the Great Port near Winchester. At stop after stop, he had outlined his strategy and made his promises to the tribes. He spoke to the Cantiaci who had fought Julius, to the wealthy Corieltauvi who grew the grain, and to the proud Iceni whom Boadicea once led to blood-reeking glory. He met with the Celtic Dobunni and red-haired Artebates, parlayed with the fearsome Brigantes of the brackened north moorlands, and outlined his plans to the seagoing, olive-complexioned Durotriges and the warrior Silures who had been led by Caratacus himself. Even some of the dark men of the west, Dumnonii whom the Romans had never been able to subdue, came to the councils and listened respectfully.

At those meetings, Carausius, magnificent in his golden circlet and imperial purple robe pinned with the silver and amber brooch that proclaimed his bloodstock as a British noble, was met with courtesy and heard with ungrudging attention. He had long since proved his abilities as a sovereign and even to the diverse and independent lords of the land, he was an impressive figure. His listeners were all leaders of men, arrogant, proud rulers in their own fiefs, unaccustomed to submission or even to hearing out another's ideas. Some were moustached, long-haired and clad in furs, others were tonsured, clean-shaven and wearing togas or tunics, but the emperor with his scarred and battered face, bull neck, huge shoulders and curling beard was the imperious overlord of war who commanded their full attention.

To them all, he gave the same message: Britain is our land. We can make it a good land, fat with sheep, grain and cattle, where men can sleep safe at night and women can walk unmolested. We need no longer be a place milked dry by distant tyrants who do not listen to our views. We can create our own kingdom, a place of peace, prosperity and justice. To attain this golden age, a state which Rome once maintained, now fallen into disarray, he told those gatherings of proud barons and jarls, we must crush the Romans this one time.

In meeting after meeting, he used his impressive presence in an orator's trick, standing suddenly to thunder at his listeners: "We must send them back to Gaul cringing and whimpering, with wounds to lick, and we will be free of their yoke for ever. They will not be able to return, because I will create wooden walls they cannot pass." And he dropped his voice in the manner of a bard. This, he told them, is how we will do it, and this is how we will keep our freedom. And he outlined his plan.

Within a week, the levies began arriving at the coastal forts, columns of long-haired warriors, tramping together, singing and chanting the infectious marching songs that made the miles flow past. The jarls had listened and called on their men. The proud princes had laid aside their differences, taken Carausius' warnings to heart and had mustered their spearmen and the specialist equipment he'd urged them to bring. Tent camps sprang up along the springy, sheep-nibbled turf downs of the south coast.

And Carausius' own officers had been busy. Papinius, charged with overseeing the transport needs of an army, had not rested and had efficiently carried out his mission. Mule trains carrying sacks of grain and great nets of forage for the animals joined convoys of creaking wagons along the roads. They were laden with barrels of salted ham, Spanish olive oil, twice-baked bread, wine and other supplies, all carried from the great granaries and warehouses of the hinterland to be stored at strongpoints and ports all along the coast.

Drovers herded their lowing cattle to the army's pens, for the soldiers needed their beef, and shepherds from the chalk downs brought in the walking mutton needed to feed the hordes of armed men gathering against the Romans. The supply convoys moved with the heavy wagons that carried military equipment: siege engines, battering rams, dismantled siege towers, ladders, catapults and artillery. Leather-shrouded carriages carried sheaves of arrows, bundles of javelins, stacked piles of curved shields and sacks and boxes of personal armour from leather, steel or bronze helmets to breastplates and even a few closely-guarded, expensive suits of linked chain mail. "Looks like someone kicked over a beehive, lord," Allectus told the emperor as he surveyed the scene unfolding under the walls of Dover's rebuilt castle.

"Yes, and we'll sting Maximian's arse," growled Carausius, who was watching an armourer sharpening edges on one of the new grindstones he'd had made.

"All working out over there?" He inclined his head towards Gaul. Allectus knew exactly what his emperor meant.

"The minute they sail, beacons will be lit by my spies on their coast. We'll know, lord," he asserted.

"Worth every denarius," said the emperor. A flurry of activity at the gate caught his eye. The tribune Quirinus was back from the Great Port south of Winchester. He saw his emperor and hurried to report, saluting with fist over his heart. Matters were in hand, he'd be returning to the port soon, he said. Carausius grunted approval and the tribune looked out at the open ground below. "Those, Caesar," he said, pointing. "So many of them?"

The emperor cracked his face into a rare grimace of pleasure. "Chariots, Quirinus, Chariots. We have a secret weapon and it's going to give the Romans a real pasting." The battle jarls of Britain had done as he'd asked. Their emperor had recalled for them the lesson of Boadicea, the warrior queen. She had cut the legions of Rome to pieces with her nimble cavalry and deadly chariots. After three centuries, the British war wagons would roll again and, Carausius hoped, history would be repeated.

"The thing is," Carausius was in an expansive mood that evening, as he sat with his officers around a chart table in his leather campaign tent, drinking good Rhenish wine from a horn beaker, "the thing is, that chariots are simply two-man mobile missile platforms. The charioteer races in, the warrior at his right hand launches arrows or javelins and then runs down the pole between the horses like an acrobat to strike down at the enemy. Then the pair move out, fast, or if the warrior wishes, he leaps out to fight on foot. The charioteer waits a short distance away, so the warrior can jump back in the chariot and get out of there if needed. It's lightning warfare and the enemy footsloggers can't catch him."

The key to the whole thing, he explained, was that the chariot had to be light in weight, because British horses were not large. They could not

237

pull the heavy four horse carriages that the Romans raced around Circus Maximus or other tracks. In any case, four horses would be unmanageable in battle conditions. Equally vital was that the chariots gave the warrior a stable platform from which to launch his missiles. Boadicea's charioteers had used wickerwork chariots with an ingenious system of rawhide straps slung from hooped willow branches to suspend the fighting platform above the chassis and soak up the bumps. The concept worked well, but only in the right conditions. The negatives were that chariots were expensive, and couldn't be used in rough or marshy terrain.

The tales about scythes on the wheel hubs chopping into the legions were mere legends, the emperor said. That wasn't an effective tactic. You couldn't drive the lightweight chariots into ranks of armoured soldiers. Anyway, you usually couldn't even get the chariots to the soldiers, because Roman officers had quickly realized that a few stakes driven into the ground in front of the first ranks of standing infantry were an effective barrier.

The chariots' main value was to deliver fast volleys of missiles at close range, their velocity boosted when the javelin thrower used the vehicle's speed to enhance his own arm strength. The warrior didn't even carry a sword, relying on his spears and, if needed, a blade tucked into a wicker scabbard woven into the chariot wall. "Fact is," said the emperor, settling his bulk more comfortably, and resettling his mutilated foot, "heavy cavalry and mounted archers long ago superseded chariots, because the horses, or even mules, are much more flexible and less likely to break down. It's the shock and fright factor of the chariots that is our best secret weapon". Carausius took a reflective swig of wine. "I wouldn't mind having some of those elephants that old Hannibal used," he murmured. "Five tons of trumpeting, grey fright-mongers. They terrify the infantry and scare off the horses, they break the enemy ranks as easily as walking.

"That old Carthaginian knew what to do. He gave the tuskers wine; they like alcohol, you know, then the handlers poked them in the ankles and that set them in a huge rage. It was just 'Hang on' as the elephants charged. Problem was, they wanted to trample anyone human, Roman or Carthaginian. Still, they would be a fine weapon, if you could get some and get them pointed the right way." The big general finished his bumper of wine and glanced at the lists of supplies and dispositions in front of him. He grunted. Forget about elephants. He had chariots. Two men and two ponies per war chariot gave him a highly mobile and effective force for specialized use. And use it, he was determined to do. He also had one or two other surprises up his sleeve for the incoming bastard Romans.

Across the Narrow Sea, the 'incoming bastard Romans,' the emperor Maximian and his general Constantius were struggling with the logistics of moving an invasion force 25 miles across a fast-flowing, treacherous strait of the ocean. On a clear day, they could see the white headlands that stood above the naval base at Dover, tantalizingly close, but out of reach without dominant sea power. Maximian had scraped together troops from a handful of legions to bring together the 4,800 men he felt were the minimum he would need to dethrone the usurper Carausius. It was, he knew, only a tenth of the numbers Julius had used when he invaded Britain, but he was confident the squabbling British tribes would be divided against their self-declared overlord. This would be more of a cutting-out expedition than a conqueror's army.

The two Romans scanned the rolls to see what legions had yielded troops. Third Gallica, those veterans of campaigns against the bandits in Gaul and Iberia, had provided the most. Then there were a few from the 12th Fulminata and the remnants of the 15th Apollinaris. Those fellows had survived the sack of their fortress by the Persians and, with a fighting retreat, had avoided being enslaved for a life of work building bridges and roads for their new masters. Maximian had used his influence with his fellow Caesar, Diocletian, to siphon off some of the 2nd Parthica, Rome's own strategic reserve, and now that the Persian campaign was at last going well, had also persuaded his co-emperor to release to him a good portion of the 3rd Augusta, bringing them halfway across the world from Damascus to northern Gaul. The emperor's eyes lit up as he noted a strong force of Batavians on the army roll. Those soldiers, based on the Rhine estuary, were specialists in making river crossings. He made a mental note to hold them in reserve until they were needed to cross the Medway or Thames to establish a foothold that would let his troops outflank the defenders. Useful.

"Some good troops, some not so good, just damned toy soldiers", Maximian griped. "There will be hard work for the tribunes to do to shape this lot up, and we don't have a lot of time." Both soldiers were aware of the dangers of the Narrow Sea, and knew they had to move the invasion force during the summer's relative calm. Maximian was also uncomfortably aware that twice, Roman troops accustomed only to the tranquil waters of Our Sea had mutinied at the thought of taking on the turbulent 'ocean' of the straits. He had no inclination to have his name added to those of Claudius and Caligula as being unable to command his own men. He had to move the troop barges over the shortest crossing on the calmest day, and he'd do it after publicly making suitable sacrifices to Jupiter. He simply had to do it soon, as the opportune time and weather to invade were ebbing faster than the surging tides.

Constantius pulled another scroll to him, and examined the admirals' reports. The invasion fleet he'd had built at Forum Hadriani was about ready, at almost 300 ships. Nearly 200 of them would be crammed with troops, the others would shuttle supplies, horses, mules, siege engines, more men and the impedimenta needed for what they hoped would be a short campaign. "We can live off the land, at this time of year there's plenty of grain in the place," Constantius muttered. "We just don't want a prolonged expedition." He rolled the scroll shut, the two men nodded at each other. "Let's move it on," said Maximian. "Bring the fleet down to Itius Portus and Bononia. We'll have to do what old Julius did, and use that place. Thank Mithras that Itius hasn't silted up."

The emperor knew his military history. He recalled that when Gaius Julius Caesar invaded Britain three centuries before, his huge fleet of small ships could not all be launched from Bononia at one time because the harbour drained dry on the ebb tide. The canny old Roman had found a harbour just up the coast, four miles east of Cape Gris Nez, where he could haul many of the specially-built invasion barges up onto the sand while using the harbour for his bigger warships and transports.

At the right time and tide, Maximian could launch off the beach, then swim out the horses and mules to the ships, hoisting them aboard into stalls. He'd also ferry out the troops he'd not been able to load into the transports that were docked in harbour. The whole fleet could sail from Itius Portus and Bononia to arrive together, not piecemeal, at the chalk cliffs after making the shortest possible crossing. Then they'd turn north to find one of the sloping beaches Caesar had discovered on his first expedition. Julius sent his ships in three widely-spaced waves, which reduced the number of ships needed as he could shuttle across, and the smaller number of men and quantities of material being landed at one time made for easier command and control, too. The general nodded to his emperor. "Yea to that, sir," he saluted. "I'll get the staff together. I expect we should have it all in place by the ides. I'll get the admirals to advise us on the most suitable time and tides around then and, the gods willing, we'll get fine weather."

XXXII. Heslus

Bringing the invasion fleet down from the Rhine and Meuse rivers went well. The ships hugged the shore closely, sailed only in daylight and enjoyed placid summer seas with enough breeze to make it a pleasant voyage. Meanwhile, Constantius split his forces and moved the larger vessels that would take livestock to the deeper harbour at Bononia, where the horse and mule lines created a farmyard smell on the clean ocean breeze. At Itius Portus, the soldiers laboured to drag the pinewood barges up onto the sand and they stocked supplies under cover on the quayside to await loading. On time, mid-month as Constantius promised, Roman efficiency had prevailed and men, beasts, impedimenta and ships were all at their allotted stations. If the weather held, they would soon form an invasion flotilla sailing north to exact the revenge of two emperors. But the gods were fickle, and the weather broke.

Shrieking gales from the Atlantic blasted in unseasonably early, died, then were replaced by battering winds and rain from the east. The seabirds wheeled far inland, coastal stands of trees bowed submissively and the strait was a sullen heave of frothing grey-green. The invasion force could only watch morosely from their sodden tents as the bad weather kept them ashore, eating their way through the stores. After eleven days, Maximian's patience broke. "We can't wait for ever. It's not that bad, it's not a long way." Constantius looked grave. "Some of the problem, lord," he said, adding a swift, "as you know," at the emperor's scowling frown, "is landing everybody if there's a surf." Maximian unrolled a well-thumbed scroll that charted the waters and shoreline of south eastern Britain.

"I've thought of that," he said. "We'll land shock troops on this beach a mile or two east of Lympne and send them to seize the port. It's not huge, but it's a foothold. We can bring in the troop transporters, disembark the first wave in port and move the perimeter out from the town. We'd have to hold the Britons off overnight, then land the second part of the force on the next tide. From there, we'll be strong enough to break out and march east along the coast and we'll be at Dover. Seize that port and we have the key to Britain in our hands. We can shuttle in auxiliaries at will if we have Dover, because whoever holds the place has the strait under his control.

"We might even be lucky and catch some of the British fleet in there, but we can't keep delaying. Carausius will have had word of our build-up and he will be moving up soldiers and supplies from all over the island. The longer we give him to prepare, the harder it gets for us."

Constantius called in the admirals, who brought some local fishermen familiar with the British waters. They said they'd sometimes run their boats ashore on the island's south coast. Landing on that shingle and sand was highly feasible, they assured the officers. Around the harbour at Lympne, the coastline had stretches of shingle beach, a shore hard-armoured with small pebbles, some of it backed by marshlands, some with firm turf above the cliffs. No, Caesar, there were no garrisons, no forts there, just a beacon at the southern headland at the foot of the wide bay.

"Then that's it," declared Maximian. "Constantius Chlorus will take the first wave of troopships into Lympne after one of the tribunes: that's you, Heslus. If you can rouse yourself from your usual elegant languor, you will lead the raiding party that will seize the harbour. You'll probably not be able to sail in, so come ashore just west of the place, and capture it from the landward side. Keep a couple of swift biremes free to bring back situation reports. They'll also be useful as markers for the crews bringing back the empty barges for the next load. I'll see to it that the pharos and other signal fires are lit the whole time, day and night, so the returning vessels will have a navigation aid, of smoke or fire.

"I personally will head the second wave of troopships, and we'll leave from Itius Portus at the same time the cavalry squadrons embark from Bononia, so we'll arrive more or less together. If we get the wind and tide right, the crossing should take just a few hours, which will give us plenty of time on the second day to disembark, sort things out and move on towards Dover."

As a gusty, grey dawn broke, Heslus and his marines sailed into the chop of the Narrow Sea, tasked with seizing the harbour at Lympne. Constantius Chlorus gave them four hours' head start, then sailed for Lympne himself with something more than one-third of the invasion fleet. His flotilla was labouring just over an hour out from Gaul when the wind rose and conditions, already marginal, abruptly worsened.

grey-green waves rolled in, breaking in towers of white foam over the barges as their captains fought frantically to avoid being swamped. The loaded troopships sat low in the water, under deadly threat from the crashing, steep-sided ranks of saltwater. The gale turned stronger and stronger, hurling itself down-strait with a force that the wide steerboards could not resist. Desperate and seasick, soldiers bailed with their leather helmets to empty over the side the sloshing water that was already knee-deep inside some vessels, and all the while, the sea exploded over the low gunwales. Finally, the armada faced its simple choice: to turn before the wind or founder in mid-strait.

The barge captains saved their ships. They were losing the fight to inch their vessels towards the white cliffs they could see to the north, and they turned downwind, and west. His shipmaster saw the others turning, and reported to Constantius. "We're have to go much more westerly than we want, lord," the mariner. "If we're lucky, we'll make land maybe ten miles further down the coast than we planned." The general didn't hesitate. "Just get us ashore without drowning every bastard man and mule, as close as you can to Lympne," he ordered. "Signal the fleet to follow us. Send one of those biremes back to Bononia to tell the emperor what's happened."

The shock troops who had gone ahead of the fleet were hardy veterans from the Third Gallica, men who had spent long years catching and crucifying the rebel peasants, runaway slaves and army deserters who roamed across Spain and Gaul. After setting off four hours ahead of their general, their dozen ships were in formation and within clear sight of the landing beaches. They could see the lit, smoking beacons that warned the enemy west and east along the coast of their arrival, but there was nothing they could do about that. As ordered by their officers, the legionaries were readied for battle, fully armed and armoured, strapped into their mail and segmentata breastplates. A mile or so more, and they'd be wading ashore.

The shipmasters one by one spotted it as they turned their eyes from what lay ahead, and each felt the clutch of fear in his chest. A dark band, blue-black, streaked and ominous, was spreading across the sky to the east. Faster than a galloping horse, the line of squalls battered in from the

German Sea. In minutes, the bay's shallow, shelving waters were whipped into a turbulence of pyramid-shaped waves, cross-currents and vicious eddies.

Three of the loaded galleys foundered within a half mile of shore, taking to the sea bed every man aboard who was weighted by his armour. Two of the other galleys turned and ran before the wind, but likely failed to clear the point. They were never seen again. Fine seamanship by the Greek and Egyptian shipmasters on the other seven vessels got them ashore, foundering and half-swamped, but with a miraculously minimal loss of lives. The tribune Heslus, soaked through and shivering under his sodden red cloak, thought bitterly that right now the Britons wouldn't think him a very formidable Red Dragon. He shook off the distractions and put the legionaries into military order on the shingly beach before marching them inland, unopposed. The terrain was rolling, with some short hills and some open, sheep-nibbled down land where a peasant's cottage with smoking chimney showed that bread was being baked. Heslus took stock. He had just more than half the number of troops he'd expected to have for the job, but they were weathered, tough and experienced in the hit and run of guerrilla tactics. They should be enough to drive off a rabble of painted savages, he thought. The carnifex and his crucifix builders would be busy in the coming days.

A rabble of tattooed and painted savages was not what was waiting for the landing party. Before the port of Lympne came in sight the Romans saw the gleam of metal and heard the blare of brass trumpets. As if they were rising out of the ground, a broad line of leather-helmeted, shield-bearing troops tramped towards them, up a small rise. They rose into sight, revealed as not one rank, but five, and not one file, but 40. Then another phalanx of similar size and order came over the brow of another green hill to the Romans' right.

Heslus was no coward, but he felt a frisson of fear at the nape of his neck. He knew his soldiers were experienced, but they had never met troops trained and disciplined in the Roman way. The irony didn't escape him. His soldiers were going to face foreign troops who used Roman tactics, and did it better. The British colonials were more Roman than his own men. He knew he was viewing Nemesis, the fate that had been ordained for him at birth, and he knew that the spinners who created the thread of his life were about to snip it short.

Coolly, suppressing panic with an almost physical effort, he began issuing orders. The Romans halted, shuffled into close order, dropped their marching packs and stepped forward into line of battle. Heslus looked through the driving rain for any scrap of terrain that might give advantage. At the moment, the numbers were about even, but he knew the Britons would be bringing up more troops. He'd be fighting a defensive battle until Constantius could arrive, and he was probably going to be more than four hours away, as he would have had to contend for longer with the Channel storm. Minerva herself only knew where he'd come ashore.

Heslus scanned the landscape. To the Romans' left was a small wooded ravine. At 300 paces distant, it might be attainable, and it could provide some flank protection for his formation. The tribune turned his men towards it. The oncoming Britons tramped forward, knocking shields together and overlapping the edge of the shield of the next soldier. He would protect his comrade's side with his shield and be protected in turn by his neighbour. All the while the two British phalanxes were heading steadily towards the invaders in a pincer that would fatally squeeze the Roman ranks.

"Third Gallica!" the tribune's voice was a bellow as he addressed the invaders. "Stay steady, pay attention to your centurions. We will hold this British rabble here until the general brings us more force, then we'll cut them down and continue on our way. It will be just a short wait. You'll have a healthy night in the open air instead of in some fleapit tavern with poxed-up whores!" Heslus heard not even a single snigger at his joke. The men, he realized, were frightened. This was outside their experience. For most, it was a view of their first and maybe of their last war hedge brought against them by enemies, and the two moving ramparts of elm, leather and bronze were closing from opposite sides. A spatter of arrows came from the Romans' left, and the shuffling legionaries slung their big shields on that side, for protection. Stay steady, Heslus thought, the ravine and wood is only another 100 paces or so. He was looking to his right, assessing how much time before the first of those Britons would be in bowshot and he could expect to be under real fire.

Ahead of him, without warning, the trees seemed to flicker in the rain and their leaves trembled. Half of his first rank, still stepping out towards

246

the cover of the trees, were thrown back by an unseen hand, a slashing storm; arrows. Men were on their knees, choking and gasping in bloody gouts. Others were tugging at arrow shafts that protruded from their thighs, necks and bellies. They had been marching with shields slung on their left, a cover against missiles from the closer British formation that menaced them there, and they had walked into a concealed battery of enemy archers. A second volley smashed into the struggling column, then the archers were stepping out of the fringe of the trees and nocking for another salvo of triple-bladed death.

Heslus' mind reeled at the suddenness of the action. Minutes before, he was marching in an empty land, now, he was beset on three sides and he knew his force was doomed. Better go down fighting. The testudo, he thought; form the armoured turtle of shields above and around his panicked column that would let it survive the arrow storm. He opened his mouth to bellow the command; it never came. An arrow smashed through his front teeth and tongue and into the roof of his mouth. Heslus, scion of a patrician family that claimed descent from Gaius Julius himself, expensively educated and beautifully mannered, died choking on a piece of smelted iron fastened to an arm's length of poplar. Worse, he died knowing failure, unable to form up his men.

His last thoughts were of his duty. As his life flowed away, his dying mind told him his voice could have saved his command from the irresistible oncoming shield walls. He registered the first screams at the impacts of the battering bronze shield bosses that struck down the fragmenting ranks of Romans, and sank into oblivion before he could feel the impacts of the down-stabbing spears and swords that hacked into his unflinching body.

In the castle at Dover, Carausius heard the horseman's report. He himself would speak to the handful of prisoners salvaged from the bloodied wreck of the Roman landing party, to see what he could learn of Maximian's plans and troop dispositions. This was obviously a probing party, or was it? Surely, Maximian wasn't mad enough to try a beach landing in these conditions? The Romans were heading towards Lympne, maybe that was their idea, but with so few troops? Well, the coastline was alerted, the beacons saw to that, and he could only await reports as his response troops were moving into position. There would be more, and soon, he knew. Maximian would not come unless he came with overwhelming force. Even with Carausius' best preparations, the Romans would be almost unstoppable. He thought bitterly of the disciplined skills with which 10,000 legionaries of the XIV Gemini, outnumbered twenty to one, had destroyed the rebel Boadicea's wild British warriors. He stirred uneasily. He was relying on a surprise weapon from the old queen's day. Would it work? Or would he witness his own troops being butchered, as were hers? Carausius physically shook himself like a dog shedding water. He had military problems to face, and pessimism and superstition were timewasting luxuries.

Where were the Romans coming ashore? It was vital he knew, to concentrate his reserves and catch them as they came onto the beach, before they gained a decent foothold. He turned to the sorceress Guinevia, who had been recording orders for the garrisons in London and Eboracum. "What do you think Maximian is doing?" he asked, frustrated. She stared at him oddly, and a small vapour cloud formed unnoticed above their heads. Suddenly, clairvoyantly, it was all outlined in his mind, so sharp and detailed that it was palpably the truth; he knew. He was absolutely certain that he knew the future. The Romans intended first to seize the lesser port of Lympne, to use it to disembark an initial landing of the first waves of troops. With that established beach head, they'd march overland on a broad front to Dover, sweeping aside the thin screen of cavalry that would oppose them, to surprise and destroy his fleet in harbour. That accomplished, they could use the port's facilities and the river wharfs for the swift disembarkations of more and more troops, with a quick turnaround of the invasion vessels to ferry more reinforcements from Bononia. With Dover in their hands, they would establish an unassailable strongpoint from which they could crush the Britons at leisure.

Those unexpected squalls had saved him as they deflected that first landing party from its target. That means, Carausius reasoned as he enjoyed the psychic clarity induced by the sorceress, that they'd been swept just a critical little way off course, down the strait. Everything was clear to him and his years of sailing the strait caused him to flash on the thoughts: 'Chances are they wouldn't try to weather Dungeness with all that offshore rip and the turbulence of the undersea ridge there. They'd have opted to run ashore where they could. Chances also are they'd have planned to arrive in two or more waves because Lympne isn't big enough to handle them all at once.' If the weather abates, he thought, and his experience in these waters told him that it soon would, they'd be able to get everyone ashore on the shingle beaches on the east side of Dungeness.

He was as certain as he breathed that Maximian would do that. "He won't want to split his forces and risk having us destroy them one piece at a time," Carausius murmured. He calmed his racing thoughts. He should expect that the Romans were about to land the first part of their force, probably in the big bay east of Dungeness. They would not dare to land the second part in darkness. Anyway, the tide would be wrong for that. It was clear to him: the first troops would hack their way ashore to establish a beach head, the second would have to wait, or stand out to sea and come ashore on the beach on the next tide, in daylight tomorrow. That should give them enough legionaries to grab Lympne despite the troops the Britons could scramble together at short notice, and then the Romans could land their heavy stuff like the artillery and siege equipment, plus livestock like the cavalry horses and transport mules at a proper harbour.

It was all clear to Carausius, and equally clear to him was what he could do to stop the invaders. He turned to the flame-haired Welsh earl Cuneglasus, a fine warrior who had earned his kingdom of Powys with his own strong sword arm and command of his wild chariot squadrons. "Use your influence with these prickly princelings," he told him. "Get the jarls and barons in here, as many of them as you can round up, as quickly as you can. I want a gathering within the hour. Don't let them waste time squabbling about who defers to whom, or who sits where, and send messengers to get word out to the others up the coast. Send for the prefects and tribunes, too. Every officer here, half an hour." His eye fell on Guinevia and he thought of their small son, who was presumably in his wicker crib with an attendant nurse. 'Take Milo away from the coast. It won't be safe here. Be ready to travel." Guinevia smiled gently and shook her head. "We shall be safe," she said calmly. "And, Caros, my place is with you." Already though, Carausius was not listening. His mind was churning with the situation at hand since he had seen the future so clearly. He turned to a tribune. "Get the fleet on full readiness, prepare the log booms to block the harbour here and across the Thames river, but don't put them in place until we know they're definitely coming. We'll deny them Dover and Londinium with just a few big trees in the right place and a few hundred men on the shore. But first, get a boom in place at Lympne, too. I want that port shut down, now. Don't wait until you see the enemy, implement that order at once. And you," he gestured at his cavalry commander, "stay with me. I have something urgent for you."

XXXIII. Lympne

Constantius Chlorus, meanwhile, was waist-deep in surging surf. The first wave of troopships was grinding ashore on a desolate bank of shingle that was barely east of a low promontory. That projection stuck out into the narrows and seemed to have created some truly foul currents and violent wave action out there. Good thing they'd not had to sail through that, he thought. The shipmasters had been obviously alarmed at the sight and had vehemently warned him against trying. They'd turned for the shore and run up the shingle, but the general's own ship had grounded short of the shore on an outer bank and he and his troops had to wade ashore through deeper water. He was losing his footing and, armoured as he was, in serious danger when an attentive ensign caught Chlorus by the tie cords of his crimson officer's cloak and half-dragged him to the shallows. Damned saltwater, everything will chafe and itch for days, the general thought. He struggled up the shingly beach and took the tribune's salute crossly, two red spots marking his pale face.

"We've sent scouts out already, lord," said the officer. "We seem to be at the arse end of nowhere. That way, north, is what looks like a big marsh, but this shingle seems to go northeast and inland. It's good footing, which could allow us to make decent progress once we get everyone landed." The general frowned.

"Get on with it," he snapped. "Get everyone ashore, it'll take hours. Set up for the night. We're here until dawn anyway; we're not going stumbling off into a bog." He gave his cloak to his servant. "Get that thing dried out, and get me another one," he ordered. "I'm soaked."

Even in the soft half-light of a summer's dusk, the British cavalry troop sent from Dover did not make an impressive sight. The ponies, shaggy moorland creatures, were so small their riders' dangling feet almost touched the ground, and behind each saddle was slung a pair of big nets untidily stuffed with forage, all of it adding to an unmilitary appearance. The riders themselves wore an assortment of armour and equipment: leather helmets with a stitched ridge, leather-reinforced trews to protect their thighs from chafing on the sheepskin horse blankets that covered their steeds' backs, small round targs as shields and breastplates of boiled leather. The most military things about them were the long lances they carried, but the overall effect was hardly parade order, as each rider led two or three mules. Those beasts of burden were loaded with leather bags full of some metallic cargo that clinked occasionally as the animals trotted.

Their appearance may have been unimpressive, but the cavalry was highly trained and efficient, and their commander had taken careful note of his emperor's orders, which were to locate but not engage the enemy, to remain unseen if possible, to scout the ground for a specified set of conditions and to dispose of the contents of the leather sacks in a particular manner.

The commander, a diligent man, saw to it that his equestrians carried out those orders scrupulously, discreetly and well. His silent scouts, their accoutrements tied with scraps of linen to prevent metal clashing on metal, went unobserved as they spotted the Romans encamped on the shingle, where they were readying for the next morning's arrival of more troops. They reported the sighting, the cavalry commander issued some quiet directions, and he and his squadron did what they were ordered to do without being detected. The entire squadron faded away into the darkness after making certain identifying marks with small cairns of piled rocks on the shoreline.

High tide came just before first light, and Maximian ordered his two fleets launched from the coast of Gaul for Lympne, trusting that the port had been seized by now. The first fleet, under Maximian's own command, set out from Itius Portus. The larger ships left the harbour in a steady procession and the smaller troop barges were manhandled down the shelving sandy beach into the now-calming waves. As the emperor sailed, he sent couriers south to inform his admirals. They and the larger transports from Bononia would carry the cavalry and heavier gear like the siege equipment, nail kegs, bridge-building materials and catapults. They'd delay their departures to allow Maximian time to disembark his troops and clear the harbour to receive the cavalry and heavy gear, for they too were headed for Lympne.

Maximian was barely clear of the shore when the bireme was sighted. "Finally," he grumbled to an aide. "Where has that bloody messenger been?" Shortly, the oared vessel pulled close alongside and the courier from Constantius made his report. The fleet had been blown off course and landed about ten miles down the coast from Lympne. The courier ship had spent the night battling wind and tide to bring the news, and the messenger did not know if the port had been seized. Perhaps the other bireme courier ship would have more news, lord. Maximian tugged at his beard. "We may well not have the port," he told his officers. "We'll go there first to investigate. Send a couple of ships northwest to contact Constantius and find out his situation. It may be we'll have to land these troops on the beach and march back to Lympne to seize the place. It's a nuisance, but it can be done."

He sent the bireme back into Bononia to apprise his officers there of the change. The cavalry and the siege train would have to follow later than planned. He'd get word to them when to leave, but it might mean the delay of a day or so. He shrugged. He could cope without the cavalry and there would be no call yet for siege engines. As he turned to watch the messengers depart, a plume of smoke caught his eye. He looked at the headland of Gris Nez, where an obvious signal fire was blazing, and swore. Eastwards, beyond the headland another and then another matching blaze and attendant smoke plume answered. Westwards, three more signals told the British across the narrows that the Roman fleet was on the water.

The heavy boom of tree trunks chained end to end was stretched across the mouth of the harbour at Lympne and the Britons had fortified the breakwater with ballistae and archers against any possible landing to remove it. In the Thames at Tilbury, grunting sailors were grumbling at Car the Bear's demands as they hauled another floating barrier of chained logs to where it could be deployed across the river in the matter of a quarter hour. The long line of signal towers stretched along the banks of the estuary would give plenty of warning of the Romans' approach. At Dover, the British fleet was putting out into the Narrow Sea and a troop of marines was already floating the port's vast boom into place as the last of the flotilla moved towards the strait. Britain was closing its sea gates, and the wooden walls of its defences were being sailed out to meet the invaders.

During the night, the warriors of Britain had also been moving into place, marching west down the high road from Dover to meet the enemy encamped on the sweeping shingle beach at Dungeness. Their cavalry scouts along the white cliffs could see more Romans sailing in mid-strait, angling towards the port at Lympne. Soon, after the invaders' reconnaissance vessels had surveyed the defences and scurried back to the main fleet, the flotilla changed direction and, sailing parallel to the shore, headed west for the landing ground their comrades had occupied.

Carausius and his general staff trotted their horses onto a small bluff above the shingle to the east of the Roman beach head. From his vantage point, the war lord in his purple cloak surveyed the terrain. This was where he'd had his cavalry commander choose a site, and it had been carefully described to him. A ragged man was brought forward to the circle of officers. "This, lord, is a cattle drover who knows these marshes," explained the tribune Cragus, "and he has shown my scouts a path through the wetlands a mile or more over there." The emperor nodded. 'Give him gold and keep him close. He is not to leave until this battle is over."

He turned to the equestrian who had chosen the site. "Where did you put them?" The horseman pointed out the markers he'd left, rocks piled in groupings. Carausius looked and nodded. "Excellent." He held out his hand to congratulate the soldier, and they grasped wrists, shaking with conspiratorial grins like mischievous schoolboys. The emperor was delighted with the dispositions and showed it. Carausius' specific, detailed instructions to his cavalry commander had urged the man to choose a place like this with care, and he had chosen well.

What the emperor was viewing around the beach head of the encamped Romans was a sweeping bay. It ended in a low headland to the south before the land turned west into the next big bay. The inverted triangle of the promontory contained along its eastern edge one of the world's largest swathes of shingle where the Romans held their beach head. Tucked inside the triangle was a vast marshland almost impassable to man or beast. Further west, the marsh ran down to the sea on the other side of the headland, meaning that the Romans had chosen to camp with reedy marsh on two sides and the strait on the third. The Britons stood astride the invaders' only feasible land route out. The confrontation would come and the battle would be fought along the wide, firm strip to the Romans' east, between marsh and sea. Behind the British defenders was the road to Dover.

The emperor set his sappers to work. They began digging deep pits about 20 feet apart and drove sharpened stakes and short-shafted spears, points upright, into the bottoms of the holes. No cavalry could cross those works. The Britons' left flank was guarded by the strait, their right flank ended at the marsh, and there, in the reedy shallows, the cavalry commander had under cover of darkness emptied the contents of the baggage mules' leather sacks. Hundreds of coltrops, horse-crippling, four-pointed spikes were concealed under the surface of the muddied water. Infantry would be slowed and too vulnerable to the archers if they tried to plunge through the mud and water, but cavalry could be used to try to turn the flank there. Now, a hidden spiked barrier marked with rocks whose significance was known only to the British awaited any flanking cavalry.

Another surprise was in store for the invaders. Concealed behind the reverse slope of a line of dunes that stretched behind the Britons' rear, a vast flood of the barons and jarls of Britain who had answered the emperor's call was arriving. They had come from their halls and fortresses in the meadows and moors of their country to repel the Romans, and they had brought the weapons used two centuries before by their great queen Boadicea. Gathering quickly, and still hidden behind the dunes were rank upon rank of the terrible war chariots of the Britons' ancestors, called to duty one more time to save the country from the ancient enemy.

Carausius paused in his anxious reconsideration of his deployments as he thought of those chariots so vital to his plans. Could they, would they carry out the task he'd set them? It was with the gods, he thought. At the same moment, on one of the rock piles that marked a limit of the cavalry trap, a white rat groomed its whiskers, and at an ancient shrine three miles away, the priestess Guinevia was sacrificing a lamb to the witch goddess Nicevenn.

The Romans had investigated the harbour at Lympne and found it barred to them by the log boom and the waiting ballistae. Maximian's signal officers each took his red woollen flags, and following the book, waved two-handed the codes that turned the fleet west to join Constantius. It would have to be a beach landing, but the sea was calmer, so the operation was feasible. The emperor sent word back by bireme to

Bononia to send on the cavalry, but to leave the siege engines behind for now. The blue sails of the Roman invasion fleet headed steadily west.

Carausius' tribunes oversaw the dispositions as they chivvied their troops into line. On this overcast day, there was no sun behind them to dazzle the Romans, as the military manuals advised in choosing a position, but the wind at least was favourable, sending dust towards the enemy. In the battle lines, behind the deep-dug pits, each man had three feet of space; each rank was six feet apart. Carausius, resplendent in his war gear, ordered a century of 80 picked men to stay with him and the Eagle standards of the legions.

He and the elite red-chevroned guard who had uncovered the lost Eagle would be front and centre of the line, at the place where the fighting would be bloodiest, for the enemy would want to capture the vaunted standards and it was the place of honour. If the battle went badly, it was also the place of most danger, but the big emperor knew his purple crest, his Eagle standards, his new linen flag with its bear emblem would stand proudly. His silver jarl's badge of office marked him as a feared lord of war and his men would take confidence from those symbols. Privately, he knew that every tiny advantage was desperately important. The Romans were a fearsome enemy, and this land battle would be his most difficult ever. He had the advantage of fighting from behind defences, but his forces would be well outnumbered. It was, he thought grimly, a time to look at the sky and ask the gods for help. By the end of the day, he might well be in chains, dead or hanging from a crucifix. This was one battle he could not afford to lose, for himself or for his country.

Carausius glanced again at the clouded sky, wondering again how many more days or mere hours he had left in this life, then shrugged aside his pessimism; time to wonder about all that after the battle. For now, he had much to do. He called to a tribune and instructed him to ensure that certain centurions had specific orders about moving men to allow the chariots through and when to do it. The wings of the line were secured by the sea and the marsh, the centre was reinforced with pits and stakes. The tribunes had mustered a reserve infantry force behind the dunes with the hidden chariots and another force was dispatched under Cragus with the cattle drover to guide their way through the marshes. A path there would bring them out behind the Romans' rear, the drover had assured them. Cragus vowed to gut the man himself if he lied.

Carausius knew he stood at the hinge of history, when a new nation could create its own future. The Britons had come together as never before to resist an invader, and here was the flower of Britain's nobility facing the power of Rome. One or other army must be broken on a lonely stretch of shingle along the southern shore of the misty northern island.

Behind the dunes, the long-moustached warrior barons from the fastnesses of Britain were gathered in front of their chariots, arranged in a half circle around a small woman. The sorceress Guinevia was calling on her witch goddess. "The hellequin Nicevenn leads the Wild Hunt that drives the damned to Hades each year, on the night of Samhain," she told them. "I am her adept, she gives me power. I am also the disciple of Myrddin, who was born of a demon and a king's daughter, and is earthlord of the sea god Mannanan mac Lir. They have embraced me with magic and the power of our British gods." She gestured slowly, pointing her finger upwards and circling it. A small vapour cloud had formed above her, at twice the height of a tall man. The armed warriors stirred uneasily.

Guinevia lowered her pointing hand. For a moment, not one of the hundreds of men or horses made a single small sound. Into that silence, as shocking as a thunderclap, Guinevia bellowed. Her voice had become harsh and gravelled, a tone that seemed to echo from the caverns of the Underworld itself. The warriors shifted uneasily and their ponies stamped and snorted as the witch's tones carried across the dunes. "I call on Nicevenn and her mounted ghouls to ride with us this day. I call on her to bring dead Boadicea and her spirit charioteers to defend Britain once again as she did with justice before. I call on Nicevenn to claim the souls of these invaders and to take them as her playthings into the deepest pit of torment and to preserve our British warriors while they carry out this task with their emperor."

The charioteers, awed and uncertain, stood mute as the words died away. A whirl of wind gusted, spinning a slender spiral of dust across the open end of the half-moon of awestruck, on-looking men. Guinevia broke the spell. "Look," she said simply, in her accustomed voice. "The goddess has heard us. Now go, and make these extortionists regret they ever heard of our land. Make them pay with their blood."

The first of Maximian's reinforcing fleet was easing into the shallows, a heartening sight for the encamped Romans. Two or three at a time, the ships crunched ashore, grinding the pebbly shore under their keels. Men handed down shields and bundles of arrows, spears and other war gear to waiting comrades, then spilled over the sides to wade ashore. Offshore, standing to in the tidal calm of slack water, dozens more of the invasion fleet lined up to disembark their cargoes and men.

An alert ensign saw the danger first as they emerged from a line of low-lying haze. From the east, running before the wind like wild geese, came the British fleet, sails stretched as outspread wings, oar blades flashing rhythmically to the boom of drums, a white feather of foam at the foot of each bow. They raced down the strait like wolves on a sheep fold, and they tore into the lines of the Roman ships, ramming them with their iron-bound prows of oak even as the stalled, hove-to barges tried to up sail and turn away. From the British warships poured volleys of darts, fire arrows and javelins, all thudding into the waists of the invaders' vessels, as archers and soldiers fired down from the fighting towers.

The civilian master mariners from Egypt and Phoenicia, from Greece and Dalmatia who worked the Roman fleet were panicked. Some turned their vessels downwind to escape, unaware that the swirling waters off the promontory concealed ship-killing ridges of rock. Others, sometimes forced at sword-point by their Roman officers, slammed their vessels onto the beach, spilling men and equipment into the shallows. Still more were simply sunk where they were rammed, their clinkered pine hulls fragile against the oaken ribs and iron-bound carvel planking of the British ships. In a half hour, it was over. Some of the invasion fleet was grounded on the beach, some was mere flotsam; the others were foundering in the sea race off the promontory.

XXXIV. Dungeness

On shore, centurions under ever more frantic orders from the despairing beachmaster were battling to restore order from the chaos of men and piles of gear scrambled onto land. Soldiers from the first expedition were wading out to help their comrades ashore when the warning shouts began and they turned to struggle to dry land again, to find weapons and meet the thunderbolt that had erupted through the British lines. A hundred or more war chariots were racing across the firm shingle, axle to axle, charioteers crouched over the reins, flogging their wild-eyed ponies into frenzies of speed. The Romans ran to form ranks, but their efforts were too late. They were still grouped and bunched, struggling with armour and weapons, when the onslaught hit. At 20 paces, as they still were galloping in, the near-naked, blue-tattooed warriors alongside the drivers launched their heavy javelins, delivering them with all their power, a force boosted by the chariots' speed. The effect was devastating.

The chariots wheeled, their iron tires spraying shingle, and the spearmen were ready with the next volley. In moments, they were balancing surefooted down the centre shaft between the horses and had launched again, then sent a third javelin. The impact of the triple strike was like a scythe through a grain field. Dead and wounded Romans were collapsed like cornstalks after a reaper's swathe. Before the invaders could rally themselves or bring up unwounded troops, the British warriors had leaped back onto their wheeled fighting platforms and were racing away. Constantius turned to his emperor, eyes wide. "Those fucking things haven't been used in centuries," he said slowly. "Where did they come from?" Maximian, teeth gritted at all the setbacks he was encountering, shook his head. "We'll take them down when the heavy cavalry get here, that's all. Let's push these bastards out of the way and go and get that damned harbour."

For the next two hours, as harried centurions struggled to dispose their men and equipment, the chariots raced in again and again to sweep the beach head troops with their volleys, although some judiciously-planted stakes ahead of the ranks and a few companies of Roman archers did much to blunt the attacks. Finally, Maximian's patience broke again. "Let's move now, shove these nuisances aside and clear the way. I'm not waiting any longer. I have enough force here to do the job."

The trumpets and the voices of the centurions joined in a cacophony of orders, and the leading ranks of legionaries formed up in wedges, small triangular formations led by one soldier, who, protected by the shields of the comrades alongside him, spearheaded his unit into the enemy lines. The fighting wedges were designed to isolate and force the enemy into restricted positions that didn't allow much freedom for hand to hand fighting, but was favourable to the Romans' thrusting, stabbing attack from behind the protection of their shields.

The legions were lined up; Maximian tapped his sword hilt for luck, then waved his ivory and gold baton of office. "Move forward!" he bellowed. His legions began their steady tramp towards the waiting Britons.

The British tribune Quirinus was beside his emperor in the front rank with the Eagles and their elite guard when the first Roman wedge arrived. The Britons' shields were edge to iron edge, their long spears bristled outwards at eye level. At Carausius' nod, he gave the orders. "Stand by, stand by!" he bellowed. "Now!!" In a disciplined movement the Britons made their spears vertical and raised their shields into the tortoise defence of the testudo. Almost at once, the hail of javelins hurled by the Romans rattled onto the armoured carapace, as Quirinus had expected and countered. "Again!" he bellowed as the second volley beat down on them. "Spears … now!"

As he had trained them, the rear ranks of his troops dropped their shields and hurled their javelins and heavy darts over their comrades and into the oncoming Romans, many of whom had lowered their shields so they could dispatch their own missiles. "Spears!" Quirinus bellowed again, and a second volley thumped into the Romans as they stumbled over their own dead and wounded.

Already, the first Romans were mere paces away from the death pits dug in front of the British ranks. They began swerving aside, breaking formation, as they were forced to funnel themselves into the narrow gaps between the pits. The cohesion of their shield wall crumbled. Men jostled each other desperately to avoid a fall onto the sharpened stakes and gaps opened in the shield wall. Quirinus bellowed the command again. "Spears! Darts!" Again, the rear ranks poured iron death from the sky and the Roman wounded and dying formed mounds of bloodied, moaning men that obstructed their comrades, but still they came on. Now they were slower and slower as some pushed over their fallen comrades, and others broke ranks to drag them back, out of the way.

Volleys of heavy javelins, darts and the weighted, three-bladed arrows of the Britons slashed and hammered into the Roman ranks. Legionaries were crumpling where they stood, unable even to fall backwards for the press of troops behind them. The sheer weight of oncoming soldiers forced the front ranks into the outnumbered British, and the defenders began to flinch away. Carausius waved the signal for the catapults to fire, and blazing buckets of pitch arced up and then down to splash across the Roman ranks.

Some legionaries fell, but snarling officers goaded and swore their men onwards, and the great phalanx of armour moved forward through the clouds of choking, dense smoke. The left wing of the Britons fell back and the Romans along the shoreline were through the blocking line of death pits. In minutes, Carausius knew, his line would crumple and be rolled up from that side. He bellowed new orders and imprecations, and the elite guard with their proud red chevrons that were testaments to their role as guardians of the sacred lost Eagle stepped forward with him and their standards into the heaving mass of the oncoming enemy.

The Britons were maddened with battle rage, each oblivious of his own safety and confident in the shield comrade who protected his right side. The unexpected surge pushed the Romans back, and the emboldened Britons began hacking and thrusting with new energy in the corpse-congested gap between two of the death pits.

Inch by inch, the Britons heaved the oncoming legionaries back, and regained their lost line and the defensive pits. Carausius and the Eagles' guard stepped aside as a rush of troops flooded back to assist, then his attention was caught by a courier. On the Roman left, the invaders were now gaining, battering the British line into submission. The emperor scanned the flank. It seemed inevitable; the British line was flanked and would surely be collapsed. Carausius turned his battered elite and his Eagles and scrambled them to the almost-surrounded ranks before they broke. He was barely in time. The big, scarred warrior king led the counter attack, hewing with Exalter over the shield wall, forcing his opponents back pace by pace. He cleared the enemy from the blood-slick gap between two pits and the Britons pushed their dead and dying enemies into them, making space to take up their stations again.

After that small gain, the next gap was cleared as the front ranks of the legion fell back in formation, and then the next, and the next reopened, too. The moment was right for Carausius' secret weapon again. He nodded to his tribune and made a gesture to the rear. Quirinus bellowed his pre-set commands, and the British arrays parted in the strategy the centurions had agreed. At the dead run, chariots raced into the just-cleared spaces, and crashed into the front ranks of the Romans. This time, the Roman ranks did not have the chariot-baffling stakes in place, but it still looked like a losing sacrifice, giving up the flimsy chariots for one small gain.

This time, however, the British warriors didn't dismount. They hurled two, three heavy javelins into the faces of the stalled legionaries, then laid about them with heavy swords and axes, hacking and chopping down into necks and heads. More Britons ran up to surround and mount the chariots, fighting down from the platforms, stabbing with long spears over the enemy shields at the cracking Roman ranks. More fiery missiles flew in. The bloodied, burned legionaries backed away through the smoke, stumbling over their tidemark of dead, retreating to the stalled ranks of their comrades.

The chariots were hauled backwards free of the litter of dead and dying, were wheeled, and then run back into their own lines. Attendants dragged out the worst of the wounded horses and harnessed fresh beasts. In minutes, the chariots that had broken the armoured ranks were moving quickly behind the British lines, swerving towards the shore, to be deployed against the flanking right wing of the oncoming Romans, who again threatened to force the Britons away from the constricting pits and into the open where they would be butchered.

White-eyed and foaming at the mouth, the half-wild ponies of the charioteers cantered down the rear of the British line to where the tide sucked at the shingle, then they wheeled directly at the rear ranks of the Britons, who gave way, opening for them and allowing them free passage to charge the Romans. Again, the chariots did their grim work.

The biting, thrashing horses and the warriors' vicious whirling blades and spears broke the ordered ranks. The Romans exacted a bitter price in men and horses, but yard by yard they were forced back until the British line was re-formed and the surviving charioteers could withdraw and regroup.

Constantius was furious. Twice more, he hurled his legionaries against the British, twice more, he was thrown back, halted by the barrage of javelins into the choke points of the constricting death pits. Worse, more and more of his men were cut down from the surviving chariots as they retreated to reform. "We need the fucking cavalry," he told his emperor. "These bastards may as well be behind stone walls. We have to get around them."

Maximian grunted. "The equestrians should be here soon." He was right. Within the hour, the blue sails of the heavy transports showed. Minutes later, so did the sails of the British fleet. The Roman ground his teeth in impotent fury as he watched the sea battle from the shore. The heavier, shallow-draft vessels of the islanders crunched through his fleet, ramming and burning, only rarely allowing themselves to be boarded. It did not take long before half of the Roman fleet was sent to the sea floor or had fled into the strait.

The surviving warships, deeper keeled than the troop barges, were running aground on sandbanks, forcing the sailors to offload their cargoes of terrified, kicking horses and mules into chest-deep water. By late afternoon, it was done and the surviving fraction of the cavalry was ashore. Maximian's dispirited, mauled force was all on the beach, only part of the great army with which he had planned to invade, but still a formidable force if he could deploy them properly. "We have to outflank them, we can't stay here on this godforsaken shingle and we can't get through their lines. We simply have to go around them with what we have left of the cavalry," he instructed Constantius.

"Send the horsemen through the edge of the marsh and sweep the Brits up from the rear. If we can roll up these bastards behind the pits, we can crush them." The general gave the orders, the brass trumpets blared and the vengeful troops moved forward for the fourth time. At a hundred paces from the waiting Britons, the Roman cavalry burst out to attack the British right, plunging into the chest-deep waters of the marsh to outflank the infantry. The first line of horses made a fine sight, surging with the water up to their sheepskin breast bands, their armoured riders waving heavy swords, yelling threats at their enemies.

Deep in the tall reeds of the marshes north of the beach, wading in a water world of swaying head-high grasses, Cragus urged on the cattle drover who was guiding him and his troop. The sounds of the battle, the clashing of metal on metal, the shouts and wails of the wounded were all carried clearly on the wind. "Keep moving, keep going forward," the officer encouraged the struggling legionaries, holding in his fears that they would be too late or not emerge in the right place. Then he heard the first horse scream, marking the moment that the gods swung the battle's fortunes to the British and the tide of victory away from the Romans. In seconds, the whole front rank of the invaders' cavalry was down and thrashing as horse after horse stepped on the crippling caltrops and was lamed. The vicious spikes struck through the horses' unguarded hoofs deep into the shock-absorbing frog and up into the coffin bone. In moments, the marsh water was red with thick blood, yet more horsemen charged in, saw their mounts crippled and were thrown into the heaving, thrashing melee.

As the dismounted, labouring cavalrymen in their heavy armour waded out of the clinging mud, they were cut down by the waiting British. Those horses not lamed were turned back shivering to safety behind the shocked ranks of infantry, who involuntarily halted. Constantius, his face purple with rage, was bellowing at his officers to move the ranks forward, but they stayed motionless, transfixed by the thrashing agonies of the men and horses who were supposed to swing the battle for them.

And, as the Romans stood stock still, Cragus and his force emerged behind them, out from the marshes they had traversed blindly to arrive miraculously on time and at the right place. Not one of Maximian's force spotted the outflanking Britons behind them as they stepped from the bulrushes and reeds, but the British tribune Quirinus did, and he alerted his emperor. Carausius, blood-streaked in the front rank of legionaries, flanked by his Eagles and the remnants of his elite, told his trumpeter to sound the command. At the blasting notes, the reserve infantry emerged from behind the dunes, and the front ranks with their warrior emperor stepped into the gaps between the death pits, which were now filled with Roman casualties.

On the right wing, the Britons shuffled sideways to their left, creating a gap between themselves and the marker stones at the edge of the marshes. Everything happened at once. The British chariots swept forward through the gap between the marker stones and their own infantry, heading at full stretch for the cowed, waiting Romans.

Awed spearmen later claimed that a mysterious, spectral shape galloped with them in a chariot drawn by white horses with blazing fire eyes. Some said they had seen it clearly, and it was the long-haired ghost of Queen Boadicea come again to cut the Romans into bloody ruin. The clatter of their wheels on the shingle was swamped by the roar of the troops of the centre, who under their warlord emperor, trotted forward in a classic shield wall, supporting the sacred Eagle that had been returned by the gods. A scant ten yards before the emperor's force clashed head on with the bristling Roman line, Cragus and his troops hit a hammer blow into Maximian's rear guard that confused and then shattered the ranks as easily as a fist closes and crushes an egg.

"We ground them into bloody offal," Carausius recalled later. He had only dim memories of his own crazed bloodlust, of his willing surrender to the mindless joy and fighting madness of violence. He'd been there at the front of the carnage with his beloved soldiers, shield-less under his eagle-crested war helm, swinging his long sword Exalter two-handed. He remembered it crashing through the cheek pieces of a Roman's helmet, spraying blood and teeth and tearing away the man's entire lower jaw so he died with a ghastly mockery of a half-grin.

There was, too, the spearman he'd gutted with an upswing that cut from the crotch, spilled the entrails and split the rib cage so it shone whitely like a woman's splayed fingers. He'd been singing, keening a battle noise to himself as he laboured like a blacksmith, beating, chopping, and swinging Exalter into blood-spurting flesh and bone, hammer blow after hammer blow tirelessly without stopping, for an hour.

It was a magical thing, to know the strength of your arms, he thought, to be an invincible lord of war surrendered to the overwhelming red bloodlust that was pounding in your ears. Time was trickling by so slowly you could see an enemy's movements almost before he made them. When their blows came they seemed to your lightning mind so laboured and deliberate you could step inside them, or deflect them while you were looking to see what was happening at your sides and could choose at leisure, step by steady step, how you'd move to parry and counter. They were good memories, he mused, as he grunted at the aches in his body, but it had been too close a contest. Only small things had won the day, but the gods had willed it.

The emperor, still stained with smoke and smeared with blood spatters, was sitting in the commander's quarters at Lympne, where a stack of reports and orders were waiting for his attention. He sighed as he recalled himself to the demands of the day. The prisoners, among them the general and emperor in waiting, Constantius Chlorus needed to be properly secured and fed. The dead had to be buried, the salvage teams must be sent out to collect war gear. Winning a battle led to more work, but it was the better option than losing, he felt. Some news was not so positive. Maximian and a medium-sized force had escaped by sea while his personal bodyguard died on the beach almost to the last man, fighting desperately to buy him time. The defeated emperor would likely come again, the Briton was sure. And a messenger brought news that made the emperor frown. Two Roman vessels blown west had survived the maelstrom of the narrows and had landed near Fishbourne, and in vengeance had sacked and burned Carausius' palace there.

A defence of the palace had been mounted by the Greek woman, the mosaic artist Claria, but it was against hopeless odds. Desperate to save the masterwork she had so painstakingly created, she had mustered a dozen household servants, including the muralist Celvinius, who had fought like a wild thing, said several slaves who'd escaped the raid. "Claria was in the courtyard at first, and we saw her shoot down three invaders with a hunting bow," they reported. The mural painter turned out to be a fighter, too.

"He had such skill with a spear that it took five Romans to finish him off," the emperor heard. "We don't know what happened to Claria, but the Romans looted the palace and burned it down. We watched from the woodlands and it was still aflame the next morning."

A pity, thought Carausius. That mosaic of the god Cupid on a dolphin was a masterpiece. Now it would never be seen again, for the magnificent palace and its contents were all gone. He had no time for regrets about the lost opulence, though it would have been a part of his legacy. Still, he thought, he could always have other memorials erected, and they'd last for hundreds of years.

For now, he had more pressing matters to concern him. He would announce that, in token of his role as British emperor, he would in future be known, not as Carausius, but in the way the sorcerer Myrddin had once named him: 'Arthur of Britain.' Something had resonated in his soul at the title, and with the triumph, it seemed oddly right. "Now," he thought, "I am no longer a Roman vassal. I am an emperor, and my son will be an emperor."

As a practical matter, he thought he should underscore the victory. He would continue the principle of harshness he'd long ago absorbed from the old crucifixioner. He'd take the defeated Caesar, Constantius Chlorus in chains to Londinium and have him publicly executed. That would send shock waves through Milan, Nicomedia, Antioch and the other seats of imperial power, but he had a fleet to keep the Romans and those threatening Saxons out of Britain for ever and a newly-united country to back it.

The legions could use a victory parade behind their proud Eagles. Allectus should mint some special donatives and it might be a good idea to erect a statue in Londinium, to commemorate the rebel queen Boadicea. He'd heard stories from his soldiers of fighting alongside a ghost chariot driven by a long-haired woman that had led the right wing's shattering strike on the Romans. Maybe there had been much magic working for the Britons that day.

Carausius fingered the large silver and amber brooch of his rank as a British jarl and smoothed the drape of his purple-banded imperial robe; Emperor of Britain. It was good to have the gods with you. In a corner of the room, a white rat preened its whiskers, curled comfortably and slept.

For now.

Post script: The Legend of Arthur

Britain's forgotten emperor Carausius and his triumphs may well be the true foundation of the legend of King Arthur, the mythic warrior who became a symbol of courage, chivalry and Christianity.

Late in the third century of the Common Era, the Belgic-born Mauseus Carausius was commander of Rome's English Channel fleet and was quietly building both his treasury and his military forces. Ordered to report for court martial by superiors nervous of his power, the burly, bear-like soldier instead declared himself emperor of Britain and northern Gaul, suborned several legions and the flotilla that controlled the Narrow Sea between the two countries and began a decade of defiance against the might of Rome.

In that time, the rebel emperor quieted the quarrelsome British tribes, unified the country and, as its first ruler (286 – 293 CE) used his navy to create and sustain the nation's independence. However, Carausius' significance in history was forgotten for centuries despite his achievements in driving off the Romans and quieting the Picts. He may also have defeated Germanic invaders, as his Saxon Shore fortifications prove that he was more than prepared to meet them. Today, his known and acclaimed triumphs are closely echoed in the stories of King Arthur.

The life purpose and the legend of Arthur, the battle leader of the British, came together when he led his nation successfully to repel invaders. That victorious 'lord of battles' was described by the monk Gildas, (circa 500 - 570 CE) who created the island's earliest written history when he penned an admonition of usurper kings, corrupt judges and foolish priests. In his sermon, Gildas described the siege of Mount Badon as the great conflict in which Anglo-Saxon invaders were routed decisively to bring peace after a long period of strife.

The north British monk's 'De Excidio et Conquestu Britanniae' ('On the Ruin and Conquest of Britain') speaks of an unnamed 'outstanding ruler' ('superbus tyrannus') who brought the British a series of victories that culminated at Badon. That event was so celebrated that Gildas did not bother to identify the location of Badon or even to name the victor, noting only that 'Arth' – Celtic for 'The Bear' – was such a great overlord that the king of Powys, Cuneglasus The Red, humbly acted as his master's charioteer. After that triumph, the very name 'Arthur' became a powerful symbol and was adopted by later rulers who wished to assume some of the glory of the legendary British champion.

Gildas' writings are valued as the earliest known recorded history of Britain, although his calendar was muddled. He wrongly dates the construction of the walls of Hadrian and Antoninus to the late fourth century, when they actually were created two centuries earlier. By his account, the ramparts were built in the years before invaders from the west and north devastated the island. In turn, the incomers were defeated in a series of battles, of which the siege at Mount Badon was among the last, and the victor of that siege united Britain.

Gildas, who was writing a century or two after the events, might have confused the dates, but he likely got the sequence right: the walls were built, the invaders came, a leader arose to drive them away. It means that Arthur may have lived considerably earlier than generally believed, at a date contemporaneous with the late third century reign of Carausius.

The vast poverty of evidence from the time means that the other histories we have are not contemporary, some being written as long as 800 years after the events they report, but they agree to the general theme: that an 'Arthur' or 'Caros' led his country against invaders in the earliest days of the nation, bringing peace. Some accounts are not written, but come from folklore, like the strong Celtic tradition which holds that the Pict Oscar, son of Ossian, was killed when he attacked the emperor Caros while he was rebuilding Hadrian's Wall.

The Welsh storyteller Geoffrey of Monmouth, writing his 'Historia Regum Britanniae' ('The History of the Kings of Britain') circa 1136 CE, also relayed a good deal of long-established folklore and described Arthur as a Briton, although some suggest the king was actually a Celt.

Carausius, the historical ruler at the heart of the legend, may well have been Celtic. Roman panegyrists who denigrated the man who seized a throne from their patrons sneeringly described him as a 'Menapian of the lowest birth,' but their views were coloured. Menapia was the River Meuse region of modern Belgium, an area settled by Celts. Some sources suggest that Carausius was recorded as the son of a ranking official from the region.

What we do know is that his rise through the Roman military to become admiral of the Channel fleet attests to his abilities, and the evidence of the literary slogans on his coinage suggests he was well-educated.

His image on those coins shows a bearded, bear-like, bull-necked soldier, and all the evidence points to his being a bold and outstanding leader of men with great personal courage and charisma. Another clue to his standing is that at his life's end he was buried in the heart of Britain as a king, and his headstone shows he was a Christian. The Carausius grave marker in Wales with its looped Chi-Ro cross is especially rare, and it and a tall milestone found in 1894 not far from Hadrian's Wall carry the only two known inscriptions to him in the nation he once ruled, because the Romans expurgated his memorials after they recaptured Britain.

The milestone, which was found on Gallows Hill, Carlisle, was saved only by chance as it was re-used, reversed in the ground. The buried portion preserved for us the glory of the redacted emperor's full name and title: 'Emperor Caesar Marcus Aurelius Mausaeus Carausius, Dutiful, Fortunate, the Unconquered Augustus.' It was recorded thus:

IMP C M AVR MAVS CARAVSIO PF INVICTO AVG

Correlations between places important in the lives of Arthur and Carausius provide other links between the mythic and the historical men. The Arthur of legend has numerous claimed resting places, but some of the most persuasive tales link him to north Wales, where Carausius was buried.

This parallels the Welsh tradition that Arthur, who 'carried the cross of Christ on his shield', was mortally wounded at the legendary battle of Camlann. That conflict has been placed in Gwynedd, whose ruling dynasty was pre-eminent among British kings. In the 19th century an antiquarian described the discovery of a Roman grave in that exact region near the sacred mountain of Snowdon, Yr Wyddfa, which legend says is the tumulus under which Arthur buried a giant he slew. The headstone, a very rare artefact, is inscribed ''Carausius lies here, in this cairn of stones' ('Carausius hic iacit in hoc congeries lapidum'). The site is of considerable significance. It is situated high on a Roman road southwest of Cwm Penmachno at the summit of a pass, and is the perfect place for a king's long sleep, a resting place chosen to overlook a sweeping expanse of his territory.

The Carausius headstone is also distinguished as the earliest found in Wales known to carry the Chi-Ro cross of a Christian, a marking that is one of only a dozen found anywhere in Britain. The man it memorialized was important enough that his gravestone and probably his bones were moved to the nearby church of St Tudclud in Penmachno. This was an important early Christian site and is the reputed burial place of the heir to the Welsh throne, Iorweth ab Owain Gwynedd, who was father of Wales' most famous monarch, Llywelyn the Great. The heir was also known as Iorweth Broken Nose and it is said he was refused the throne because of his misshapen face. Whether the long-ago royal was ugly or not, locals believe that two powerful rulers are interred in their ancient graveyard: the Roman admiral and emperor who united Britain and the Celtic prince whose son united Wales. The Carausian gravestone can be viewed in the church at Penmachno, which reopened in 2010 after a 15-year hiatus; the milestone bearing the lost emperor's titles is in the Tullie House Museum, Carlisle.

There are other, tantalizing geographic links. One of them, mentioned in a 1622 history, is in Oxfordshire. It recalled memories of the long-dead emperor and spoke of the 'entrenched sconce of Caraus' camp,' a fortification near the church of St Laurence at Caversfield, which may once have been called Carausiusfeld. This church was built around 800 CE, likely on an earlier edifice, and is close to where the casualties of an ancient battle were buried. In 1620, a hoard of Carausian coins was found nearby, at Steeple Clayton. Folklore holds that the usurper emperor was treacherously defeated in battle at nearby Bicester, a theme which reflects the long-held belief that Carausius was betrayed by his closest aide. This, history says, was a man known as 'Allectus,' a term which means simply 'chosen' or 'elected,' and which may not even be a proper name. (Another version of Carausius' end is that he was assassinated by Allectus after the fall of Bononia.)

Equally, the site of Arthur's greatest battle, the siege at Mount Badon, (Mons Badonicus) is not known. Some scholars, associating the Germanic word 'bath/baden' with 'Badon' theorize that Buxton, Derbyshire, site of a spring whose sacred waters were adopted by the

Romans as a spa, was the site of the Badon conflict and this fits neatly with the northern focus of this narrative. Others, arguing for Badbury or Bardon, place the siege in places as diverse as Bath, Coalville, Linlithgow, the Cotswolds, Dorset and Swindon. However, over the centuries the battles and the victorious king's story have been recorded only in oral tradition, not in written chronicles, so the fog of myth obscures our view of the landscape of history.

The real story of Arthur, Guinevere and Merlin, reflected here in the characters of Carausius, Guinevia and Myrddin, will possibly never be known. As it is sometimes advisable to ignore the opinions of academics whose conjectures may be no more valid than those of other people, I respectfully suggest that the Carausius of history is the king whose deeds prompted the legend of Arthur.

What is certain is that in 2010, the discovery of a hoard of Carausian coins buried in a Somerset meadow brought attention again to Britain's Forgotten Emperor and inspired this book. I hope it revives interest in the sailor who created a nation and a navy that has kept it unconquered for nearly a thousand years.

Historical and other notes:

Although this book follows the general outline of the life of Carausius, the narrative does take a few small liberties with history. Briefly, the admiral emperor may have been a humbly-born Menapian, from what is now Belgium, if his enemies' version of history is to be believed. Or, he may have been nobly born. His later actions in referencing poetry on his coinage, indicates a higher level of education than would be expected from a peasant upbringing. Some sources attribute Roman ancestry to him, which may be supported by his name, a classic Latin one (and not related to the much-later French 'carousser' – 'to quaff.') Other sources say he was a British or Irish prince.

Even by Roman historians' disparaging accounts, he was a skilled river pilot who joined the Roman army and became a successful soldier, then admiral of Rome's British Channel fleet, based in Boulogne/Bononia. Additionally, the evidence points to him being a charismatic leader. Around 284 CE, he was accused of diverting pirate loot to himself, and was summoned for court martial and likely execution, which may have been a political move to rid the emperor of a rival. Carausius' response was to seize power in northern Gaul and Britain, places where he commanded legions as well as a fleet. His ambition was to extend his military sway beyond the pale of Boulogne, even to Rome itself, but he was frustrated by the emperor Maximian, who was tasked with bringing the renegade to heel. The Roman's first endeavour, in 289 CE, was a failure. The new fleet he had built was either destroyed by storms or more probably was defeated by the seasoned flotilla Carausius took with him when he defected.

Carausius reinforced his military position with the popular support he gained by tapping into the Britons' discontent with their avaricious Roman overlords, and he skilfully used propaganda on his coinage to suggest he was a messiah returned to save the nation. The self-proclaimed emperor became the first ruler of a unified Britain, and entrenched himself behind the chain of forts he built along the south eastern coast. These Saxon Shore fortifications were intended to guard against an expected Roman attempt to retake Britain as well as to repel Saxon or Alemanni invaders.

Maximian had to wait four years after that failed invasion before he could drive Carausius out of Gaul. He retook Boulogne, besieging it and sealing the harbour against relief or escape by sea, an event this book placed in the narrative earlier than its actual chronology. In history, Boulogne fell in 293 CE, the year of Carausius' demise. The loss of the port and the weakening of Carausius' position probably caused a power struggle with his chief functionary Allectus, and led to the usurper emperor's death that same year.

He had ruled a united Britain for seven years when he was either assassinated by Allectus or, more probably, betrayed by him at a battle near Bicester. Allectus, whose identity is obscure (the word itself simply means 'chosen' or 'elected') took power, announced himself as 'consul' and 'Augustus arrived' on coinage. He began work in 294 CE on a great building in London that went unfinished, as his reign lasted for only three years. A Roman expedition defeated him after a sea battle off Chichester, and a land engagement near Silchester. Constantius, now Caesar, landed in Britain after the fighting was over and signalled his triumph with a famous medal declaring himself 'Restorer of the Eternal Light' ('Redditor lucis aeternae') meaning 'of Rome.'

The Eagle found by Carausius in the Blue John mine, one of the stately holes of Derbyshire, is a fiction, although there was a Ninth Hispania legion based at York and sent south to suppress the Boadicean uprising in 71 AD. The British queen routed that force with very great losses near the Suffolk village of Great Wratting. Later, the legion was deployed to the Danube, where its history vanished into the mists. It was not mentioned in an army list compiled around 170 CE. A search for the Eagle of the Ninth was the subject of a 1954 novel whose author said she had been inspired by the discovery of a wingless bronze eagle at Silchester. That artefact is presently on display at the Museum of Reading, and is not a legionary standard.

Also on exhibit, in the British Museum, are some of the 800 Carausian coins that were among a hoard of 52,500 Romano-British pieces of silver and gold discovered in a Somerset field in the summer of 2010. Such coins, the Penmachno headstone and a single milestone uncovered near Carlisle, are the only known memorials of Britain's lost emperor.

I should make a small apology for the use of some modernisms in this book. In the interests of clarity and to prevent the need frequently to thumb back to a reference page, I opted not to use many possibly-unfamiliar Latin place names from Britain or France, making just a few exceptions that are intended to retain the flavour of the narrative. Two of those exceptions are Eboracum, which is 21st century York, and Bononia, the French seaport of Boulogne-sur-Mer.

To establish the locales: the tale begins in the year 270 CE near Oceli Promontorium, now known as the great Yorkshire sea cliff Flamborough Head, and follows Carausius across the North Sea to Forum Hadriani, today's Dutch town of Voorburg. Forum Hadriani ('Hadrian's Market') was then the northernmost Roman settlement on the continent of Europe and was a key military post in the defences of the eastern border of the empire. Later, when the story is set in Britain's Peak District, locations include the Roman camp at Navio, which is in the Derbyshire hamlet of Brough. The fort exists today as just a few stones and an earthwork containing traces of the underground strong room. The nearby Blue John mine where the fictional Eagle was hidden is still in operation. The Romans smelted silver from the region's lead mines, including a major working at Lutudarense, now called Matlock Bath. This village is near the pleasant Regency spa town of Buxton which the Romans knew as Aquae Arnemetiae, or 'the Waters of (the Celtic goddess) Arnemetia.' To end the tutorial, Gaul is of course modern France, and Menapia, home of the real Carausius, was a region of what is now Belgium. The palace at Fishbourne, near Chichester, was destroyed in Carausius' time, but its ruins and fine mosaics are real enough and are a major tourist attraction today. The battles on the shingle of Dungeness and in the waters off Portland Bill, as recounted here, are fictional. But, they could well have happened, just as Carausius, the forgotten emperor of Britain, may be the lord of war whose exploits are the true source of the legend of King Arthur.

Printed in Great Britain
by Amazon